Believing BAILEY

By

Linda Kage

OMNIFIC PUBLISHING
LOS ANGELES

Omnific Publishing
2355 Westwood Blvd., Suite 506
Los Angeles, CA 90064
www.omnificpublishing.com

First Omnific ebook edition, November 2017
First Omnific trade paperback edition, November 2017

Library of Congress Cataloguing-in-Publication Data

Kage, Linda.
Believing Bailey / Linda Kage – 1st ed. isbn: 978-1-623422-51-6
1. New Adult Romance — Fiction. 2. Falsely Accused— Fiction.
3. Redemption— Fiction. 4. College — Fiction. I. Title

10 9 8 7 6 5 4 3 2 1

Book Cover Design by Linda Kage and Amy Brokaw

Printed in the United States of America

For Holly

(Or as Sadie calls you: Cat Kitty!)

Chapter 1
BAILEY

This party sucked so bad. Even the beer was stale.

I seemed to be the only person bothered by the taste, though. Everyone else in the crammed fraternity house was chugging it as if it were, well, *good* beer.

Wrinkling my nose, I lifted the red SOLO cup higher so there'd be a longer stream to watch as I poured the contents into the sink.

Behind me, some frat boy called, "Hey! What're you doing? That's good beer."

"Debatable," I murmured as I finished emptying my cup and then tossed the wasted shell into a nearby trashcan. Dusting my hands dry on my denim-covered hips, I glanced around, searching for some kind of entertainment. *Any* kind of entertainment.

A keg stand was taking place in the other half of a kitchen with cheers of, "Drink, drink, drink," chorusing throughout the room. But meh. Boring.

I'd just left the half-dressed drunk girls dancing in the living room, and didn't want to witness that atrocity again.

Out the window, I saw a group of guys playing bean bag toss on the back lawn. I could've headed that way and joined their game, but the wussies I'd defeated last week had been nothing but sore losers; they'd called me some really nasty, lame names just because someone with ovaries had kicked their asses. So I had no desire to play against those no-aim idiots again.

A couple made out in the corner, the guy skimming his hand up the girl's thigh until his fingers disappeared under the hem of her short skirt.

I rolled my eyes. There was absolutely no guy I'd met on campus this year that I could even remotely consider hooking up with. I had a bad feeling the cowboy I'd been chasing last year must've graduated because I hadn't spotted him once this semester, and it was November. So that crossed all possible plans of hanky panky off my list.

There was no reason for me to hang around here at all, except I didn't want to go home.

They were home. All disgustingly happy four of them.

My roommates.

I couldn't even express how excited I was that my two best friends—along with their perfect, superhot boyfriends—and I were now living together under one roof so I could continually watch Paige and Tess snuggle with their men non-stop morning, noon and night for seven days a week with no rest for the weary.

The joy. Really. It was too much to even contain.

It didn't matter that it'd been my idea for the three of us to rent an apartment together, or to sweeten the pot, I'd said, "Sure, invite your guys to live with us too." How the devil was I to know I'd find myself existing in a hell filled with a perpetual Valentine's Day? I mean, seriously, those two couples were so freaking in love it was maddening.

They might as well just tack a neon flashing sign to my bedroom door that said, "The Loser Loner Sleeps Here."

It was supposed to be awesome that I'd snagged the master bedroom, which had its own private bath and walk-in closet plus a sweet view of the park across the street. But really it just felt extra huge and lonely in there all by myself while I would lie awake at night staring up at my ceiling and listening to murmured voices seep through the walls on either side of me as my coupled up best friends snuggled in for the night with their soulmates.

Plus, it also felt kind of selfish to hog the biggest room to myself since I obviously needed the least amount of space. Tess and Paige insisted I keep it, though, so each night it just stretched bigger and emptier and lonelier.

Not that I actually wanted my own boyfriend. Ick. The one time I'd tried that in high school, it'd been a disaster of epic proportions. So, yeah, no permanent man for me, thank you.

But still.

There was just something about being left out of the couple club that made me cantankerous. That made me feel lacking. This evening had been particularly unpleasant. They'd wanted to rent a movie together. Paige and Logan had curled up on the couch, Jonah and Tess had snuggled together on the love seat, and I'd been left with the lazy boy and a bowl full of popcorn to keep myself company, which I'd polished off within the first ten minutes.

Watching the two couples tangled together, kissing every few seconds, constantly touching their other half, and so obviously in love, had made me puke a little in my mouth (and made me so jealous I'd wanted to ax someone), so I'd abandoned them about five minutes after that and found my way here to this dreadfully dull frat party.

Okay, dull might be a bit of an understatement. I mean, no one else around me appeared bored, so it was probably just me, and it only seemed lifeless to me because Tess and Paige weren't around.

I wandered into a new room as if I was searching for something or someone, though I wasn't. I'd never felt so restless and solitary in my whole damn life. I missed hanging with my two besties.

But I was happy they were happy so I'd stop whining about that. Really. I just needed, I don't know, *something*. Not a man. But something to give me a reason to wake up each morning, something to make all this *living* business worthwhile. A goal maybe.

Yeah, a goal sounded good, like something to work toward and keep my mind busy, aside from school and my part-time job. Something that actually interested me.

Yes, perfect. I was totally going to come up with a cool, stimulating goal. Like…some goal. I wasn't exactly sure what *kind* of goal exactly, but—

When I spotted a cowboy hat from the corner of my eye, I paused everything.

Because cowboy hat? *Cowboy hat*!

I did a double take and my mouth fell open.

There was my goal. My cowboy.

Holy hedgehog on a Friday at church, he was *here*! The cowboy I'd first seen a year ago and had been hunting ever since just so I could introduce myself to him and see if the rest of him turned out to be as good as my first impression had been was standing twenty-freaking-feet away. Right in front of me.

Decked out in a cowboy hat, long-sleeved checkered top, big-ass shiny belt buckle, snug Wranglers, and perfect leather boots, he was it, everything I'd ever dreamed I wanted in a guy. His hair was dark and just long enough for the ends to curl out the edges of his hat and make him even more deadly gorgeous. And he was smart enough to be drinking from a longneck bottle, not that stale keg swill they were serving.

Had I just said I didn't want a boyfriend? Well, forget all that, because this guy, yeah, this guy was my soulmate. I just knew it.

I know, I know. No one likes all that love at first sight BS. But just work with me here. In my fantasies, it could be so. In reality… well, let's not go there, because I was operating purely in fantasyland at the moment.

As I blinked repeatedly, simply gaping at him, my legs decided they no longer worked, because they weren't moving, weren't hurdling drunken idiots or karate kicking dancing girls out of my path to get to him. They were locked and frozen in place, unable to do much more than knock my knees together unsteadily.

Okay, so maybe goals were scary things, because I could not approach my cowboy. My soulmate. What if he turned out to be an asshat? Or worse. What if he was perfect? Then he'd certainly never want anything to do with a mess like me.

Intimidated beyond speech and petrified motionless, I watched him take a drink and then grin at something the blurry person next to him had just said, and oh, angels tumbled from heaven. That smile. It hitched up a little higher on the right side, making it crookedly adorable and sexy at the same time, with a slight laugh line crinkling the corner, telling me he probably smiled a lot.

I whimpered. My ovaries might've melted. My panties grew suddenly uncomfortable. My body was ready for him.

Then he turned, and holy cheese on crackers, his *butt*. His butt in Wranglers was epic. It was every cowboy groupie's dream come true. And I was the ultimate cowboy groupie.

My mouth watered and fingers itched to grasp until *what*? His butt started moving away.

Why was his butt leaving me?

"No. *Wait!*" Frantic and a little hoarse, my voice cracked as I finally lurched forward and lifted my hand, waving him to stop, as if that would actually waylay the guy twenty feet away with his back to me. "Shit."

Screw my apprehensions; the scrapper in me kicked to life. He was not getting away this time.

I'd spotted him only a handful of times in the past year since I'd been feverishly hunting him, and he'd escaped me—unknowingly, since he'd never been aware I was pursuing him—every single time. He was like a ninja cowboy or something. But not tonight. Tonight he was getting roped and hogtied until I at least got to speak to him and introduce myself.

Just as he disappeared into a back hall, someone—someone who I swear had a death wish—stepped into my path.

This time, my legs were working just fine and my brakes were non-existent. I plowed right into the girl, making her jostle her drink and slosh foamy beer over her hand and down her arm until it dripped from her elbow.

"Hey," she complained, while I yelled, "*Dammit.*"

The girl sent me a startled glance, and I calmed enough to say, "I mean, sorry. Excuse me." Darting around her, I let out a growl when I found two guys in my way. Scrambling around them, I weaved my way through the maze of irritating humans, trying to pop up onto my tiptoes and peek over them so I could see the hall my cowboy had slipped into. But I couldn't see anything past shoulders and chins and chests, which only made me clench my teeth harder.

This was so not the time to be short. Curse my parents for passing me short genes.

Okay, maybe not really. I loved my father to bits. And speaking ill of my mother just felt wrong, may she rest in peace.

Finally, I had a clear shot into the hallway, but, no.

It was empty. Totally and completely empty, just like my room at night when I listened to Tess and Paige through the walls as they whispered sweet nothings to their boyfriends.

My heart stalled in my chest.

He had escaped again, the slippery cowboy. I kind of wanted to curse him too—why couldn't he have just stayed still five seconds longer, damn him? —but he was way too sexy to be damning and I already felt guilty enough for cursing my parents seconds ago, so I bit my tongue.

After a second of panting and resting my hands on my knees to collect my breath, I straightened and fisted them at my hips, once again renewed with determination.

He was not getting away again. That was my new life motto.

There were a total of seven escape hatches—fine, they were just boring old *doors*—down this hall. I'd just check them all. But as I neared the first one, the door opened and a very non-cowboy-looking guy exited.

His eyes widened and he jerked to a stop when he saw me hurl myself toward him before I realized, fudge, he wasn't who I wanted.

"Shit."

We both stopped in time to prevent a collision, but the cup in his hand had some powerful forward momentum going on, and his grip on it was obviously not so stellar, so it kept tumbling forward.

It slipped right out of his hand, tipped toward me, and splashed its entire contents down the front of my shirt with cold, wet, stinky stale keg beer.

My gasp was legendary. "Oh my God, that's cold!"

"Fuck, I'm sorry. I'm so sorry."

I didn't pay the apologizing klutz much mind; I was too busy gaping down at my soaked shirt in horror.

"Here. I'm sorry."

The guy ducked back through the doorway, disappearing momentarily, before he returned with a hand towel and started dabbing it against my wet chest to soak up the beer.

It'd been a good two and a half years since anyone had gotten that close to my breasts, and the shock of familiarity made me jerk backward and give him a censorious glare. "Really?"

"What?" he slurred, lifting his face and blinking cluelessly. Thick, stubby lashes fanned over the most electric blue pair of eyes I'd ever seen, and for a moment I was once again struck dumb, staring at them, because wow, those were some really blue eyes.

A second later, I scowled even harder at him for distracting me, and I arched my eyebrows tellingly before motioning to my chest where his hand still was, before he seemed to realize he'd been groping me.

With a chagrined wince-slash-grin, he jerked the towel from my chest and extended to my hand so I could snag it from him and pat myself dry.

"Sorry," he offered again while I muttered curses under my breath, and beer dripped down my stomach into the waistband of my jeans. "I'll buy you a new top. I swear. Just look me up tomorrow when I'm sober, and I'll get all your details or take you shopping or whatever. Whatever you want, I'll fix this. The name's Beckett. Beckett Hilliard, and I live here. Just call the house and ask for me, and I'll take care of everything. I'm not just saying that, either. I won't flake out on you or—"

Lifting my hand to stop him because his drunken rambling was making me dizzy, I said, "Look…Bucket."

"Beckett," he corrected.

I blinked. "Huh?"

"My name is Beckett. Not Bucket."

"Well, it sounded like you said Bucket." I clenched my fingers around the damp hand towel I was still holding. Each second I stood here arguing with a bucket of Beckett, my cowboy was getting farther and farther away

He wrinkled his nose. "What the fuck kind of name is Bucket?"

I growled and threw up my hands. "Well, what the fuck kind of name is *Beckett*?"

His prickled offence was immediate. Drawing back his shoulders, he said, "It's a family name."

I rolled my eyes. Oh geez. He really was a filthy rich little frat boy, wasn't he? I took an extra second to scan him over, and yep. Ick. Tall, slim and perfectly fit, he wore a collared polo shirt with one of those mini alligator patches over his heart, khaki pants and loafers. The only thing to complete the package would have been if his hair had been all gelled and slicked back into neat perfection, but the light brown mess was spiked out in a couple oddball places as if he'd drunkenly mussed it. Other than that, he resembled the epitome cliché of every rich son being funded through med or law school by his corporate CEO daddy.

Gag me.

"It means bee cottage," he told me. "Or maybe dweller near the brook." Frowning as if confused, he shook his head. "I'm not sure exactly. I found so many different meanings—"

"Oh my God!" I clutched my head, trying to block out the rambling. "I don't have time for this. He's getting away."

Beckett—not Bucket—stopped blathering. "Who's getting away?"

"The *cowboy*." I scowled at all the closed doorways in the hall. Which one had he taken?

"You mean Chance?"

"What?" I jerked my attention to Beckett so fast he reared backward. "You *know* him? The cowboy?"

After a couple blinks, he snickered. "Uh…yeah. Everyone knows Chance. He's in the fraternity."

Chance. That sounded about right. My cowboy could totally rock a name like Chance. Rugged yet loyal. Faithful and trustworthy, but also full of hard muscles and a look in his eyes that said he was a handful.

A sexy handful.

Sexy Chance was the perfect name for him.

But, wait. Had Bucket just said fraternity? Yeah, no. No way. Not *my* cowboy.

I snorted. "I don't think so."

Bucket frowned as if confused. "Cowboy hat, boots, plaid shirts with the snaps, Wranglers, big belt buckle. The whole shebang." He cupped his hands around an imaginary buckle at his waist to demonstrate.

I frowned at him, in clear denial. But no. *My* soulmate in a gross fraternity? I think not. My cowboy could not be a frat boy. Life wouldn't be that cruel.

Stupid Bucket was just drunk and confused. That was all.

"Did you see him?" I demanded, ready to grab his shirt and start shaking. I glanced past him toward the doorway he'd just exited. As soon as I found Chance, I'd get all this fraternity misunderstanding sorted out. "Did he go in there?"

"In here?" He laughed. "Yeah, no. We didn't take a piss together, sorry."

Dammit. That was just a bathroom.

Okay, so six exits left to check.

"Thanks." I tossed the damp hand towel at Bucket's chest and turned away to try the door directly across from this one.

Locked. Grr.

When I started toward the next, Bucket called after me. "Hey. What about your shirt?"

I rolled my eyes and tried the next door down. "It'll wash." The latch turned in my hand, making my heartrate jack with excitement.

Pushing my way into the dark room, I saw another door across the floor that led into a lightened area, so I hurried toward it only to find yet one more bathroom. Dammit! How many freaking bathrooms were in this place?

Behind me, a shadow fell over the opened doorway into the hall. "Hey. Girl with the rainbow hair."

Oh my God, really?

Bucket had *followed* me? What was wrong with this guy?

Rolling my eyes and not wanting to deal with him anymore, I hurried deeper into the bathroom so I could jerk open the shower curtain and duck inside. I'd just climbed into the bathtub and concealed myself when I heard the bathroom door creak open wider.

"If you're really looking for Chance, I could take you to him and—oh! Shit, I thought she came in here. Damn, I must be drunker than I thought."

I bit my lip, forcing myself not to react, though now I kind of wanted to throw open the shower curtain and screech, "take me to him *now*!" But that might look a little too desperate. Plus, I didn't want to explain why I'd been hiding in the bathtub in the first place. Embarrassing.

There was a shuffling on the other side of the curtain, telling me he was leaving, thank God, and then I heard him in the outer room heading toward the exit. Just a few more seconds of hiding out here and I'd be able to escape this little space that was beginning to suffocate me with its noxious fumes of Axe body spray and the hint of dirty socks.

Maybe I could "accidentally" bump into Beckett—and no longer Bucket, because if he could get me to my cowboy, he couldn't be that bad—in the hall and give him another chance to help me find Chance. Yeah, that sounded good. He had poured beer all over me, so he owed me. I could—

"Hey there, Beck. I thought that was you I saw come in here."

I frowned as a woman's voice entered the outer room and the only exit from this bathroom. She sounded all purry and husky-voiced like a woman on the prowl, trying to catch herself a good time.

The door from the hallway into the room closed with a click before the lock sounded.

Oh no. This could not be happening.

I'd just wanted to find my cowboy; how the hell had I gotten myself stuck in a stinking bathtub listening to some horny chick trying to hook up with a drunk idiot?

I had the worst luck ever.

Chapter 2
BAILEY

I peeked out the crack of the curtain and saw shadows through the opening of the bathroom door as the light in the outer room—which must be a bedroom, since I barely made out the corner of a bed—came on.

"Hey, did you see a girl with rainbow-colored hair out there?" I heard Beckett ask the girl. "I'm talking red, orange, yellow green, a freaking rainbow."

"No," the girl drew out, sounding amused. Then she asked, "Are you having hallucinations? Been taking the good drugs tonight, honey?"

"Yeah, maybe. I mean, no. No drugs. Just too much beer. But I…" I could almost picture him scratching his head and gazing around the room, confused. "I swore she came in here."

"Sounds like maybe you need to sit down until you get your head cleared." Bedsprings squeaked, like someone sitting on the mattress.

"Oh my God," I whispered, squeezing my eyes closed. I did not like where this was going.

"There," the girl murmured. Seemed like she was running her fingers through his hair or something, some kind of soothing motion to calm him, because the next thing she said was, "Better?"

Beckett let out a satisfied groan.

My eyebrows sprang up into my hairline, and my curiosity got the better of me. I just had to know what the heck she was doing that he seemed to like so much. Biting my lip and wincing as if that would make me somehow quieter, I gently and slowly moved the shower curtain aside and then stepped out of the tub as easily as possible. Then I just as gingerly made my way to the door, where yes, I could see through the crack perfectly without being spotted.

I'd been right on the first count. Beckett had sat on the bed, his feet were still flat on the floor and he was upright. Maybe the chick had nudged him down there, I have no idea, but she remained standing by his side where she was running her fingers through his hair, which was causing all his groaning and making him close his eyes and tip his head back. The dude kind of had a nice jawline when he tilted it like that.

"I don't know what's wrong with me tonight," he confessed, the ache in his voice making me blink and see him as an actual person instead of a drunk frat boy. "I told myself I was going to stop drinking this much. I'm so fucked up."

"Aww, you poor thing," the girl cooed, cupping his cheek. "I know exactly what's wrong with you. We all heard how Jana broke up with you."

With a noncommittal sound, he shrugged and opened his eyes to look at her. "It was mutual," he slurred as if he'd been trained to say that.

"Of course it was, baby." She was coddling him now and had stopped stroking his face so she could curl her fingers around his chin and force him to keep looking at her. "You want to know a secret?"

His eyebrows crinkled before he admitted, "I don't know."

I watched his face, and for some reason I got the feeling he didn't really like this girl much. Not sure what exactly gave me that impression, but I was kind of sucked into the moment, reading how much she was trying to play him and get him into her clutches while he was subtly resisting. It was like watching a live soap opera, and I had to know what would happen next. I actually craved some popcorn and Skittles right about now to really enjoy the show.

The still-nameless girl leaned down toward him as if she was going to kiss him but then she veered her mouth to his ear so she could whisper loud enough for me to hear her from across the room. "I always thought Jana was a bitch."

Beckett pulled back and frowned at her as if affronted for his ex-girlfriend's sake. "I thought you two were friends."

She smiled cattily. "Tonight we're not."

With a frown, I judged her. I judged her harshly. But what a terrible thing to say about a friend. I would never, ever say a thing like that about Tess or Paige. I wasn't even sure what her words meant, they just sounded all kinds of wrong and back-stabberish to me.

Even Beckett crinkled his eyebrows as if confused. "What does that mean?"

See, even he was confused. You go, Beckett. Let her know how wrong she is for bashing her "friend."

But the chick only chuckled and let go of his chin so she could pat his cheek. "It means, tonight I'm Team Beckett."

Then she got down on her knees between his partially spread thighs and reached for the fly of his jeans.

Holy shit!

As if reading my mind, a similarly shocked Beckett reared back and gasped, "Holy shit." Then he reached the girl's shoulder. "Melody, what the hell are you… I'm way too drunk for this. I can't—"

"Shh." She pulled his hand off her and smiled up at him. "Don't worry about it, baby. I'm sober enough for the both of us. I'll take care of everything. Just relax."

"Yeah, but—" He sucked in a startled breath and gripped the sheets on either side of him with both hands as his head fell back and he gritted his teeth. I strained to see what she'd just done, but her back and long black hair obstructed my view. Not that I really had to see to know.

Melody had obviously gotten her hand into his pants, a fact confirmed with she gasped in awe. "Damn, I knew it. I knew you'd be big. Yes. So big." She looked up at him. "Think I could fit all this bad boy in my mouth?"

He shook his head no. I wasn't sure if he was saying no, she couldn't, or no, he didn't want her to even try. But then he mumbled, "You shouldn't. Jana—"

"Is no longer your girlfriend," Melody reminded him. "In fact, I saw her here with Davon tonight."

"Davon?" He frowned as if confused.

"Mmm hmm," Witch Melody seemed a little too pleased to report as she walked her fingers up Beckett's thigh. "So there's no reason at all for me not to do this." Then she bent her head, and I couldn't see, but I knew exactly what she did.

Beckett's mouth fell open as he gasped.

I slapped my hand over my own mouth, unable to believe what I was watching, what I was *stuck* watching.

Okay, maybe stuck was the wrong word. I could totally look away. Oh, dear Lord. Why wasn't I looking away? I spun around because that was the right thing to do; I shouldn't be watching this. But then I could still hear the quiet suction of Melody's mouth and the rising of Beckett's breathing. So I transferred my hands from my mouth to over my ears.

Three seconds later, I felt like a total moron for standing in a bathroom with my hands over my ears. I slowly removed them, and the silence that followed unnerved me. Panic welled. What if they were done and heading to the bathroom to clean up now? I whirled around to check.

Nope, Melody was still going at it.

And Beckett continued to seem confused by the whole thing. He shook his head and gaped down at the top of Melody's head. "Melody," he tried again, grasping her shoulder. "This really isn't—" But she did something to make him grunt away his protest and grip his own hair with his free hand. Then she grasped his other hand he'd had on her shoulder and physically pinned his fingers to the bed as her head made this up and down motioned away from and toward his lap.

He whimpered out the last of his resistance before letting his torso fall backwards onto the bed and moaning, "What the fuck is happening?"

I almost felt sorry for him. I mean, he was trying—failing spectacularly, but still trying—to tell this Melody idiot no, and she was totally ignoring him. It kind of made me want to pop out of the bathroom and pull her off him by the hair, muttering, "Are you deaf, honey? He doesn't want this."

But then, he stopped complaining and was now just letting it happen, even lifting his hips toward her face and breathing harder, muttering a couple, "shits" and "Oh, Jesuses."

I turned away again, feeling hot and ashamed, only to turn back, equal parts curious and gawker-horrified. Only to turn away again. After going through this routine a few more times, practically spinning in a circle with my indecision over whether to keep watching or not, I decided I needed to know when they were finished in order to best plan my escape, so I watched.

"God, you taste good." Melody lifted her face to grin at him as if refreshed. After wiping the back of her hand across her mouth, she lifted her skirt up to her waist, shimmied a pair of thong panties over her hips until she was flashing her bare butt my way, and then kicking them off. Shocked by her audacity, I backed away from the crack, freshly stunned by what I was watching, only to step forward again, shamefully unable to stop looking.

Melody climbed onto the mattress over Beckett. "It's got me so wet, baby. I want to feel you come inside me."

My mouth fell open as she settled right over his lap and her skirt fell back down around her, thank God covering her bare bits from my peeping Tom eyes.

Beckett started to sit up, slurring, "But I don't—"

"Shh." Melody set her hand against his chest, pushing him right back down onto his back. "It's okay. I have everything covered, even protection."

And she pulled a condom from her cleavage.

Beckett seemed to panic, looking around the walls as if searching for something to help him, to save him. "Jesus, Melody. I don't even know whose room this is."

She giggled and cooed, "Doesn't that make it so much more exciting?" as she tore open the package with her teeth.

The condom disappeared from my view as she obviously put it on him. I bit my lip, wondering what I should do. Should I help him? Stop this right here? Make her behave?

My skin crackled with anxiety. I was already highly uncomfortable from being forced to stay in here while something that private and intimate was going on right on the other side of the mostly open door, but something about Beckett's reactions were telling me he didn't want to have sex with her. My gut churned, not sure what I should do.

But then it was too late. She lowered herself onto his lap, and they both groaned. He gripped her hip, his fingers digging into the cloth of her skirt.

She moaned and began to move…fast. Like that ridiculous bouncing you see on movies. I turned away and pressed my hand to my mouth. Behind me, Melody cried, “Yes. Yes. Yes,” making me wrinkle my nose and grimace from the absurdity of it all. “I knew you’d feel this good. Oh God… Beck.”

I rolled my eyes. But really? She sounded so freaking fake. She had to be putting on a stupid, lying show because, how could it possibly feel that—

“Jesus…Christ,” Beckett bit out, making me turn back to look again, because his voice sounded too appealing for me to stay away. And yeah, despite what was happening, appealing was totally the right word to explain him. In the throes of pleasure, he was magnificent. Arching his neck back so I could see the straining muscles in his throat tighten like cords, he lifted his face with a rapture that seemed to coil through me as if I were experiencing it with him. Then he hissed, “It’s been too long since I did this. *Fuck*. Harder. Go rougher.”

Melody changed her speed, not focusing so much on speed but the force with which she slammed down onto him, and I jerked away from the crack to stop watching, feeling like the dirty voyeur I was. My cheeks heated with shame and embarrassment. What was worse, my nipples hardened, which I totally blamed on my shirt and bra that Beck had spilled beer on and left cold and wet and *not* on the fact I was listening to sex sounds.

I guess Beckett—the bucket head—didn’t want saving after all. The stupid boy. How dare he make me feel as if he’d needed me to do something for him?

Humiliated because I’d actually wanted to stop her for him, I sent a sharp glare toward the crack in the door as Melody’s moaning became obnoxious. “Yes. There. Right there. Don’t stop. Oh, fuck, you really are as good as Jana said you were. Beck! if feels so fucking good.”

I crossed my arms over my chest and would’ve sniffed moodily if I hadn’t been worried it’d give my presence away.

If I’d wanted to listen to this kind of nonsense, I would’ve just stayed home and eavesdropped on Tess or Paige. Though honestly, I’d never actually heard either of my roommates getting it on with their boyfriends. I bet they didn’t sound like a calf being slaughtered when they came, though, not like Melody did.

She was really carrying on now. Whatever Beckett was doing *right there*, it was good. Real good. It made me ache a little in the center of my chest, and wish someone would touch me in the right spot and make me—

But that was stupid. So stupid. Never in my life would I be resentful of a girl making those kind of awful noises. Except…

Dammit. Sometimes I really hated my uber curious nature. I couldn't help but return to the crack and peek out. I still couldn't see details, both were in the same position as before, Beckett stretched out supine on his back with Melody sitting upright on his lap facing him. Though now, his hand was no longer clutching the sheets or his hair. It had disappeared between their bodies, somewhere around the vicinity where they were joined. I didn't know where the hell he was touching her, but it was obviously hitting *the right spot.*

Melody was such a lucky bitch. It was no fair.

The one and only time I'd ever had sex, the guy had not touched me anywhere down there, except with his gross pecker. He hadn't really touched me anywhere with his hands. He'd used them to brace himself above me until he'd rutted his way into a climax. And in return, I had laid there, turning my head aside and biting my lip against the pain, hoping it would end soon, which thankfully, it had.

Beckett and Melody were not ending soon. And Melody didn't seem to be hurting at all. In fact, the woman threw her head back and brayed out the worst sound of pleasure I'd ever heard a woman make in my life.

Holy shit, but if that's what happened to every girl when she orgasmed, maybe I shouldn't be so bitter that I'd never had one. It had to be the ugliest, most mortifying thing I'd ever seen.

Poor Beckett.

Except he didn't seem to mind. While Melody went into heifer mode on top of him, braying and snorting, he seemed to grow more tense and hungry under her until, whoa…

Now there was a magical-looking orgasm. When Beckett came, his entire face transformed into this thing of beauty as if he'd just been released from the worst torture and his soul had just been set free from eternal damnation. His lips parted and eyes widened. Maybe he was seeing God. I don't know. But it was hot. And it made me feel strange and even more uncomfortable.

I couldn't believe I was watching this. It was, hell, I didn't even know. But I felt slimy and gross and yet I was way too captivated to look away, because it was so spectacular.

Before I realized what I was doing, I pulled my cell phone from my back pocket and turned it to mute before taking a picture. Then I frowned at what I'd done.

Okay, something was seriously wrong with me. Without even checking the results, I stuffed the phone back into my pocket and shook my head, mortified I'd actually just done that.

But for the briefest, most forbidden second, I'd wondered what it would've felt like if Beckett had been inside *me* while that had been happening to him, and I'd been jealous. Which was stupid. I was so stupid. And weird. I needed to get out of her before I combusted from all the strange stupid, weird emotions tripping through me.

On the bed, Melody and Beckett finished. Melody collapsed on top of him, burying her face into the crook of his neck, murmuring something that sounded like praise. And suddenly, I remembered just how messy sex was, you know, down there. Their next stop would no doubt be the bathroom, to clean up. I didn't want to be in here when that happened, and I wasn't going back behind the shower curtain.

I needed to escape. Now.

Since this had to be the best opportunity while they were both still recovering, I held my breath and eased opened the door enough to wedge myself through. My heart pounded like a resounding kettle drum; I was so sure they'd hear it. But the couple on the bed didn't seem to notice anything at all when I joined them in the room. So I began to tiptoe toward the door, watching them the entire time.

Just as I reached the exit, unlocked it as quietly as possible, and began to creep it open, I looked back just as Beckett's eyes came open languidly, and he focused on me over Melody's shoulder.

His hand lifted limply about a foot above the mattress before he pointed at me, very clearly seeing me.

My heart pounded in triple time as I froze in my tracks. Then I did the craziest thing in the world. I set my pointer finger against my lips, begging him to stay quiet.

Shocking the shit out of me, he repeated the action, pressing his finger to his own lips. The glazed expression on his face told me just how much he was out of it. I rolled my eyes—stupid boy—and hurried from the room, silently shutting the door and hurrying away.

I rushed all the way down the hallway and back into the main part of the frat house. The blast of music and people shocked my senses. I gaped at the blur of activity, feeling too off balance to return to this after seeing what I'd just seen. Then I shook my head, and stumbled through bodies until I found an exit to the outside.

The cool breeze against my chest reminded me my shirt was still wet from the beer Beckett had spilled on me. It felt so surreal that it hadn't even dried yet, while an entire universe of things had seemed to happen since the moment I'd been soaked. Time was so weird. Just like this moment. It was peculiar and bizarre and weird. Even my hands looked weird when I looked down at them to find them shaking.

I didn't know how to deal with this. So I ran to my car, three blocks away through the freezing cold night, and I didn't stop until I was home and in my bed with the covers tucked way up to my chin as I huddled into myself and stared wide-eyed at the ceiling of my room.

But my heart didn't stop pounding. It kept thumping fast through most of the night as I lay wide-awake, wondering what the heck had just happened to me.

More importantly, what had I just become?

Chapter 3
BECKETT

Regret tasted like regurgitated alcohol. In fact, I think everything I'd drunk tonight was about to revisit the outside world for real. I'm not sure which cheapskate had ordered the keg for the party, but this shit was rank. And okay, maybe I'd had too much of it as well.

My stomach roiled and nausea rose. I tried to sit up, roll off the bed and stumble toward the bathroom, but a weight on top of me kept me pinned to the mattress.

"Mmph. What?" I cracked open bleary eyes to find a face full of dark hair.

Melody.

Jesus, I'd forgotten about her, which was fairly awful since I think I was still inside her.

Oh damn, here came more regret. I'd just slept with Melody. Melody Fairfield. I'd never even liked Melody, which made the need to get my cock out of her even more urgent.

Fumbling until I found her shoulders, I gripped her gently trying to get her attention or pry her off me or something. "I need to..."

"Hmm?" She lifted her face to smile blissfully at me. "What's wrong, baby?"

Oh, God, she was calling me baby. I was two point five seconds from upchucking all over her. "Bathroom," was all I could mumble.

"Oh." I must've looked green enough to get my point across because her eyes flew open wide. She sat up and shimmied off me so I could roll over onto my stomach and crawl to the edge of the bed. I hit the floor on both feet but by the time I made it to the bathroom, I was on my hands and knees crawling. I slumped to the toilet and pushed up the lid with just enough time to hang my head miserably and puke.

My stomach seized and lungs burned by the time I was finished. At some point, Melody must've come to the doorway to check on me because I heard an, "Eww, gross," before her shadow disappeared again.

Limp and drained with the room spinning around me, I rested my cheek on the porcelain rim until I felt enough energy to claw my way up the side of the sink and turn the water on. After splashing two handfuls onto my face, I cupped more in my palms and drank what I could capture. After that, I groaned pathetically and propped my forehead against the mirrored cabinet above the sink before opening the door and checking for painkillers inside.

I found two Tylenol capsules and swallowed them dry. Then I turned to escape the bathroom because it smelled like bile in here, but my pants sagged around my knees tripping me up. I grasped the doorway just in time to keep from tumbling face first to the floor.

Glancing down, I found I was still wearing a condom. Classy.

Well, at least I'd been safe. Thank God. Though that was the only relief I felt, because I still couldn't believe I'd just been with Melody. *Melody* of all people. Fake and conniving, she usually inspired me to become scarce whenever she'd hung out with Jana. I'd have to be pretty damn drunk to ever have sex with her.

Then again, I think I was pretty damn drunk.

The bedroom slanted sideways when I peered into it. A foggy version of Melody rose from the bed and came toward me.

"Beckett, baby. You feeling better yet?"

Again with the baby. I winced, hoping she didn't touch me, because that might induce more nausea. "I still have my condom on," I stated the obvious. I have no idea why I said that. It sounded dumb as soon at the words slurred their way from my lips. But I don't think I could even begin to recover from the trauma of fucking her until I got the foul thing off me, so it's presence still on me really, *really* bothered me.

"Want me to take care of it?" She began to reach forward.

Oh, hell, no.

I managed to lift my hand, politely warding her off. But the mere idea of her skin making any more contact with my skin made my stomach revolt. "Nah. I got it. Thanks."

She nodded and stepped back. When she spotted her panties on the floor, she bent down to pick them up, affording me with a view of her bare ass as she did so.

She had a nice ass. She had a nice everything really—appearance wise. But my stomach heaved again, realizing what I'd just done. *Who* I'd just done.

This was bad. This was so fucking bad. How was I going to get past this? What if she wanted to, like, date me now? I couldn't even contemplate the idea of dating Melody Fairfield, and yet I couldn't have sex with a girl and then avoid her for the rest of my life, which is more what I really wanted to do. Except avoiding someone I'd had sex with wasn't in my DNA. I couldn't just hit it and quit it. To me, that was jerkish. And I wasn't a jerk…typically. But I think I was going to become one after this, which made the good boy in me whine at the whole ugliness of my situation.

I was so fucking fucked right now. Why had I let her do what she'd done?

Melody stepped into her panties and began to draw them up her legs, so I reached down to ease off my condom. Just as I got it fully removed, a knock sounded on the door and it began to open.

"Mel?" a voice asked, just as some dude I'd never met before poked his head inside. "You in here?"

I froze, condom in hand. And Melody lifted her face, her panties halfway up her legs.

The guy blinked. "*Melody*?"

A beat passed as he stepped fully into the room, took me in from head to toe, pausing at my exposed dick, then shut the door at his back with a thunk. "What the fuck?

She burst into tears and raced to him, flinging herself into his arms. "Radley," she sobbed, burying her face in his chest as her arms wound around his neck. "Oh, thank God. *Thank God!* I need you. It was horrible. So horrible."

Radley seemed to be about as taken aback by her behavior as I was. He stiffened before reluctantly pulling her closer and kissing her hair. "It's okay, baby? What happened? What'd he do to you?"

I shook my head, baffled. What the hell were those two even talking about? And who *was* this guy? Most importantly, why had Melody just called sex with me horrible when she'd just toted me the best she'd ever had literally minutes ago?

I was too confused and still too drunk to sort through any of it. So I just stared at them, my junk still hanging out, used condom clutched in one hand, and mouth falling open stupidly.

Over Melody's shoulder, Radley pinned his gaze on me just as I decided I should probably zip up now. "What did you do to my girlfriend?" he demanded.

Wait. Did he say...

Girlfriend?

I nearly swallowed my tongue. I had no idea Melody had a boyfriend.

"Um." Shit. Why hadn't she told me she had a boyfriend?

I shifted a step back, already lifting my hands in peace, though one hand was still full of the condom I'd just used on his girlfriend, which he immediately zeroed his attention onto.

No.

No, no, no, no.

Melody clutched him harder, clinging dramatically as her weeping rose louder. "He...he made me do it," she wailed. "I didn't want to, but he...he f-forced me. I t-tried to stop him, I did. But I couldn't. Oh my God, I couldn't stop him. He held me down, and he," She paused to hiccup pathetically. "He wouldn't stop."

My mouth fell open wider as I stared at her, unable to believe what she'd just said, too shocked to even react to it.

But seriously. Had she really just done what it sounded like she'd done?

"*You*," Radley, the boyfriend snarled. When he set Melody aside and pointed at me, I stumbled back into the bathroom, shaking my head.

"No," I said. "I didn't. She's lying. I would never..."

But he was already slowly advancing on me, trapping me in the bathroom. I tripped in reverse until I bumped into the sink. Then I lifted my hands, already cringing. I tossed down the stupid condom, flinging it out of sight. "I didn't…didn't even know she had a boyfriend."

Dude, Radley was massive, and there were three of him wavering around in my drunk vision. I was able to focus on his hand—er, all three of them— right before he cracked his knuckles and curled the fingers into a fist. "Boyfriend or not, you still never force a woman."

Yes, exactly. I knew that. I knew that better than anyone. But I'd never forced a girl in my life, and I especially hadn't forced Melody. I hadn't even *wanted* Melody.

This was all wrong.

I shook my head, but Radley swung, anyway.

The impact rattled through my teeth and down to my feet, shuddering through my jaw and reverberating into my spine. Blood filled my mouth. My head felt broken. I tried to shake it off, to clear my vision. Nothing helped. Pain throbbed through my brain.

And Radley swung again.

"I didn't," I tried to tell him, but my tongue wasn't working right, my vision wasn't working right. My thoughts weren't working right.

Radley hit me a third time, this one in the ribs. I tried to defend myself, lift my arm to block the next blow, shove him backward. But it all felt useless. My limbs weren't freaking cooperating.

Everything went gray. Then black. The last thing I remembered was the cold tile floor slamming against my cheek and a shoe ramming into my back before there was nothing.

* * *

I came awake one wheezing breath after another. Everything ached. I wanted to curl into a ball and die. After the slightest movement of drawing my knees up toward my chest, I gasped from the waves of agony that rippled through my chest.

I tried to blink my eyes open but one of them wasn't working. My head felt like a big swollen ball of ouch.

"What…?"

"Man, you fucked up. You fucked up so bad, Hilliard. I can't, I mean, I knew you were going on a downward spiral, but this is bad. You went off the deep end this time."

I knew that voice. It was my best friend from our fraternity. Max.

After an extreme effort of will, I turned my head toward him and tilted my face enough to see a somewhat blurry view of him through my better eye. "What happened?" I rasped, barely able to talk.

It felt as if I'd just been hit by a freight train.

"Dude." He shook his head and took a step away from me. "You fucked up. You fucked up big time. I mean, Melody *Fairfield*? Do you know what her brother's going to do when he finds out about this?"

I groaned and reclosed my eye, beginning to remember fragments. Melody on top of me, riding me, coming with me inside her. Then the puking and the boyfriend and him beating me unconscious. Oh yeah, and her accusing me of rape. Couldn't forget that part.

Christ on a crutch. This was fucked up.

"University police is here," Thomas—the president of my fraternity—announced, appearing in the doorway of the room. He sent me a contemptuous glance that confused me since Thomas and I had always gotten along. Then he returned his attention to Max and added, "Lucky for him since Melody's brother just showed up too."

I closed my eyes and groaned.

This was all too much. A girl crying rape against me, her brother and university police showing up, my body feeling like a used battering ram, and the alcohol I still hadn't completely flushed from my system still wanting to vacate me. Curling onto my side, despite how much it hurt, I hugged my sore ribs and vomited some more.

Chapter 4
BAILEY

I woke up well before my alarm went off, my mind still reeling and the words "Oh my God, what did I watch?" still spinning through my head.

I felt vile and strange for so avidly having observed something so base and primal. I'd never even seen porn before.

Well, I had now, I guess. A real live version, though I hadn't exactly seen genitals or anything revealing. But I'd known exactly what they'd been doing, and my eyes had been plastered to the crack in that door, because I'd wanted to see what would happen next.

I was such a bad, depraved girl.

Needing to shower and wash the bad off, I hurried into my private bath, but as I stripped, I found myself covering body parts as if someone were watching *me*.

Then I stepped into the tub and started the water, turning it to scorching.

I tried to reason the guilt away. I mean, it wasn't as if I'd had a choice in the matter after I'd gotten stuck in the bathroom while they'd been just outside in the bedroom, doing what they'd been doing. Okay, sure, if I hadn't been a big weenie and hidden from the drunk guy in the first place, I probably wouldn't have found myself in this mess at all, and I certainly hadn't needed to *watch* everything. I could've stayed in a back corner and patiently waited until they were done. Or hey, I could've announced my presence at any time. That would've stopped them. Why the heck hadn't I just done that? Why had I stayed quiet and watched?

Because I was a filthy little creeper, that's why.

I stayed under the spray of the water for longer than I needed to, cleaning everything twice. But I still felt vile afterward. I'd made plenty of wrong decisions in my life, but this one kind of felt worse than the others. If I'd been Tess or Paige, I never would've been caught in that predicament. Why the hell couldn't I just be more like Tess or Paige?

Why did I have to be stuck as loser Bailey of all people? Gah, life was no fair. Why did I always have to be so *me*? It sucked. This entire situation just sucked!

Suddenly mad at the world for making me the way I was so I wouldn't have to be mad at myself for simply being the way I was, I frowned and turned the water off, then jerked open the curtain. But that only reminded me of another curtain I'd opened less than ten hours ago, and *that* memory cracked open another: the expression on Beckett's face when he'd come inside Melody. Which made me throb in the most inappropriate places.

Shuddering, I scrubbed dry and jerked my underwear on before opening the door and finding an outfit to wear in my huge closet. By the time I made my way to the kitchen, it was still early, even too early for anyone else in the apartment to be awake. It was a Sunday morning, so they were probably all going to sleep in anyway, unless they had to work today, the same as I did.

Regardless, I kept the light off as not to wake anyone, though all their room doors had been closed when I'd stepped into the hall. I found the refrigerator by feel and rubbed my eyes against the blare of the interior light as I opened the door. Shivering when chilly air wafted out to greet me, I stared inside stupidly, trying to wake my brain enough to decide what I wanted for breakfast. All the while, it felt so surreal that I was going to eat breakfast like everything was normal when nothing felt normal at all.

Every resident of the apartment marked their food with a black sharpie, except for Tess. Being her usual perky self, Tess used a bright green marker to scrawl her name across her things in her bubbly penmanship, and then she dashed a smiley face underneath. Miss Optimism herself.

Why couldn't I be more like her?

I scanned the items in Jonah's corner. He always stocked the best munchies. But when I saw a chocolate caramel swirled snack pack, which I would've nabbed on any other morning, I didn't reach for it. Already feeling bad enough today as it was, I just couldn't add thievery to my list of crimes, though I'd stolen from him plenty in the past and never felt bad about it before.

Yeah, I must really be off my game today.

I settled for bread and made myself some toast with butter. Then I poured a glass of milk and sat at the table to stare blindly at the kitchen cabinets and counters while I ate, tasting nothing.

I still kept seeing flashes form the night before, Melody's long dark glossy hair swaying as she bounced on Beckett's lap, Beckett's groan and that look on his face when he came, the way she'd told him how she knew she'd get him sooner or later and how worth it it'd been after they were done. Every sight, sound, and smell seemed permanently imprinted on the inside of my eyelids. Okay, maybe not the sounds and smells. Not sure how to imprint those on eyelids, but every sense from the night before was firmly stuck in my memory banks forever, that was for damn sure.

"Morning."

The kitchen light flicked on, and I nearly jumped out of my skin as Logan, Paige's boyfriend, shuffled into the room rubbing his eyes.

Pressing my hand to my still-racing heart, I gasped, "Hey," and watched him alertly as he proceeded to fix two cups of coffee.

"How was the party last night?" he asked, his back to me as he worked.

My eyes sprang open wide. "What? Nothing happened. Why are you asking?"

Oh my God, what did he know?

He paused and sent me an odd look over his shoulder. "Huh?"

I blinked, realizing he'd just been trying to make polite conversation. He really knew nothing. So I forced a yawn to make it seem as if my brain was still too sluggish with sleep to function properly. Then I said, "I'm sorry, what did you ask?"

He tipped his head to the side as if trying to figure me out. But then he turned back to his coffee. "Just wondering if you had any fun at the party you left in such a hurry to attend."

"Oh." Had I left in a rush? I guess I *had* felt the urgent need to flee. Watching Tess and Jonah and Paige and Logan together had been making me stir-crazy. But I'd had no idea they could tell I'd been frantic to escape. Yikes. I needed to work on that. The last thing I wanted to reveal was how much their lovey-dovey ways bothered me.

"Fine. It was fine," I started to answer before shrugging and adding, "Boring." Well, it had been boring right up to the point I'd bumped into that drunk into the hallway, who'd spilled beer on me, followed me into a back room and then proceeded to have sex with another girl while I was trapped in the bathroom and forced to watch the whole thing. But yeah, before that. Boring. "I left early." Sending Logan a tight smile, I might've even fanned my eyelashes innocently.

His eyebrows crinkled, totally not buying it. "You weren't back by the time we went to bed."

"Oh…" Crap, maybe I hadn't left early. Honestly, I had no idea how long I'd been at the party before I'd bumped into Beckett, or how long spying on him and Melody had taken. Time made no sense at the moment. "I, uh, I drove around a while before coming home."

Wait, that hadn't sounded like I had delayed in coming home, had it? Like I hadn't wanted to be around him and his lovey-doving on Paige all the time? I mean, I *hadn't* wanted to be around it, but I didn't want *him* to know that. If anyone ever found out how truly jealous I was, I think my life would cease to exist as I knew it.

"Oh," he said, nodding at my answer. I don't think he knew how to reply, so he smiled vaguely, finished fixing his two cups of coffee, then picked them both up and nodded my way before fleeing the kitchen.

I blew out a long breath, feeling way too strung out and on edge for so early in the morning. I really needed to get my act together or someone in this house was going to realize something was up with me.

Focusing on my breathing and trying to calm myself, I had another few minutes of reprieve, alone with my stirring thoughts and deep-even breaths before Tess and Jonah joined me, holding hands and talking quietly together as they entered the kitchen.

Tess's face brightened when she saw me. "Morning, Bailey. Did you have fun at the party last night?"

Christ on a cracker, why did everyone want to know so much about that stupid damn party?

Fine. Maybe they were just being nice and trying to act interested in my life. I was being paranoid. I got that. No one actually *knew* what I'd seen. I just had to act cool, play this off naturally. No problem.

Except I sucked at acting. I was a bit too open and honest for that shit, like the brutally embarrassingly open, honest type. I couldn't be chill when I felt like a fembot in the presence of a strip teasing Austin Powers. My head was probably seconds from doing a three-sixty and my chest would no doubt explode right after that, rolling smoke from my ears.

I mumbled a non-answer and nodded. Tess didn't have a chance to press for more information because Jonah had already opened the refrigerator door and was asking her what she wanted to eat.

While they were couple-cooking their breakfast, I slipped out of the kitchen. Once back in my room, I gathered my things and decided to head to work early. There was always stock in the back my boss Vivian wanted put out that no one ever put out on the display racks. Maybe I could do that. I didn't realize I was over an hour earlier than usual until I left my room and bumped into Paige who was heading toward the bathroom with her towel and clothes bundled to her chest.

"Hey, you're up and around early today," she said on a smile. "Must not have stayed at the party until the wee hours last night, huh?"

"I, uh…I have some stock to sort through. My boss asked me to come in early," I lied, cringing internally because I hated to lie. Like I said, I was usually too brutally honest for people's comfort. "Have a good day."

Yeah, I'm lying through my teeth, but have a good day.

Geesh, I felt like a great big fraud of a human being.

I rushed out of there and arrived at the clothing outlet store I worked at before it had even opened. After blindly gathering armfuls of clothes in the back, I hauled them into the front and put them on hangers before tagging them and hanging them on racks. Finding myself near the storefront windows, I people-watched as I worked. But everyone I saw pass I wondered about. What kind of expression did they make when they came? Did they heave out ugly sounds, the same way Melody had? Or make the sexy, heavy breathing and occasional scintillating groans that Beck had?

Not that anything about anything I'd seen last night had been sexy. It'd been awful, and invasive, and embarrassing, and I was going to stop thinking about it.

Right…now.

My internal command didn't work.

I kept wondering where he'd touched her that had set her off and how big he'd really been to impress her so much. Why hadn't they kissed even once? Kissing had been the only half-decent thing I'd ever done with Dale, my first and only experience with the opposite sex. And why had going down on Beck made Melody wet? Blowjobs had always seemed like they'd be an annoying chore to me, not something that was actually enjoyable for the girl.

More and more thoughts like those plagued me for the rest of the day. I couldn't even fully appreciate the praise Vivian gave me when she showed up to find what I'd done for her.

I have no idea why I was so obsessed with last night. I'm sure people had walked in on couples having sex plenty in their lives, and they'd never thought about it again. But this was a first for me. A big first. And it'd been so unlike the one sexual encounter I'd had myself. Dale had been the one to pressure me into it until I'd finally sighed and said, "Whatever," so he'd shut up already. But last night, Beckett hadn't pressured Melody at all. Actually, it'd been quite the other way around. I'd never seen a girl so bold and aggressive for sex before.

I was kind of jealous of her for going forth and making sure she got what she wanted, except I thought her whole approach had come off as sleazy and underhanded. Beckett had been way too drunk to be making any such decision, and she hadn't listened to a single protest he'd made. I don't think I'd ever be able to come onto a guy unless I knew one hundred percent beyond a shadow of a doubt that he wanted me back.

But I guess Melody was just tons more confident than I was. A bitch, in my opinion, but still admirably confident.

By the time I made it back home to my apartment that evening, my spinning brain had mellowed some, but I was still quiet and thoughtful as I unlocked my door and tromped up the steps.

We had a second floor apartment. The door to the outside opened on the ground level and immediately veered up a stairwell to our living room. One of the two openings into the living room led into the kitchen, while the other led into a hallway to get to the bedrooms and bathrooms. When I'd first found the place to rent, I thought the whole second-floor aspect had been cool. But after living here for six months, climbing these stairs every day was becoming a pain in the ass.

I was the first to make it back home, so I found my way into the kitchen to start supper. I wasn't typically a big cooker, but I needed to keep my mind busy.

I chopped vegetables, browned beef, boiled potatoes. Before I knew it, everything was beginning to smell and look a lot like stew. My dad had always been big on making stews and soups and chilis when I'd been growing up. That little link to home comforted my nerves and by the time roommates started trickling in, I think I was finally feeling more like myself again.

At least I thought I was, until supper started and Tess tossed me a concerned glance. "You doing okay, Bailey? You're awfully quiet tonight."

Honestly, no one had been talking about much. The guys had been regaling the girls with stories of their different gym teachers from grade school. Typically, I would've come up with some sarcastic, witty quip to knock one or both of the boyfriends' egos down a peg or two, just for funsies, but tonight, not so much.

As everyone grew quiet and regarded me curiously, I lifted my face from my soup and said, "Hmm? I'm sorry, what?"

"Is everything okay?" Paige asked this time. Now both women looked concerned.

I nodded immediately. "Oh, sure. Just fine. Why?" No way was I going to tell them about my voyeuristic adventures the night before, and definitely not in front of their boyfriends. Logan and Jonah thought I was cracked already. Who knew how they'd react if they learned I was a freaky pervert too.

Everyone was still staring; my two friends seemed like they might want to try to resuscitate me as if I was flat lining or something. It freaked me out. Geesh, I wasn't usually *that* much of a loudmouth at supper.

Wait, was I?

Oh, probably. Whatever. I still wasn't acting *that* weird. I just needed the attention off me.

"Good Lord," I squawked, making shooing motions at them. "Do I have a unicorn horn growing from my forehead or something? Why are you all gawking like that at me? I'm *fine*."

"Sorry," Tess rushed to transfer her gaze to her food. She'd always been sensitive to a person's emotions like that. "You were just acting off."

"Well, *Off* is my middle name, so how is that really unusual for me?"

The guys snickered. I flipped them off for agreeing with me so quickly. Jonah rolled his eyes and sent me his own bird in return.

"Did everything go okay for you at the party last night?" Paige asked, wiping her mouth with a napkin.

I swerved my attention to her and instantly scowled. She was a little too perceptive sometimes.

"Because I heard a rumor at the coffee shop today that some girl was raped there."

My jaw dropped open. "Say *what*? Last night?"

"Oh my Lord." Tess covered her mouth with one hand while reaching for my arm with the other. "And you were there all by yourself. *Bailey*. You could've..." When she went pale with all the possibilities of what could've happened to me, I snorted.

"I was fine." But I whipped my attention back to Paige. "I wonder where..." Then I shook my head. How freaky. A rape. What if it had happened in one of those other rooms down the hall I'd been about to search? What if Beckett accidently trapping me in that bathroom had kept me from running into the rapist myself?

Even though I'd just tried to reassure Tess that I'd been totally fine, I shuddered and rubbed my hands over the skin prickling on my arms, trying not to dwell on how lucky I'd been.

"You are *not* going to one of those frat parties by yourself again," Tess stated sternly, her gaze boring into mine.

When I sighed and rolled my eyes, she growled. "I'm serious. This isn't something to brush off. There are some true monsters out there."

Realizing it wasn't a joking matter, it really really wasn't, because Paige had been attacked just last year at a frat party, I nodded, and murmured, "You're right. I'm sorry."

"Good." Tess nodded, appeased. "Now. If you simply must go to another one of those stupid parties, one of more of us will go with you. Not that I know why you want to attend them, anyway. I never had any fun at one."

At the first college party Tess had attended, she'd gotten drunk by the same guy who'd pushed himself on Paige later that year, but

I'd been there to pull her away before he could try anything on Tess. So yeah, I couldn't imagine she had any fond party memories. But all this just meant I was once again forced to be their lame fifth wheel.

If only I had—

Wait.

For some reason, this made me think of the cowboy. I gasped, completely having forgotten about him until now. I couldn't believe I hadn't thought of my soulmate all day long, not since Beckett had followed me into that room. But now… Now I gasped and slapped my hands down on the table, making both couples jump.

"I saw the cowboy last night," I blurted, "And guess what? I think his name is Chance. Isn't that awesome? I love the name Chance."

"You what? Oh my goodness!" Tess clasped her hands to her cheeks. "You actually *talked* to him?"

My shoulders slumped. "No. We didn't talk. He got away again. But some drunk idiot told me his name was Chance." Then I frowned, picturing my unreliable source of information. Could I really believe anything Beckett had told me? He'd been mostly out of it. I shook my head and rolled my eyes. "He also tried to tell me the cowboy was in his fraternity, but there was no way I could believe that." I snorted. "Could you just imagine *my* soulmate being a frat brat? No way."

Paige and Tess exchanged knowing glances, but I ignored them. They just didn't understand. So what if the cowboy being my soulmate was a crazy daydream? It made me feel better to talk in certainties.

"Why the heck didn't you say anything sooner?" Tess finally asked.

"Oh, I, uh." I frowned, unable to reveal what had distracted me from my cowboy sighting. So I lamely concluded with, "I forgot."

Tess and Paige exchanged another glance, this one more on the confused side. I understood their bewilderment. After I'd talked about nothing but the cowboy for an entire year, it was pretty much unheard of for me to forget I'd had another encounter with him.

Paige was the first to recover. "Did you get his last name?"

I slumped, a bit defeated. It'd taken me a year to get his *first* name, and she was already demanding a last? Some people just couldn't enjoy a small victory for five seconds, could they?

"Maybe you could look up his first name in the campus directory," Jonah suggested.

I sat up straighter in my chair, not even considering that option. "Oh my God," I said. What if I actually found him there and maybe got an address too? "Yes! Perfect idea."

My head went a little dizzy from excitement.

"Ooh! Go look now," Tess encouraged. "We'll clean the dishes."

So, while Tess and Paige waved me from the kitchen, I shoved back my chair and popped to my feet, wondering blindly where I'd left my laptop. I ran straight to my room, but didn't spot it on my bed, or in my backpack until I remembered I'd been on Facebook last night before they'd popped the movie in, at which point I'd set my computer on the floor between the lazy boy and love seat.

Hurrying into the living room, I flopped onto the lazy boy before leaning over the armrest and tugging my laptop into my lap.

The television was on, airing the evening news, but I paid it no mind as I flipped up the lid and waited for the screen to pop to life and ask for my password.

Just as it did, the reporter on the news said, "Police are finally revealing the name of the suspect involved in the rape reported at a Granton University fraternity party last night."

Intrigued, I looked up just as the mugshot of man in a prison orange jumpsuit popped onto the screen, a man whose face looked as if it'd been beaten to a bloody pulp, but a face I remembered clearly.

"Beckett Hilliard was arrested last night for the rape of Melody Fairfield, where the crime was reported as taking place in a back bedroom of the Alpha Gamma Rho fraternity..."

"What?" I shook my head, unable to stop staring. What the hell was this?

Bucket was the big, awful rapist everyone was talking about?

"No freaking way," I uttered.

Chapter 5

BECKETT

Monday morning, thirty-three hours after I'd been arrested, someone finally opened my retaining cell.

"Hilliard," the voice blaring my name made me jump. "Approach the door. It's time for your first appearance."

I remained seated a second longer as nerves jumbled in my stomach. I wasn't sure if the idea of attending my arraignment was relieving or dooming. I just knew it had me on edge. I'd taken enough law classes to know I'd be told what charges had been filed against me, what my bail had been set for, and then I'd be asked to enter my plea. But other than that, I had no idea how this worked.

But I guessed I better find out before they had to come in here for me and taser me from my cot. So I stood and shuffled toward the doors until it opened and a correctional officer waiting on the other side held up a set of handcuffs.

I gulped, still unable to quite believe this was happening. I'd been arrested one other time this summer, for assault, but I'd been bailed out before spending any actual time behind bars. Other than that, I'd never even gotten a speeding ticket before. Now I was in jail for rape. Unreal.

As I turned around and placed my hands together behind my back, I thought back to my one phone call I'd made two nights ago when I'd first been brought in.

Worst fucking call of my life. My dad had answered. Couldn't have been Mom. No. There was no reason to go easy on Beckett, not after that night I'd had with some lying chick accusing me of the worse crime ever, then her stupid naïve boyfriend beating the crap out of me, and then the cops hauling me off to jail in the back of a police car while all my fraternity brothers had watched with judgmental jeers. So yeah, let's go straight to hard-ass dad picking up the phone first. Sure.

"Dad." My voice had cracked on his name, and even though I knew he'd take it the worst, I was still relieved to hear his voice. I was suddenly just a kid, needing his parents. I wanted to be home with him. I wanted to be crawling into bed with him and Mom and telling them all about the nightmare I'd just had so they could soothe my fears away.

"Beck?" I heard shuffling. He and Mom were probably already in bed. I could picture him sitting up and putting on his glasses to read the time on his bedside clock. "What's going on? It's after midnight. Is everything okay?"

"Umm." I shook my head before I could say the words. "Actually, no. I'm not okay. I'm kind of…" Shit, there was no easy way to say this. "I'm in jail."

"*What*? Jesus, Beckett. What did you do? Drunk driving? Drunken disorderly conduct? I knew you had to be partying nonstop in that fraternity of yours."

I closed my eyes and rested my forehead on the wall in front of me. My brain was still spinning from drinking and my bones hurt from Melody's boyfriend. But all that was minor compared to the ping in my heart, too scared to tell my father the truth.

"Beck? Are you still there?"

"Yeah," I croaked. "Trust me. I'm not going anywhere." My laugh was dry and bitter and short lived. "But no. No, I wasn't arrested for drunk driving." I could only wish that had been the charge.

"Then…?"

I drew in a breath. This right here would be the test of all tests. After everything my family had been through lately, I'd definitely know where their loyalties lay.

"Beck? What were you arrested for?"

"Rape," I whispered.

A pause followed before he said, "Excuse me?"

"Dad, you know I didn't do it. I would never. You know me. I'm your son. This is just one big, fucked up misunderstanding. Her boyfriend showed up, so she freaked and started spouting out these lies, and..."

And holy shit, I'd just admitted to my dad I was a cheater. Fuck, I'd never cheated on a girl before or assisted in a cheating, but now I was in jail and telling my father all about my cheating ways. How was this happening?

I stopped blathering and panted for breath, worried about his response. When he didn't have one, and ten seconds later he *still* hadn't spoken, I winced. "Dad?"

He cleared his throat. "You will be held accountable for your actions, son. May God have mercy on your soul." Then he had hung up on me.

I stared blankly at the wall as the dial tone echoed through my ear. My own father hadn't believed me. I mean, he had reason to not believe any guy accused of rape. After what had happened to Britt, sure. But still. I was his fucking son. His flesh and blood. He *knew* better. He knew *me*.

Which made me wonder if this was about what he believed at all.

His complete lack of faith, or at least his lack of support, pulverized me. I was still reeling all the way to the courthouse thirty-three hours later. I didn't know how a judge or anyone else would be able to support me me if my own father refused to.

When they led me before the bench and I looked into the condemning eyes of the lady in black robes, I knew...there would be no mercy for me today. Just from the way she narrowed her eyes, I knew she was a man-hater.

"Beckett Aaron Hilliard, you have been accused of multiple counts of forcible rape."

"Multiple?" I croaked, not expecting that part. How the hell many times had Melody said I raped her?

Judge Gudrun stared down her nose at me with a stony expression. "In this case, each instance of penetration serves as a count of rape."

I gulped, feeling doomed. "Oh." In my mind, I tried to calculate how many times Melody had bounced on my lap. I'd been pretty drunk; it had felt as if it'd taken me forever to come. How many penetrations did that make? Hundreds? Thousands?

Holy shit, I was going to spend the rest of my life in jail.

"How do you plead?" Her honor's booming voice startled me.

"I, uh, I didn't rape her?" I asked more than answered.

Her nose wrinkled with distaste, "Your answer is either guilty, non-guilty, or no contest."

"Oh, sorry. Not guilty then." I ducked my head, feeling like a moron. I wasn't in the right frame of mind for this right now. What kind of idiot bombed his own hearing?

"Then your trial is set to take place on…" She sent the lady sitting in a cubicle next to her a seeking glance, and that woman promptly handed her a sheet of paper, which she glanced at briefly before spitting out a date that left my head as soon as I heard it. "Do you have an attorney or do you need one assigned to you?"

The question came at me so fast I had no idea how to answer. "Uh." How the hell did I answer? I didn't have a lawyer, I had no idea how to find one, especially from jail, or how I could afford one. My family likely wasn't going to help me out. But weren't court-assigned lawyers the crappy ones? What choice did I have but to go that route?

"I…I… I guess I need one assigned," I finally said.

Judge Gudrun nodded and made a note on her sheet. "Alright then. Your bail is set for fifty thousand, but I'm going to raise it to seventy-five."

Seventy-five? Seventy-five thousand *dollars*? Holy fuck. That was a lot of money. I didn't have that kind of money. And I already knew no one would be willing to front it for me.

My shoulders slumped low. I was going to be stuck in jail until the trial took place. Oh shit, when had she said that was again? I suddenly felt like hyperventilating.

Before I knew it, the officer who'd escorted me here was telling me to stand, and we were leaving the courthouse.

I sat in the back of the patrol car and stared out the window at freedom all the way back to the jail. Every car we passed, or person I saw walking down the sidewalks, the bicyclists who zipped by, I envied. They had no idea how precious just being able to stand at the crosswalk, waiting for the light to change, was. All it'd take was one spoiled college girl's lie to take it all away.

Once we returned to the police station, I wasn't taken back to my old cell, where I'd been stewing all night and through another day by myself alone, waiting for my Monday morning arraignment.

No. The officer opened another door, only for me to peer inside and see dozens of other guys. I scuttled backward, away from them, confused.

"This isn't where I was before," I said, my heartrate jacking into my throat with a jarring force.

"I know." The officer nudged me forward. "That was your classification cell until your hearing. Now…" He spread out a hand, inviting me inside. "You're in general population."

I gulped. General population. I wasn't ready for general population. And I certainly wasn't ready for the jailer to push me through the doorway with enough force to send me stumbling inside. "Got a new rapist for you guys," He called just as the door banged shut. "Enjoy."

I spun around and gaped at him with wide eyes through the door as he grinned demonically and waved his fingers at me. Holy shit, he couldn't do that. Could he?

My skin buzzed with fear as I spun around to take in the convicts surrounding me who'd just heard I was a rapist.

When one huge, burly guy with a beard and long hair came strolling forward, his eyes narrowed, I froze and held my breath.

"A rapist, huh?" he asked quietly as he cracked his knuckles. I was really coming to hate it when people cracked their knuckles. "I don't like rapists."

Yeah, well…I didn't either. Not that anyone in this room cared or even bothered to learn that. They became a bit too preoccupied with beating the crap out of me.

Chapter 6

BAILEY

I was the biggest coward I knew. That was all.

I woke up Monday morning after seeing the news report about Beckett the night before with every intention of skipping class and going straight to the police department to give them my statement, but…yeah, I couldn't.

Seriously, how did you confess to complete strangers the most embarrassing thing you'd ever done?

I had no idea, that's why I didn't do it.

Instead of driving to the station or even class, I'd found myself at a beauty salon, and the next thing I knew, I was getting my hair dyed a pale blonde and then asking the lady to put some curl in it. Which was why I suddenly wanted a scarf to cover my head as I entered my apartment that afternoon. Not that my new do looked bad. It was actually kind of cute; totally Bailey approved. It seemed to make the contours of my face seem more cheerfully adorable than the chubby round blob they usually felt like. I should've tried curly blonde ages ago.

But it was also a dead-giveaway that something was bothering me.

While some people redecorated or ate or cleaned in times of great distress, I dyed my hair. Like in the tenth grade, for example, Chrissy Jackson called me a fat bitch and got all her friends to call me one too until someone had scratched it into my locker door. And my hair went pitch black with a streak of red. Then, during the summer between my junior and senior year, I lost my virginity—horrid event—so my hair suddenly became an array of brown, black, blonde, red, and mahogany of every shade. Then seven months ago, I learned my mother hadn't actually died when I was too young to remember her. I'd been seven when she had passed and I'd just been so traumatized by the whole event that I'd pretty much wiped all memory of her from my existence. Learning that doozey had prompted me into dying my hair every freaking color of the rainbow.

The reason why I dyed my hair during these times wasn't that complicated. I just needed an extreme change to deal with my own overwhelming emotions, because I really couldn't deal with them at all.

Paige might not be quite so tuned in to the hair-dyeing aspect about me since she hadn't even known me a year and half yet, but Tess, yeah, Tess would know something was up. Tess had known me my whole damn life. She'd figure it out immediately.

Oh, who the hell was I kidding? All of them already knew something was up. But now I'd just gone and proven them right with blinding pale ringlets of blonde wrapped around my head.

Holding my breath, I tiptoed up the steps where I could already hear the television and murmured voices of more than one of my roommates in the front room, hanging out.

"Holy wow," Tess was saying, but I hadn't cleared the landing yet, so I knew she wasn't talking about my hair.

"What?" Jonah asked her.

"I think this rape thing is going to blow up to be bigger than either the shooting or the theater burning down," she answered.

Hearing the word rape made me hurry up the steps just in time to see her curled on the couch where she was cozied next to her boyfriend and was shifting the screen of her laptop around to show him what she'd been seeing.

"Just look at all the memes they've made already."

Forgetting my hair, I dashed behind them to peer over their shoulders for a glimpse of the screen myself, and my mouth dropped open as I saw all these pictures of Beckett with messages below and above him, damning him for all eternity as they called him evil, vile things.

My stomach surged with unease. A great big *guilty* unease.

Tess shook her head. "Granton's going to have the worst reputation of any college in the history of ever."

I nodded mutely. Our poor university really did have enough to contend with already. At the beginning of last year, some eerie strange kid who'd lived in our dorm building and I'd met a handful of times had gone on a shooting spree and killed eleven students. Then, last semester, protestors had accidentally burned down the Performing Arts Theater, which resulted in the deaths of three more people. Now *this* was being talked about everywhere. It seemed as if every time Granton University was mentioned on the news, something awful had happened.

"And it looks like we made the national news again," Paige spoke up from the love seat, where she was watching the television. She lifted the remote and turned up the volume just as a CNN reporter mentioned Beckett.

"Hilliard, a senior at Granton, had his arraignment this morning, where the judge lifted his bail to seventy-five thousand. After he pled innocent, Judge Gudrun set his trial to take place in late spring."

My mouth fell open. His bail had been *raised*? This made no sense. None of it. I shook my head, wondering how this could be. He was innocent. Why had they raised his bail? Why weren't they setting him free?

"Great," Logan muttered from next to Paige. "I can just hear enrollment numbers drop another twenty percent. I bet they'll raise tuition again to try to make up the difference."

"Fuck tuition," I exploded, gaping at the national news reporter who was detailing all of Beckett's allegations as if they were freaking fact. "They're crucifying his poor reputation."

How would he ever recover from this?

A stunned silence followed my outburst as everyone turned to gape at me. Then Tess screeched, "Oh my God! Your hair."

"And fuck my hair." I motioned toward the television. "Why are they *doing* that to him?"

Four pair of eyes blinked dumbly. Then the two couples shot each other confused glances before Paige discretely cleared her throat and hedged, "Umm, because he's a rapist, maybe?"

Realizing I'd just completely ousted myself, I flushed hotly before stuttering a second, then saying, "B-but what if he's not? I mean, has he been found guilty yet? Has he *confessed*? They just said he pled innocent, didn't they?"

Of course, he would plead innocent. He *was* innocent. I'd been there. I knew he was innocent. I'd seen and heard the whole thing. He had *not* raped that Melody girl. And he'd been in no condition after that encounter to go off and rape her or anyone else later after I'd left either. This was all just bullshit.

My stomach churned with guilt as I glanced at the picture they showed of Beckett. There was really only one reason he was in jail right now.

Because I hadn't been able to tell anyone, not even my best friends, what I'd seen.

To be honest, or maybe just really hopeful, I hadn't thought this would blow up as big as it had. The guy was innocent; there could be absolutely no evidence against him, right? So how could he still be in jail? How could this make the national news? How come I kept feeling guiltier and guiltier every second of the day, as if my little confession would be the only thing to get him free? That couldn't be the case. There had to be *something* else to help him.

Right?

I gulped and looked down just as a new nasty meme popped up on Tess's Facebook feed. It didn't seem to matter if what he'd done was true or not. Social media had found him guilty; he was as good as fucked. Poor guy.

"Bailey?" Paige said slowly, making me jump and remember everyone was still staring me at me.

Tired of faking it, I just clutched my new curly blonde hair in my hands and gave up. "I don't know what to do," I confessed.

No, actually, I *did* know what I needed to do. I just didn't know if I had to nerve. Was I really supposed to waltz into the police department and tell some cop I'd watched two people have sex? Confessing that was exactly the kind of mortifying thing I had nightmares about, right next to dreaming about showing up to school naked and dreaming about making out with one of my brothers. Who could confess that kind of shit?

"Okay, that's it." Tess plopped her laptop onto Jonah's lap and sprang to her feet, before rounding the couch to grip my arm "We are girl talking, and you are going to tell us what's going on. Right now." Then she motioned toward Paige to follow us before she dragged me down the hall.

Twenty minutes later, in the privacy of my room with my door shut and the boyfriends locked out, I hugged my pillow to my chest and tried to hide my face in it while my two best friends gaped at me as if I were insane.

"Bailey! You have to tell the police."

I lifted my face in order to shake my head. "I don't know, are you sure? What if they don't need me and my story is completely irrelevant and I just look like a freaking voyeur for going to them and telling them what I watched?"

"You *need* to tell them," Tess stated more adamantly.

"I don't think I can." I sighed and buried my face back into the pillow, where everything was soft and nice and smelled like shampoo. I should live in that pillow forever. Pillow paradise.

"Beckett Hilliard's freedom is at stake," Paige said.

The words came so plainly and practically and yet they hit the mark harder than anything, because dammit, she was right. I couldn't do this to that poor guy. I lifted my face from the pillow, returning to reality.

I should've known the moment Beckett had spilled beer down the front of my shirt he would forever more be a pain in my ass. Stupid, idiot boy. He really, *really* should've stopped Melody when she'd unzipped his pants, like I knew he'd wanted to, so I didn't have to be stuck in this predicament right now. Hell, so *he* wouldn't be stuck in it.

Who knew one spilled beer would tie two complete strangers together so inexplicably.

I blew out a breath, but had no other choice except to admit, "Okay." Then my stomach churned as a new idea hit me. "Oh God, you guys are going to tell your men about this, aren't you?"

They were going to know I was a voyeur. They'd probably wonder how many times I'd spied on *them* having sex.

I was never going to live this down.

Chapter 7
BECKETT

Infirmaries weren't such bad places. You got your own private cell, no one tried to kill you, and, okay, honestly, nothing topped the no-one-tried-to-kill-you aspect. That was my favorite part of the whole place, I was not getting beaten to a bloody pulp.

Sure, it hurt to breathe, I was pissing blood, and the nurses—I guessed that was what you called the guards who patched you up—were less than gentle. But I was not afraid for my life in here. I felt safe and secure.

I kind of wanted to stay here forever.

My welcoming committee in general population hadn't been lying; they really, *really* hadn't liked rapists, or even accused rapists for that matter. I was lucky to survive that encounter before a pair of correctional officers caught on as to what was happening and put a stop to it. Since then, I'd been safe, in complete utter pain from head to toe, but still safe, in my cozy, little infirmary cell.

In the next chamber over, another convict groaned and clutched his abdomen before complaining about a stomachache. I turned my head aside on the cot where I lay flat on my back and watched him from my one good eye.

Yeah, just when one eye had healed from Melody's boyfriend, the other one got jacked with. Karma hated me, apparently.

But karma didn't seem to favor this dude either. His face was pale, and sweat poured from his temples. He actually looked like he really did hurt as he started to complain loudly, demanding help, before he was harshly told to zip it.

I returned my attention back to the gray concrete ceiling and tried to make myself picture some pleasant images swimming around up there, except my mind conjured nothing, just cold, lifeless gray concrete. But no one was kicking me in the ribs or bashing my skull against the floor, so it wasn't too bad.

I smiled at that, then winced as I drew in too deep of a breath, making my chest fill with fire and pressure. I quickly exhaled and concentrated on shortening each breath. The grumbling by my neighbor began to grow monotonous until it became almost a rhythmic kind of background chatter and began to lull me into sleep. As soon as my eyes grew heavy and my head became muzzy, however, someone pounded on the bars a foot from my face, jarring me awake.

"Hey, Hilliard."

My one working eye flew open and my startled heart slammed itself against my ribcage, making me gasp as my entire chest constricted.

"Your lawyer's here. He's coming in there with you, so don't try any funny business, okay?"

I have no idea what business they thought I could even attempt in this condition that was remotely humorous, but I lifted my arm from the bed just enough to give the guard a thumb's up. I wasn't exactly planning on preforming any stand-up comedy, so all was good.

"He's pretty much out of it," the guard told someone next to him as he unlocked my cage and swung the door open. "Hasn't said a word since they brought him in here half dead yesterday afternoon except to answer direct questions."

"Thank you, Harold," the guy next to him answered before I heard his footsteps echo across the floor as he entered my cell and then my line of sight. My lawyer looked young, like rookie young, or maybe he just had one of those pudgy baby faces and he was really fifty-five or something. I don't know. But he seemed nervous as he eyed me, swinging his briefcase around like a shield to hold in between me and him.

I guess being beat half to death the day before made me look pretty badass, I don't know, but my appearance sure seemed to intimidate the hell out of him.

"H-hey, Beckett," he started haltingly as he latched his fingers around the back of the chair that was sitting at my bedside and then dragged it another five feet away from me before taking a seat in it and settling his briefcase on this lap.

"Hey," I rasped back, my voice nothing short of a hoarse whisper. I cleared it before motioning to my bedside table. "I'd offer you a drink, but they only gave me one cup."

The man let out a nervous chuckle as he glanced around my sparse cell.

"This is a first for me," he admitted. "And definitely the most unorthodox visit I've ever paid one of my clients, but they assured me it was safe."

I blinked, not sure how to take that. It was so bizarre for anyone to think of me as dangerous in the first place, but even doubly so because of the state I was in. The worst damage I could do right now was bleed on him.

Life had turned so strange in the past few days. This whole new world was foreign.

Instead of reassuring him, though, that I wasn't a serial killer and wanted to eat his liver with some fava beans and a nice chianti, I asked, "You my lawyer?"

"Oh!" He jolted, and his face brightened as if embarrassed. "Yes, sorry. I'm Ron Stempy. I work for the state's legal defense, and I've been assigned to your case."

"This your first case?" I guessed.

He blinked, appearing surprised by the question. "It's my seventh, actually."

"Oh. Good," I rasped, giving him a thumbs up. "You're an old pro then," while inside, I wept.

They'd sent a damn rookie to defend me? I was so fucked.

Stempy seemed encouraged by my sarcasm though. Maybe it'd sounded genuine to him. I'm not sure, but it made him shed some of his tension and reservations as he snapped open his briefcase and began to extract papers. "I've been going over your testimony and that of the victim, and I have a few more questions if that's okay."

I wanted to argue that Melody wasn't exactly what I'd call a *victim*, but I still felt sluggish from the sleep that had just tried to claim me. I wasn't in the right frame of mind to argue about shit. So I slurred, "Sure, I'd love to answer questions." Not like I had much else to do. The gray ceiling I'd been so busy staring at wasn't going anywhere.

Stempy's smile looked forced. "Okay, then." He drew in a deep breath. "Let's start from the beginning. The room you and Miss Fairfield were found in together; it wasn't yours. Was that her brother's room? Did you follow her in there?"

"No." I shook my head and winced when pain reverberated through my skull, like an echo of the way it had rung yesterday when they'd slammed me face first into the floor. "I don't know whose room it was. And I didn't follow her. She followed *me*."

Stempy flipped through the report he was perusing before looking up and lifting a surprised eyebrow. "She followed *you* into the room?" He scratched out a quick note. "Then why did you go into that room to begin with if you didn't even know whose room it was?"

"Thought I was following the girl with the rainbow hair."

"Rainbow hair?" A frown creased Stempy's face as he flipped a few more pages before pausing and reading. Then he said. "You mentioned a rainbow-headed girl somewhere else. In the initial investigation when the police questioned you, they asked if any other witness had been present. You said, 'Yeah, the girl with the rainbow-colored hair. After it was over, I opened my eyes and there she was in the room with us, creeping through as if she didn't want to get caught. When she saw me looking at her, she put her finger to her lips, asking me to keep quiet. She wasn't a hallucination."

Clicking his pen as he paused from reading the account, quoting me word for word, Stempy frowned. "Why did you say she wasn't a hallucination?"

I shrugged. "Well, she couldn't have been. I saw her. I talked to her. I spilled beer on her shirt and tried to help her pat it dry. I felt, you know, a live, corporeal person. She couldn't have been a mirage. But then I followed her into that room, and suddenly she was gone, like, I don't know, she disappeared into thin air. When Melody showed up, I asked her if she'd seen the rainbow-haired girl, but she seemed to think I was hallucinating things. But I wasn't. Rainbow-hair girl was real. I saw her before, and then again after it was over, leaving the room. So she must've been hiding or something, behind the shower curtain, I don't know. But she was *there*."

I snapped my fingers. "And Melody very clearly locked the door when she came in, but her boyfriend opened it afterward, so someone—the rainbow-haired girl—had to have unlocked it when she left."

"And what did this corporeal girl look like?"

"I just said, she had rainbow-hair." Why would a person need any more information that that? But it got me a short frown, so I squinted my eyes, trying to remember more, except I only came up with a vague outline of her. "Short," I added. "Full figured."

"So she was fat?"

I frowned at Stempy, not liking that word because he made her sound bad. I hadn't remembered anything bad about the way rainbow-hair had been shaped, so I settled for saying, "Not boney."

"Chubby, then," the lawyer decided, writing that down.

He didn't notice the glare I sent him, which was probably for the best. I didn't especially want to get on the bad side of the only guy willing to defend me. And yet I couldn't handle him focusing on her weight when there had been so much more about her that seemed tons more prominent.

"She was very dynamic," I said. "Energetic. Like a spunky little spitfire that could either be the life of a party and have you rolling with laughter, or your worst nightmare if you ever pissed her off."

I'd only spent two minutes in her company, yet I knew what I said was true without a doubt. And also completely irreverent. The blank glance Stempy sent me told me personality was not going to help him physically pick her out of a line-up. But sadly, that was basically all I remembered about her.

Rubbing a spot on the center of his forehead as if a headache were growing, Stempy sighed. "How much did you say you had to drink that night?"

I narrowed my eyes. "I was fucked up. I know that. But I remember everything, and I didn't hallucinate anyone."

I felt as if I was being too adamant, which probably came across as really fake, but I couldn't help it. My freaking attorney was looking at me like I was a total liar. My hopes sank and I found myself rubbing my own head as it began to pound miserably. Then I winced when I hit a sore spot, so I dropped my hand lamely back to the mattress.

No one was going to believe me, were they? I suddenly understood how Harrison Ford had felt on *The Fugitive* when he'd tried to convince everyone a one-armed man had killed his wife.

I kind of wanted to stand up and shout, *"You find this man, er, rainbow-haired girl. You* find *this girl."*

She was obviously the key to everything.

"So, this girl," Stempy was saying, shaking his head as if my answers were too complicated for him to comprehend. "You followed this girl—with the rainbow-colored hair—into the room, but you didn't know her?"

"Right." I nodded. See my answers weren't confusing at all.

Stempy sighed. "If you didn't know her, then why did you follow her into someone-else-you-didn't -know's bedroom?"

"I told you." I stared at him as if he'd lost his mind. "I spilled beer on her. I was trying to apologize and offer to buy her a new shirt, but she veered off into that room, running away from me. I don't know why it was so important to me; I just wanted to make everything right with her."

Stempy lifted his hand to stop me. Then he said, "Okay, obviously we need to start further back than the beginning. *When* did you spill beer on the rainbow-colored hair girl?"

Oh, right. Maybe I did need to explain more. I could suddenly see why he was so lost. "Okay, yeah." I nodded. "So my fraternity threw a party that night. Obviously I attended *and* drank alcohol there. I was really drunk, and at one point I needed to take a piss. I went to the bathroom, but when I came out, holding my beer, she was right there."

"The rainbow-haired girl, not Melody?"

I nodded. "Right. And I mean, she was, like, *right* there. So we both jerked to a halt to keep from running into each other, but I lost hold of my cup and spilled my beer all down the front of her shirt. Cool shirt, too. It said *This is my Day Drinking Shirt.*"

When Stempy blinked at me blankly, not impressed, I added, "You know from the song 'Day Drinking' by the band Little Big Town?" I nodded respectfully. I totally meshed with Rainbow-Hair's taste in music.

But Stempy obviously wasn't a country music fan. I cleared my throat. "Anyway, I offered to buy her a new shirt." And maybe get my own while I was at it. I really had liked that shirt.

"You offered to buy her a new shirt?" My attorney seemed dubious.

I shrugged. "Sure." It seemed embarrassing to admit now that I'd wanted to find out where she'd gotten hers so I could get my own. So I added, "I was really drunk."

Stempy nodded. "Ah."

"But she seemed distracted, was looking for someone. And she took off before I could somehow make things right between us for getting her all wet. So when she went into the bedroom, I don't know, I just followed her. It was dark in there, but the bathroom light was on further inside the room, so I thought she'd gone into the bathroom. But when I got there, nothing."

Stempy looked up from his notetaking, his eyebrows raised. "Was there another exit from that bathroom?"

"No." I said. "It was the strangest thing. When I turned to leave though, Melody was there, entering the room and turning the light on."

"So *Melody* turned the bedroom light on, not you?"

I thought that was a weird question, but I nodded. "Yeah."

"You're sure?"

Blinking about how much of a big deal he was making over a light switch, I took a second to think it through, and I was still sure. "Yes."

"And what did you say to her when she did that?"

"I didn't say anything. She's the one who talked to me, saying she thought it was me she'd seen enter the room."

Nodding, Stempy scribbled more notes. "And how did you answer?"

"I told her I was looking for the rainbow-haired girl. And she asked what kind of drugs I was taking, like I'd hallucinated her. But I told Melody I wasn't on anything, I don't do drugs, I was just really drunk. And she said she was sober enough for the both of us. Or wait." I frowned, trying to recall the sequence of events correctly. "Maybe she said that later."

Stempy looked up. "But she definitely said it. She told you she was sober."

"Yeah." I bobbed my head. "She wanted me to sit down because I was so drunk I was weaving on my feet. She came over and nudged me to sit on the edge of the bed."

"*She's* the one who nudged *you* down?"

I watched him write all this, wondering why it mattered, but I murmured, "Right. And then…" I squinted, trying to remember. When Stempy lifted his face, I started talking again. "Then she ran her hands through my hair, telling me she knew why I was so drunk, because she'd heard my girlfriend and I had broken up, like I was drowning my miseries in alcohol or something."

"And were you?"

I shrugged and looked up at the gray ceiling. "I don't know. Maybe." Among other reasons.

"Okay. And then what happened?"

"I'm not—" This was where things got a little foggier for me, but I didn't want Stempy to think I had blocks in my memory so I hurried to say, "She said something really off, like she confessed she didn't like Jana. That's my ex I just broke up with. But her and Jana were supposed to be friends. It was just…" I shook my head. "It seemed skeevy to me. When I asked her what she meant, she said she was on Team Beckett. And then she reached for my fly and unzipped my jeans."

Stempy gaped at me as if engrossed in some raunchy locker room talk. "What? Just like that?"

I shrugged. "Just like that. It shocked the shit out of me too."

"How did you respond?" he asked, as if he were a fellow fraternity brother eager to hear what happened next, not so much like a lawyer mapping out my defense.

"I…" I snapped my fingers and pointed. "*That's* when I told her I was too drunk to, you know, engage in such activities. But she assured me she was sober enough to take care of everything. I still kind of resisted, though. I didn't want…"

When my voice trailed off, Stempy pressed, "You didn't want what?"

I gulped, feeling bad about confessing this. "I've never really been that into her. So I didn't want to do anything with her to give her the impression I wanted to start, you know, a relationship. But she distracted me by telling me Jana was somewhere at the party with this guy named Davon, and while I was digesting that, she went down on me."

Stempy's mouth fell open. "And when you say she went down on you, you mean…?"

I lifted an eyebrow. "She gave me a fucking blow job."

He gaped at me a moment before shaking his head. "You didn't stop her?"

"Uh." I think that answer was obvious.

Stempy actually blushed before pointing at me and muttering, "Right. Freshly single, drunk college guy. Why would you stop her?" Then he cleared his throat, straightened his tie. "So, uh, she instigated the actual…?" He motioned with his hands.

"She instigated *everything*. Before I could, you know, ejaculate, she stopped sucking on me and said she wanted to feel me come inside her. I kind of resisted again then, but she said she'd take care of everything, and she pulled a condom from her cleavage."

"Wait. From *her* cleavage?" Stempy asked, and started writing again, as if he'd just realized he needed to take notes.

"Yes, from her cleavage," I repeated. "Then she pushed me down onto my back, pinned one of my hand to the mattress and climbed onto my lap where she fucked me into oblivion."

"So…" Stempy paused scribbling to wipe at a bead of sweat trailing down his temple. "She, uh, she was on top?"

"She was on top," I confirmed. "The entire duration. We finished about the same time, and when it was over, she collapsed on me with her face, you know, right up there next to mine. Then she said something along the lines that she couldn't believe she'd finally gotten to be with me and she knew I'd be as good as she'd heard I was." I rolled my eyes. "Not that I believed her, but…" With a shrug, I admitted, "I mean, it wasn't awful to hear, but it sounded kind of cheesy, like a lame line to me. So I closed my eyes to block her, and I passed out for maybe a few minutes. Not like a full pass-out, but like a half-out-of-it daze. You know, that downtime afterward, when it's all quiet and peaceful and shit?"

When Stempy nodded vigorously, I grinned. "Yeah. Anyway, I was half out of it but thought I heard something at the door, except I remembered Melody locking it, so I looked up to make sure no one was coming in, when there she was."

"The rainbow-haired girl?"

"Yes." I nodded. "I think she was leaving, not entering. I don't know where she'd been the whole time, but she had to have been in there somewhere with us, right, because the door had been locked. When she looked at me and realized I saw her, she froze and pressed one finger to her lips, asking me to keep quiet. So, hell, I don't know why, but I put my finger to my lips too. And she left. I reclosed my eyes and slumped back onto the bed until my stomach revolted and I had to puke."

Stempy winced, because yeah, vomiting totally ruined the dirty sexy parts of my story.

"I was still swaying in the bathroom doorway after I'd finished puking when her boyfriend showed, which I'd had no idea she *had* a fucking boyfriend. As soon as she saw him, everything about her transformed. The waterworks started, she began shaking and crying, and that's when she cried rape, so he wouldn't think she'd willingly cheated on him."

"Well…" Stempy said, clearing his throat and straightening his suit jacket. "After seeing what he did to you, I can see why she would've been afraid to admit to cheating."

"You think?" I muttered, still not too happy I'd received her cheating-beating instead.

"Yes, so, I guess this is all I need to know for now." He set his pen back inside the briefcase. "If I come up with any more questions or learn any new information, I'll be in contact."

As he settled his notes and papers back into pockets and folders, my heart jerked with nerves. I couldn't tell if he was optimistic about my future or not.

"Do you think we have a chance of winning?" I finally asked, dying to know his thoughts.

"That depends." He snapped his briefcase closed and eyed me over the top of the closed lid. "When I came in here, it was a straight-up he-said, she-said case with you ranting about hallucinations of girls with rainbow-colored hair."

"But—"

He lifted a finger to hush me, so I did. And a slow smile spread across his face. "But now…" He added slowly, making me feel hope bloom in the pit of my stomach, because this was one time I actually liked hearing the word *but*. "Now I might have something. Are you absolutely positive your fingerprints would not be found on the condom wrapper, or the light switch, or doorknob of that room?"

I blinked, thinking it through. Then something powerful and bright flared through me, as I said, "No. There's no way. I didn't touch any of those things. And I'd never been in that room before."

He nodded again, looking triumphant. "Well, she's claiming *you* are the one to turn the light on, shut the door, and produce the condom, so if someone dusted for fingerprints, this could prove which one of you is actually telling the truth."

"Oh, thank God," I breathed. "So you…did anyone dust those things for fingerprints?"

Stempy's face fell. "Well, no. No one went that deep into investigating things on the night of the event, and I'm sure the doorknob and light switch in that room have been touched by too many people since then to catch either yours or her prints. And I have no idea if anyone even *kept* the condom wrapper that was found."

"What?" I croaked. "But you said…you said—"

"I said *if*." Stempy raised a finger, watching me closely. "*If* I questioned Miss Fairfield again and got to her believe fingerprints *had* been gathered, would she slip up and admit she'd been lying?"

My shoulders slumped and the flame of hope inside me fluttered back down to a small ember. "That's a pretty *iffy* if."

Stempy winced. "Yes. Yes, it is, especially since the first time I questioned her, I cautioned her that lying about this would be perjury and could land her in jail if a false testimony was ever discovered, so yeah, now she has some pretty strong motivation to stick with her story, no matter what."

Dammit. I closed my eyes. "So, then, what now?"

"Now…" Stempy let out a long, drained sigh. "Now, we hope your hallucination wasn't really a hallucination, and that there really is a rainbow-haired girl floating around Granton University somewhere."

Chapter 8
BAILEY

I wound a strand of my new blonde hair around my finger and eyed the Granton Police Station from the outside. It was a square, two-story building made of light brick with a glassed entrance. The place had been built about fifteen years ago and looked modern-ish, so it didn't have an intimidating vibe to it at all.

So why the hell was I too scared to march up that front walk and go inside?

Because I was a big ol' pansy, that's why.

Tess had offered to go with me. Hell, Paige had offered to go with me. Jonah had mostly just snickered and leered while Logan had blushed and refused to make direct eye contact. But I had declined the offers, flipped off Jonah and sent him a dirty scowl, and then arrived at the police station by myself, my palms sweaty and knees knocking.

I stood there another minute before bolstering myself, drawing in a deep breath and holding it, then placing one foot in front of the other. Twenty-eight steps later, I exhaled and reached out to open the door.

When I pushed through the entrance, I stopped just inside, braced for the finger-pointing and name-calling. But no one screamed voyeur or pervert, and I was able to take another shaky breath before looking around the fairly empty vestibule before spotting a cubicle with a single person sitting inside, typing at a computer.

I walked to her slowly and discreetly cleared my throat before she looked up at me.

"Hey, um, hi." I cleared my throat again. "I need to talk to someone about some information I have on the Beckett Hilliard rape case."

"*Oh*!" The woman seemed surprised by my offer, but she quickly said, "Okay, sure. Let me see if I can get a detective for you. Go ahead and take a seat. Someone will be with you in a minute."

It felt as if I was at a freaking doctor's appointment. I glanced behind me, and what do you know, there was even a few chairs with a table and magazines on them to thumb through. How surreal. Trying to convince myself I was really here for a root canal and not to confess I was a dirty awful voyeur, I sat in the stiff blue chair and picked up a *Highlights* magazine, then flipped through it until I found the Hidden Pictures page.

They needed some elevator music up in this place to really complete the waiting-room mood.

I'd just found a birthday cake hidden in a wall next to a swimming pool when I heard footsteps approaching. When I looked up from the page, a man in slacks and a polo shirt but a gun and badge strapped to his waist nodded to me.

"Ma'am," he said politely. "I'm Detective Rice. Someone said you were here about the Hilliard case?"

"Yes, I—" Flushing, I tossed the *Highlights* down, hoping he didn't think I was an idiot for browsing through a kid's magazine.

Oh, who was I kidding? I *was* an idiot. A complete and utter nitwit. This was a big, huge, important deal, and I was just a stupid little college girl who'd watched two people have sex. Detective Rice looked so professional and authoritative with his salt-and-pepper hair and shrewd pale eyes that looked as if they saw everything as he ushered me down a hall to his office, while I wore polka dot leggings with an oversized long-sleeved shirt bearing a picture of a Grumpy Cat that said *I had fun once; it was awful.*

"I don't think I got your name," Detective Rice said as he motioned me into the windowless room toward a chair by a messy desk and shut us inside alone.

"Oh! Sorry. I'm Bailey. Bailey Prescott. I'm nervous. I don't know how to do this. I—"

With a placating smile, he lifted a hand, and I instantly fell quiet, swallowing down my blubbering, moronic words.

"It's okay, Miss Prescott. I understand how difficult this must be for you. And I appreciate the courage you have to come forward. We'll take this as slow as you need to."

"Okay." I nodded gratefully and eased out a settled breath as I sank into the chair and then clutched the seat under me with both hands, so very glad he was being nice and accommodating about this. Maybe I could confess my sins after all.

Until he sat in his chair and picked up a notebook, saying, "Now you're claiming Beckett Hilliard raped you too, right?"

My mouth fell open. "What? *No*! Not at all."

Detective Rice's face lifted, filling with surprise, "But the secretary said—"

"I have *information* about the case," I butted in, staring at him as if he'd lost his mind, "Information that he *didn't* rape Melody What's-her-face. Not that I'd been raped too. Good Lord, *no*! He didn't rape me. He didn't rape *anyone*. I was there that night. I saw them. He didn't lay a single malicious hand on her, and she was willing, the whole time. *She* instigated it."

The older man stared at me a good five seconds longer before he murmured, "You witnessed the entire event?"

Hey, the way he said it actually didn't sound so bad. *Witnessing an event* seemed so much better than ogling a couple doing the horizontal tango. So, yeah, I'd *witnessed*. I loved that word.

"Yes," I breathed in relief. "I witnessed everything from the moment she entered the room until they were done. And he did not rape her. Not even close."

"Holy—Wait one second." He held up a finger before grabbing his phone and dialing a single number.

"Yes, sir?" a voice asked through the speaker on the base of the phone.

"Sandy," Detective Rice asked the base. "Did I read it correctly on the schedule today that Stempy was going to stop by to see his client?"

"He's here right now, signing out, actually."

"Good." Detective Rice glanced my way. "Could you send him back? I believe there's someone in my office he'd be very interested in questioning with me."

"Yes, sir."

Detective Rice disconnected the speaker, and I gulped, wondering—though mostly worrying over—who Stempy was.

"You have impeccable timing, Miss Prescott," Detective Rice announced. "Beckett Hilliard's lawyer is here visiting him. He probably would've contacted you later with more questions, but now that he's here, we can both just talk to you together."

"Oh," I said in a small voice. So I was going to get grilled by a cop and a lawyer together. That was just great. Awesome. They should toss in a priest too and really make the inquisition complete. Then again, this had to be better than answering questions more than once, right? So sure, bring on more people. The more people to hear about my debaucheries, the merrier.

Oh God, I think I was going to throw up all over the floor. When a knock came on the door, my stomach actually lurched. No! Don't throw up, stomach. Please don't throw up.

Detective Rice stood and answered the door. I swear, the guy that entered seemed so young he had peach fuzz growing from his face. He looked as young as I was.

"Ron Stempy," Detective Rice introduced before swinging his hand my way, "Bailey Prescott. She claims she saw everything that happened on the night of the Hilliard rape."

I frowned, tempted to correct him and say there had been no rape, but Stempy's startled reaction stole my attention.

"She…?" He swung my way so fast I pulled back in my chair away from him. Then he froze and blinked at me a moment before blurting, "But she's blonde." Then he shook his head as if in denial and directly accused me, "You're *blonde*."

My hand went to my curls. "I…yeah. I just got it dyed." What the hell did he have against my blonde curls? I thought they looked cute.

"You…" He stared stupidly another ten seconds before repeating. "You dyed it? What…." He shook his head again and flushed. "I'm sorry, I know this is an off-the-wall question, but when did you dye it, exactly?"

"Yesterday," I said slowly, pressing my locks protectively to my head, and wondering if it was a crime to be blonde. A wild thought raced through my head that they were going to hold me down and shave me bald for dying my hair.

But the lawyer nodded as if pleased by my answer, then bit his lip before asking. "And what color was it before, if you don't mind me asking?"

I squinted at him, wondering why this was so important. "It was a lot of colors, dyed like a rainbow, actually."

He hissed out a sudden, relieved sounding breath. And from the look in his eye, I got the feeling this guy suddenly wanted to hug me. "Oh God," he panted out, most unprofessionally. "Miss Prescott, you are exactly the girl I want to talk to."

* * *

An hour later, I left the police department, feeling, I don't know. Relieved mostly. A good kind of relieved. I didn't feel all that scummy either. Okay, kind of scummy, even though the detective and lawyer both had been quite professional about questioning me. There'd been a few times when we'd all blushed and cleared our throats before continuing, but they hadn't made me out to be a dirty voyeur peeping tom sicko at any point, so that was sweet.

Mr. Stempy seemed a lot more excited about what I had to say than Detective Rice. He smiled as if relieved when I said things like Melody instigated everything and she'd been on top. And one time, when he asked if I knew who'd provided the condom, he'd actually victory-fisted himself before hissing *yes* under his breath after I answered that Melody had pulled a condom from her cleavage.

The most embarrassing part came at the end when Detective Rice politely thanked me and told me someone would be in contact if they had any more questions.

I glanced between the two, startled it was over. They hadn't tied me to a chair in a mirror-windowed room as they played good-cop, bad-cop or given me a lie-detector test or anything.

"That's it?" I blurted, confused.

Mr. Stempy smiled as if amused. "Someone will probably be in contact with more questions."

I nodded and rose to my feet. "So, um, he'll be released then, right?"

The two men exchanged an uncertain glance before the lawyer sighed. "It's hard to say. This started out as a simple she-said, he-said case. Now it's a she-said, he-said, *she*-said situation, so…"

"So no one *believes* me?" I said, dumbfounded, gaping at him.

It'd taken me all the courage I had to come in here and confess this to them, and now…now it was my word against stupid Melody What's-her-face's?

Fuck that shit!

An incredulous anger rose in my chest. I turned my opened-mouth stare from the detective to the lawyer before Mr. Stempy lifted his hands peaceably.

"Now, that's not entirely the case, Miss Prescott. It's not that we don't believe you. It's just…there are conflicting accounts of what happened, so it'll be harder to determine who's telling the truth."

"*I* am!" I boomed, pressing my finger into my chest before pointing at both of them and demanding, "I didn't have to come here. I didn't have to tell you people anything. Do you *know* how hard it was for me to walk into this police station today and tell you what I saw? It would've been so much easier just to keep my mouth shut."

"Now, just calm down, Miss Prescott." The cop waved me quiet as if I were turning hysterical or something.

I frowned at them both and sniffed out my resentment before folding my arms tightly over my chest. "I don't know why I bothered if no one was going to believe me. I don't even know that stupid drunk boy. But I didn't think he deserved to go to jail just because some conniving whore lied about him, so I put myself out there to help him out, except *now* you're telling me I didn't help shit? What the fuck?"

"You *are* helping him," Beckett's lawyer insisted, keeping his voice all monotone and placating, trying to calm me down. It only made me scowl at him harder. He winced. "It's just… We have to work with facts, things that *can't* be disputed, and words can always be disputed. So while your words *do* help some, it'd just be *more* helpful if there was some evidence, like a video or…or…"

My mind clicked, suddenly remembering. "A picture?" I asked, already reaching for my cell phone in my back pocket. "Would a picture help?"

I couldn't believe I'd totally forgotten about taking that picture.

Both men surged forward as I logged into my phone and tapped my photo app.

"You took a picture?" Detective Rice asked incredulously.

"Yeah, well…" My face flushed hot. Okay, this was awkward, until Mr. Stempy actually gave a little hop of excitement.

"If you have a picture, a good, clear picture with her on top of him, this could do it, this might really get him free."

Awkward moment gone, because the lawyer's enthusiasm wiped it away, I bit my lip, hoping to God I'd gotten a good, clear shot.

"I'm not sure," I admitted. "I never looked at the results."

My photos appeared; I chose the newest one because I hadn't taken a picture of anything since then.

And…

"Oh, shit," I blurted when noise and blurry movement immediately blared from the screen of the phone. "I must've changed the setting to *video* by accident."

Oh, my God. This was so freaking embarrassing. I'd taken a *video* of two people having sex.

When I instinctively tried to turn it away and hide the evidence, both men reached out to stop me. "No, wait! This is even better. Start it over again."

I blinked as Mr. Stempy reached over and pushed *play* one more time. Was he freaking serious? They actually expected me to stand between them while we all merrily watched a sex tape together?

Um, okay.

Melody's horrific grunts filled the office, and I swear, even my teeth blushed.

This. Was. Awkward.

"There." Detective Rice moved in even closer to me, hovering over my shoulder on one side as he pointed at the screen while Mr. Stempy shifted in from the other, sandwiching me between them.

Really, really awkward.

"It focuses for a second. You can barely see Hillard's face through the crack in the door, but you can't tell who's on top of him."

Oh my God. How could they sound so clinical and un-bothered by those sounds?

"But she has long, straight, dark hair like Melody Fairfield," Mr. Stempy argued.

"There's no way to know it's really her," the detective stated firmly.

Mr. Stempy jabbed a finger back toward the screen. "She's on top, though, just like Hilliard and Miss Prescott claimed, which Miss Fairfield completely denies happened."

The two men frowned at each other just as Melody really started wailing, and Beckett gave a shout of pleasure.

Oh, hell, please open up and swallow me now, world.

"Wha…?" Both men frowned when the frame moved, going blurry and then the screen became completely dark.

"I thought I'd only taken a quick picture," I explained, my face all hot and flushy. "So I shoved the phone back into my pocket about as soon as I got it into focus."

Stempy held up a hand when I began to lower the phone. "Wait, the video's still going, though. Maybe we can hear—"

Before he could even finish his hope, a muffled female voice called, "Oh my God, that was so good. I can't believe I, Melody Fairfield, finally caught the elusive Beckett Hilliard. And holy shit, Jana was so right about you. You fuck like a goddamn animal."

Beckett's answer was a faint groan as if he were in pain, and then the video finally ran out of steam and shut off.

I lifted my face, no longer so mortified, because I was too busy sharing a shocked glance with Detective Rice and Mr. Stempy. All three of our mouths had fallen open, none of us quite able to believe what we'd just heard.

"Okay, maybe it *was* Melody Fairfield with Beckett Hilliard in the video," Detective Rice finally allowed, "But who's to say this video was taken on the night of the…"

His words faded off, as I pointed to the date and exact time, along with the town's name, posted above the video.

He blinked, then cleared his throat and said, "I'm going to need you to forward that video to me, please."

Beckett's lawyer nodded. "Me too."

It wasn't until after I'd left them, made it to my car and started the engine that I realized I'd just shared a sex tape I'd filmed with two complete strangers.

Life was so weird.

Chapter 9
BAILEY

"So, did you tell them?"

I pulled my lap blanket more firmly over me and grabbed another handful of potato chips—my comfort food. Across the room, *Ferris Bueller's Day Off* played on the television. It'd been a good escape for all of an hour until Tess had come barreling up the stairs, out of breath, her red hair flying out behind her and her cheeks pink from the outdoors cold.

"Yes," I muttered before cramming more Doritos into my mouth. "It's done."

"So…?" She dropped her book bag to the floor and spread her arms, waiting for me to elaborate.

I lifted and eyebrow and crunched noisily. "So…*what*?"

"Oh my God, Bailey? So what *happened*? Did you free him? Are you okay? Did they make you feel dirty and wrong? I kept worrying the whole day that they'd make you feel like the one who did something bad. I totally should've gone with you. I can't believe you—"

"Holy jeez!" I said to hush her. "It went fine. They were really cool, and I actually feel better about it now."

Tess glanced at the movie, where Ferris was currently singing *Twist and Shout* on a parade float, then her gaze ran over the blanket wrapped around me to the nearly empty bag on my lap. She knew I didn't feel totally better yet.

"Okay, fine." I sighed. Sometimes it sucked to have such an intuitive friend. "I have no idea what's happened to the case. I don't know if they freed him instantly, or not? I just...They took my report and then sent the little woman on her way, and it's killing me that I don't know how anything went down from there."

"Well, obviously, they released him, right?" Tess seemed so certain of her statement until she focused on my face. Then her lips parted and her head swayed back and forth with denial. "Right?"

"I don't..." I shook my head. "I don't know." After they'd seen my video, I would think so, yes, but no one said so one way or another. I opened my mouth to tell Tess that, but then I realized she didn't know about the video. Because I hadn't known about it the last time I'd seen her. I couldn't admit that part. Even taking a picture of what I'd seen was humiliating enough, but actually having a *video* of it? No. Sweet innocent Tess didn't need to know that part.

Okay, fine her sweet innocence had nothing to do with it. I just didn't want her knowing how truly depraved I was.

So I stuck with, "I don't know what happened to him, and it's driving me crazy."

"Well." Tess nodded thoughtfully before saying, "You're Bailey; you're not afraid to find this stuff out. And you know which fraternity house he lives in, so..."

Holy geez, she was right. I whipped the blanket off me and accidently sent the bag of Doritos flying across the room as I jumped to my feet.

"I'm going over there," I announced, my big declaration losing some of its bravado with the nacho-flavored corn chips raining down on the floor around us.

Tess blinked at the mess before saying, "I'll go with you."

I started to nod—a little excited to do this with her since we'd always gone on such adventures together—until we heard the door open below us and then bang shut before heavy footsteps started up the stairwell. Definitely not the tread of either Paige or Logan, which meant Jonah was home.

My shoulders slumped.

I knew he made Tess blindingly happy and treated her right, but the bastard had stolen my best friend from me. We used to be inseparable and did everything together. Now *they* were inseparable and did everything together. I honestly couldn't remember when

Tess and I had last gone out on a just-Tess-and-Bailey outing. She didn't seem to miss them, so I didn't complain.

Okay, I complained, but it was the teasing kind of complaint that told them I wasn't the least bit bothered and totally didn't feel left out, even though I totally was and totally did.

Tess's entire face brightened when Jonah's head appeared and then his whole body as he rose from the stairwell and joined us in the front room, and I knew I'd never let her really know how lonely I'd become.

"Nah, I got this one," I said, though I'm not sure why I even bothered. Tess was no longer paying me any attention; she was too busy throwing her arms around Jonah as he wrapped his arms right back around her and picked her up off her feet to give her a big welcoming smooch.

I sighed and moved past them to the wall full of hooks holding coats and jackets and purses with floor mats under them to house shoes.

After I shoved my feet into a pair of fur-lined ankle boots, I reached for my coat. I'd just shrugged it on and was buttoning it up, when Tess realized I was leaving.

"Oh! Bailey."

I winced over at her. "Is it okay if I do this one by myself? He only met me the once and doesn't know you, so…"

"Oh." She nodded instantly. "Sure. That makes sense. After being accused of what he's been accused of and spending the last few days in jail, being visited by a stranger might be…" She shook her head, not sure which term to use.

I nodded, totally understanding. There were a lot of things happening these days that needed new terms that probably hadn't even been invented yet.

"Thanks," I said. "I'll be back in a bit."

Then I grabbed my purse and hurried down the stairs.

I didn't think about what I was going to say to Beckett once I saw him, not until I actually reached the Alpha Gamma Rho house and was walking up between the white pillars of its front porch.

Holy criminy, what the heck *should* I say?

Hey, I was just curious what happened to you, so okay, it looks like your free now. I guess I'll be going. Nice to see you again, bye.

Hmm.

Yeah, I think that needed some work.

I could, uh, well…

The first thing that came to mind was an apology. I mean, I'd spied on the guy having sex. Then I'd waited over twenty-four hours to go to the police for him after I'd discovered he'd been arrested. Oh, and let's not forget I'd called him stupid multiple times in my head, though he really had been. I hadn't stopped Melody from going down on him when he'd been too drunk and horny-male to stop her himself.

So, yeah, I was here to say sorry. Good idea.

Before I could think it through any more than that, I knocked on the door and held my breath. I wasn't sure exactly how I was going to word it. Apologizing really didn't seem like everything I wanted to do here. It just seemed like, well, something was binding us together now, a single event that had turned into something bigger than it ever should've been. It felt odd to never talk to him again after that. I'd kind of saved him; I sort of felt responsible for him now.

But I couldn't tell a guy I'd only talked to for two minutes that I was actually worried about him. So yeah, I was just going to apologize. I mean, an apology was good enough, right? He'd had to spend twenty-four extra hours he'd in a jail cell because of my cowardice.

Oh, Lord. What if Bubba had gotten his hands on Beckett in that time and made him his little prison wife? My stomach lurched with unease. Hopefully Bubba didn't work quite that fast, although damn, Beckett did kind of have one of those pretty-boy faces, a decent body, and his eyes… He had awesome eyes.

Fuck. I better at least have saved him from the honeymoon with Bubba.

Approaching footsteps sounded from inside, and my palms began to sweat. Okay, so how many apologies did I have to make again? Two? Three?

God, I hated apologizing. I always started stuttering and fumbling and totally butchered them to hell. Beckett deserved a nice eloquent, sincere beg of forgiveness. All I could be was honest and awkward as hell.

The door opened. I swallowed my tongue, expecting it to be him for some reason.

But it wasn't him. It wasn't Beckett Hilliard at all.

Instead, the first thing my gaze greeted was a row of shiny pearl snap buttons running up a light blue shirt. I blinked and looked down. Enormous gold belt buckle. Snug Wrangler jeans. Silver-tipped cowboy boots.

Oh my God, *cowboy boots*!

I zipped my attention up and gaped into the eyes of the cowboy. *My* cowboy.

Holy shit, I'd totally forgotten about him and Beckett's insistence that he actually belonged to the Alpha Gamma Rho fraternity.

I shook my head. Seriously, what was my soulmate doing in a fraternity? This wasn't right at all.

But then he smiled and I forgot about all that, because oh wow. He had a warm greeting smile as he slumped one shoulder against one side of the doorframe and then reached out to grip the other side with his hand, his boots crossing at the ankles.

"Well, hello there, sweetheart," he cooed, his voice deep and penetrating. Oh God, how it penetrated. "What's a pretty little thing like yourself doing on our doorstep?"

Oh, cheese and rice, he'd just called me pretty. Excuse me while I fainted.

My heart fluttered and smile bloomed as my face grew warm. But really, this was all too much to take in. My soulmate, the man of my dreams, the elusive cowboy I'd been chasing for a year was standing right in front of me—touching distance away—looking at me, *smiling* at me, and calling me pretty.

I just, I could do nothing but soak it all in.

When I soaked the moment in a bit *too* awkwardly long, gazing at him with probably a bit *too* much adoration, his grin turned cocky and one sexy eyebrow arched up into his hairline.

"What's the problem? Cat got your tongue, darlin'?"

"I, uh." Oh hell. I'd totally forgotten what I'd come here to do. I knew I'd had a determined mission in mind when I'd knocked on this door, but yeah, it was long gone.

Whoops.

I almost giggled at my silly self. I was so forgetful. Oh well. It couldn't have been that important. Maybe I could get the cowboy to spank me for my wandering brain and—

What? No!

Where had that thought come from? Bad Bailey.

I cleared my throat, thinking I should probably say something worthwhile and stop ogling the poor guy. I'd have the rest of my life to look at him, didn't want to wear the sight out all in the first thirty seconds of officially meeting my soulmate. Though, wow, this was one sight I'd have no qualms about wearing out. He was just so yummy. So cowboy. So…

I shuddered and kept gazing at him like a moron.

He chuckled, because he knew…oh, he knew exactly what I was thinking and feeling. And it was a little bit thrilling. My blood thickened in my veins, and I swear my body grew prepared for him, ready for whatever he wanted to do.

"So, are you here to see someone specific?" he asked, his gaze telling me he didn't care who I was here for, because *he* was going to be the one I was going to see. "Or did you just want to browse through your choices?"

Oh, I didn't need to browse. I'd already made my choice, thank you very much. I opened my mouth, but the only words I could think to say were, *Will you marry me*?

Except that wasn't right.

Dammit, why the hell was I here again?

Ooh, Beckett. Yes. Good Bailey. My rational brain returning just in time, I snapped my fingers and blurted, "Beckett."

The cowboy's arm immediately jerked from the doorframe, and he straightened from the jamb to look imposingly taller as his smile fell dead. "Excuse me?"

Wow. That had made him immediately icy. I shrank back, wondering what I'd done that was so wrong. "I… I need to talk to Beck," I said. "Is he…" The cowboy's glare grew more ominous, so I swallowed and finished in a small voice, "Here?"

"Why…" He stepped outside onto the veranda with me to tower a good foot taller than me and glared shrewdly as he asked, "would that motherfucking raping son of a bitch be *here*?"

His voice was so deadly and steely soft that I shuddered.

"I." I gulped unsteadily before it struck me. "Wait. Didn't his case get dropped?"

"Dropped?" The cowboy boomed. "Why the fuck would his case get dropped? After what that piece of shit did to my sister, he better *die* in that jail cell."

Chapter 10
BAILEY

Thud.

That was the sound my jaw made when it hit the ground from dropping my mouth open so far, or you know, the sound it would've made if my mouth literally could've done that, which it totally would have, if it could have. But didn't.

"Oh my God," I breathed, my eyes the size of golf balls—again, not literally. "You're Melody's *brother*?"

Eww.

Without my permission, my nose wrinkled. No way in hell did I want that skanky piece of trash as a sister-in-law. Talk about worst Thanksgiving dinners ever.

This was just no fair. Life couldn't be this cruel.

My cowboy, my soulmate. He was right here. He'd called me pretty. How the hell was he related to *her*?

I knew he couldn't help it. No one chose blood, buts still, he seemed pretty defensive of her, like he liked her or supported her or believed her story or whatever, which was just totally wrong.

But maybe that was because he didn't know the truth.

Ooh, that must be it. He just didn't know what she was really like.

I needed to fix this, to set him straight.

"I'm so sorry," I started, almost feeling the urge to reach out and grip his arm in comfort. "I hate to be the one to tell you this, but he really didn't rape her. Beckett, I mean. He didn't force her or pressure her or manipulate her in any way. *She* was the one to push for it, to instigate it, to, hell, she put the damn condom on him."

The cowboy tipped his head slightly and squinted a moment before murmuring, "What did you just say?"

I flushed. No way was I going to repeat all that, especially to the girl's brother. So I simply cleared my throat, and confessed. "I was there. I saw everything. And your sister..." I shrugged. Well, she was a lying, awful whore. Not that'd I'd say that to him verbally, though I'm pretty sure he got the message loud and clear, especially when his face turned purple and his teeth clenched together into a snarl as he growled, "Listen here, you lying little bitch."

I sucked in an entire lungful with the gasp I produced.

But...what? How...?

My soulmate...

He'd just called me a—

"I don't know who the fuck you think you are—"

I shoved him. Right in the chest, both hand flat against his shirt, with all my might.

No one, and I mean no one, called me a bitch—especially a *lying* bitch—and got away with it. Chance—or whatever the hell his stupid name was—the fucking hot cowboy I'd wanted for over a year, was now dead to me.

As he stumbled back inside the fraternity from the force of my shove, I poked my finger at his nose and followed him in, staying in his face so he would remember everything I had to say.

"I am Bailey *Fucking* Prescott, you asshole. And no one calls me a lying bitch. You want to see a lying bitch, why don't you talk to your *sister*, because she fucking lied out her pretty, straight *lying* teeth. Beck didn't touch a hair on her head. I was *there*. I saw everything that happened, and he did *not* rape her. End of story."

He grabbed my hand. Hard. Like hard enough to hurt and make me gasp as my bones just seemed to crumple together under the force of his grip.

"Listen here, *bitch*." He forced me backward right out the door with the force of his hold on my hand alone. "You don't come here and talk about my sister like that. Someone needs to set you straight and shut your big, fucking lard-ass mouth permanently because Melody would never—"

"Hey, hey, hey!" Some guy jumped between us and manually nudged the cowboy away from me. "Take it easy, man."

"Get this stupid, fat cunt out of my face!" Pointing at me over the interloper's shoulder, he cleared the phlegm from his throat and spat at my eyes.

It went into one, splattered across my nose and some even went up my nostrils.

Gasping and shuddering from the utter grossness of it all, I squeezed my eyes shut and lifted my hands blindly, gagging out my horror.

Before I could see again, the fraternity door slammed shut. I didn't realize the other frat boy had stayed outside with me until he said, "Here," and a piece of cotton cloth was shoved into my hand.

I had no idea if it was a tissue, used underwear, or what, but I gratefully said, "Thank you," and wiped the slime off my face.

Sure, I'd always dreamed of swapping spit with my cowboy, but this wasn't exactly how I'd pictured it going down.

"Are you okay?"

I finished cleaning up my face, then blew out a breath and batted the wrinkles out of my shirt, straightened my spine and brushed some stray moisture from my eyes. Not sure why they were wet to begin with, but whatever. Then I blew out a big breath before lifting my face and saying, "Of course I'm fine."

I was.

Really.

Not.

Then I narrowed my eyes and sent a contemptuous glare toward the closed door. "But that bastard's definitely not my soulmate anymore, that's for damn sure."

They guy who'd saved me blinked. "What?" He had shaggy blond hair and a wrinkled shirt with blue jeans and work boots. I frowned at him a moment, thinking he looked a little too farm boy to be in a fraternity. Then I shook my head.

"Nothing."

He watched me a moment before shoving his hands into his pockets and shivering from the cold. "What you just said." He motioned over his shoulder with his thumb. "To Chance. About seeing what happened with Beck. Was that true?"

I scowled. "Of course it was true. Why would I lie about that?" Did he know a lot of girls who openly confessed to being voyeurs?

The guy shrugged and looked momentarily thoughtful, but not in a good way, like my news disturbed him. "Beck was never the type, you know, to force a girl. I don't think I every really, fully believed he'd rape anyone. But if it's true, and he's really innocent…" He shook his head. "Then Beck is fucking screwed. They'll never let him back in the fraternity, and Chance…Chance'll be gunning for him. He'd never believe anything bad about his sister."

Yeah, I'd kind of caught on to that fact about good old Chance. I wiped at my face again, feeling phantom traces of spit still on my cheek. "Well, it sounds like Beck's screwed then. Because he totally didn't rape her." My shoulders sagged. "He really hasn't been released from jail yet? I went to the police *hours* ago with my story. I would've thought they'd let him go by now."

The blonde fraternity dude shook his head. "I haven't heard about him being released. And if he does get free, he won't be welcome back here. It wouldn't matter if he was innocent or not. This has caused too much damaged to our name." He looked worried as he said that, but I had the feeling he wouldn't go out of his way to help his friend Beck, either.

Poor Beck.

I took a step back, ready to get away from this place. "Well, thanks again for the…" I finally looked down at what I was holding and blinked at the red and white hanky. It was exactly like the one my dad always carried.

What the hell was this preppy frat boy doing, carrying around something that was so country?

He took the wadded piece of cloth back and shoved it into his pocket. I stared at him strangely another second and then turned away to hurry off the porch.

I didn't breathe easily again until I'd returned to my car and had the heater on. And even though I positioned the vents so warmth blew right on my face, I felt icy cold and numb all the way to my bones.

I plodded up the steps of my apartment when I got home, still bone-cold dazed, and stopped at the top of the landing. Tess, or someone—though it was probably Tess—had cleaned up my potato chip disaster I'd abandoned earlier and then folded my blanket and placed it neatly on the back of the couch. The room was quiet and television turned off. I could hear voices from the kitchen; they were probably eating together, like a big, happy two-couple family.

They'd be just fine without their fifth-wheel Bailey tonight, so I trudged to my room and went straight to the bath, where I stripped down and stepped into the shower. I turned the water as hot as I could get it without burning off layers of skin and then scrubbed at my face for a good five minutes until tears began to drip down my cheeks. Hugging myself, I sat on the floor of the bathtub under the hot spray and cried for a bit longer.

But seriously, who knew learning your soulmate was really an asshole could be so devastating?

Chapter 11

BECKETT

"What's wrong?" demanded the correctional officer who was standing behind me as I tried to piss. "Thought you said you had to take a leak?"

I did. I still had to. It was just, I wasn't really used to the audience. Stage freight and all that. Gritting my teeth, I tried not to think about the uniformed guard breathing down my neck and finally got a trickle to come. Didn't hurt as bad this time. I risked a glance down and the stream wasn't even tinged pink. My kidneys must be getting better. My eye certainly was; I could finally see out of both of them again. I was still sore and bruised as hell but I felt a hundred times better today.

When I finished, I stepped back and zipped, only for the guard to glance past me and into the little bowl I'd had to pee into.

"Looks like you're getting better," he congratulated, patting me on the back hard enough to jar my tender ribs and make me want to weep from the pain. "No more blood in the urine."

I gulped and sent him a sickened nod. Getting better meant one thing. It meant—

"We can get you back to general population now."

That.

Fuckity, fuck, fuck. I didn't want to go back to general population. I suddenly wished my piss had been a dark, scarlet red. I didn't want to leave my safe, comfy infirmary.

"But—" I glanced longingly into the cell that I'd stayed in for two nights as the guard nudged me past it.

"Don't worry. We'll put you in a different pod this time around."

Oh joy. A whole new group of convicts could kick my ass now.

"Can't let you stay here forever," the guard added, pressing on a button and then waiting until someone in control unlocked the door in front of us. As it swung open to lead into a hall, I resisted without meaning to, wanting to argue that yes, yes they could totally let me stay here forever. I was fine with staying.

"Move it, Hilliard," he ordered.

Heaving out a sad sigh, I nodded and fell obediently into step, but it didn't take long for my breathing to pick up, my vision to waver, and my body to go from ice cold to burning hot and back to ice cold again. After everything went totally gray and then came back blurry, I shook my head, trying to see better, expect I just couldn't. My body was going into panic mode whether I liked it or not.

My heart was beating too fast, my hands were shaking too hard. If they put me back in with general population now, I think I'd literally scare myself to death. This was what I'd always imagined a heart attack would feel like.

"Here we are."

Oh, shit. We were here already? Was this guy going to make another big announcement about me being a rapist? Were they going to start on me in the first thirty seconds again? What if I didn't survive the beating this time?

Anxiety attack, here I come.

The door swung open, and I whimpered, fucking wussy-ass whimpered.

Yeah, they were going to kick my ass immediately.

When I didn't enter immediately enough, the guard shoved me forward. I stumbled inside the pod and about two dozen guys stopped what they were doing to stare.

One scary-looking shaved-head motherfucker playing cards at a table snickered. "Nice," he said before turning away disinterested and threw down two of his cards, demanding more.

Most everyone else lost interested as well. My equilibrium was still whack and everything went blurry and tipsy. My breathing wouldn't slow down, but a hope bloomed inside my chest. Maybe they were going to leave me alone this time. God, I hoped so.

I started toward the side. The walls seemed like much safer places than out in the middle of everything. But some scrawny, drugged-up looking creep fell into step behind me.

"Hey, you're that rapist, ain't you?"

Dammit, how did he know that?

"I saw you on the TV."

Oh.

I ignored him and carried on, no idea where I was going, just trying to get away from him, though there really was no going anywhere away. We were stuck in the same big pod together, a room full of thieves, drug dealers, real rapists, and probably even murderers.

"Hey." He poked me directly in the center of the back.

I paused and glanced back.

He was grossly skinny and slimy, as if he didn't bathe often. His dark hair was matted and long. I tried to keep from grimacing as he moved in closer.

"Pussy sure do feel better when it don't want you in there, don't it?" Then he cackled, showing off a mouth full of back rotting teeth and jabbed his elbow companionably at me.

"Eww." This time, I couldn't resist revealing the disgust that oozed off me. I winced, revolted, and turned my face aside to keep from looking at this sick bastard straight in the eye.

But, yeah, that offended him.

"Hey," he roared, stepping up into my face, even though he was nearly a foot shorter than me. "Don't you be acting like you're better than me, you pretty, rich little fucker. We in a whole new world now, princess. And you're just a pathetic little shit stain here."

I blinked, wondering why he'd called me rich. No one had ever called me that before. While I was still pondering that one, the bald guy who'd been playing cards, threw down his entire hand and pushed to his feet, glaring our way.

"New boy giving you some trouble, Hopps?"

"Yeah," the guy in my face sneered, blowing his putrid breath in my face and making me gag. "He's fucking disrespecting me."

"Yo, no one disrespects Hopps," Bald-guy told me, nudging the tiny druggie aside so he could get into my face. He was considerably taller than Hopps. And wider too. Hell, he was considerably taller and wider than *me*.

His fellow card players from the table had risen as well and were gathering behind him, and yep, one was cracking his knuckles.

Dammit, not the knuckle cracking. I could almost feel my nose breaking already.

My shoulders fell. I didn't bother to gush out an apology. It wasn't because I was trying to be a brave idiot either. I would've babbled one out on my hands and knees if I'd thought it'd do any good. But I knew, just from looking into this guy's eyes, they were going to kick my ass no matter what I said.

"Well..." he demanded. "You mute or what? Say something already."

I opened my mouth, but before I could say anything, the intercom beeped. "Hilliard," a voice boomed overhead. "Approach the door."

When no one in the entire pod reacted and the guy in my face didn't move, I pointed toward the exit. "That...that's me. I gotta go now."

I slipped by him along the wall and then then jumped free to hurry toward the door. No one followed me, and my breath stuttered with relief. My eyes might've even started watering I was so grateful.

I didn't even care what the guards had in mind for me; I'd been saved from an ass-beating. So life was good.

"What's going on?" I asked as soon as they'd marched me a good thirty feet down the hall away from my pod. Were they taking me back to the infirmary? I could totally handle that.

"You got another hearing," a guy I'd never met before announced.

I blinked. "I do?" Then I shook my head. "Are you sure? I didn't think I had anything else for months to come."

The guard only shrugged. "Your name's on the docket."

Well, okay then. It honestly didn't matter to me if they'd made a mistake or not. If it saved me from broken bones, mistakes were good.

So back into the police car I went, handcuffs, orange jumpsuit and all. The ride through town toward the courthouse made me blink. I was already growing used to being inside all day; it seemed so bright out here. About the time my eyes finally adjusted, we had arrived at our destination and I was paraded through a sally port and in through the back entrance of the courthouse. After I was ushered into the same room where I'd had my first hearing, I saw my lawyer across the crowd and blinked.

Well, hell, maybe I *did* have another appearance today.

But why?

I tried to catch Stempy's eye, figure out what was happening, but he seemed preoccupied with some paperwork he was reading from his opened briefcase. So I sat where I was told to sit, and waited.

I wasn't the first case this time around, and I had to wait through three other grueling hearings before my name was called. My handler who'd been sitting next to me nudged me into a stand, and I lumbered clumsily in my ankle cuffs toward Stempy.

"What in God's name is going on?" I hissed as soon as I sat at the defendant's table with him. Good things did not happen to me when I was in this courtroom. I couldn't even imagine what sentence they'd afflict on me this time around.

Raise my bail another fifty grand? Decide to forgo a trial and deem my guilty now? Decide hangings were back in style and just string me up in the courtyard out back?

But Stempy's eyes lit with glee as he leaned toward me. "Sorry, I didn't have time to give you a heads' up. But some new evidence has come to light, prompting a new hearing."

"New…?" I shook my head, not understanding.

"Rainbow-hair girl," he whispered, grinning. "Well, she's a blonde now, but that's neither here nor there. She came forward."

"She…" My chest squeezed with excitement. "Holy shit! She did? So I'm free? Are we here to free me?"

Stempy winced. "I'm not exactly certain. After we passed on this new information to the county attorney, and we all questioned Melody Fairfield again, she still refused to admit to lying, but her story no longer holds water, and when we caught her in a few lies, she just broke down crying, so it's possible the prosecutor might still take the case to trial."

My chest seized. Rainbow-hair girl had come to my rescue, yet I might still be stuck in jail until Spring? No! I'd never make it that long. I couldn't even last five minutes in that place without someone cracking their knuckles and wanting to cause me extreme bodily harm.

"Since the evidence is so strong, the judge might release you on O.R. and—"

"Wait. What does O.R. mean?"

"Release you of your own recognizance. You can go free without having to pay your bail, but you'll still have to go through with the trial and possibly check in with a reporting officer until then."

I was already nodding, more than okay with that option. Any route that didn't send me back to jail was fine with me. "I can do that," I assured him eagerly.

But he didn't seem so optimistic. "That's only one thing that might happen."

Shit. I should've known there would be more possible outcomes. "What else could happen?" My eyes begged him to say something good, like they might give me a free puppy or a million dollars for mistakenly imprisoning me. I just couldn't handle an option that sent me back to jail.

But the same lady judge who hated my guts called for our attention, and my hearing began.

"Mr. Hilliard," she greeted, clutching her gavel as if she wanted to chuck it at my head. She narrowed her eyes with that I-hate-rapists-and-all-men glare she was so good at giving. "Back so soon?" I shrugged, biting back the instinctive playful need I wanted to reply, saying I'd just missed her. But I worried that might sound too smug, or male, for her taste. Besides, I was still worried about the "other" things that could happen that Stempy hadn't been able to tell me about.

Judge Gudrun turned her attention to the county attorney across the aisle from us. "Councilor, I believe this hearing was scheduled because new information came to light."

"That's right, your honor." He took to his feet and cleared his throat, then shuffled through some papers and fiddled with his glasses, perching them just right on his nose.

I held my breath and gritted my teeth, willing him to just spit it out already. Was it puppies or more trips to the infirmary for me?

"Your honor, due to lack of evidence, the state drops their charges against Beckett Aaron Hilliard."

My mouth snapped open. I whipped my gaze toward Stempy. "What—?"

He grabbed my arm and waved me quiet before I could ask if what I'd heard meant what I thought it meant. My pulse began to race. It had sounded like I'd just been freed completely, no O.R., no supervision, no check-ins or urine tests. Holy shit, the idea of going completely free seemed almost foreign to me. If every charge was really dropped, what did that mean for me now?

Would I just return to school as if the past few days had never happened? Would my family let me back into their fold? Would the fraternity—umm, no. Chance would push to keep me out of the fraternity. And they'd probably listen to him. That fake bastard had wormed his way into being their golden boy.

I'd have to find a new place to live, probably a new place to work. The university barn tended to only employ AGR boys.

Whether I liked it or not, things had just changed. My entire life was different now.

Judge Gudrun started talking again then, but the words couldn't seem to focus in my head. All I kept hearing was, "the state drops their charges," and I couldn't focus past that, because that sounded good. I needed something good. I needed something good more than I needed my next breath. When the judge slapped her gavel against its block, I jumped and turned to Stempy again for translation.

He finally turned to me, holding out his hand with a big gleaming smile on his face.

"Well, I have to say that was the best win I've had. Beckett, thank you. You're actually one of the ones I like to defend."

I shook my head as I took his hand. "So this means I'm free, right? Completely totally free?"

He laughed. "Yep, completely and totally free? Just like that?"

"Yep, just like that."

"No O.R.?"

"Nope. You can return to your life now. They'll take you back to the jail where you can collect your personal affects and sign out."

I stared at him as if he spoke a foreign language. But free? I was really free?

For some reason, I couldn't yet trust it.

Chapter 12
BECKETT

It felt strange changing back into the clothes I'd been wearing the night I'd been with Melody. I actually wanted to set them on fire and watch them burn to ash, incinerate any kind of reminder of her and what I'd been through these last few days.

The things they'd taken from my pockets had been stored in a manila envelope that they returned to me next. After slipping my wallet, loose change, and keys back where they belonged, I tried my phone, but it was dead.

Okay, so I guess I was walking back to campus.

Typically, a walk like this would've been invigorating. I would've grinned the entire trek and lifted my face to the cold breeze and swam in the feeling of being free again. But I still felt like shit. My face was bruised and battered, my ribs ached and made my breathing wheeze, and I walked with a limp because my fellow convicts had kicked me pretty good in my knee.

Also, I'd been arrested without a coat, so I was a popsicle by the time I reached Alpha Gamma Rho. When I saw the white pillars rising up in front of the front door, I wanted to weep with relief. I stepped onto the porch, groaning from the aches and pains, just wanting to get inside to the warmth and sit somewhere soft for a minute.

I wasn't even thinking about Chance and what he might do, so when I opened the door and saw Max first thing, lounging with his feet up, watching TV, I grinned, just happy to see my bud.

But his eyes flew open wide, and he jumped to his feet, already looking around for other people.

"Beck?" he hissed on an exaggerated whisper. "What the hell are you doing here?"

"They dropped my case," I said. "All the evidence showed I told the truth."

"Well, you can't stay here." He wasn't looking at me as he hurried forward and took my arm as if to usher me right back out the door. "If Chance saw you—"

"I can handle the cowboy," I muttered, pulling my arm from his grip and glaring at him. Honestly, I doubted I could handle Chance, especially in the shape I was in. We were the same height but he outweighed me by a good thirty pounds.

I was too ticked at Max to really think about that, though. He hadn't said one thing about my fucking mutilated face, or how glad he was to see me free, or that hey, he was sorry he never got around to visiting me and showing his support.

"All my shit is here," I said. Where else did he think I'd go? "My truck's parked out back. My—"

"We boxed up your stuff already," Max rushed to say, finally looking at me long enough to pull back in surprise before scanning my wounds from head to toe. Then he sighed and more quietly added, "I put it all in the bed of your truck."

"So, there's no way they'll let me back into the fraternity?" I gulped, dreading his answer.

His eyes widened. "Dude, there's no way they'll let you back into the *university*." He glanced into the kitchen to make sure it was clear before he dragged me inside. Then he picked up a piece of mail and handed it to me. It had my name on it, but it had already been opened. "Man, I'm sorry."

I looked at him before tugging the envelope free of his grip and pulling out the letter inside. Granton University had officially kicked me out, and then gone as far as to warn me there would be legal consequences if I ever stepped foot on campus again.

Holy shit. I didn't even know you could get a restraining order from a college. This sucked.

It sucked more than I thought it could.

Max shifted closer. "You need to go. I'm sorry, man, but I can't be found talking to you."

I looked up at him but didn't really see him. Was Max breaking up with me too? He was the only friend I'd been certain I could rely on.

"But…?" What the hell was I supposed to do? I grabbed his arm. "Wait, you don't actually think I did it, do you? You don't think I'm a—"

"No!" Max whispered harshly before glancing around to make sure once more we weren't spotted together. "I knew you were innocent. But that chick showing up, claiming she saw everything, really cemented it for me."

"What chick?" I asked, shaking my head.

He shrugged. "I don't know. Never seen her before. Short, blonde, chubby thing. Said her name was Bailey Prescott and that she'd seen the whole thing between you and Melody. She came here looking for you and almost got into a knock-down, drag-out fight with Chance because she was so adamant about defending your innocence."

I shook my head, wondering who the hell Bailey Prescott was. The only girl I thought had seen me and Melody was—oh wait. I suddenly remembered Stempy mentioning she no longer had rainbow hair.

Warmth and soothing relief filled me to learn she'd come here too to defend me, since apparently even Max didn't feel so inclined to back me up.

I suddenly wanted to find Bailey Prescott and give her a big thank you hug. I owed her my entire life.

"…Still have to go now. I can't be seen with you," Max was saying, making me frown at him. Fine. If he didn't want to help me out, I guess I was out of here. "You really need to go before Chance catches you."

I waved him silent, rolling my eyes. "Whatever," I said. "I'll see you around." Or not. Probably not. I had a feeling Max didn't want anything else to do with me.

I headed out the back door, and sighed with another bout of relief when I saw my truck…until I realized a word had been keyed into the side.

Rapist.

Oh no. Fuck no. They'd mutilated my baby. I slowed the closer I got to it, only to realize most of the boxes my shit that had been packed in to the bed of the truck had been pulled open and broken or strewn about, my favorite jeans cut into shreds and the blanket I'd had on my bed splattered with some kind of red paint.

I didn't even want to know what *those* said.

My tires hadn't been slashed, though, so I unlocked the door and gunned the engine, plugging my phone into my car charger before I was even a block down the road.

I wanted to go home, but I still wasn't sure how my family would receive me. Maybe I should call first. I didn't know, but I did know before I did anything, I needed to regroup.

I found a cheap motel on the edge of town. As soon as I stepped inside to ask about renting a room, the lady at the desk pointed and said, "No. You're that rapist on the television. You get out of here before I call the police."

The couple who'd been trying to enter behind me, backed away, staring at me as if I were, well, a rapist.

I hurried from the motel and raced back to my truck, my face getting hotter and hotter as more people in the parking lot gaped at the word on the side of my truck and back to me, recognition lighting their gazes.

Whipping on a ball cap as soon as I climbed back into my truck, I cranked the engine and drove out of town, taking dirt roads until I knew I was absolutely alone. Then I found my pocket knife in my glove compartment and climbed out of the truck while it was still running.

My heart sank as I read the word gouged into the white paint job. "I'm so sorry, baby," I said, my voice choking up as I flicked open the knife and proceeded to scratch through the word *rapist* until there was no way to determine what it had said before.

It was going to take me months to afford a new paint job to fix this.

My heart still felt broken as I returned to town and tried a new hotel, wearing my hat low along with an undamaged hoodie I'd found in the back seat of my truck.

I got further without any complications this time, all the way up to the point that I needed to pay for a room. When I took out my debit card, the guy swiped it. Then swiped it again before telling me the charge was declined. I didn't have a credit card, so I opened my wallet for cash, and had just barely enough to cover the fee.

Grateful I'd gotten a room, I hurried, grabbing enough from my truck to get me through the night, and immediately tried my phone. For some reason, I feared it'd be out of service too, but it worked, thank God. I looked up my bank account first.

It'd been cleared out. Completely. I stared at the zero balance in shock, unable to believe what I was seeing. When I'd opened the account in middle school, I'd shared it with my dad so he could put some occasional funds in for me. I must've forgotten to take his name off, because there was no way anyone else could've wiped out my money like that.

But the thing was, he hadn't given me money since I'd gone off to college. All the funds I'd had in there was from my work at the University barn.

Feeling not only abandoned but now betrayed by my family, I started to dial home, but then disconnected, not sure I could talk rationally to them just yet. I couldn't believe they'd stolen from me.

So I called my boss at the barn instead, only to be frostily told I was no longer employed there.

I wiped a trembling hand over my face, wondering what to do next. Who to go to for help. I'd never realized how having people in your life was such a big deal until there were no people there for you at all. Contacting any of my fraternity brothers was out of the question, and that had pretty much been the only clique I'd hung with.

I ended up calling Jana. I knew we'd broken up, but we'd been together for a year. She would know better than anyone that I wasn't a monster. And we hadn't even broken up for really strong reasons. There'd been no big, nasty, ugly fight where we now hated each other's guts. We were still friends.

I thought.

I hoped.

I'd just grown distracted after all the problems had started at home, feeling like I needed to be there, while she'd felt as if I needed to be more mentally with *her*. That was how she'd worded it anyway. It had sounded like a pretty selfish excuse to me. When I'd needed her support most, she'd flaked on me. But hell, maybe she'd support me now. Maybe—

"You fucking prick bastard," she growled, answering on the third ring.

"Jana," I breathed her name in relief, glad she'd actually picked up the phone.

"How dare you call me? How fucking dare you? I mean, seriously, Beck. *Melody*? Melody the fucking slut *Fairfield*?"

Ah, shit. I hadn't thought of the scenario where she'd believe me but still be pissed because of my lousy taste in rebound partners. Not that I'd picked Melody, exactly, but—

"Lose my number," Jana growled.

"No, wait! I need—"

She hung up before I could plead my case.

So, yeah, I guess Jana wasn't going to be supportive this time around either. I'd been an idiot for even trying her.

I sighed and fisted my hand before setting it against my forehead. What the fuck was I supposed to do now? I had no money, no family, no friends, no job, no place to stay after tomorrow when the hotel kicked me out. I had nothing but the broken junk in the back of my vandalized truck.

For some reason, I thought of rainbow-hair girl. What had Max said her name was?

Bailey something? Bailey…Prescott. That was it.

I logged into the Facebook app on my phone to see if I could find her, but before I could even think about searching, the newsfeed had me freezing.

"Holy shit," I uttered.

Everyone hated me. They hated me and wanted me to die a slow, agonizing death with parts of my body cut off and burned before putting me out of my misery.

Silently, I turned my phone off and placed it face down on the mattress of the bed beside me.

This was worse than I ever could've imagined.

Chapter 13
BAILEY

I felt groggy and sore when I woke. Sleep had come in sporadic bursts here and there throughout the night.

And it was all Chance "The Cowboy" Fairfield's fault.

It'd been a day and a half since he'd spit on me, and it was still bothering me.

I was a realist. Logically, I knew I had never stood a chance in hell with a guy like him. All that 'he was my soulmate' bullshit I'd spewed about him had been just that. Bullshit. A pipedream if you will. It'd been fun to imagine the what-if of being with him.

In real life, I didn't even want a boyfriend really. I don't think, anyway. And even if I did, a hot cocky cowboy like him wouldn't even have given me the time of day. I mean, I wasn't pretty, or tall, or slim, or smart, and I didn't have a sparkling personality on top of that.

At best, I could hope he didn't have very high standards and would settle for a one-night stand with me, and then I'd maybe get to try sex out once more in my life, see if it was better or still sucked as bad as the first time. But yeah, I never really honestly thought there'd ever be anything more than that between us. Not in reality. But the pipe dream had been fun. It had filled the hours and given me something to focus on.

Why the hell had he gone and opened the door to that fraternity house to ruin it all?

At first, it'd been cool. He'd called me pretty, and I'd thought holy shit, maybe he would be willing for a little hot nooky with me. Maybe he'd show me that sex wasn't such an awful, icky sport after all.

Except it'd gone horribly, awfully wrong. Then he'd called me… well, everything he'd called me, and he'd crushed my pipedream. A year of what-ifs surrounding him, and he'd shattered them all in ten seconds flat.

Bastard.

Now I had to come up with a whole new pipedream to keep my company on lonely nights.

I was still trying to deny the fact that he'd ever made me cry in my shower as I applied a thicker layer of eyeliner to my lashes than usual. People didn't make me cry. And I didn't want a jerk with an even worse sister to be one of them.

Stepping back, I inspected myself in the mirror. Satisfied with the results, I tossed down the eyeliner and found my book bag and coat before hurrying from the apartment without even going near the kitchen. I was congratulating myself on escaping without talking to anyone or answering any questions when I heard a call from behind me.

Curses. I was only five feet from my car too.

Gritting my teeth and muttering under my breath, I spun around to find Tess hurrying after me. "Can I ride to class with you today?" she asked, opening the passenger's side door before I could even answer.

I frowned. "Where's Jonah?" She usually rode to campus with him.

She sighed. "I wanted to ride with you today."

I let out a grumble of defeat and tossed my things into the backseat before sliding behind the wheel. She popped into the passenger seat.

"Well?" she was demanding even as I turned on the car. "You worked so late yesterday, we didn't get a chance talk last night about what happened the night before that. Was he there? Did you talk to him?"

Oh, he'd been there all right, I wanted to answer bitterly. And unfortunately, yes, I'd talked to the bastard. But then I realized she was asking about Beckett. Not the cowboy.

"Oh. Yeah, no. He wasn't there. I think he's still in jail, actually."

"What?" Her face fell. "Really? But your testimony—"

"Well, it turns out my testimony doesn't mean shit," I answered bitterly. "Believe it or not, some people actually think *I'm* the liar."

Some people in stupid cowboy hats, wearing stupid belt buckles and stupid boots.

Tess just blinked before saying, "Why would you lie? You don't even know Beckett Hilliard."

I know, right!

I shrugged as I pulled onto the road and headed toward campus. "Don't know," I mumbled. I was tired of thinking about it. I was tired of cowboys, and non-rapists, and every fraternity ever invented. I was just…done. Done with them all.

Good night.

"Jonah still planning on going home with you for Thanksgiving?" I asked, needing a topic change more than I needed anything right then.

"Uh…" Tess blinked, not expecting that. "Yeah, of course. There's nowhere else he'd go."

I nodded. "Yeah. Makes sense." Well, poop. That conversation didn't last long. Now what did we talk about?

Usually, I was bursting at the seams for the chance to tell Tess something or other, and now that I had her exclusively to myself, I kind of just wanted to be alone.

Sadly, I think I was still licking my wounds.

Stupid jerk cowboy, calling me a lying, fat bitch.

Tess kept sending me covert glances, looking concerned. I knew she wanted to ask what was wrong with me, but that wasn't Tess's style. Open direct confrontation was more my style. So we arrived to campus in silence.

Though she always rode with Jonah, she shared more classes with me. We still had a few general ed courses we'd signed up to take with each other, and today we had three classes together. Two right in a row, then a lunch break, and the third after that.

The first two passed with relative boredom. The guy in front of us in speech class tried to ask out this girl next to him, but she shot him down hard, which had been entertaining, but other than that, it'd been blah, blah, blah.

At lunch, we went to the food court at the student union and once we were in line behind a chatty pair of girls, I leaned in closer to Tess and finally admitted, "Does today just feel weird to you?"

She nodded. "It does. But why?"

I started to shrug, not sure. I knew why I was in a funk. But why was Tess feeling it too?

In front of us, I overheard some girl say, "I can't believe they let that Hilliard rapist free. It's so scary."

Gasping, I turned fully toward them to listen in.

But Beckett had been *released*? This was amazing! Thank God. Why hadn't I heard—

"Poor Melody," the girl's friend cooed.

I sent Tess a significant glance and gave her an eye roll. *Poor Melody my ass*. That liar deserved some of her own time in jail if you asked me.

"Ohmigod, did you hear who got him out, claiming she was a *witness*," the first friend asked.

I paused, opening my mouth, as she made air quotes around the word witness.

The second girl grabbed first girl's arm. "No. Who?"

"Bailey Prescott."

Holy shit, they were talking about me. And why had she said Bailey Prescott as if she were tasting something nasty?

Shaking her head, the second girl dumbly said, "Who's Bailey Prescott?"

"You know, that cray-cray rainbow-haired chunk who sits behind us in American History class with that mute redheaded friend of hers."

"What?! *That* mouthy opinionated fat cow got him free?"

Say whaaaaaat?

Had they just called me—I stepped forward, but Tess grabbed my arm and dug her fingers in, forcing me not to react or intercede.

"Oh my God, how could they let *her* even testify on his behalf?"

Excuse me?

My back straightened as shock pierced through every organ of my body. Were mouthy, opinionated fat cows not even allowed to go to the police with evidence to help an investigation now?

"You just *know* she lied for him, probably because she had a crush on him or something, thinking he'd give her the time of day if she saved him."

What. The. Hell?

Tess tried to drag me away, but I was rooted to the spot, determined to listen to what else these two girls had to say about me.

Girl one was shaking her head sadly. "It's so pathetic when ugly girls don't even care if a guy is a sexist rapist asshole, but they still lie for him anyway just to get a little attention."

I was ugly?

I mean, I'd always known I'd never be a skin and bones Miss Universe, but I'd never considered myself flat-out *ugly* before.

Ugly felt so extreme.

But apparently, I was mouthy, opinionated, fat, pathetic, and ugly too boot.

Holy shit.

"Well, she's always been an attention whore, so it's really not that shocking if you think about it." Girl Two was twining a piece of dark hair around her finger, and I suddenly wanted to leap forward and just grab it and pull…pull so hard it ripped the roots from her pretty little skinny-headed scalp.

This time, when Tess yanked on my arm, I let her drag me away. I stared sightlessly ahead as she towed me across campus. It didn't occur to me that she wasn't leading me to our next class together but rather out into the parking lot where my car was until she was digging into my book bag hanging limping from my shoulder for my keys.

Then she pushed me into the passenger seat and hurried around to the driver's side herself. The car started, and she backed from the parking spot.

"I'm sorry," she finally said, filling the silence so abruptly that I jumped. I looked across the interior of the car to find tears glittering in her eyes.

I shook my head. "What're *you* sorry for?" And why the hell was she crying?

"I didn't…" She paused to choke on her words, before wiping tears off her cheeks with her fingertips and continuing. "I didn't stand up for you. I didn't…I didn't defend you to those stupid… those stupid *bitches*."

My eyebrows arched. Tess never called anyone a bitch. She really *was* upset.

Still too numb by what I'd just heard to share her distress, I shrugged. "I would never expect you to." That's not who she was.

Tess was a bleeding-heart pacifist who avoided confrontations and bringing any kind of attention to herself. Just because she hadn't made a spectacle on my behalf just now didn't mean I thought she loved me any less. The only thing I was assured of at the moment was that Tess still loved me.

With a sniff, she glanced at me and wiped her face again. "But you would've stood up for me. You would've said something to them and put them in their place for hurting me. You would've—"

"That's just because I'm an attention whore," I cut in bitterly before turning my gaze sharply to stare out the side window. "All us crazy pathetic, mouthy, opinioned fat cows are, you know."

"*Arg.*" Tess gritted her teeth as she turned a corner before hissing a stream of curse words. My eyebrows lifted, kind of impressed by her litany. It was rare—beyond rare—when Tess cussed, but she was dropping f-bombs like a pro right now. Finally, she glanced at me, her eyes shot through with anger as she pulled onto our street. "You are none of those things, Bailey, do you hear me? Those vile slugs don't know you. They don't—"

"You don't have to defend me to me, Tess. I know I'm not perfect."

"Well, I know you're not perfect too," Tess snapped as she pulled to a stop at the curb in front of our house and turned to face me fully. "I know you better than anyone. You're brash and impetuous with no filter whatsoever. Whatever you're thinking spills from your mouth, and you stick your nose where it doesn't belong more often than not. You can drive me crazy with your smart-alecky wisecracks and snap judgements. And you—"

"Gee, you're making me feel like a paragon of perfection right now, bestie," I muttered, glancing away and blinking rapidly because listening to her list my faults stung a million times worse than knowing those two jerks from campus thought I was an ugly fat cow.

But Tess gripped my arm with force yet compassion, making me glance at her. Her smile was watery but genuine when she said, "But you're the most loyal friend a person could ever have. You protect those in your tribe whole-heartedly. You'd sacrifice your own happiness to make sure one of your people was content. And you've been known to make me laugh until I've shot milk from my nose."

I cracked a smile at that one and nudged my elbow at her. "And it was strawberry milk at that."

Tess groaned and dabbed gingerly at her nose, even though that particular event had happened back when we'd been eight. "Yeah, I think the strawberry aspect made it sting more."

My shoulders loosened and I couldn't help but drop some of the depression that had been gripping me. How did Tess always make my heart happy just by being herself? I guess that was what made her a true friend. Merely being in her company and having her attention eased my soul.

But thinking of the word attention made me remember the term attention whore those girls had called me. Had I been so lonely lately, upset with all Tess's time with Jonah, because I really was a dirty, hog of an attention whore? I glanced at her, feeling like a shitty awful friend for wanting more of her lately. I should've been truly, deep-in-my-heart happy for her because she had more people to love her, not jealous. Ugh, I really was the worst.

Mood plummeting once again, I smiled sadly and reached out to pat her arm. "Thank you for being with me today. I don't know how I would've gotten through that scene without you there."

Tess's eyes bugged as she stared at my hand until I felt the need to pull away.

Okay, so maybe I wasn't a touchy-feely person. I didn't hug or comfort or receive affection or any of that emotional shit. It probably was really strange that I reached for her.

Maybe I was losing my mind.

"I think I'm going to go do some homework in my room," I said, needing a break from life. "Thank Jonah for letting me hog you so much today."

"*Bailey*," Tess said, looking shocked by my words. "You didn't hog me. Hey! Don't leave. Seriously, sweetie, what is going on with you? Something is wrong. And I know it's not just those stupid girls from school. You didn't even let Chrissy Jackson and her band of shrews get to you sophomore year when they decided to bully you."

Actually, they *had* gotten to me. Deep in my core, they'd made me believe I was worthless and would never find true love or be successful or gain a friend outside Tess. I'd just refused to let those wounds show. I'd buckled down and turned sassier than ever to show them they couldn't touch my spirit, though they'd actually shattered it.

But Tess was right. The girls on campus today would've normally turned me even mouthier than usual. No, this was, I don't even know. I wasn't sure if I could attribute the mood to the cowboy either. To be sadly honest, I think it had originated from the night I'd seen Beckett Hilliard make Melody Fairfield come like a heifer being slaughtered on an alter to the sex gods.

He hadn't even looked like he'd done much of anything for her, but she'd seemed to like it so much. She'd gone ugly crazy with lust. It didn't seem right. Why had it hurt and felt so uncomfortable for me the one time I'd tried it, yet *she'd* had the best orgasm of her life?

I knew Tess and Paige liked sex. Their men treated them good and cherished my two friends. But I had always kind of thought the fact that they were so in love had kind of blinded them to how good it really wasn't.

But then Melody the skanky whore Fairfield had come along and proved to me that love had nothing to do with a good orgasm. And I felt broken inside.

Maybe I just wasn't meant to be a sexual being. I mean, I certainly didn't have a magazine-cover-worthy provocative shape to lure a man in. I didn't flirt well, or at all. And I, well, I don't know but it sucked to realize I didn't have any of that and probably never would.

It was like I'd been slapped with a hard dose of reality that I'd be alone and lonely for the rest of my life for a reason; because I was just that lacking. No sex, no companionship, no anything seemed to lurk in my future. And it scared me. I felt worthless. And alone.

Doomed to wander the earth this way for all eternity.

But I looked at Tess dead in the eye, and I couldn't tell her that, none of it. She'd just shrug it off and say, "*You're not worthless.*" Then maybe she'd get offended because she wouldn't think our friendship was helping me feel loved enough, or something like that, when that wasn't it at all. I just…it was something inside—something about who I was—that felt broken. And I think only *I* could fix it.

Except I didn't know how.

Maybe it wasn't even fixable. Maybe I was just destined to be sexually defunct and relationship-dead for the rest of my life.

"I think this whole rape case still has me wigging out," I said instead. Hey, it was kind of true. I wasn't sure what had happened to Beckett. I doubt he was at the fraternity now. Should I still try to look him up? The first time had gone wrong enough that I almost didn't want to take the chance again. But a niggle at my conscience told me to find him. "I think I'm going to go to my room and find out where Beck is."

Tess immediately nodded, her big blue eyes still worried though. "Want me to help?"

I smiled gratefully but shook my head. "No. Go cuddle with your man. I really do feel bad about taking you away from him today."

"Bailey," she groaned. "You did *not* take me away from him. He knows you need some extra attention lately. It's fine. Don't—"

"Well, I'm fine," I reassured her. "So stop worrying so much about me. I'll see you at supper. You're cooking tonight, right?"

She nodded mutely, so I grinned and said, "Great." Then I pushed open the car door and hurried up to our apartment alone.

Once in my room, I settled myself comfortably on my bed and pulled my computer onto my lap. But Beckett Hilliard wasn't even in the Granton University student directory anymore. And when I logged onto Facebook to find his account—which hadn't been hard since all the dirty nasty memes against him had been linked to his name—it had been deleted.

"Dammit," I muttered, wondering where he was.

All the google searches only went to articles about the rape and his being set free. After scrolling through about twenty pages of that, I gave up with a groan and slapped my laptop closed before falling onto my back and staring up at the ceiling.

But when I did that, I only remembered what Beckett had looked like when he'd come, his mouth gasping open and his eyes wide with shock as he lay in this very position and stared at the ceiling of that fraternity room.

Then I remembered the disgust in Chance Fairfield's eyes when he'd called me a lying bitch and spat in my face.

I shuddered and sat up. I wanted to find another human—preferably Tess or Paige—be in their company, and not feel so alone. But I was too worried it'd only make me feel more worthless about myself, so I decided to do some homework.

That lasted for a couple hours before it felt like my brain was mush from studying so long. I slapped my Electronic devices and Circuits textbook shut and crawled off my bed, realizing evening was falling and I'd missed lunch. That never happened. Like ever. I loved food too much.

And now I was worried about myself. I really was in a strange funk. I'd already been wondering while I'd been studying all afternoon which color I wanted to make my hair next.

Shaking my head, I decided I was going to make a huge, raving snack and veg out in front of another eighties movie. I'd have to pull out the big guns this time and put on *Princess Bride* I think. Yes, definitely, that's what I was going to watch.

But I didn't even make it ten steps out of my door when it happened.

I was approaching Paige and Logan's room to pass by their door when I heard giggling from inside. The door was eighty percent shut but open enough to let the sound out clearly.

And then I heard Paige say, "Logan, shhh…" in a reprimanding voice as I passed. "What if Bailey hears?"

I slowed to a stop. But then hurried back in to gear, afraid I'd be caught "hearing" them.

I knew—I knew oh-so very logically—that Paige didn't mean anything bad by what she said. She hadn't suggested I was a dirty, rotten voyeur or that I was purposefully out and about trying to creep in on her with her man, like all I did these days was spy on other couples having sex. Hell, for all I knew, she was trying to be considerate of my feelings because she knew I'd had a rough day and worried I'd feel worse after hearing two people being happy together and laughing.

But it still stung. Oh damn, how it stung.

I suddenly didn't feel welcome anywhere in the world.

After all the ugly, fat cow talk, I was just too tender to take any more. Throat burning and eyes watering, I hurried into the front room until I hit the stairwell. Then I grabbed my coat off the hook as I passed and rushed down to the front door. Not even my room would provide a very good sanctuary right now. I'd only be able to hear their muffled talk more clearly through the cold lonely wall.

Thinking about the park bench across the street that I never saw anyone sitting at, I shoved my way outside with a good bit of force, wanting to be all the way removed from the apartment before I really burst forth and started shedding tears.

But a big black mass of something standing on the steps with its arm raised as if to knock blocked my path.

I shrieked but still didn't stop in time to keep from plowing into it.

"What the…?" He tried to grab my arms to steady me, I think, but he didn't have any kind of solid footing himself to be steadying anyone.

So we both went tumbling down, me on top, and him landing on the cold hard, solid ground.

"Holy fuck," I groaned, feeling dazed, even though I'd had a cushiony person to land on, though he wasn't really all that cushiony. He was a bit too hard and muscled to provide any kind of soft-padded landing. I felt jarred right down to my teeth.

Moaning, I sat up and crawled off him just as he seemed to get his wind back and let out his own chuff of pain.

Since the day had worn down to evening, and the sky was gray and muggy, I didn't see him in crisp, bright detail. But I still knew who he was.

He wore a black hoodie with the three bright white Greek letters stretching across his chest and a ball cap over his head. His face was covered in bruises, ranging from green, dying older ones to a couple fresh deep purples beauties. He looked basically nothing like he had the one night I'd met him, and yet I still recognized him immediately. I grabbed his arm to make sure he hadn't passed out on me, and he opened his eyes. They were still just as startling blue as they'd been before.

An instant moment of relief filled me. He was okay—well alive anyway. He was free, and out of jail, and now I could stop worrying about where he was or what he was doing. Except with that relief came a spot of irritation. I didn't know this guy from Adam, why the hell had he inspired any kind of worry in me in the first place?

So I let out a groan and shook my head. "Jesus Christ, Bucket. You sure have a bad habit of loitering in doorways when I'm in a hurry to get through them, don't you?"

Chapter 14
BECKETT

Fuck, I think I just broke one of my bruised ribs. For the longest second, I couldn't breathe, couldn't move past the pain. I could just lay on the cold, hard ground, hugging myself.

The weight on top of me shifted and scurried off, the girl babbling something that totally didn't penetrate the agony surrounding my synapses. No idea what she said.

Then small fingers gripped my arm with a firm, sturdy pressure, and I cracked my eyes open wide enough for her entire face to flood my field of vision as she leaned down to get a look at me. She said something else that didn't get through before she leaned in closer and said loudly enough for me to finally hear, "Holy shit, are you okay?"

"Fine," I gasped, still clutching my ribs. Yeah, I was just dandy. Or I would be in a couple years, possibly decades.

"Well, you look like hell." She tightened her grip and tugged me upright into a sitting position. The blood rushed from my brain, causing sharp daggers to pierce my temples.

I whimpered and wavered until the ache dulled enough for me to function. "Yeah, well I wouldn't recommend jail for any kind of beauty regimen retreat, that's for damn sure."

The girl laughed, making me focus on her looks for the first time. She was a cute thing, with a round face and cheeks that had probably gotten pinched and smooshed a lot when she was young. Her eyes were big and smoky gray with these long-ass lashes that swept gracefully over them and briefly brushed the tops of her cheeks before she opened her eyes again. Her hair was shoulder-length, blonde and curly, the fun bobbing, kinky kind of curls that always made me want to play with them.

I realized I was staring when she shook her head with a baffled kind of frown, glanced around us and asked, "What're you doing here?"

The blunt question startled me out of my daze, but it wasn't delivered with a rude vibe or anything, it was just really direct, more direct and familiar than I was expecting. So I cleared my throat as I picked myself up off the ground, dusting dirt and leaves and grass from my ass as I went.

"Sorry," I said. "I, uh, I just…" I glanced at the door to the apartment I'd been prepared to knock on. "Is Bailey home?"

When she didn't answer, I turned to find her setting her hand on her cocked hip and frowning at me.

Worried I'd messed up somehow with that question, I gulped and glanced around before asking, "What?"

She rolled her eyes and sighed. "Wow. Save a guy's life and he completely forgets what you look like. I feel so special right now, Bucket. Thanks."

The name Bucket caused my eyes to widen. I scanned her from head to toe but didn't recognize a single thing about her from the one night we'd met except her height. "You…" Clearing my throat, I started again. "Sorry, I just, your hair—the rainbow hair, I mean—was the only thing I really remembered about you. And now that you dyed it, well…" I shrugged lamely.

Yes, I was an idiot.

Bailey touched the side of her head, her scowl only deepening. "Why is everyone so obsessed about me dying my hair? Does it look that bad?"

"What? *No*," I said immediately, worried I'd offended her. This girl had saved my life, the last thing I wanted to do was upset her in any way. "It's beautiful. The curls. They're…" I motioned to my own head, stupidly drawing rings around my scalp with my finger before adding, "I've always liked curls."

Realizing how strange I sounded, I winced.

Bailey lifted an eyebrow and stared at me as if I'd lost my mind. But she didn't seem leery or afraid, which, after the hassle I'd had yesterday getting a hotel room, was actually awesome. I would take the you're-so-whack stare any day of the week over the please-don't-rape-me cower.

"So my friend said you stopped by the fraternity," I started over, feeling like I was bombing this whole conversation the more I spoke. Then I sniffed. "Well, *ex*-friend. *Acquaintance*," I corrected.

It felt weird to call Max a mere acquaintance. We'd known each other since freshman year when we'd rushed Alpha Gamma Rho together. We'd mucked horse stalls out at the University barn together, gotten drunk together, played wingman with girls for each other. And now he didn't want to get caught even talking to me.

It seemed so bizarre that this girl I didn't even know wasn't glancing around to make sure no one driving by on the street caught me anywhere near her when my own so-called best friend had.

Yeah, thanks a lot, you fucking *friend*.

"So you found my address and came to find out what I wanted from *you*?" she asked slowly, still gazing at me as if I'd lost my mind.

I shrugged. "And to say thank you," I added. "Mostly to say thank you. So…thank you."

I kind of half-nodded, half-bowed to her, like I wanted to treat her like royalty but felt weird about it. She blinked, letting me know I was totally weird.

I cleared my throat and shoved my hands into the front pocket of my hoodie. "Why were you trying to find *me*?"

Eyes widening, she jerked her head back and forth, shaking it madly. "N-nothing. I mean, no reason."

I squinted. She gulped. Then she winced and let out a defeated sigh before admitting, "I wanted to apologize."

My eyebrows jerked up. "For what?" Her apologizing made no sense whatsoever.

Flushing, she looked away and hugged herself. "Because," she muttered before pinching her brow into a frown and scowling directly at me, "Because I waited so long, you know, to come forward and help you."

My mouth fell open. I gaped at her mutely, long enough for her to start squirming uncomfortably under my stunned stare. Then I shook my head and blurted, "That's not…you can't…don't *ever* be sorry about coming forward. You *saved* me. I don't think you really realize how much you honestly rescued me. I don't care if it took you a day or a year, I am forever in your debt for what you did. You didn't know me, you had no obligation whatsoever to put yourself out there for me. Yet you did. That's what matters."

As if uncomfortable by my praise, she hugged herself. "Well, I pretty much *had* to." She shrugged one shoulder. "No one else was going to. I'm the only one who actually saw you, you know…" She glanced away, blushing. "I'm the only one who witnessed what happened."

It struck me then, like really struck me, this girl had seen me have sex.

The moment instantly grew, like, fifty times more intimate. The air seemed to suck in around us, and this strange heat bloomed deep in the pit of my stomach, like almost at the base of my cock. Then the nerve endings in my extremities gave a tingling shudder, especially when her gray eyes ran over me as if remembering exactly what she'd seen me do with Melody.

Something must be really fucked up with my brain because for the briefest moment this overwhelming thought struck me, and I couldn't help but wonder if she'd liked what she'd seen. She'd watched me come, listened to my panting breaths as my muscles had coiled for an orgasm, she'd maybe even smelled my release permeate the air. Had that disgusted her? Or intrigued her?

Then my thoughts went even more depraved; I wondered what she looked like when *she* came. I could damn near picture those full lush lips parting, that pert chin arching up and those long lashes fanning over her gray-gray eyes before her breath caught and—

Damn it to hell, I should *not* be thinking about this. What in God's name was wrong with me?

Since my encounter with Melody had led to everything that it'd led to, sex should be the very last thing on my mind. In fact, I might very well refrain from it for the rest of my life. No woman on earth was worth the hell I'd just been through.

Shaking my head to jostle my thoughts from the gutter, I refocused on Bailey's face. She was staring at me with wide eyes as if she knew exactly what I'd been thinking—not scared of it, but maybe just intimidated as in a flattered, oh-my-God-was-he-really-just-thinking-about-me-like-that kind of way. Which didn't help my growing erection die down in the least.

"Can I ask you for a huge favor?" I blurted, needing a distraction as I bent one leg strangely to create more space in my jeans and hopefully hide any bulges in case she dropped her gaze, to say, my lap region. Then I flushed hard, realizing what I'd just said. This was totally not the way I'd planned on begging for her help. Wincing, I added, "Even though I'm the one who owes *you* my life and you owe me completely nothing."

Her eyes narrowed suspiciously. "What kind of favor?"

"Can you, um…" I drew in a breath, worried she would deny me outright without even giving me a chance to plead my case. "Could you come with me sometime to my parents' place and help me convince them I'm innocent. They kind of, um, didn't believe me the first time I called."

Her mouth dropped open. "Your own *parents* didn't believe you? Why the hell would your parents not believe you?" Suddenly, she took a wary step back, the first time she'd ever seemed concerned about her own safety in my presence. Not that I blamed her. If a guy's own parents could think he was a rapist, he was probably a pretty despicable guy.

I winced, biting back the urge to reassure her I was safe and that she had no reason to be afraid of me, maybe even confess my true motive. But that was more embarrassing than letting her think I was repugnant enough to lose my family's faith.

I drew in a deep breath, kept my hands firmly in my front hoodie pockets and explained, "They have a good reason. It doesn't have anything to do with me personally, and it's complicated, so—"

Bailey waved me quiet. "You know what, just tell me about it on the way. Do you want to take my ride or yours?"

My mouth fell open as I gaped at her. "What?"

"You can tell me about all your family drama on the way to your parents' place," she enunciated more slowly.

The joy of her agreeing so readily to go with me was eclipsed by my confusion.

"Like what? You want to go *right now*? Right *now*, right now?" My heart picked up speed just thinking about seeing my mom and dad that quickly. Was I really ready to face them so soon?

Bailey merely shrugged as if it were no big deal. "Sure. Why not?"

I glanced around at the darkening evening. "It's almost night."

Bailey tipped her head to the side as if confused. "Do they not answer their door after sun sets?" Then she lowered her voice in a conspiratorial fashion. "They're not, like, afraid of werewolves of vampires, are they?"

I shook my head, blinking over such a ridiculous notion. "Umm, no. Of course not. I mean, maybe they are of vacuum cleaner salesmen, but it's just...they live over an hour away. It'd probably be over a three-hour trip. We might not make it back until after midnight tonight."

Bailey shrugged. "So?"

I swallowed, growing nervous. What if Mom and Dad still turned me out after I showed up for a face-to-face with them? What would I—?

No, I wasn't even going to entertain those kinds of thoughts. They'd let me back in. They *had* to. I was their son. They loved me and had always supported and protected me.

I focused on Bailey and panicked. "Don't you have to get up early for classes?" I asked, almost praying she said yes and cancelled on me, or at least postponed until I felt more mentally prepared.

A shadow of emotion crossed her face—something filled with pain and heartache—before she coughed into her hand and said, "I was planning on skipping tomorrow. You?"

Me? What about me? When I realized she was asking about my class scheduled, I flushed, immediately uncomfortable. Ducking my head, I kicked at the ground and admitted, "I, uh, I'm not enrolled at Granton anymore. They've forbidden from even stepping foot on their campus."

Her mouth dropped open. "Are you freaking kidding me?" she demanded. When I gave a brief, shame-filled shrug, she sniffed. "Well, that's just bullshit."

I looked up fully, surprised she was so affronted on my behalf.

I'm not gonna lie, it felt nice to know someone was on my side. I suddenly wanted to hug her. But then my mind immediately wondered how soft she'd feel in my arms. Her pillowy breasts would be nice mashed against my chest. And I bet her hair would smell sweet if I buried my nose into those funky, fun blonde curls. I straightened and scratched at the back of my neck, trying to dispel such thoughts from my brain.

With a grateful smile, I admitted, "I agree." It was all total bullshit.

"Well..." Bailey nodded and blew out a breath. "I guess my questions remains. Who's gonna drive?"

"I-I'll drive," I offered, even as I wondered how much gas I had in my tank and cash I had in my wallet. Renting that hotel room the night before had pretty much drained me, and I was positive I wouldn't make it to Mom and Dad's house with the amount of gas I currently had in my truck, much less back to Granton again.

But Bailey clasped her hands together and said, "All right then," as if it were all decided, which I guess it was. "Let's head out."

So I pointed out the way and led her from the door I'd never even gotten to knock on. She followed me across the dark street to my truck. I had an older model truck, no electronic key fob, so I walked around to the passenger side first to unlock her door for her. Then, since I was already there, I opened it and held it for her while she climbed in.

She was a petite thing and my truck was lifted, but she had no qualms about gipping the doorframe and hauling herself up into the cab, making it inside on the first try. She seemed fine about getting into a truck alone with me too, which blew my mind. She was probably the only person on the face of the planet who knew without a doubt I wasn't a rapist. She was the only person in the world who actually seemed to still trust me and have any kind of faith in me.

You really never realized how precious a person's trust and faith in you was until you didn't have it anymore. I didn't want to lose it with Bailey either, so I'm pretty sure I was willing to do just about anything to keep her believing in me.

Chapter 15
BAILEY

"So…?" I held my hands in front of the heater's blower on the dash of Beckett's truck before rubbing my warmed palms together and dropping them back into my lap. "You were going to fill me in on your family drama."

I was still a little shocked at myself for so readily going anywhere with him, but then…I guess I'd been craving an escape to get away from school and even my apartment for a while, so when he'd asked his request to get me out of town, it had felt like a big, fat blinking sign. I jumped all over the offer without even thinking it through. Then again, making rash decisions was my thing, so… huh, I guess it wasn't that surprising after all, though it *was* weird sitting quietly in a truck with a guy I knew basically nothing about, expect how pretty he was when he came.

Beckett glanced across the cab at me, looking distinctly uncomfortable. "Uh…" But then his gaze lit when he caught sight of a gas station. "Hold that thought. I need to fill up."

When he parked in front of a gas pump and killed the engine, he pulled his wallet from his back pocket before filing through the bills inside. I arched up enough to catch sight of a five, three ones, and nothing else. He snapped the wallet back together and sent me a quick glance.

I sank back into my seat, attempting to look innocent and unassuming, even though questions flooded the tip of my tongue. There was no way he'd be able to fill the gas tank on eight dollars. The gauge had showed we were at just under a quarter tank, and with an hour-long ride, I wasn't so sure eight dollars would get us there and back.

I wanted to ask why he wasn't pulling out a credit or debit card. I wanted to know if he needed me to pay. I had no problems with chipping in gas money. But he didn't ask for help and I didn't offer any. He seemed so embarrassed by his financial situation I kept my mouth shut, which was a rare event in and of itself. I never kept quiet when really curious thoughts bombarded me.

But I sat in the quiet cab of his truck like a good girl who really wasn't nosy as he murmured, "Be right back," and pushed the door open.

I watched from my seat as he went inside to pay, then filled the engine with exactly eight dollars' worth of gas.

When Beckett returned, sliding behind the wheel, and started the engine, he sent me an uneasy glance before asking, "Are you warm enough?" Then he fiddled with the heater controls. I think he wanted me to say no so he'd have a reason to change the temperature, and do something, *anything* to avoid the elephant in the truck.

But I said, "I'm fine," to which he muttered a disappointed, "Oh," and dropped his hand from the heater controls.

"Want some music on?" he asked next, already going for the radio next. "Country station, right?"

Man, he really did not want to tell me about his family situation. The boy was procrastinating big time. That only made me more eager to know everything.

Besides, if I was supposed to step into the lion's den with him, it seemed logical that I learned what I was heading into. Honestly, it was only fair. Plus it would help curb some of the raging curiosity in me, because I felt like I might blow any second from the insane need to *know*.

"What I don't get," I said, "Is how your parents, who should know you better than just about anyone, thought you were even *capable* of rape. Are you sure there's not something you need to tell me about you?"

He sighed and settled both hands on the steering wheel. "I only talked to my dad on the phone about it," he finally admitted. "And he never came right out and said, 'I don't believe you.' He was more 'you need to take responsibility for your actions,' and he said that *after* I told him Melody already had a boyfriend when we—"

"Melody already had a boyfriend?" I squawked. "When you two..." I motioned back and forth with my fingers.

Beckett glanced at me, frowning as if he thought I should already know this. "Yeah. Why do you think she cried rape in the first place? After you left the door unlocked, *he* came in looking for her. As soon as he found us together, she immediately started bawling and claiming I forced her."

"Holy shit." I stared forward out the dark windshield and watched the glowing reflection of the approaching highway signs zip by on the side of the road. "She's even more wicked than I originally thought. I had no idea she had a boyfriend when she came onto you."

"Yeah," Beckett muttered bitterly. "Neither did I."

I turned to watch his profile as he focused on the road ahead. "So none of this would've happened if I'd just relocked the door behind me, huh?"

He glanced over, meeting my gaze before scowling and shaking his head. "No. None of this would've happened if *Melody* had just been faithful to her boyfriend and left me the hell alone. None of this would've happened if *I* had just told her no like I'd wanted to. None of this would've happened if she'd just manned up and admitted to cheating on him. *You* did nothing wrong whatsoever."

I sank lower into my seat, feeling the urge to argue that point. It felt as if I'd done plenty wrong. I'd spied on him having sex, I'd remained quiet and hidden when he'd tried to tell her no, I'd taken not only a picture but a freaking video of it. I'd left the door unlocked so they would get caught together, and then...then...I'd left him hanging in jail for longer than I should have.

Hugging myself and feeling vile, I muttered, "Why *didn't* you just tell her no? It was obvious the whole time that you wanted her to leave you alone."

He reached up and reshaped the bill of his hat with his hand in a nervous gesture before quietly admitting, "I don't know. Because I'm stupid. I was drunk. I'm a guy. I didn't want to be alone. Take your pick." Then he wiped his hand over his face before releasing a pent-up breath. "Trust me, if I had to do it all over again, I'd have run out of that room screaming as soon she entered it, or I would've hidden with you in the…" He paused to glance at me. "Where the hell did you hide the whole time, anyway?"

"Bathroom," I admitted ruefully.

He nodded. "Behind the shower curtain?"

"Yep."

"Ah." Snapping his fingers, he said, "I knew it." Then he frowned slightly and tipped me a sideways glance. "But why were you running from me in the first place?"

"Because I was looking for…" Well, it didn't matter who I'd been looking for now. "And you were drunk and annoying and I didn't want to deal with you, so it seemed like an easier plan to just avoid you."

His eyebrows arched, probably surprised by my blunt honestly, but he didn't seem offended. Usually people were offended when I spoke my mind. It kind of warmed my soul that Beckett wasn't. "Well, I guess that makes sense," was all he said before, squinting and asking, "Who were you looking for again? I can't remember."

When he glanced at me, I refused to answer. He squinted even more before snapping his fingers. Then his eyes grew wide and his mouth opened, but no words came.

"Yeah…" I said slowly. "*Him.*"

The fucking bastard cowboy.

Beckett cringed. "You must know Melody then too, huh? Was she…? I mean, are you two friends?"

I snorted. "Hell, no. And no again, I had no clue who she was when she walked into that room. I didn't even know her brother. I was just trying to catch up with him so I could meet him, because I thought he was…" I sighed. "Never mind. It doesn't matter now."

Appearing regretful, Beckett bit his lip. "Sorry. I guess I ruined that for you, didn't I, because that'd be an awkward introduction if you did meet him now. *Hey, I'm the girl who outed your lying sister. You come here often*?"

I huffed out an amused sound, because he'd been not-far from the mark. But then I sobered, remembering exactly how close to the mark he'd been. "Yeah," I murmured. "Well, we *did* meet, and it *was* awkward."

Beckett zipped his gaze my way only for some kind of realization to slimmer through his eyes. "That's right. Max said you two got into it." He winced. "It was a pretty bad confrontation, huh?"

"He spit on me."

"Really? Shit. I'm sorry."

"Wasn't your fault," I muttered. "I blame his sister. And him. Nasty family, those Fairfields."

Beck bit his lip as if he wanted to smile and agree but figured it was probably a bad time to do so. "Well, thank you for defending me to him."

I shrugged and slumped even more into my seat until my restraining belt was nearly around my neck. "It was stupid of me to be so eager to meet him," I rolled my eyes, "just because I have some dumb cowboy fetish."

We were both silent a minute before Beckett cleared his throat. "Would it make you feel better to know he's from the city?"

Frowning, I turned to narrow my eyes at him. "Excuse me?"

Beck shrugged. "Chance. The cowboy. He's a fake. I mean, he was. When he started at Granton, he was a total city slicker, never even been on a horse or seen a farm in real life." He rolled his eyes. "But one day, I guess he just up and decided he wanted to ride bulls in the rodeo, so he changed his whole persona. To be fair, he's tried really hard since then to be *country*, but…" With another lift of the shoulders, Beckett let me know it was all a guise.

I gaped at him unable to believe my ears. Unable to believe any of it. "But…But…" I'd chased him for a year, thinking he was totally genuine. "His accent," I argued.

Huffing out an amused sniff, Beck grinned. "Yeah. That's put on to get chicks." When my mouth fell open, he glanced at me and grinned wider, "Guess it works, huh?"

"That fucking bastard," I breathed, making Beck laugh aloud. I scowled at him. "Why is this so funny to you?"

His grin dropped. "Sorry, sorry," he gushed. "It's just…sorry." He lifted one hand off the steering wheel to seek peace. "It gives me a personal thrill every time he loses an admirer. Damn fake gets more pussy than he should."

Still scowling at him, I crossed my arms over my chest. I don't know if I was so upset because I'd fallen for the "cowboy's" fake front or because Beckett seemed so gleeful about my stupidity. "I should've known he wasn't real," I muttered, deriding myself even as I glared at the driver. "I mean; the guy was in a freaking *fraternity*. What true country boy would be in an icky, gross fraternity?"

Beck sent me an odd glance and his mouth opened as if he wanted to naysay me. But then he pressed his lips back together, probably remembering he was no longer in a fraternity himself and therefore didn't need to loyally defend it or its members.

"But enough about that," I spoke up. "When are you going to stop avoiding the subject of your family and tell me what's going on there? We're probably already halfway to their place; don't you think it'd be wise for me to know what kind of mess I'm going to be walking into with you, so I don't step into some sticky, taboo topic by accident. Because if you must know, I'm pretty awesome as shoving my foot right into my mouth pretty much every time I talk."

"Yeah," he admitted on a harassed sigh. "Shit, yeah, you should probably know what's going on."

But then he didn't speak, and I lifted my eyebrows and both hands before saying, "Any time now. You have a captive audience."

"Damn," he hissed under his breath before whipping off his ball cap and scratching the back of his head, and then fitting it back onto his scalp. "My parents really aren't in a situation where they can support an accused rapist because this summer my sixteen-year-old sister Brittany really *was* raped." He glanced significantly at me before quietly adding, "And no one believed her. Well, except me and my parents. The guy—her attacker is a pretty big deal in our area. His dad is my dad's boss, actually. Er, he *was* my dad's boss. Dad kind of lost his job over the whole thing."

"Holy shit," I breathed. "Beck, that's…oh my God, that's so shitty."

He nodded. "It was my fault Dad lost his job. His boss had convinced Britt and my parents to keep it quiet. But I…" He shrugged. "I just couldn't. That motherfucker destroyed her. She stopped talking, stopped eating, began to have these nervous breakdowns. She holed herself up in her room and wouldn't come out. They finally put her into a mental health facility after she tried to kill herself."

"Oh God." I covered my gaping mouth with my hands.

"The rape kit they did on her *showed* signs of extreme force, but the prick just claimed she asked for it rough." Beck shook his head and clenched his teeth. "I couldn't let that go. How could I fucking let that go?" He looked at me with hard eyes as if he expected me to actually answer.

I shook my head, agreeing, "You couldn't."

He nodded. "So I beat the fucking shit out of him." His chin trembled and voice cracked as he finished, "And Dad got fired."

"Damn." I didn't know what else to say as Beck took a couple seconds to get himself under control. He cleared his throat and wiped the back of his hand across his cheek. "Freshly out of work and my Dad had to spend fifteen hundred dollars to bail me out of jail. They were already getting swamped under with the extra care they were paying to get Britt some help. None of the charges against me stuck since that prick had swung first, but it had already caused enough damage. Mr. Raider pulled some strings and my dad still can't find anyone to hire him. Mom's pay at the hair salon where she works certainly isn't covering all the bills. I offered to take off school this semester to get a job to help with everything, but they still weren't too happy with me. They told me to go back to Granton at the beginning of the semester and not get into any more trouble." Beckett sucked his bottom lip in between his teeth. "But going to classes and keeping up with the fraternity like life was normal while I knew my family was going into crisis mode, especially with some of it being my fault, sent me into a tailspin. I started drinking more than I should've, lost my girlfriend because I was so out of sorts, and I got reprimanded at work for showing up late and hungover. So, yeah…"

He glanced at me, and his bright blue eyes seemed so watery and sad that I almost wanted to start crying for him.

"It's not so much that I think they truly believe I'm a rapist now. This is more about whether they can deal with one more screw up from me. Instead of helping them through all this shit, I've only caused more problems. It would totally serve me right if they washed their hands of me completely."

I nodded, understanding his concerns. I'd worry about how my dad would receive me after all that too. It didn't matter if I was completely innocent of the crime or not. If I'd stupidly gotten myself into a bad situation, I could see him shaking his head in disappointment and muttering, "Well, you got yourself into this one, Bailey Rae. Now get yourself out."

A sudden thought struck me. Frowning, I sent Beckett a sidelong glance. "Hey, if trying to convince them of your innocence isn't what this trip is really about, then why am I coming with you?"

Beckett blew out a long breath and his shoulders fell a good two inches before he slid me a long, tired glance. "Believe it or not, you seem to be the only person who believes in me right now. And I'm scared to death. I have no idea what they're going to do when I show up on their doorstep." He shook his head, his throat constricting as he swallowed. "I can't face them alone," he admitted. "I need your support."

Chapter 16
BECKETT

The silence that filled the cab after confessing to Bailey Prescott what a damn coward I was kind of unnerved me.

But then she shrugged and said "Oh," so matter of factly that I had to blink. "Why didn't you just say that in the first place?"

I shook my head slowly, not sure how to answer. She seemed so blunt and open and honest, and no-big-deal about it that I decided to go the same route. "Asking you to come with me and hold my hand while I faced my mommy and daddy because I was too scared to do it by myself sounded pretty lame to me. And besides, I'm basically a complete stranger to you. We only met once, and that one encounter landed you in a whole mess of problems. I seem to get everyone around me mixed up in the worst kinds of situations, so it'd actually be smart of you to stay away from me. I didn't think the complete truth would help my cause any."

Bailey nodded as if thinking that through. "Makes sense," she said. Then her entire brow crinkled. "Wait. I don't have to literally *hold* your hand, do I? Because," she shook her head emphatically, wrinkling her nose. "I'm not much of a hand-holder."

I laughed. It wasn't at all a laughing situation. But this girl had managed to make me laugh. "No," I told her. "We definitely don't literally have to hold hands."

"Oh." Her shoulders sagged in relief. "Cool." But then she began to chew on her thumbnails. "So how much farther now?"

I focused on where we were. Shit. "A couple miles," I realized. "Maybe five."

She nodded and repeated, "Cool."

Cool. Not quite the word I would've used. I would've gone more with *holy shit* or *I think I'm going to puke.*

I straightened my hat and arched the bill under my palm so it would arch just right.

"You're nervous," Bailey said.

I sent her a distracted glance. "What?"

She motioned to her own forehead. "You're playing with your hat. You did that earlier. That means you're nervous, right?"

Dropping my hand and clearing my throat, I readjusted myself in my seat. "I don't know. I've never noticed before."

"Yep, you're definitely nervous," she stated definitively.

I sent her a brief scowl for making it so clearly obvious because her saying it aloud ramped up the nerves in me until they were at hyper-fear. Then I turned down the dirt road to my farm.

Bailey straightened in her seat, looking around, not that she could see much, it was full night now, and a dark moonless night at that. "This is a dirt road," she blurted the obvious, spinning in her seat to gape at me. "You live in the country."

I didn't answer. Her declaration didn't seem like something that needed answering.

She blinked at me as if seeing me for the first time. "What did you say your dad did again?"

I hadn't said. "He worked at an implement store, selling large farm equipment. He was there for twenty-two years."

"Holy hell," she breathed, still ogling me.

I glanced at her frowning. "What?"

But she only shook her head. "Nothing." She shook her head one more time and went back to staring strangely out the window.

I turned my truck into our long driveway and started fiddling with my hat again. When Bailey glanced at me with raised eyebrows, I sneered irritably at her and dropped my hand, snapping, "I can't help it, okay?"

She shrugged. "Then keep playing with it. Doesn't bother me." She said it simply as she leaned forward to peer up at our farm, where my parents' two-story house rose from the top of a slight hill and the driveway wound a circle around it. "So bizarre," she murmured.

"What is?" I asked, finding a good spot to stop and kill the engine. Pepper, our old collie, starting barking from around the corner of the house and I could barely make out his white and brown coat of fur darting through the night toward my truck.

Bailey blinked at him as if seeing a ghost. "It's all just so strangely similar to *my* home. Two-story house out in the middle of nowhere, sitting on a hill. We even have a dog. Humphrey's a Labrador, though."

I nodded. "We had a cholate lab before Pepper. Her name was Sal."

Bailey seemed dazed as he met my gaze. "Humphrey's a yellow."

"They claim those are supposed to be the smartest," I murmured, not sure what else to say.

Pepper reached the truck and jumped up onto the driver's side door. I heard his claws dig into the paintjob, and I began to cringe until I remembered, oh right, it didn't matter. My baby was scratched all to hell anyway.

"Seriously, who *are* you?" Bailey blurted, making me raise my eyebrows at her.

"What do you mean?"

"The first night I met you, I took you for a preppy, rich city boy whose big, important daddy was probably paying your way through pre-med or something."

I made a face. "Really? Whatever gave you that idea?"

"Because you…your…" She jabbed her hand my way as if her stuttering and fumbling motions made all the sense in the world. "And the fact you're in a fraternity," she finished, dropping her hand.

I grinned. She was so clueless it was actually cute. With a small shake of my head, I said, "You need to get out more." Then maybe she'd learn not everything was so black and white or even so clichély stuffed into neat, recognizable little groups.

Poor Bailey and her preconceived notions about things.

Still shifting my head back and forth and unable to stop smiling over her utter naivety, I pushed open and door and jumped out to scratch Pepper under the chin when he planted his front paws onto my hip. "Hey, boy. I missed you."

At least he was glad to see me, which reminded me where I was and what I was doing here. Suddenly sober again, I gulped and looked up at the darkened porch of my childhood home. I'm not sure how long I stood there, unable to move. But Bailey's voice from next to me jarred me from my reserve when she said, "Well, hi there, big fellow. Aren't you a friendly thing. Yes, you are."

I glanced over to find Pepper loving on her, his paws nearly resting on her boobs, as she scratched him vigorously behind the ears.

"Pepper," I reprimanded, grabbing his collar and pulling him off her. "Down. No jumping on visitors."

"Oh, he's fine," Bailey reassured even as she dusted paw prints off her stomach. "He reminds me of Humphrey. Never met a human he didn't love."

"Yeah. That's Pepper for sure." I petted his coat, though my gaze strayed toward the house.

When I didn't move, just kept petting the dog, Bailey cleared her throat. "Well, shall we?" She made a sweeping motion toward the front porch.

I sighed and barely took my hat off before resettling it on my head. "Yeah. I guess." But I just couldn't make myself start walking.

Bailey groaned. "Dammit, Bucket," she muttered, grabbing my arm. "Get your ass into gear already." She marched forward, pretty much dragging me along with her. "They're your *parents*. What do you think they're going to do; stab you in the heart with a meat clever? Geez Louise."

Up the porch she went, forcing me to trip along behind her. When we reached the front entrance, she raised her hand and knocked on the door before I could even catch my breath.

"Holy shit," I gasped. She'd already knocked on the door. This was happening. This was really happening, right now, whether I was ready or not.

I don't think I was ready. "Holy shit," I said again, my breathing bursting out of control and my vision graying in and corners. "What if…what if—"

"Hey." Bailey took my hand and squeezed my fingers, making me zip my attention to our clasped hands. I distinctly remembered her saying she didn't want to hold my hand, so I looked up at her with confusion. But her gray eyes were nothing but steady and concerned when she quietly ordered, "Just breathe."

I breathed, and my vision blinked back to full focus.

The front door opened, spreading light from inside out onto the porch. I let go of Bailey's hand and blinked into the brightness until I made out my mother's form.

My mom. She'd read me bedtime stories and cooked me chicken noodle soup when I'd been sick. I'd sat on her lap on Christmas Eve's trying to stay awake late so I could get a look at Santa Claus and I'd had my knuckles swatted by her when I'd tried to steal turkey early on Thanksgiving. She'd raised me and clothed me and taught me and loved me. I just wanted to rush to her and hug her and let all the bad shit in my life melt away.

But I remained rooted where I stood, only managing a breathless, uncertain, "Hi."

When she finally recognized me in the dark, her lashes fluttered rapidly and she pressed a hand to her mouth before whispering, "Beckett."

I jammed my hands into the front pockets of my hoodie and shifted weight from one foot to the other. "They let me go. Someone—a witness—came forward with the truth, and they let me go."

"That would be me," Bailey spoke up, stepping forward and lifting her hand to wave at my mom. I glanced at her, a little surprised she was still here. As soon as I'd seen my mother's worn, pale face, I'd forgotten everything else.

Mom sent her a perplexed glance, so Bailey quickly added, "I'm here to tell you undeniably without question that your son is completely innocent of everything he was charged with."

After another second of gazing at Bailey, my mom said, "Do you really think I need a complete stranger to convince me my son isn't a rapist?"

"I, um." Bailey blushed madly and said, "No?" as if guessing before she turned to me with a sheepish wince.

Mom focused on me as well. "What're you doing here, Beck?" she asked as if too weary to deal with me.

She looked as if she'd lost weight since the last time I'd seen her a few weeks ago, and gained a handful of wrinkles. Exhaustion had literally gouged out creasing into her pale skin. When I'd last called home the night I'd returned from a livestock judging contest for my fraternity to report the runner up place I'd won, Mom had told me how many problems she'd been having with her hands while she'd cutting hair. She feared she might be getting carpel tunnel. If that happened, she'd lose her job and there would be no money coming in at all.

Too many woes were piling onto her. And here I was, adding more weight onto her shoulders. I realized despite whether she wanted to support me or not, she might not be capable of emotionally weathering one more problem.

My hopes sank. "I…" Dammit, my voice was going hoarse. After a little cough, I tried again. "Can we come inside?" I asked.

She sighed as if she might give into temptation and allow me through the door, but then she drew herself up straight and shook her head. "No. No, I don't think that's a very good idea." Her hands began to shake and chin trembled, letting me know she didn't want to turn me out, but then she explained, "Britt is home."

"She is?" I sucked in a breath. "Is she…how is she?" If she was home, she had to be getting better, right? That was good news.

But my mother didn't look optimistic. Her eyes glazed with tears as she glanced away. "We just got her back last week, and so far we've been able to keep this trouble you got yourself tangled in from her, but it's been all over the news, Beck. She's going to find out eventually, and we have no idea how she's going to react. She's in a very fragile state right now. Just hearing the word rape could…" She shuddered and shook her head. "No, I'm sorry, baby, but we can't have you here right now."

I felt punched in the chest by her words, but I nodded because, shit, "I understand," I said. Britt needed them more than I did. Except fuck, I really needed my parents, too. What the hell was I supposed to do until…Until when? "So…you'll just call when it's safe to come home?" I asked.

She stared at me a full ten seconds, disappointment brightening her tired eyes, until she wiped a tear off her cheek. "Beckett, we told you to go back to school, focus on your studies and stay out of trouble. Why couldn't you have just *stayed* out of trouble? That's all we needed you to do." She clenched her teeth, anger showing through her pain.

"But, I didn't…" I shook my head, wanting to insist I hadn't done anything wrong. I was innocent.

Except she hit me with the knockout blow. "Your father said you admitted to being with a girl who already had a boyfriend." Suddenly, she didn't appear so beaten and drained. The last tear to fall from her eye shimmered with outrage. She was pissed and unable to believe the son she'd raised to be a decent man could out so wrong and do something so awful.

Shame lanced me. I couldn't believe my mother knew this about me. It was humiliating. Hanging my head, I admitted, "I didn't *know* she had a boyfriend."

"Which means you didn't bother getting to know her at all before having sex with her? Is that right?"

Fuck. No one could make a guy feel guilty and remorseful like his mama could. "No, ma'am," I admitted.

"Then this is *your* problem to deal with." She held her chin up in that way that told me nothing was going to change her mind. I felt as if I were basically dead to her now. "We cannot help you. If your father was here, he'd say the same thing."

I swallowed, lost. But I whispered, "Okay," because how the hell was I supposed to argue with my mother when I'd been the one to fuck up?

I started to turn away, only to pause, remembering one thing. "My checking account."

Mom flushed bright pink, but quickly cleared her throat. "We were behind on bills. You were in jail. We thought we'd have time to pay it back before you got out."

I stared at her, not sure what to think or feel about that. I'd been offering to help them for months, most of that money had even been saved expressly to help them, so I shouldn't be mad they'd finally accepted it, even though I needed it now more than I'd ever needed it before. But it still felt like a theft to me. I'd worked for that money, hours of sweat and blisters and sore muscles, only for them to take it behind my back without even letting me know. It was almost as if they'd betrayed me.

But I lifted my hand and nodded, saying, "It's okay. Don't worry about it. After putting Dad out of work and losing you guys more than I could ever repay, it's the least I can do."

I just didn't know what I was going to do with myself now.

Mom nodded briefly, not making eye contact. She started to shut the door, before pausing and saying, "Take care of yourself, Beckett."

Then she shut me out of her life forever.

Darkness wrapped around me as the cold November air seeped straight into my lungs and froze my very soul.

My parents had forsaken me.

Chapter 17
BAILEY

"What the hell?" I shrieked, making a comatose-looking Beck jump out of his skin.

He swerved around to blink at me in a daze, and I had a feeling he'd completely forgotten I was there, standing on his parents' dark porch with him.

"How could she just— your own mother! Oh my God. That sucked ass. I was just kidding about the meat cleaver to the heart bit, but that…" That had definitely been a meat cleaver of a blow straight to his heart.

He said nothing; he just stared at me until he turned away robotically and walked off the porch, down the front steps and moved stiffly toward his truck. But he stopped when he reached it, as if he'd forgotten how to lift his arm and open the door. He just stood there, hands at his sides, facing the damn driver's side door. Pepper, the collie, even came up and sniffed his fingers before licking his knuckles and begging for attention, but he didn't respond.

I had no idea what to do. I didn't deal with emotional shit. But Beck's zombie mode was freaking me out. I could only handle it for about two minutes before I whispered, "Beckett?"

He turned his head, and his head only, to look at me.

I swallowed, uncertain, before I asked, "What are you going to do now?"

He contemplated me ten seconds longer, looking straight into my eyes with that zoned-out dead stare before his shoulders crumpled and he shook, lowering his face into his trembling hands.

His chest heaved as he tried to console himself, but his agony just seemed to grow exponentially. When his knees gave out and he started to slump to the ground, I leapt forward to catch two handfuls of the front of his hoodie. "Whoa there. Hey." I could barely keep him on his feet so I nudged him against the truck, propping him up so he could lean against it heavily.

"Why don't I drive?" I offered lamely. He didn't argue or agree, so I said aloud to myself, "Yes, Bailey. That's a brilliant idea. Why *don't* you drive?"

After manually taking Beck's arm, I walked him around to the passenger's side. I only had to open the door to get him to mechanically climb inside, thank goodness, because I had no idea how I was going to stuff him in there if he hadn't been willing.

Then I hurried around to the driver's side. I'd driven some of my brothers' trucks before, but it always felt like I was sitting up in a tractor-trailer, steering a damn train when I did. Same deal in Beck's truck, I had to adjust the seat way forward because there was no way my short legs could reach the pedals from where he'd set it.

Then I started the engine and glanced over at my rider. He looked drained and beaten and completely out of touch with reality.

"Put your seatbelt on," I said quietly.

He did. So I geared the engine into drive and got us the hell off his parents' property.

The drive back to Granton was quiet and dismal. Every time I looked over at Beck, he was gazing out the passenger's side window. I could tell he wasn't asleep because he was sitting upright, alert enough not to slump. But he still seemed to have checked out. I even stopped for more gas, and he didn't seem to notice.

So I let him be until we neared the city limits. "Where are you staying?" I asked.

He shook his head.

Well, shit.

After drawing in a long, sympathetic breath, I nodded. Okay, so he'd lost his home at his parents' place and at the fraternity, and his parents had wiped out his back account so he had no money to rent a hotel room. His ex-friend, acquaintance he'd spoken of probably couldn't put him up for the night because I think he'd been from the fraternity too. So that left…nowhere.

I blew out a breath, out of options and not sure where to take him. He probably shouldn't be alone. He was in no state to take care of himself.

"Is there anyone I can call for you?" I asked, already knowing the answer. If he'd asked *me* to go with him to his parents' place for moral support, that pretty much meant he had no one to call.

One harsh, bitter laugh from him was the only answer I got.

"All right then." I tried to look at this from all angles and find something good he could still rely upon. But he was out of housing, money, school, friends, and family. But he had…hmm, this truck! Yes, a truck was something. And what else? A job, maybe?

"Where're you working?" I asked. Of course he had a job. Unless missing work because he was busy being arrested and gaining the reputation as the area's worst rapist had gotten him fired.

I cringed, even as he turned to look at me. "I was a student employee for the university."

Which meant he no longer had a job because he was no longer a student.

My shoulders slumped. "Well, fuck. I guess you're going to have to come back to my place and crash for a few days until you figure things out."

He merely blinked at me as if I spoke a foreign language.

"We'll have to keep quiet when we come in, though. My roommates are probably all asleep."

Beck turned to look back out his passenger side window. My heart broke for him. I'd be a mess too if my family had turned me out. I wanted to reach out and grip his arm comfortingly and tell him everything was going to be okay. But what the hell did I know? His future looked completely and utterly hopeless.

I couldn't exactly tell him *that* to cheer him up, so I kept my trap shut and pulled into an open parking spot across the street from my apartment. After shutting off the engine, I sighed and pocketed his keys, trying to plan out how I was going to haul his comatose ass up to my room.

But after I opened my door, climbed out, and started around to his side, he was already getting out himself. "Oh," I said, skidding to a halt when we came almost nose to nose with each other. Then I straightened and took his hand. "This way."

I have no idea why I held his hand. I guess I didn't trust him to wander off and get himself lost in the dark, thought honestly, I think I really did it because I wanted him to physically feel me and know I was there for him.

He blindly followed where I led, gripping my hand as if it were his only lifeline. At my door, he stopped when I stopped to unlock it. Then he moved when I moved, stepping inside. It was like leading one of those trained, seeing eye dogs.

I didn't have to hush him because I knew there was no chance of him talking, anyway. We moved quietly up the stairs, through the darkened front room, then down the hall past Paige and Logan's until we reached mine. After turning the handle, I pushed inside, leading him through the doorway.

Not sure what do to next, I let go of his hand to shut the door and then turned on a dim night lamp next to my bed.

I was going to say something about finding him a pillow and some extra blankets so he could crash on the floor, but the words stalled in my throat. His face was bruised and his shoulder slumped as he cradled his ribs. He looked so broken and defeated, I shook my head. I couldn't make him sleep on the floor. I'd settled him down on the bed and then go curl up on the couch myself.

But first. "Sit down before you pass out," I told him. When I took his arm and physically urged him to take a seat on the edge of the bed, he looked as me while he sank down onto the mattress.

"Last time a girl said that to me and pushed me down onto a bed I landed in jail."

Then he cracked off a short bitter laugh before his face contorted with pain, as if he might start crying. But he didn't cry. His shoulders jerked and he hiccupped a sob before shuddering out a breath. When he inhaled again, it sounded like a dry heave.

His face turned red and he gritted his teeth before clutching his chest and gasping, "Fuck, I can't breathe."

He'd briefly had this problem right before his mom had answered the door tonight. Remembering that I'd helped it pass by grabbing his hand, I cupped his cheeks in both hands and forced his face up so he'd look me straight in the eye.

"Yes, you can," I said sternly. "Just breathe."

His chest gave another huge, sputtering heave, but he breathed.

"Now exhale," I ordered.

He did, closing his eyes and leaning forward to rest his forehead against my chest. My arms just naturally went around his head until I was hugging him to me. It was the oddest thing ever. I never hugged anyone, but it was like I couldn't *not* hug Beck. He needed it. And I could tell he really did need it too because his arms went around me until he was clutching the back of my coat and holding onto to me for dear life as he shook in my arms and pressed his cheek firmly to my breasts.

When he sniffed, I cooed, "Shh. It's okay. It's all okay now."

Nothing was okay, but I think he needed to hear me say it was, anyway.

I petted his hair and ached deep inside for him. His entire world was shattered, and his core foundation—his own family—had just crumbled under him. I couldn't even imagine how devastating that was.

I just held him and consoled him as best I could by running my hand over his head. A crick started to grow in my back and my thighs began to burn from holding the awkward position. I didn't think he could be too comfortable how he was either, so I said, "Do you want to lay down?"

He didn't answer but gradually started to shift across the bed, lowering himself as he went. The problem was he didn't release his grip on me, so I stumbled along with him, nearly falling on top of him as he stretched out.

He didn't seem to want to unbury his face from my boobs, but I knew there was nothing sexual in his touch. He was seeking solace, nothing more.

Wiggling around until we were settled and cozy, we wound up with me on my back and him draped half on top of me, finally turning his face enough to the side that his cheek was nestled against my heartbeat. His arm stayed tightly wrapped around me as the occasional shudder wracked his body. That lasted a good half hour before his breathing deepened and he fell asleep. I kept stroking his hair though, I think I'd become addicted to doing that.

My fingers didn't want to stop comforting him, they might have even kept going after I eventually fell asleep.

My last hazy thought before I dropped off was how strange life was. I'd had exactly two encounters with this guy and yet I oddly felt closer to him than I could remember feeling to anyone. My arms tightened around him, hugging him just a little closer to me. In his sleep, he sighed as if comforted. Warmed from the inside out, I fell into a deep and heavy, dreamless sleep.

Chapter 18
BECKETT

I woke to light. An almost cheerful light.

It was strange. I was bruised, sore, stiff, my head was pounding, my eyes felt swollen, my throat was painfully dry, I'd been turned out and rejected by everyone I thought I could rely on and yet I felt at peace. I don't know if it was the cheerful sunlight streaming in through the window, the softness of the pillow under my head, the warmth of the blankets on top of me, or the comforting texture of the human flesh under my fingers.

My hand stroked idly up the flesh, running briefly over a more-wrinkled nubby area, until I decided it was an arm I was touching with an elbow in the middle. My lashes fluttered open to an eyeful of kinky blonde curls.

I released the arm I was holding so I could curl some of the hair around my finger and then watch it spring up and bounce a few times. A small smile lit my lips. I couldn't remember feeling this content for a long time, maybe even before Melody Fairfield had destroyed my life. I closed my eyes, delighting in the warmth of the sunshine and grateful for the softness of the mattress under my tender ribs.

But the moment was ruined when the owner of the arm and hair moved, letting out a moan of protest before flopping onto her back, nearly flattening me in the process and stretching her arms above her head—almost taking out my eye that time—and arching her back. Her breasts lifted, pressing snug against the cotton of her shirt, and things in me stirred, giving their own little morning stretch of approval.

I opened my mouth to say hello, but that seemed like the lamest greeting to give someone after they'd just selflessly nursed you through the night and single-handedly kept you from having a complete mental breakdown. So I closed my mouth and tried to cough some morning dryness from my throat.

Bailey squeaked her surprise, nearly tumbling from the bed and not-nearly, but actually catching me in the ribs this time with her elbow.

I sucked in a breath and curled into a ball around the pain, cradling my side with both hands.

"Holy shit," she yelped, sitting upright to gape at me. "I totally forgot you were here."

I intended to apologize for scaring her, but Jesus Christ, I hurt.

"Are you okay?" she finally asked, worry sparking her gray eyes, before she reached out her hand to touch my arm, only to pull back again.

I nodded and tried to straighten so she wouldn't be able to tell how much my side still throbbed.

She continued to frown with worry, watching me closely. I focused on her face and felt a sharp, stabbing embarrassment. I'd completely freaked out all over her. I'd taken charity from her and stayed at her place, which I never would've done in a normal frame of mind. I'd hugged her, clung to her really, and weakly let her comfort me. And I barely knew her.

I had no idea what to say and had to look away. I kind of would've loved it if the earth would crack open right about now and suck me down forever. Anything to escape this humiliating, humbling moment.

"I need to use the bathroom," she said abruptly as if she too felt the urgent need to escape.

After scampering off the bed, she darted, still in the clothes she'd worn the night before through a partially opened doorway before snapping it shut.

Sitting up, I looked around her bedroom. She was an eclectic kind of girl. Star Wars and Marvel bobble heads sat on shelves in front of posters on the wall of country western music groups, which were tacked next to a plaque for winning sub-state in high school basketball, while Chucks and cowboy boots and high heels lay scattered across the floor in front of a huge open treasure chest-looking trunk that had all sorts of clothes hanging over the side, from black, white and greys to pinks, reds, blues and browns.

From first glance, she appeared to be an assortment of everything.

Behind the door, the toilet flushed and then the faucet ran before Bailey reappeared, stepping into the room and trying to smooth down her wild locks. "Do you need to go?" she asked, motioning behind her and into the bathroom.

I did, but I shook my head no. It was as if accepting one more thing from her—even the use of her facilities—was too much.

"Are you hungry?" she asked next, shifting her weight from one foot to the other and rubbing her stomach.

I couldn't remember the last time I'd eaten, but oddly enough, I wasn't hungry. So I opened my mouth and rasped the words, "I'm fine."

There was so much I knew I should say. Thank you. Sorry. Thank you again. But the words didn't come, and I felt even more lacking.

Bailey cleared her throat, and I knew my muteness was only making her feel more uneasy. "Well, you should eat anyway." She glanced at the clock on the wall. "All my roommates have probably left for the day. I'm going to go to the kitchen and grab us some breakfast." When I didn't respond, she lifted her eyebrows and added, "Okay?"

I moved my head up and down to mollify her, and she finally left the room. That's when I swung my feet over the side of the mattress and lowered them to the floor before rising to a stooped-over stand. My ribs screamed in protest, so I hugged them close as I looked down at myself.

I was still wearing everything, even my sneakers, from the night before. I blinked at them, wondering if I'd ever slept in my shoes before. Unable to remember a time when I had, I glanced up and spotted my keys on the nightstand.

I grabbed them and took my first halting step toward the door. Ten more later, I could finally straighten my back fully, and five more after that, I reached out and turned the handle before opening up and glancing into a quiet hall.

It looked safe, so I stepped from her room and headed toward what looked like an opening of a living room. I didn't remember much of the floorplan from the night before. It'd been dark and I'd been out of it.

Another rash of embarrassment heated my cheeks. I couldn't believe the way I'd reacted. I'd never been so needy and overcome before. Yes, my mother's rejection had staggered me, but I should've been able to weather it.

I hadn't, and I hated that weakness about me.

Once I hit the living room, noises from one direction told me the kitchen was that way where Bailey was making breakfast. I went the other way, hurrying toward a banister that wrapped around a descending stairwell. After easing down the steps, I pulled open the door, burrowed deeper into my hoodie at the blast of cold morning air, and I stepped outside.

My truck sat across the street. I ignored the scratch marks starting from the front fender and ended halfway down the side of the bed, and unlocked the door before climbing inside and starting the engine.

Before pulling out into the street, I looked up at the apartment I'd stayed in overnight and shook my head, feeling shitty.

I hadn't thanked her, not for a single thing. I had no idea where I'd be right now if she hadn't pulled me together and brought me back to her place, if she hadn't held me while I'd fallen apart and let me sleep comforted in her arms. She deserved more than me taking off without even a thank you, and yet she deserved more than me sticking around too.

I wasn't in a position where I could repay her for anything. Right now, I could only take. Someone as giving and supportive as her didn't need a *me* in her life.

When I checked my fuel level, I cursed under my breath to see it nearly at a full tank. I vaguely recalled Bailey filling it up for me. Dammit, was there anything she *hadn't* done for me last night?

I wasn't her responsibility. Actually, I wasn't anyone's responsibly. Not anymore. I needed to take care of myself. As I turned a corner at the end of the block and glanced into the rearview mirror, the flapping lid of a box in the bed caught my attention.

First thing first, I should probably find a place for my shit. Leaving it out in the open much longer would only invite thieves. So after finding the first dumpster I saw behind a business building, I pulled up next to it and got out to sort my things.

Most of it had been broken or destroyed, so it was fairly easy to weed out the clothes and amenities I could salvage. Those went into the backseat as I tossed the rest into the trash. When I came across my electronic tablet, lap top computer and a watch I'd never worn, and none of them had been destroyed, I paused, looking them over before an idea hit.

Once the bed of my truck was clean, I found a pawnshop. I sat outside the store for nearly an hour, going through files and pictures, emailing the ones I wanted to keep to myself before deleting the rest and wiping all my personal shit from everything. Then I untethered my internet connection to them from my phone and hugged both tablet and computer to my chest for a few seconds in farewell.

The pawnshop owner offered me a pathetically low price for them, but I wasn't in a position to haggle. As he counted up my cash, he squinted at me and tipped his head to the side.

"You look awfully familiar. Do I know you?"

I dipped my chin down so the bill of my hat would cover more of my face. "Don't think so," I mumbled, hoping like hell he didn't recognize me from the news. I needed that money he was only seconds away from handing me; if he realized who I was, I wasn't so sure he'd be willing to buy my things any longer. People could be so finicky when dealing with a news-reported rapist.

But he never figured it out, just frowned and shook his head before scratching his chin and handing me the dirty, tattered stack of bills across the counter.

"Thank you." I took them with a suddenly shaking hand and sent him a nod of gratitude before I got the hell out of there.

Food was my next stop, so I pulled into the first fast food joint I could find. My stomach jolted as soon as I stepped inside the restaurant. It had to have been over twenty-four hours since I'd last eaten. Keeping my hat pulled low and the hoodie of my sweatshirt up around my neck, obscuring most of my face, I ordered off the dollar menu and sat in the corner with the most shadows. It was past the noon hour rush, and business had slowed, but stray people would trickle in every few minutes.

I was nearly finished, polishing off my fries and sucking the last of my drink through the straw when a mother entered, her young daughter dancing around her and already begging for the toy from the happy meal. I started to smile, charmed by her enthusiasm before a great big swell of panic hit, straight in my chest.

I suddenly pictured someone else recognizing me and pointing, then shouting *rapist*. The mom would gasp and grab her daughter, clutching her close, terrifying the poor kid who'd been so eager only a second before. Panic and chaos would ensue, all happiness and smiles suddenly gone, just because I was sitting here, eating my meal.

I don't think I belonged out in public among people anymore.

The last fry felt extra dry going down. I stood and rushed to pack away what was left, stuffing the last of my fries into the pocket of my hoodie for later, then I threw my trash away and hurried back to the bathrooms to clean up before I left.

I changed outfits, then washed my face and hands. Once I left the restaurant, I started to jog toward my truck, but a shout from the opened window of another truck sitting in the drive though waylaid me.

At first, all they hollered was, "Hey, you!" so I kept going without even glancing back. But then I heard a car door slam and footsteps before someone added, "Beckett Hilliard."

I looked back on instinct, hearing my name, and saw Chance Fairfield rushing toward me, followed by a couple other guys from our fraternity who must've been riding with him.

At first, I could only blink dumbly. But seriously, what were the odds of running into him of all people in a town this big? The campus wasn't even anywhere near here, and he should've been in class this time of day. Right?

I took too long cursing my luck. It gave him ample opportunity to run right up into my space, threatening and already rearing his arm back.

"You are so dead, you motherfucker," he growled before plowing a fist into my jaw.

I'm not gonna lie, it rang my bell.

I thought I was going to pass out or at the very least puke. But from the corner of my throbbing eye, I saw him swing again and I ducked at the last moment. The air from his jab swept across my cheek he was so close to the mark, but at least he missed.

"Hey, hey, hey," I said, lifting my hands, and trying to reason with him. "You just need to calm down and listen to me a second. I didn't force her to do anything."

But, oh, was *that* the wrong thing to say. He cried out his rage and steamrolled his entire body toward me, bowing his head and using his shoulder as a battering ram to tackle me to the ground.

I landed with a bone-jarring thud, splitting pain through my ribs. It stole my breath and gave the cowboy time for a couple more punches before I couldn't handle it anymore. I hurt so fucking bad, I needed him off me or I just knew I was going to die. I bucked him away, shoving, and kicking, and punching blindly in a wild desperation to be free. I knew I hit a couple of solid lands because I felt the firm give of flesh under my knuckles and heard his grunt of surprise.

When I successfully got my feet planted on his abdomen and kicked him off away, he tumbled backward, landing ass first on the asphalt about three yards away. But as soon as I rolled into my hands and knees and tried to push to my feet, two of my ex-fraternity brothers grabbed my arms to prevent me from escaping. The bastards hauled me upright, keeping hold of me as Chance staggered to his feet.

My nose felt broken, and I tasted that all too familiar metallic flavor. The cowboy didn't look so good himself, though. He shook his head and wiped a handful of blood from his upper lip.

I shook my head, struggling against my captors as he stormed menacingly closer. "You're so wrong about this, Fairfield," I tried. "You're going to feel like shit when you realize how wrong you are. She *lied*."

He only snarled, curling back his lips to flash his teeth. "My sister doesn't *lie*." And he jacked me in the jaw.

My vision blinked out, then blinked back on, but everything was blurry and I felt really dizzy. When he reared back his arm again, I shook my head and whimpered out a single plea through bloody lips. "Stop."

"Oh my God!" a female voice suddenly cried. "You boys stop that. Stop that this instant. Leave that young man alone. I'm calling the police."

The two people holding my arms suddenly jumped away from me, letting go quickly enough that I slumped to my knees.

Chance turned tail and ran off behind them toward his truck where I vaguely made out Max standing and watching with large eyes as if he wanted to hurry away with them but also wanted to check on me. He made eye contact with me briefly, and when I mouthed his name, his eyes flooded with regret before he spun away and followed the other three to the truck, where they climbed inside and squealed the tires in their hurry to leave.

I stared after them, panting heavily and clutching my ribs as I remained slumped on my knees.

"Are you all right? Don't move. I'm going to call you an ambulance."

"I'm fine," I croaked, looking up to find the same woman who'd entered earlier with her excited daughter. The girl was now clutching the woman's legs and looking scared out of her mind. "No ambulance," I assured them, lifting a hand to wave the offer away. "I'm okay, ma'am. But thank you."

The kid still looked scared out of her wits. She held her happy meal to her chest, the paper bag rattling noisily from the force with which she shook.

I offered the girl a small smile. "Did you get the toy you wanted?"

I didn't realize what a dumb question that was until the mom paused in her dialing to blink at me. The kid stared at me as if I'd lost my mind.

I guess I could no longer smile and talk to little kids, a fact proven true when the mom sucked in a sudden breath a second later. I lifted my face, noticing recognition widening her eyes.

"Oh, Lord. You're… oh, my God." She grabbed her daughter harshly and yanked her away from me before spinning them both away and hurrying to her SUV across the parking lot, while her kid cried, "But, mom. That man's bleeding."

They rushed from of the parking lot almost as quickly as Chance and Max and his crew had.

I sat there a few seconds longer before pulling myself together and slowly pushing myself to my feet. My truck was only about twenty feet away, but it felt like a damn mile. I really didn't think my body could take much more abuse. Once I reached my ride, climbed behind the wheel, and pulled the door shut, I just sat there, resting my head back and closing my eyes. That one small walk felt as if it'd taken all the energy I had.

But I knew I couldn't stay here much longer. Being recognized seemed to come with nothing but pain. I needed to find somewhere to go that was away from people. Away from pain.

I meandered out of town, out toward the university barn where I used to work, idly daydreaming about how I'd give anything to be shoveling the shit out of horse stalls right now. I let myself yearn for my old life, wishing it could all return to normal again as I turned deeper into the country and headed out to the University lake, which was really a small pond that all us aggie students went bass fishing from occasionally.

It was rarely ever used, and certainly not during typical school hours, so I knew I'd find the place empty. I parked near the shore and killed the engine to regroup.

For the longest time, I sat watching the occasional, lazy ripples across the surface of the water, or a wood duck float by. It was peaceful and beautiful and so out of place from all the ugliness surrounding me lately. But like Bailey's bedroom this morning, it almost felt too peaceful for me now.

I didn't belong here anymore than I belonged out in public or in that perfect bedroom of hers with her. Wetness trickled down my cheek as I wondered if there was *anywhere* I belonged. Would anyone care at all if I just ceased to exist?

That thought was depressing, so I closed my eyes and tilted my head back. I tried to nap in the driver's seat but it wouldn't incline very far due to all my personal effects I had piled in the back, and besides there was no getting my ribs comfortable on such a hard surface.

The sun began to slide down in the sky, evening rose, and I knew I wouldn't be able to stand sleeping here all night.

I started the truck and headed back toward Granton. Not sure why I stuck around the area, there was nothing for me here. I could literally go anywhere in the world, there were no ties holding me down. I wouldn't get far with the money I had, but there was no reason whatsoever for me to stay.

Except maybe for one.

I found myself back at her apartment twenty minutes later. Turning the truck off, I stared up at her place, my chest constricting with the idea of going to her right now. I had enough funds to last me a couple more nights at a hotel, but I needed to think bigger than that, plan for further into the future than a day or two.

Bailey had said the night before that I could stay at her place until I got back on my feet. At least I'm pretty sure I remembered her saying that; I hadn't been too with it.

Besides, something ached in me, deep inside, feeling hollow at the thought of never seeing her again. I wasn't sure if it was because I'd ditched out on her without saying goodbye, or something else. But I felt drawn here. Maybe I could just tell her thank you.

The only problem was I didn't want to bother her. I barely knew her and she'd already done so much for me. *Too much.* I just couldn't let myself become *that* obligated to anyone. It felt wrong. Not to mention the fact I wasn't sure if I could ever look her in the eye again for the way I'd wigged out on her.

But I opened my doors, yearning and nearly desperate to see those springing blonde curls and those big gray eyes. I had this feeling she'd scold me when she saw me, mad because I'd taken off without saying goodbye, and I almost smiled at the image. Except smiling felt wrong too. Being around anything that brought me any kind of joy seemed inappropriate, so I veered away from her place instead of going toward it.

I entered the quiet park across the street and sat gingerly on the first bench I came across, not sure what the hell I was going to do.

Chapter 19
BAILEY

He'd vanished. The stupid boy had just up and disappeared on me when I'd been trying to take care of him.

Who the hell did that?

It pissed me off, but only because I refused to admit how much Beck's disappearance worried the shit out of me, and kind of hurt my feeling too. He was in no position to be out on his own right now. How dare he skip out after the night we'd shared! And why would he leave me? Had I done something wrong?

Dammit.

What did he think he was doing anyway, taking off like that? He had nowhere to *go*!

I drove around, looking for him for a while. But I didn't really know anything about him, had no idea where he'd go. Cursing him up one side and down another, I returned home and paced my place. I hoped he'd return, like he'd only gone out to run an errand or something. But by the time all my roommates made it home, Beck still hadn't showed up.

Once more, I was unusually quiet and stressing out big time. I bypassed supper, which only prompted another visit to my room from Tess and Paige. I couldn't quite look Paige in the eye. I wasn't mad at her, but it felt weird to look at her, thinking she might worry about me creeping on her and Logan now. And Tess. I couldn't tell

Tess where I'd gone the night before or what I'd done. I always told her everything, never kept shit to myself.

Why couldn't I tell even Tess what was going on?

Life had just gotten so fucked up. I didn't know what was happening to me or anyone else.

I hated that.

Tess felt the need to tell Paige what we'd overheard the day before on campus—damn, had that only been yesterday—and Paige had gotten loyally offended on my behalf, but none of that seemed to matter.

I wanted to know where Beck was. I *needed* to know. How dare that bastard just up and disappear without even telling me he was leaving or where he was going? Didn't he realize he was my responsibility now?

Idiot!

My friends talked around me for a good hour and didn't seem to notice how distracted I was. They thought they had all my problems figured out. They said I should just ignore all the nasty gossip about me and carry on as usual; it would die down soon enough.

Sure, sounded good to me. Whatever. I nodded and agreed in order to make them happy. God, I was such a shitty friend.

Honestly, I didn't know how to talk about this. I didn't know how to explain Beck or the protective need I felt to take care of him. How could I tell them something I didn't understand myself?

Wanting him here so I could keep watch over him felt like an obsession, and obsessions were bad. If they knew how bad off I'd become, they'd try to intervene and stop me. I couldn't stop. I had to worry about him. I had to find him. I had to *fix* him.

"Fucking bastard," I muttered hours later after Tess and Paige had left, and they'd all gone to bed. I was the only one left in my apartment wide-awake and unable to sleep, pacing my room and wondering where the hell he was staying tonight. "Doesn't he even care what he's *doing* to me?" I demanded aloud.

Obviously, he didn't. Frustrated beyond all get-out, I yanked open the curtains to my window, needing a change of scenery before I drove myself crazy.

"Where are you, you stupid bucket-head?" I muttered, plunking my forehead against the pane glass as I stared sightlessly down at the park across the street.

A loneliness crept into my veins, and suddenly I wasn't sure if I was so upset because I was really all that worried about his welfare or because I felt abandoned.

But that last part was just stupid.

How could I *miss* him enough to feel abandoned? I didn't even *know* him. I just needed to cut this shit out and get over him already.

Except the ache in my chest wasn't listening to the rational reasoning part of my brain, and it could only remember the way he'd so trustingly curled into me and clung to me, needing me, relying on me to see him through. And the stupid little ache missed those precious moments.

I felt as sad at that guy sitting out there on the never-used park bench all by himself with the streetlamp spraying down on him and showing off how solitary and alone he looked. Wondering what had put that dude in such a funk, I studied him until my eyes started to squint, realizing how familiar his silhouette seemed. And then I was gasping as my mouth fell open because I realized I knew that silhouette with the ball cap on his head and his hoodie's hood hanging down his back.

"Oh, that *turd*!" I growled, fisting my hands down at my sides before spinning for the door and racing from my room. I didn't bother with shoes or a coat or stocking cap, or anything. I was too mad, and relieved, and ecstatic to see him again.

Ground moisture instantly soaked through my socks as I stepped outside. The cold blew right into my lungs, but I barely felt that either. Darting down the sidewalk and across the street, I scowled at him until I was only a couple feet away.

"Where the *hell* have you been?"

He lifted his head, and I faltered my lecture because he looked so gosh-darn defeated.

I ground my teeth, determined to give him a piece of my mind, anyway. "You had me worried sick. Do you even know what I went through, looking for you and wondering what had happened to you?"

"I'm sorry," he said with a heartfelt simplicity.

I opened my mouth, wanting to rage and lecture more, but dammit, why did he have to look so much like a kicked puppy? "Oh, just shut up. Let's get inside before we both freaking freeze to death."

Except the stupid, idiot boy shook his head. "No. You've already done so much for me. Too much. I can't. I'll never be able to repay you. I don't want…I can't…"

I blew out a frustrated breath and shook my head sadly. He reminded me of myself, a little too proud to accept help and awkward about thanking people. But right now, it wasn't working for me.

"Then why are you sitting outside my apartment like a lost little kitten?"

If anything, he looked even more lost than before. Glancing around the dark, empty park, he admitted, "I don't know."

I groaned, "Well, can you *not-know* inside, where it's warm? I've ruined my socks and forgot to grab my damn coat." Taking his arm, I yanked him up into a stand and started to march back in the direction of home.

He followed willingly for a couple feet, but then he resisted, saying, "Bailey."

I groaned and glared over my shoulder at him. "What?"

He shook his head, seeming upset and regretful. "I never said thank you. For last night."

I sniffed and rolled my eyes. "Just save it. After the way you ditched out on me this morning without a goodbye or fuck-you, or anything, I don't even want to hear how *grateful* you are."

"I *am* grateful," he insisted softly. "I was just…Jesus," he glanced around as if devastated. "You saved my life. Y-you've just done too much for me. How can I…how can I take *more* from you? I don't want to use you like that."

"You're not—" Realizing I wasn't going to convince him he wasn't using me, I groaned and cut myself off, trying a new track. "Fine. Pay me back, then. I don't care. Just get your ass into gear, Hilliard. I'm *cold*."

He started to move, even as he asked, "But *how* am I supposed to pay you back? I don't *have* anything anymore."

"I don't know," I answered distractedly as I opened the door and tugged him into the apartment. "We'll figure something out. Later."

I led him up the stairs and back to my room. Once I nudged him inside in front of me, I closed us alone in my room and turned on the light, ready to scold him some more, even as I ripped off my wet socks.

But when he turned to look at me, my mouth fell open.

"Oh my God, your *face*." I pointed at him, trying to catch my breath. "What the hell happened? Half those bruises were *not* there this morning."

An amused smile came over him before he glanced down at his hands where there was a cut on his knuckles. "It was the strangest thing. I ran across the cowboy of all people at McDonalds when I was getting myself some lunch." Smile stretching wider, he shrugged helplessly at me. "Apparently, this town just isn't big enough for the two of us."

I blinked at him. "Seriously?" I finally asked. "You just *accidently* ran across him? You didn't seek him out?"

His eyes widened. "Why the fuck would I seek him out?"

"I thought he was the reason you were kicked out of your fraternity. And you know, deep down, he has to be aware his sister's lying. If he'd gone the justice route and stuck up for you instead of being stupidly loyal to her, you might not have been kicked out of school or the fraternity or—"

Beck lifted his hands, stopping me mid-talk. "Trust me, I didn't go on a revenge-seeking mission. I was perfectly content with never seeing him again." With a wince, he shifted and clutched his side.

"What's wrong?" I demanded, approaching him. "Where does it hurt?"

"I'm fine," he insisted, though his face was pale and he couldn't hide the pain from his eyes. "Just bruised, maybe cracked a few ribs."

"Let me see." I reached out. He lifted his arm to block me, but I batted the annoying limb out of my way and yanked up his hoodie. Underneath was a white t-shirt, so I yanked that up too, only to gasp from the amount of bruises on his side.

"They're not all from today," he insisted, as if that made any kind of difference. "Actually I don't know if any of them are from today. I think all of them came from Melody's boyfriend and my ex-fellow inmates. I was just kidding about them being cracked. I'm sure they're only bruised."

I sucked in a wince. "Holy shit, Beckett. These look nasty. I was about to make a nest of blankets on the floor for you, but I can't let you to sleep on the hard floor in this condition."

He pulled his shirt and hoodie down to cover the discolored skin. "Yes, you can. It's fine. I'll be fine."

"Whatever. Just get on the bed already," I groused, pointing it out to him. He opened his mouth to argue, but I help up a hand.

"We both slept there together last night, and no one died. It'll be fine."

He frowned and closed his mouth, then took a deep breath before tipping his head and quietly asking, "Why are you doing all this for me?"

I huffed out a laugh and shook my head. But he just kept watching me, waiting for a serious answer, so I sighed and admitted, "I have no idea. I don't think I could explain it if I had to."

His eyes squinted slightly as he if were peering straight into my innermost feelings. Then he nodded slowly. "Okay," he said simply. His gaze slid toward the bed. I couldn't tell from his expression if he was dreading getting on the mattress with me or if he was actually looking forward to a comfortable place to sleep.

But then he turned back to me and pointed toward the bathroom. "That's a bathroom, right? Do you mind if I…?"

"Oh!" I have no idea why I was surprised by the notion, but I flushed and quickly nodded. "Yeah, sure. Go ahead."

He murmured his thanks and disappeared behind the door. A few minutes later, I heard water running and then he re-emerged. He'd taken off his shoes and shed his hoodie. He looked thinner and more vulnerable in just the T-shirt. The need to go to him and wrap my arm around him, offering comfort, rose in me.

I was afraid this guy might be turning me into a hugger. I'm not sure if I liked that or not.

Ignoring the impulse, I moved away from him to grab a pair of pajamas and darted into the bathroom myself. I spent more time in there than I needed to, nervous about climbing under the covers with him.

We'd done this the night before, but this time we'd both be cognizant and fully aware of what was happening. It suddenly made everything feel so much more intimate.

Cursing myself for being such a weenie, I yanked open the door to find he'd already crawled under the covers. But he wasn't asleep. He instantly sat upright, his bright blue eyes wide and worried as if he were scared shitless he'd done something wrong. The blankets fell down his chest, pooling around his waist, and I blinked over how spectacularly beautiful he was, even bruised and half-beaten to death.

There was a gorgeous guy in my bed. How freaking bizarre was that?

"Is this okay?" he asked uncertainly, poised as if ready to jump off the mattress if need be.

I started to nod, but then felt funny about admitting just *how* okay I thought he looked in my sheets. Cheeks flushing, I said, "Can you move to the other side?" hoping the question would hide what I was really thinking.

"Oh! Yeah, sure." He hurried to scoot over. "I'm sorry, was I on your side?"

I should've gone with that theory, yes, he'd taken my side, but instead, I stupidly admitted, "I have no idea. I've always slept in the middle."

When he glanced at me as if confused why I'd made him move, I cleared my throat and flushed even harder. "That side just looked better," I mumbled.

Yes, I was a moron.

"Oh." He still looked perplexed, but he said, "Okay," and settled onto the new side without argument.

I just stood there, watching, unable to move. Was I really supposed to just tiptoe over there now with my bare feet and oversized T-shirt and crawl into bed with him?

Ugh, I guess so. After turning off the main light, I haltingly started forward, gaining Beckett's attention. His lips parted and his shoulders rose half an inch as if he were drawing in a deep breath. His eyes followed me as I moved around to the side I'd just stolen from him and lifted the sheet enough to slide under the covers.

I reached for the nightlight and clicked that off. Then I lay stiffly, staring through the dark up at the ceiling. Thirty seconds later, I frowned and shifted. Then I squirmed again. Okay, this wasn't working.

"Actually, can we change sides?"

He huffed out a laugh but said, "Yep."

I hopped out of bed and raced around in the dark to the other side. When I heard Beckett shift back to his original spot, I crawled in with him again. Almost as soon as I sank into the cushion, I moaned. "Oh God, yes. This is definitely better."

"It is, isn't it?" he murmured.

His voice raced through me, making me shiver. Damn. Oh, damn. We'd just picked sides of the bed.

I shifted around some more, getting comfortable even though this was all so awkward and new. For some reason, we both ended up on our sides facing each other, him resting his cheek against one pillow, me resting mine against another. Neither of us spoke as we just watched each other through the moonlight filtering through the window that I'd forgotten to draw the curtains closed to.

Finally, he whispered, "Thank you, Bailey."

I closed my eyes briefly and shook my head. "I really don't want a thank you."

"Then what do you want?"

My eyes sprang open. I knew he wasn't offering sexual favors, or anything like that, in exchange for room and board, and that's not what I wanted from him, anyway.

Well, not really.

But a small, guilty, private part of me ached for something close to that.

What did I want, he'd asked. What did I really want more than anything else on earth?

I wanted some kind of connection to another human being, physical contact, emotional ties, a spiritual bond, *anything*. I knew I complained about what Tess and Paige had with their guys. But that was only because deep down, I wanted what they had. I wanted to know I was capable of being loved. I wanted to feel I was sensual enough to turn a man on and get turned on myself by him. I wanted the whole nine yards of an ooey-gooey, gag-me relationship.

As Beck Hilliard's bright blue eyes bored into mine and his question echoed through my head, I could think of no other answer but that.

I wanted to fall in love.

But I couldn't tell *him* that. He was too busy dealing with his life falling apart around him to worry about my stupid little malfunctions.

So I sniffed and rolled my eyes. "I just want Melody Fairfield and her brother Chance to get what's coming to them. I want the world to know—really know—how much of a big-fat liar *she* is. I want them to stop picking on you and realize how wrong they all were."

I wanted all the idiot sheep on campus to believe *me* when I said Beck was innocent.

Beck chuckled softly. "Yeah. You and me both. Though if it makes you feel any better, I'm pretty sure I made him bleed today."

I gasped in pleasure. "Did you? That's so awesome. Thank you." Then I scowled as I pictured the cowboy. "I still can't believe he spit on me." Or more aptly, I couldn't believe I'd spent a year pinning my silly hopes on such a jerk who would spit on girl.

Oh well. I was done with that. Over it. (Not really. Being spit on stayed with you a while.) I was so moving on. (I still hated him. He'd hurt me big time.)

Focusing on Beck, I sighed. I could even see some of his bruises in the dark. Poor guy. "I never told you how sorry I was about what your parents did to you. That really sucked."

"It's fine." He shrugged and lowered his gaze before looking up and meeting my eyes. "No, actually, it's not fucking fine at all. I think the moment my mother shut the door in my face was the absolute worst moment of my life, even worse than when Melody called me a rapist."

With a nod, I whispered, "I bet. I can't imagine what I'd do if my dad ever did that to me."

"We take them for granted, you know. Our parents. We assume they'll always be there, always support us, always back us up. But honestly, they don't *have* to. They don't have to do any of that shit. Some of them come with a breaking point where they say enough is enough. It was a brutal lesson to learn I crossed that point."

He looked so devastated; I knew I had to change the subject, if only for my own peace of mind. It tore *me* up just thinking about what had happened to him; I could only guess what it did to him.

Wanting to distract him, and say something witty and fun and happy, anything to lighten the mood—that's what Tess would've done for me—I opened my mouth and, "My mom died when I was seven," I blurted.

Then I frowned at myself. Wait, that wasn't light or witty or even remotely happy. What the hell, Bailey?

But Beck watched me, a captive audience, so I cleared my throat. "I don't remember her. At all. We were in a car accident together, Mom and I. I guess she died instantly, but I was trapped inside with her for a while. It must've done something traumatic to me." I shrugged. "I don't know, because I don't remember it, and I don't remember her either. I mean, I remember nothing about her. I was seven when she died, I should have memories, right? But I don't. It's like I completely wiped all existence of her from my memory banks." Then I nudged his arm and snickered, "How's that for a sucky, ungrateful daughter?"

Beck just stared at me as if not comprehending. "I'm confused," he finally admitted. "How could you completely forget her?"

"I don't know," I admitted. "The brain is a crazy, complicated thing, I guess. My dad and brothers played it off like I'd been too young to have memories of her when she died, which probably didn't help me remember anything, but Tess and I got into this huge fight last year and she accidently blurted out how old I'd *really* been, so—"

"Wait, who's Tess?"

I stopped talking, completely thrown off guard as I blinked stupidly at him.

He wrinkled his brow and asked, "What?"

It seemed impossible that he didn't know who Tess was. Tess was my foundation, my go-to person. She was the best part of me.

Shaking my head, I said, "She's my best friend. She's been my friend since forever, since we were babies. *She* even remembers my mom. She's actually one of my roommates here in the apartment: her and her boyfriend Jonah and our other friend Paige along with Paige's boyfriend Logan."

Now Beck seemed even more confused. "You live with two couples?" His nose wrinkled. "Oh, that's got to suck."

I snorted, a little happy he actually got it. "You have no idea."

He grinned back, before shaking his head and frowning. "Now why would Tess do that do you? Seems like kind of a shitty move to wait all this time before telling you."

"I deserved it," I assured him. "Trust me. I was the sucky friend first."

He scowled as if he couldn't believe that, but I nodded. "I was. But in any case, the truth came out, so I visited my mom's grave at the cemetery. Can you believe I'd been out there dozens of times in my life and I'd never paid attention to the year she died on her tombstone before? I mean, how blind can one person get? I felt so stupid and…and…"

"Betrayed?" Beck guessed.

I swallowed and stared at him. "Yeah," I admitted softly. "I felt a little betrayed too. Why hadn't anyone just told me?"

"They probably thought they were protecting you, though yeah, it was still pretty awful and stupid of them. I mean, they had to know you'd find out eventually."

"And what the hell did they think they were protecting me from?" I sniffed. "Did they think I wasn't strong enough to handle the truth? I mean, screw that shit. I *thrive* off the goddamn truth."

Laughing softly, Beckett nodded. "Yeah, *that* I believe."

I scowled and demanded, "What the hell does that mean? What's wrong with being honest?"

He shook his head but kept grinning. "Nothing at all," he assured me. "I love your brand of honesty. You're so transparent I'm pretty sure I don't have to ever guess what you're thinking."

If only he knew how transparent and honest I'd been before he'd come into my life. Even I knew I blurted out too much of my honesty before. I'd actually clamped up quite a bit since meeting him. But I didn't tell him how I no longer divulged every detail of my life to Tess anymore, or how every thought in my head no longer spilled from my mouth. I thought shit through first—like, now for example; I wasn't telling him how much I wanted to lean forward and press my mouth to his, just because it seemed like it'd feel right.

He had a pretty-shaped mouth and his electric blue eyes looked like they were practically dancing right now. I felt *close* to him. And a kiss seemed like the perfect way to show that.

But instead, I cleared my throat and repositioned myself on the bed as if I was trying to get comfortable. "I don't have classes tomorrow, since you know, it's Saturday. But I do have to get up early to go to work."

He sighed out a breath as if sad that meant our talk was over. "Okay." His voice was quiet and eyes somber as he leaned in toward me. I froze, holding my breath and wondering, oh my God, was *he* going to kiss *me*, right before he pressed his lips chastely to the center of my forehead.

I nearly wept.

"I'll let you get some sleep then," he whispered.

I blinked at him, feeling rejected because he'd made such a friendly gesture, a friendly *platonic* gesture that was in no way whatsoever sexual or passionate, probably because he didn't feel sexual or passionate about me, period.

Though, honestly, how could he? He was this gorgeous, electric-blue-eyed piece of man candy, and I was, well, I was me. The short, opinioned, fat, ugly cow, according to a couple lovely classmates, who didn't know when to keep her mouth shut and was willing to lie for a rapist in order to score a simple date.

I shuddered and closed my eyes, turning my back to him so he wouldn't see if a tear or two slipped out. "Good night," I said as cheerfully as I could muster.

Except, in return, he sounded pretty somber when he murmured, "'Night, Bailey."

Chapter 20
BECKETT

I waited until her breathing changed before I reached out and touched her hair as softly as I could without waking her. She didn't stir, so I curled a couple more strands around my finger, wondering what she'd do if I ever touched her like this when she was awake.

It would've been nice if I could say she was hard to read, but Bailey was unfortunately all too easy to read. She said what she thought and did what she said, and the unfortunate part was I'm pretty damn certain she didn't think about me that way in the least. She definitely would've done something about it by now.

Shaking my head even as I scooted in closer behind her just to get close enough to smell her hair, I closed my eyes and inhaled deeply. Yeah, Bailey Prescott wasn't really the type to stand around, waiting for the guy to come to her. Hell, she probably just grabbed his face and yanked him down to her if she ever wanted a kiss.

I grinned over the image until it struck me she'd never do that to me, because obviously, she didn't feel that way about me, so it would behoove me to behave honorably around her. This was the girl I owed my life to; it'd be sleazy to put the moves on her when I knew she wasn't interested, not to mention the tiny fact it'd make things extremely weird between us and she'd probably end up kicking me out on my ass and I'd be completely homeless and destitute.

Oh, and I'm sure the fact she saw me have sex with someone else minutes after meeting her didn't help matters either.

And even, despite all that, if she did perchance welcome an advance from me, what could I ever offer her in return? I had nothing.

So yeah, letting her know I thought of her that way was totally off the table.

But when she fell asleep next to me, all soft and innocent and beautiful, it was hard not to imagine a what-if. She was the most unusual girl I'd ever met. So far, I'd seen her be bold and sassy, then helpful and supportive, onto kind and caring, only to go bossy with a hint of compassionate concern. I didn't even know someone could talk with bossy sass while they were worried about you, but she nailed it.

I kind of dug that. A lot. It made her even more beautiful to me. Someone so take-charge but with a soft center, made the male in me challenged to break past her mouthy demands and find that purr inside.

She murmured something in her sleep and rolled back around to face me. I held my breath, afraid I'd woken her, but her breathing remained deep and even, brushing across my face, so I relaxed fractionally, even as I felt like slime for groping her hair while she was unconscious.

"Sorry," I whispered, cringing.

But, dammit, her face looked so soft and smooth and one curly lock from her bangs had fallen over her eye. I studied it, wondering if it was bothering her, tickling her nose or anything. I bet it was bothering her. Helping things out, I reached over and flicked the curl away from her closed eyelids, then I let the backs of my fingers linger and brush every so softly against her cheek.

Holy shit, I'd been right. Skin as soft as satin. I wanted her to cuddle against me so I could hold her the same way I had the night before. She needed to be closer, right up against me.

But that was wrong, and I was an ass for thinking about her this way after she she'd been nothing but hospitable and generous and wonderful to me.

Gritting my teeth, I turned away so I could stop tempting myself. I fell asleep like a good boy, I swear. But when I woke again hours later, in the middle of the night, I'd turned her way again in my sleep and shifted closer until my hand was on her hip and her ass was snuggled into my lap.

My erection was thick and heavy in my sweatpants, throbbing like a son of bitch, and there's no way she would've missed it trying to gouge out a path between her cheeks if she'd been awake.

Holding my breath, I eased backward away from her sweet tush before rolling around to face the other way. Then I reached down and squeezed myself, trying to turn it off.

Didn't work.

It was a long, painful time later before I could get back to sleep.

* * *

I woke to the muffled sound of a hair dryer. It made me think I was home, and Brittany was breaking the rules again, hogging the bathroom before I had my turn. I was the older one and didn't take as long as she did, so Mom had made a rule that I had first dibs for the bathroom every morning. Britt wasn't even allowed go in until I was finished.

Groaning, I rolled onto my stomach and prepared to push up onto my elbows so I could yell at Mom and tattle on my sister, when I realized I wasn't home.

I could never go home again.

Instead, I gazed around Bailey's room, feeling empty.

The hair dryer in the bathroom shut off. I rested my head back on the pillow and listened to her complete the last of her primping. She was getting ready for work, I knew. It felt strange not to be up and about preparing for my own job at the barn. I couldn't remember the last time I'd slept in and lazed the morning away in bed.

Instead of being grateful, I wished I had something to do, somewhere to be. But there was nothing.

Bailey opened the door, and I was struck with a fresh wave of wants. Taking back my earlier wish to get up and head off, I suddenly decided, no, I wouldn't mind staying right where I was if she joined me. She could stroll that petite body of hers over here, crawl on top of me and—Eh, no. I'm not sure if I could ever handle the girl being on top again. Not after Melody.

So, I'd just roll Bailey over onto her back and sink into her softness, pressing my mouth to hers and burying my fingers in all that curly blonde—

"Morning," she said, barely paying me any attention as she swept briskly toward a purse on a chair in the corner and started to gather her things. "I need to be at work in half an hour, so I'm going to head out in a few minutes." She paused and sent me an uncertain glance. "Do you plan on staying here?"

"I…" I had no idea. I didn't want to think about the rest of the day, but I did know I didn't want to be out in public. "Would that be okay?" I hedged.

Her shoulder relaxed as if my response relieved her, and she nodded. "Yes. Just…" Then she winced and glanced toward the closed door of the bedroom before she moved closer to me and lowered her voice. "There's just one thing."

When she cringed, I shook my head. "What's that?"

"My, uh, my roommates have no idea you've stayed here these past two nights, so—"

I sat up and threw the covers off me, hissing, "Bailey, what the *hell*?" How could they not know at all? "Is there a possibility they wouldn't be okay with this?" I demanded.

When she bit her lip, I closed my eyes and groaned. Yep, I was going to get kicked out of here any minute.

"I don't think so," she rushed to reassure me, only to make a face and add, "But I don't know for sure. They know you're not a rapist. I mean, I assured them of that, so you don't have to worry about that, but…"

"But they don't know me," I said the obvious for her. And I didn't blame them. I wouldn't be comfortable with some stranger hanging out in my apartment all day with no one home to supervise him, reason number one why I'd always locked my fraternity-room door.

"Maybe if you just stay in here until I get back," she started.

But I was already shaking my head no. "Bailey, this isn't like sneaking a puppy into your room. You shouldn't keep something like this from your roommates."

"I know," she whined, scowling at me. "But now isn't the time, what if they say no? Where would you go?"

I opened my mouth to answer until I realized I didn't have an answer. Sighing, I buried my face into my hands and scrubbed them up and down, wincing when I hit a bruise. What a mess.

"How about you just stay in here today. They all have to work too, so we'll wait until this evening when they're all home. Then we can broach the subject with them then? Okay?"

I looked at her. "And if they say no tonight? Then where am I supposed to go? I can't…" I glanced around her room, feeling hopeless. There didn't seem to be any light at the end of the tunnel.

Bailey set her hand on my shoulder and I felt immediately comforted. "Let's just take baby steps and worry about today right now. We'll deal with tomorrow when it comes."

I nodded, feeling defeated and said, "Okay."

She nodded, smiling. "Okay. I'll be right back with some breakfast and maybe enough food to last you through the day.

I gave a humorless laugh. "Same concept, but it still beats being in jail, I guess."

Her face fell. "You're not…" Running her fingers gently over my hair, she said, "If you go out, could you at least leave me a note, letting me know?"

"I won't go out," I promised her.

Her hand made one last sweep over my head, and then she was leaving to bring me back some food. She brought me plenty. I could only shake my head and wonder how long she planned on being gone. But then she said she'd be back by four and she really was gone.

About half an hour later, I was sure I was alone in the apartment. But I stayed in Bailey's room and ate an orange and two granola bars before downing a bottle of water.

She had a small television in here, so I watched a morning show, then a noon show, and finally an afternoon show, before growing drowsy and taking a small nap, but I woke up feeling worse than before. I hated doing nothing all day; it always left me drained and groggier than ever. Besides, I think it'd been just enough days after being beaten for me to reach the zenith of soreness. Every muscle throbbed.

I crawled out of bed and shuffled toward the bathroom. But when I opened Bailey's medicine cabinet, there wasn't any kind of pain reliever inside. A shiver wracked my body. I pressed my hand to my forehead and wondered if I had a fever. The sore, shaky muscles and shivering felt like the stirrings of a cold.

Rubbing my hands up and down my arms, I returned to Bailey's room but didn't find any kind of pill bottles on her dresser, so I crept to the bedroom door and slowly poked my head into the hall. No one seemed to be home yet, thought it was getting to be that time. I really felt shitty, so I took the chance and stepped from her room.

I found another bathroom within ten seconds and then some ibuprofen fifteen seconds after that. But as I was unscrewing the lid, I saw a whole row of prescription bottles lining the top shelf. I popped two pills into my mouth, swallowing them dry, before reaching up to examine one of the bottles.

They were written out for a Jonah Abbott and seemed to be some powerful, highly-addictive pain medicine. I pulled down a few more bottles, whistling lowly under my breath. This Jonah dude must've gotten hurt pretty bad to need all this shit. It'd been prescribed to him back in February.

February. That had been back when the gunman had taken out some students on campus. I hadn't known anyone who'd been killed or even injured in the massacre, but I wondered if this Jonah guy had been involved in all that.

He'd barely used half the contents from each bottle, and I wondered what it'd be like if a person just took them, all of them, swallowing them down two at a time. Would the pain would just disappear? Would they drift off peacefully, completely unaware of how fatally they'd just overdosed?

For a minute, I stared at the bottles, imagining it. It could all be over, just like that. The misery and uncertainty and loss. No one would even miss me. Hell, they'd probably be relieved I was gone so I could stop bothering them. I'm sure Bailey could do without me leeching off her. My parents would be free of me causing them any more trouble. And I could stop feeling so betrayed and abandoned and hated. I could end all this right now. Right here.

I put my palm against the cap of one bottle as if to unscrew it.

"Oh my God, what the hell do you think you're doing?" a high voice shrieked.

I jumped so hard, I dropped the bottle and guiltily darted my gaze to Bailey who was standing frozen in the bathroom door and gaping at me in pale, frozen horror.

Chapter 21
BAILEY

I couldn't believe my eyes. I just…I couldn't.

Beckett was standing there, surrounded by bottles of prescription pills and staring at them with longing and temptation.

"Oh my God, *ohmigod*!" I shrieked, hurrying to him and snagging the bottle he hadn't dropped from his hand. "How many have you taken?"

I needed to get him to the hospital. Right now. They'd have to pump his stomach, get every single pill out. Oh my God, but what if I was too late? What if—

"None," he said, shaking his head in instant denial. "I didn't take any. I mean, I took two ibuprofens, but that was it. I was in pain. I just wanted…" He shook his head some more.

But he looked so guilty and caught-in-the-act. I didn't think I could believe him. I rattled the prescription bottle in his face. "Then why did you pull all these down?"

"I…" He looked at the bottle, his expression filled with even more mortification and guilt.

"Oh my God," I whispered, terrified to my core. Helping him through a hard time was one thing, but going on suicide watch for him was quite another.

When he looked at me, though, he could only shake his head. "I was just looking at them. Curious," he tried to explain. "I wasn't going to take them. I swear, I didn't take any."

I threw down the bottle into the sink and gripped his arms, shaking him roughly. "Then look me in the eye and *swear* to me that taking all these didn't even cross your mind."

He looked at me, his bright blue eyes so red and tormented. When his face crumpled with defeat, I knew it had crossed his mind.

"Oh, Beck."

"I didn't take any," he swore.

"But what about tomorrow?" I exploded. "What happens when I leave you alone again? How the hell can I not worry it won't cross your mind tomorrow, but maybe just a little more persistently the next time? Holy shit, Beck, I can't deal with this. I can't…I don't do drama and emotion and freaking nervous breakdowns. I can't even deal with my own hard times. When the going gets tough, I run to the hair salon and get my hair dyed. I can't deal with anything! Now you're standing here, contemplating *suicide* and I'm the only fucking person on the planet who actually gives a shit enough to want to stop you. Oh my fucking God!"

I let him go to grip my head and spin away, unable to look at him. "Don't do this to me. How could you…" I whirled back. "What do you think it would've done to me to come in here and find you dead just now?"

"Jesus," he breathed, stepping close to touch the side of my head. "I wouldn't do that to you, Bailey. I won't. I swear it. I don't know what I was thinking. The thought just barely crossed my mind." His lips parted with a terrible kind of realization before he quietly added, "And it wasn't terrible."

"Yes, it goddamn well *is* terrible," I shrieked like a banshee, basically screaming at the top of my lungs. "Suicide is bad, Beck. But *yours* would shatter me. Don't you ever fucking do that to me again. I will strangle you to within an inch of your life, and then I'll resuscitate you and force you back to life. Because *that's* what you're going to do. *Do you hear me*? You're going to fucking live!"

"Yes, I hear you," he hollered right back, his voice booming deep as his eyes narrowed with irritation and his brow puckered madly. "You're fucking screaming in my face. I think everyone in the goddamn city heard you. *Now hear me*. I didn't take any. I'm not going to. And your yelling at me is probably the worst way ever to talk a guy off the ledge if he really *were* going to do any of that shit."

"Well, excuse me if I yell when I get scared," I yelled.

"Well, stop being scared, dammit, because I told you it was fine. I'm fine."

"Except fine never really *means* fine."

We were both screaming these things at the tops of our voices, right into the other's faces. I'd had this kind of screaming match with brothers before. But it'd certainly never made me feel so exhilarated. I swear, Beckett's bright blue eyes flashed with the same kind of adrenaline rush as he stepped closer to me.

"*My* fine means fine," He shouted.

"Oh my God, what is going on?"

When the voice came from the doorway, Beck and I sprang apart as if we'd been caught canoodling or something.

Paige and Logan stood in the doorway, gaping us before Jonah's face appeared over their shoulders.

"Are those my old pills?"

I linked my hands together behind my back and dug the toe of one shoe into the floor in front of me. "Oh, hey, guys…" I said slowly. "You're, uh, you're home early."

Nothing to see here. I hadn't just been screaming into the face of the stowaway boy I'd been stashing in our apartment for the past few nights without their knowledge. Nope, not me.

"We're actually home late," Paige answered slowly, lifting her eyes from the pills scattered on the floor before glancing questionably at Beck and turning to rest her attention on me.

I glanced at the time. Shit, she was right. Oh, God. This was so embarrassing. How long had I been yelling at Beck and getting strangely turned on by it?

"Oh," I said in a small voice. Then I motioned to Beck. "This is—"

"Beckett Hilliard," Logan answered for me.

Beck glanced at him, then blinked before tipping his head as if he recognized my roommate. "Designated Dave?" he asked, confused.

"My name's actually Logan."

That only seemed to perplex Beck more. "Really?" I knew he wanted to know why everyone called Logan Designated Dave, but he refrained, only glancing at me to let me know he had no clue what to say next.

I was going to let them know Beck was going to stay with us for a while and was trying to think up how to say it even as I opened my mouth. But Tess's voice came from somewhere in the back of the crowd. "Can we move this to the living room so I can see what's going on?"

Her request actually worked. Paige and Logan backed from the doorway and disappeared for a few seconds.

Beck and I exchanged chagrined glances. Then he hurried to scoop up all the pill bottles and put them back onto the shelf in the cabinet. After that, he blew out a cheekful of air, silently letting me know he was ready to do this. So I took his hand and led him from the bathroom.

He didn't pull away. If anything, he leaned in closer as if to talk into my ear before I heard, "I thought you weren't a hand holder."

I scowled at him over my shoulder, hissing, "Just go with it. And let me do the talking." Then I dragged him down the hall more harshly than before so it'd look like I was in control and herding him along rather than I just wanted to hold his hand for moral support, because I was suddenly nervous about facing my friends and really needed some moral support to survive this.

We reached the end of the hall and turned into the main room, only to find all four of my roommates standing in a semi-circle in the opening, waiting for us. In tandem, Beckett and I pulled back, surprised they were right there.

The two couples peered curiously at Beck. Tess even went as far as to gasp a surprised, "*Oh*," before stepping protectively closer to Jonah.

I glanced at her to find her blushing madly.

Tess wasn't intimidated by him because he was bruised and battered to hell. She usually stepped forward to help injured souls. No, hot guys were what made her shy.

Realizing she considered Beckett attractive made a spark of jealousy flicker through me. And that made no sense. I frowned at myself for the knee-jerk emotion.

It all gave Beck enough time to tighten his grip around my hand and blurt, "I stayed here the last two nights."

I spun to him. "What the hell!"

He only rolled his eyes. "Oh, like you would've been any more tactful."

My mouth fell open. How the hell did he know I completely lacked tact? The guy had known me for only a few days.

Not right.

Paige cleared her throat before saying, "I wasn't aware you two knew each other." She glanced at Tess for confirmation, but Tess only ducked her head so her red hair would hide most of her face. Paige turned back to me, wide-eyed. "I thought he wasn't there when you tried to find him at his fraternity."

"He wasn't." I glanced at Beck, but now that he'd already pushed me into the hot seat, he was being mute. The butthead. I turned back to the group, who suddenly felt like a freaking firing squad aiming their rifles—er, questioning stares—at me. "But then he contacted me, and I, uh, I assisted him with something, and after that, he really needed a place to stay, so…" I spread my arms to encompass the room, letting them know I'd let him stay here.

"You never told us he contacted you," Tess finally said, lifting her face and blinking at me as if I'd lied to her.

I guess omitting that fact was a lie. Oh, crap. I'd never lied to Tess before. And I had no way to justify myself. I squeezed my fingers more snuggly around Beckett's and mumbled, "Sorry."

"I can't believe you let him sleep under our roof without even consulting us first," Jonah said, his voice stern and eyes hard with disapproval.

I gave him an indignant sniff before straightening my back. "Excuse me. I didn't realize I had to ask." Of course, I'd known I should've asked. It was only considerate to my roommates, whom I respected. But going with this reaction helped me feel not so shitty about how I'd treated my friends these last few days by not sharing anything with them. "It's not like he really *is* a rapist," I snapped. Then I narrowed my eyes at Jonah, daring him to say he didn't believe me in that department.

He heaved out an irritated sigh. "I know you said he was innocent, but damn, Bailey, we don't know him. I don't feel comfortable letting a stranger stay in my home, with my girlfriend here. I should've gotten a say in that."

Speaking of his girlfriend…

"Tess?" I whirled toward her. She was the biggest bleeding heart of the group. She'd talk some sense into her boyfriend. But she bit her lip and winced.

I groaned. "No. Not you too."

"I'm sorry," she gushed, "But if anyone else found out he'd been staying here, do you know what this would do to *you*, Bailey? All the rumors going around that you lied for him because you liked him and wanted him to date you would look true."

"What rumors?" Beck turned to me. When he saw my irritated scowl, he must've realized what Tess said was true. His eyebrows lifted in scolding. "You didn't tell me you were getting backlash over this."

I sighed and rolled my eyes. "Because it's not a big deal. Just a bunch of gossip and speculation. The story sounds juicier if I'm a liar who's desperately in love with you."

"*What*? Jesus, Bailey." He let go of my hand and took a step backward away from me as if I suddenly had leprosy. Running his hand through his hair, he insisted. "I can't stay here now. I can't put your reputation in danger."

"Oh, whatever," I snapped, grabbing his elbow to keep him from going anywhere. "The gossip isn't going to miraculously stop if you leave."

"But it'll sure as hell get worse if anyone found out I *have* been staying here. Christ, I gotta..." He tried to pull his arm free from me, but I refused to let him go. "*I need to leave*," he growled.

"No, you fucking don't!" I exploded, "Especially not after I came home to find you trying to kill yourself."

His mouth fell open as he gaped at me. Then he darted a glanced to Paige, Logan, Jonah and Tess as Paige uttered, "Say *what*?"

"I-I wasn't trying to kill myself," he rushed to explain to them before tightening his jaw and sending me a hard stare for outing him. "I was just—"

"Just what?" I growled. "Exploring your options? Suicide is not an option, Beck."

"Well, what the hell else am I supposed to do?" he cried, pulling hard enough to get loose of me. His eyes turned watery as his bottom quivered. "There's nothing left for me here. I'm not doing any good for anyone." Motioning to me, he looked even more tormented. "I'm not doing any good for *you*. Everything and everyone would be better off if I was just gone."

"No, I would not," I rasped meaningfully as I shook my head. "I would most definitely not be better off if you were gone. I'd be a fucking failure, that's what I'd be. Helping you through this has felt like the only thing I've ever done right. If you took your own life, you'd take that away from me." Gritting my teeth, I growled, "Don't you goddamn dare take that away from me."

A tear trickled down his cheek. "I'm a burden to you."

I shook my head. "No. You're my friend. Friends aren't burdens."

He covered his face with both hands to hide the evidence of his feelings as his shoulders shook and a sob wracked his frame. "Christ, Bailey. Don't say that. I don't deserve it."

"Well, too bad. I disagree. And besides, even if you didn't deserve it, I'm sure no one really deserves half the lucky shit they get in life."

There was only one thing that had ever worked before when he'd been this down, so I did that. Opening my arms, I wrapped them around him and hugged him.

He immediately hugged me back, burying his face in my hair and shuddering against me as he rasped, "I'm sorry," into my hair. "I'm so sorry. I really wasn't going to do anything. It was just a thought. Just a stupid, passing thought. I promise you, I won't ever hurt myself."

I patted his back, letting him know all was forgiven and forgotten.

Behind us, I heard Tess say, "Is she hugging him? Am I seeing things, or is she really, honestly hugging him?"

"I think she's really, honestly hugging him," Paige whispered back.

Beck lifted his face from my shoulder and quickly mopped his cheeks with his fingers before he cast a horrified glance at our audience. Just as swiftly, he stepped back, turning away to hide his misery.

I took in my roommates, looking each one in the eye, one after another. "Well?" I asked. "His life has completely derailed on him. He has no money, no job, no family, no friends, and no place else on the planet to go. The university kicked him out, and his emotional stability is zilch. Are you really going to kick him out after that?"

I knew I had my two friends' support then. They both looked beseechingly to their boyfriends.

Jonah sighed and muttered a curse under his breath.

Logan eyed Beck as he rubbed his hand over the inside of this wrist. Then he said, "What about a compromise?"

Beck glanced at him as he lowered his brow, untrusting. "What kind of compromise?"

Logan studied his other three roommates before drawing in a breath. "I think we're all in agreement we don't want to put him out on the street. We'd like to help him as much as you do until he gets back on his feet, but there's still a measure of unease, since he's an unknown. How about he be here in the evenings and overnight," he motioned toward me, "when Bailey's here. Then, while we're all in class and working during the day and the apartment's empty, he finds somewhere else to go."

Beck and the other three, all nodded, agreeing with that idea, but I cried, "No way. Yesterday, when he left during the day, he got the shit beat out of him. The news made everyone believe he's a rapist, so that's what everyone who crosses his path thinks of him. He's not safe out there."

Beckett scowled at me. Just like a guy, thinking he didn't need any protection and could take care of himself. "I'll be fine."

I gaped at him, unable to believe he was okay with this. Why was everyone against me? Beck needed a safe place at all hours. They were being such idiots right now. Did no one else realize how much danger he'd be in out there?

Obviously, they didn't because they just kept staring at me, waiting for me to give in, already.

Knowing I couldn't win this round, I threw my hands in the air and groused, "Well, if no one minds his face looking like ground chuck for the rest of his life because everyone and their dog wants a piece of him, far be it for me to care. But just for the record, I think this is a stupid plan. He should be allowed to stay here at all hours."

Then folding my arms over my chest, I stormed from the room, muttering over my shoulder. "I'm making supper tonight. No one help me." They'd all just try to make something stupid for us to eat, anyway. Humph.

Chapter 22
BECKETT

No, this wasn't awkward at all.

As Bailey marched from the living room, I glanced uneasily at the four people who remained. Her roommates. They all stared at me as if they expected me to tug a knife from my pocket and start slitting at my wrists. What's worse, they were all strangers, well except for Designated Dave, who wasn't really Dave after all—strange, that—and I barely knew him anyway. But he and the other three had now just seen me lose my shit all over the place. How was that for a first impression?

It was so nice to meet you too.

If I hadn't wanted to die before, I kind of did now, from utter mortification.

"I'm…" I inched backward away from them and hooked my thumb over my shoulder. "I'm just, yeah, I'm gonna go. I'll be in Bailey's room."

The short redhead grabbed her boyfriend's arm and popped up onto her toes so she could hiss loudly enough into his ear for me to hear, "Should he be alone right now? I don't think he should be alone right now."

Oh, boy.

The big guy turned his gaze to me in a resigned but determined kind of way, like he really didn't care what I did, but he was still fully prepared to physically strong-arm me into staying, even if it meant pinning me to the floor and sitting on me if necessary, just to make his girlfriend happy.

I lifted my hands, still creeping small steps backward, preparing to make a break for it if need be. "Look, I'm fine. Really. I'm not actually suicidal or anything. I just…" They were all three still staring at me as if I was totally suicidal. I jerked a hesitant glance toward the big guy—Jonah. "I'm really sorry I got into your pills. I had a headache."

When I motioned to my bruised face in the hopes they would believe I honestly did feel like shit, no one's expression lit with an *ah, I get it* nod. Bummer. I kept bumbling through my explanation.

"And Bailey didn't have any aspirin in her bathroom. So I checked the one in the hall, where I saw all the bottles on the top shelf. I was just curious what they were for. But all the sudden, Bailey was there, screaming, and it made me jump. The bottles when flying, and…"

Yeah, my explanation started to run dry.

But Jonah nodded his forgiveness, which rocked. Truly. "I broke my femur," he explained.

"Ah." I nodded too. Then I winced; a broken femur probably hurt big time. I totally sympathized with any kind of pain right now.

"But when Bailey first confronted you about the pills," the dark-headed girl—Paige—said, making my stomach pitch because, shit, she was really going to go there, wasn't she? "You said…" She paused and swallowed audibly when I pierced her with a glance, begging her with my expression to please, God, shut up about that already. But she shared a look with Designated Dave—er, Logan—which seemed to bolster her resolve before she turned back to me. "You said there was nothing left for you. You seemed so broken. I mean, you really seemed—"

I lifted my hands and glanced away, still unable to deal with that moment of complete humiliation. "I'm fine," I rasped. "Seriously. It was…" I shook my head, not sure how to explain it. "It was just a bad moment. You know those moments, when stray thoughts flit through your head, and then they're gone and you're like, weird. Why did I think that? Because, in all honestly, I would never do that. Th-that's what that was. Just a small hiccup in my head. I'm really not like that."

I shrugged helplessly. A week ago, I never would've thought I'd be trying to convince complete strangers I wasn't going to kill myself. The bizarreness of it all suddenly left me too flabbergasted to continue. I just stared at the brunette, lost.

Unfortunately, she still looked concerned. "Regardless," she said as kindly as possible, even sending me a bolstering smile before she glanced at her boyfriend and took his hand. "Logan and Jonah have a friend named Samantha. She's not technically a psychiatrist, but she helps people all the same. And she's really cool. She helped them both through some rough issues. If you'd like her number, I'm sure she'd be more than willing to talk with you, too."

Yeah, until she found out I was the famous rapist of Granton University.

As if reading my mind, Paige more firmly said, "She *would* help you."

For some reason, that just made me feel shittier though. I shouldn't need help. I should be able to handle this and get my own shit together.

I blinked and then flushed hotly. "Okay, uh, well, thank you, but…" I glanced around, looking for Bailey, or someone, anyone to pop forward and tell these people I was fine. But dammit to hell, I wasn't fine, was I? Clearing my throat, I gave Paige a humble kind of *I give up* nod before saying, "Thank you for the offer. I'll keep it in mind."

Bailey reentered the living room, clapping her hands. "Okay, food's ready! Let's eat."

Jonah frowned. "But you left, like, only two minutes ago to go fix supper."

She sent him a nasty smirk. "What can I say; I cook fast."

"What the hell *did* you cook?"

"Hot dogs and cold baked beans from a can. Are you coming or not?"

"Jesus, *I* could've made that," Jonah huffed but stomped toward the kitchen, clearly not about to turn down any kind of meal.

The others almost obediently filed after him until it was only me and Bailey left in the living room. She glanced at me and held out her hand, beckoning me forward. "Come on. Let's eat."

I shuffled a step back and shook my head. "I'm not very hungry."

And I'd already reached my threshold of awkward for the day. I wasn't exactly looking for *more* by staying in the company of her and her roommates. They'd just seen me fucking cry.

Before this whole fiasco started, I think the last time I'd cried had been when I was ten-years old and our Lab, Sal, had died. And even then, I'd run to my room and slammed the door to bawl on my bed with a pillow over my head so no one could see me.

I wasn't a fan of this open weeping bullshit. I pretty much wanted to sink through the floor and cease to be seen by anyone else ever again.

But Bailey only snorted. "I went through the whole process of making you food; you're eating, dammit." She latched a firm hand around my arm and dragged me from the living room.

It didn't seem to matter if I mentioned that hotdogs and cold baked beans weren't exactly a "whole process" or not; she was determined.

So, six of us sat down to supper. Every seat at the dining room table was full. I had a feeling Bailey always sat on the end where she currently was in order to let each couple sit together on one side or another. So that meant I was left at the other end, opposite her.

I actually appreciated that. Facing the others was not high on my list of wishes at the moment. Still, sitting here at a table with these people was so freaking uncomfortable. And they were all so strangely silent.

Until Bailey gave a dramatic sigh and said, "For the love of God, someone say something before I start in again about how I think we should totally hook Jonah's friend Aubrey up with Logan's brother's Jake."

"Oh, Jesus," the big guy groaned, covering his eyes before saying, "How many times do I have to tell you, just because they're both gay, doesn't automatically mean they should hook up."

"But—"

"Would *you* try just any guy simply because he was hetero?" At Bailey's scowl, Jonah added, "Jake's an athlete. Aubrey's into drama. They wouldn't get along."

"Well, we wouldn't know that for sure unless we at least *introduced* them, now would we?" Bailey mumbled, before moodily clinking her spoon into a pile of pork and beans on her plate. "I'm just saying, it wouldn't hurt to try hooking them up."

"Oh, Lord," Jonah groaned.

"I'm going to have to agree with Abbott on this one," Designated Dave—er, Logan—finally spoke up. "I think my brother's a little bit too elitist for Aubrey's taste."

"You mean, he's a total freaking snob? Yeah, that's for damn sure." Bailey pointed her spoon at Logan. "I can't believe you're still giving that entire hoity toity family of yours another chance to be in your life after they kicked you out for, how many years? They seem so frigid and uptight whenever they come to visit you."

Logan breathed out a sigh. "That's just the way they are," he explained. "It's a work in progress. We'll get there. Someday." I could almost hear him silently add *hopefully*, and it made me think of my own family.

"Well, I don't know how you could ever forgive them for the way they disowned you. I mean—Oh!"

Her gaze veered to me, and I could actually hear her thoughts. The word *disowned* had immediately made her think of me. My own stomach knotted at the memory, but it also had me glancing sideways as Logan and wondering what had happened there to make his family turn him out. He'd always been so quiet and straight-laced whenever I'd seen him at parties. Hell, my parents probably would've adored a son like him.

"I just had the strangest thought," Bailey announced, "Xander killed someone and didn't go to jail, while Beckett committed no crime and *did* go jail. Isn't that crazy ironic?"

I had no idea who Xander was, so I didn't have an answer. But strangely enough, no one else at the table could seem to reply, either. They all froze with another awkward silence. I glanced around, wondering what I was missing.

"Shit," Bailey added a second later. "That was inconsiderate, wasn't it?"

The redhead—Tess, I think her name was—nodded and held her fingers an inch apart. "A lil' bit, yes."

"Sorry." Wincing, Bailey swung around to plead to the other couple. "I'm so sorry."

Logan lifted a hand, immediately excusing her. "It's fine."

"It was self-defense." Paige turned to me of all people as if it was vital for her to convince me of that. Then she frowned and said, "Kind of. They were just drunk teenagers who got into a fistfight, and he was knocked to the ground, where he hit his head and died. Total freak accident."

Her eyes were a dark pleading brown as if she *needed* me to understand that the murder committed had been totally innocent. "Okay," I answered, nodding to let her know I wasn't about to question her. But then I had to glance around and ask, "Who's Xander?"

Logan made an amused, but also kind of pain-filled sound before lifting his hand. "I am. My name is Logan Xander."

I blinked, wondering why the hell everyone at the fraternity called him Designated Dave then. I'd met him a few times when I'd been drunk off my ass. He was a sober driver who gave people lifts home from parties. I'd used his services before, and remembered him being nothing but quiet and considerate to the drunk idiots he helped, while they weren't always that great in return. But now that I thought about it, it'd been a while since I'd seen him working the parties. He'd probably met Paige and—

It suddenly clicked in my head what Bailey and Paige had said *Xander* had done. My eyes widened. "Holy shit," I blurted. He's accidently murdered someone in an innocent fistfight. "That had to suck. I've been in fights plenty in my life. I can't even imagine what would've happened if any of them had ended that way." Then another awful thought struck. "Was he a friend?"

It had mainly been friends I'd fought with. Damn, if I'd accidentally killed a friend—

I suddenly realized my question had the same awkwardly quiet response Bailey's initial foray into this conversation had brought. I glanced around, wondering why that was such a bad question until Paige cleared her throat and quietly admitted, "It was my brother."

Oh…shit. Logan had killed Paige's brother…and now they were dating. I bet that was quite a story.

My mouth opened, and I could feel the foot being inserted.

"I-I'm so sorry," I fumbled out, but that felt like the lamest apology a person could give at a time like this.

I glanced at Bailey, seeking help out of this. But she only waved a hand, unconcerned. "Don't worry about it. I spread more awkwardness than this around the table on a nightly basis."

"She really does," Jonah agreed dryly.

Bailey scowled at him. "Suck it, asshole. You're just jealous."

When he chuckled in return and flipped her off, I figured those two probably swapped insults regularly. Tess, stuck in the middle of them—both literally and figuratively since she was the best friend of Bailey and girlfriend of Jonah and they were currently sitting on either side of her—didn't seem concerned by their bickering at all, which supported my theory.

I watched the redhead for a second. She seemed so quiet and shy, it was hard to imagine her as Bailey's best friend. They were like polar opposites.

She must've felt my gaze on her, though, because she glanced over, only for her eyes to widen and her face to brighten with embarrassment before she quickly darted her face downward again.

I blinked. Huh. I didn't think Bailey's best friend liked me. And I didn't like *that*. Jana's friends had always adored me—

And where had that thought come from? I wasn't *dating* Bailey. Why did I feel the need to make her friend like me?

Like a wakeup call, that thought kept me quiet throughout the rest of the meal. I didn't need to try to fit in with these people. I was just here temporarily, and then I'd move on. I'd already learned the hard way that putting any kind of trust or expectations in others—ahem, thanks a fucking lot, *Max*—was a bad idea. So I decided not to let myself get too close to Bailey's people.

When I finished eating, however, I offered to clean the dishes, still hoping to catch some favor with the redhead. I just couldn't help it. It was as sickness. I must be one of those needy, approval-seeking dorks and just hadn't realized it until now. But Tess didn't seem to catch my efforts. She trucked it out of there with her boyfriend and the other couple.

Bailey, however, lingered behind. When I stood to pick up a handful of dirty dishes, she did the same.

"Hey, you don't have to help," I scolded lightly. "You cooked, so you should be excused from cleaning duty."

She laughed. "Yeah, I really *cooked*. Besides, I don't mind."

Since I liked her company, I stopped protesting.

We gathered and loaded the dishwasher together, standing on either side of it to file in plates and cups. At one point when she leaned down to slot some silverware into the holder, a curly lock of her hair slid down into her eye. She brushed it away without even seeming to notice, but I couldn't take my attention off that lock as it tangled around a mass of other curls over her ear.

"What colors have you dyed your hair?" I asked without thinking.

She glanced up. "What?"

I shrugged and cleared my throat, backing up a step to appear more casual and less interested. I waved my hand toward her head. "You said earlier you dyed your hair when the going got tough."

"Oh." She went back to work loading dishes. "Well, you saw the rainbow."

"I did." I nodded.

"And before that, it was another mix of colors like brown, blond and red, regular hair colors but a bunch of different thin strips of them. Then once, it was pitch black with a streak of red. I tried to make it completely red like Tess's once but that didn't work. And I was a brunette once."

"What's the original color?"

She glanced at me and winked. "Oh, I'd have to kill you if I told you that."

I sniffed out an amused smile, but another part of me stirred because I knew another way I could find out her true hair color.

But that was wrong to think, and I was going to stop thinking it.

Except I really *couldn't* stop thinking about that.

Returning my focus to the dishes, I thought about it until we were completely finished cleaning the kitchen.

Bailey grinned companionable at me as she dusted her hands together with a satisfied air of completion. Yeah, she had no idea what was going on in my brain right then. "All right. Good job. Let's see what the others are up to."

I nodded and followed her to the opening of the kitchen, where she stopped abruptly.

"What's wrong?" I asked, peering past her and into the living room, where the other two couples were watching a movie, it seemed.

"Dear God," I murmured. "Do we have to go in there with them while they're like that?" I leaned in toward her to lower my voice, and caught a whiff of her—the same fragrance I'd breathed from my pillow for the past two nights. "I might get hives."

She snorted out a laugh. "Get used to it, Bud. They do this all the time. And we're big home-bodies, so when I say all the time, I mean *all* the time."

I shuddered in revulsion, even though the idea of snuggling up on a couch wrapped around Bailey while we watched a movie every evening didn't sound repulsive in the least.

"How do you stand it?" I whispered.

"I don't." She widened her eyes to the point it made her look insane. "Can't you tell?"

I laughed.

She relaxed her eyes and grinned. "I tried hanging out in my room mostly, but lately, I've been getting restless and going out by myself, finding parties where drunk guys throw their beer on me and then chase me into back bedrooms where they then force me to watch them making it with stupid, lying chicks."

"Dear God." I groaned and slapped a hand over my face. "Don't remind me of that. Worst night ever. I doubt I'll ever drink again."

"You really shouldn't," Bailey advised, nudging her elbow at me. "Don't you know dirty viper sluts like to take advantage of pretty, vulnerable boys like you when you're too drunk to know what's going on?"

I started to grin before growing serious and saying, "Hey, it's not cool to victim blame."

She grinned back only to force a straight face too. "Sorry. You're right. That was uncalled for."

Simultaneously, she and I both grinned again together at the same time.

Nodding my head toward the couple-palooza going on in the living room, I lowered my voice some more and said, "Let's go hang out in your room."

Then I froze, wondering if that sounded too suggestive.

But relief showed in her gaze. "God, yes," she said as if that were the best idea ever.

We snuck into the living room, and no one noticed us darting past them behind their couches and loveseats. Then we hurried into the hall and down toward her room. Bailey entered first, and I shut the door behind us, pressing my spine to the closed entrance. She skipped to her bed and fell down on it, holding her stomach and grinning when she rolled onto her back to grin my way.

"Oh, this is so much better," she moaned in a pleased way that made my dick jump to attention. Her blonde curls splayed across the mattress, and this vision entered my head where I prowled toward her and crawled on top of her, covering her whole body with mine before I sank my fingers into that hair and kissed her endlessly.

Nerves jumped in my stomach as I slowly neared the bed to sit gingerly on the corner, purposefully keeping my distance.

"I hung out a lot in my room at the frat house," I said idly, smoothing my hand over the coverlet of her bed. "There was always so many people coming and going at all hours. My room was my only sanctuary."

She nodded, pulling herself into a sit and crisscrossing her legs so that we were on opposite sides of the mattress, facing each other. "I had a quiet little sanctuary at home." She rolled her eyes. "With four butthead brothers, not even my room was safe, so I went somewhere else where no one would ever find me."

"Where was that?"

With a secretive smile, she shook her head. "No way. No one knows that. Not even Tess."

I grinned back, wanting to know where her secret place was now more than ever. Hell, I wanted to know everything. So I said, "Four brothers, huh? Wow. No sisters?"

She shook her head. "Nope. I'm the only girl."

"They youngest?" I guessed.

"Yes," she lamented. "Being the youngest and only girl is a recipe for disaster, I'm telling you. Especially with my mom gone. You should've seen them freak out when I got my first period."

I chuckled. "I'll bet. What're your brothers' names?"

"Let's see. There's Brock, Braiden, Booth, Blaine, and then me."

I started to nod, before freezing. "All Bs," I said, straightening with surprise.

She groaned and fell forward to hide her face in the mattress before sitting up and scowling. "Don't you dare say that's fucking cute. I will cut you."

"Oh, trust me. I would never. Because I totally understand." I pressed a hand to my heart. "There's me, Beckett, and my sister, Brittany. Then my mom and dad are Brian and Brenda."

Bailey gasped. "My dad's name is Ben, and my mom was Bonnie. Oh my God. You're from a B family too. You *do* understand."

"Hell, yes, I understand," I insisted. "And it's awful. Everyone else is all like, 'oh, that's so adorable,'" I mimicked before making a grimace.

Pointing at me, Bailey growled, "But it's not. Not even a little. It makes people never take you seriously, or they make fun of you, or worse, think you're all just so freaking delightful and take stupid matching pictures of your cuteness all bunched together." She sniffed in outrage. "Like I want to be smashed between my stinky brothers that much."

"Annoying as hell," I finished, nodding in total agreement.

"Exactly."

"I'm never doing that to my children." I shook my head, adamant.

"Hell, I'll even refuse to date a guy whose name *starts* with B," she added.

"Good idea," I seconded, until wait…I frowned. *My* name started with a B.

But she didn't seem to notice that point. She held out a fist for me to bump. "To anti-B-hood!"

I chuckled and bumped my fist against hers. We shared a smile for…I don't even know how long. But it was warm and carefree and felt nice.

I don't know who spoke first after that, or what we even discussed. But it was nothing but comfortable and relaxed. The topics skipped to strange, everyday shit, sometimes funny, sometimes annoyances we shared. We just swapped stories and compared opinions until Bailey yawned and glanced at her wrist before her eyes went huge.

"Holy shit. I had no idea it was so late."

She hopped off the bed and hurried into the bathroom. When she came out in her comfy conservative pajamas, I wanted to cuddle with her more than was humanly decent. But that was bad. It had to be bad, right?

I sat up and scooted off the bed. "Do you mind if I borrow your shower?" I asked, scratching the back of my neck as I grew not-so comfortable, wanting things I knew I shouldn't.

"Sure." She waved her hand to the bathroom door. "You know where it is. Help yourself to whatever."

I nodded my thanks and escaped the bedroom. For some reason, I took my time. This going to bed with her every night was getting harder and harder to handle. I wanted her more every time we lay down next to each other. I admired her and ached and dreamed about something happening between us, even while I knew I shouldn't.

Luckily, she was asleep when I finished my shower, so I was able to crawl onto my side and watch her for a while, before I whispered, "Thank you."

That moment hours ago when I'd stood in the other bathroom, staring at those pills and feelings tempted, seemed like a lifetime ago. Bailey had made it all disappear and at the moment, I couldn't even remember why I'd even had the thought. I certainly wouldn't again, that was for sure. I had something to live for now. Something huge and important.

I was going to recover from this and come out better at the other end just so Bailey could claim with confidence how much she'd saved me.

I would do it all for her.

Chapter 23

BAILEY

"What the heck are you looking for?" Tess asked, sending me a strange glance.

I pulled back around to face the table we were sitting at with a sigh, realizing this really was the fifth time I'd scoped out the student union's food court, searching for Beck, even though I knew he wouldn't come near campus.

Damn, I was an idiot.

"I don't know," I admitted, only to whirl to her. "Are you sure he's going to be okay out of the apartment today?"

Yesterday—Sunday—hadn't been so bad. I'd only had to work in the morning at the store and Logan had been home then. He'd offered to stick around so Beck wouldn't have to vacate the apartment. But today—Monday—we'd all had classes. So Beckett had waved me goodbye at the door when I'd left, letting me know he'd return in the evening when I was home again.

"I'm sure Beck will be fine." Tess patted my arm, totally placating me. "He's an adult. He can take care of himself for one day."

I rolled my eyes. "Except the last time he left the apartment, he was beat up by the freaking cowboy."

"The cowboy?" Tess shook her head and frowned in confusion. "Wait. Back up a second. Do you mean *your* cowboy? How the heck does *he* fit into all this?"

Ah, crap. I'd forgotten I hadn't told her how my year-long cowboy obsession had fallen through. I mean, seriously though, how much humiliating stuff could I reveal about myself? It was bad enough she knew I was a voyeur. I didn't want her realizing just how awful my snap judgement in that guy had been too. I liked Tess thinking good things about me, like I was loyal and stood up for people I believed in, not that I was a stupid idiot who made such bad choices.

But as she blinked at me, waiting for an answer, I sighed. "It turns out the cowboy's name is Chance *Fairfield*. And he *did* belong in the same fraternity as Beckett."

"Fairfield," she said slowly, wrinkling her nose as if trying to recall why that name sounded familiar.

"As in Melody Fairfield," I explained dryly. "The girl who cried rape on Beck. The cowboy's *her* big brother."

"Oh..." Tess's mouth fell open. Then she gulped. "Oh my God, really?"

"Yeah." I nodded. It needed no more explanation than that.

"Oh man." She shook her head as if she couldn't quite comprehend what I'd just told her, or maybe she comprehended it just fine and was realizing just how much this had to be affecting me. "Bailey, I—"

I lifted a hand to stop her, not wanting to hear the pity. "It's fine," I said, standing and grabbing my lunch tray to turn it in at the washing station.

Tess hurried after me. The best feature about her was that she didn't press issues, something I appreciated greatly at the moment. Except as soon as we stepped from the student union, she looped her arm through mine, surprising me enough to send her a startled glance.

"Seriously, Bailey. Are you going to be okay? So much has been happening to you lately."

An empty hopelessness weighed down heavily inside me. And for the briefest moment, I wondered if I really would ever be okay again. But just as quickly as the sensation came, it passed and I waved a hand. "I'll be fine. You just worry too much."

"I know, but this time it feels..."

When her voice trailed off, I glanced at her to realize she was squinting and staring past me at something. "I-isn't that *him*?" She whispered the last word as if scandalized.

I whirled around, expecting to find Beckett. I was actually fully prepared to storm to him and demand to know what he was doing here on campus, endangering himself.

But Beck wasn't the *him* Tess was referring to.

Chance Fairfield strolled down the sidewalk toward us with none other than his sister Melody at his side. He hadn't noticed us yet, but it was only a matter of seconds before he did.

"Holy hell," I breathed. "Search for the guy for a year and nothing. But suddenly when I *don't* want to see him anymore, he's freaking everywhere. And with *her* of all people."

"Her?" Tess's eyes widened at they landed on Melody. "You mean…?"

I nodded. "His sister, yes."

At that moment, both brother and sister looked up, spotting us.

"Let's go this way," I told Tess, hooking my arm through hers and dragging her off in any direction that would help us avoid the Fairfields. Except the cowboy darted into our path.

I tried to evade him again, steering Tess a different direction. But she wasn't prepared for the sharp change in course and stumbled into me, slowing us both down enough for the cowboy to make a barricade of himself right in front of us. We jerked to a halt, Tess gasping her surprise at the way he glared at me.

As she shifted closer to me—probably to seek protection and give it both—Chance snarled, "What the fuck are *you* doing here?" He sported a black eye, courtesy of Beck, and I couldn't help but feel a thrill knowing Beck had hurt him back.

"I go to this school," I answered the obvious before sniffing and rolling my eyes. "Moron."

Melody finally reached us, hearing the tail end of my "compliment."

"Who the hell is this chunk?" she asked.

Tess took hold of my arm, obviously offended on my behalf, as Chance snickered and motioned to me with his chin before answering, "Don't you know? This is the lying bitch who got Hilliard out of jail."

Mouth dropping open and eyes bulging wide, Tess turned to ask, "Did he just call you what I think he just called you?"

I didn't get a chance to answer before Melody interrupted us, squawking, "*What?* But she doesn't have rainbow-colored hair."

Wow, she was a quick one, she was.

I sent her a saccharine smile. "Well, some things change, sweetheart. Too bad my first impression of you didn't. Turns out you really *are* a manipulative whore."

"Hey," Chance growled, stepping intimidatingly closer, which made Tess squeeze right up against me, her breathing picking up as she grew more anxious. "Watch your mouth, cunt. My sister's been through enough."

I bit the inside of my lip before nodding to agree. "You know, you're right. I bet she has." Meanwhile, I whipped my phone from my back pocket and slid my finger across the screen until I was looking up my videos. "I'm sure cheating on her boyfriend takes *a lot* out of a girl."

Then I pressed *play*, making her caterwauling orgasm screech through the speakers of my phone.

"Oh, my God. Oh, my God, Beck. Right there. Right fucking there. Fuuuuck. It feels so good," she bleated. "Fuck me, fuck me, fuck—"

Gasping, Melody snagged the phone from my hand and threw it on the ground before crushing it under her boot heel.

It happened so fast I could only gape, with Tess standing frozen speechless next to me.

Even Chance looked struck dumb as he ogled the shattered phone. Then he lifted his eyes to his sister, and I could tell—hell, anyone watching could tell—he knew without a shadow of a doubt his precious sister was a liar.

She hadn't been raped at all.

"If you showed this to anyone—" she started, pinning me with a death glare.

But I laughed in her face. "I showed it to the police, you idiot. How do you think I got Beck out of a jail? And why the hell did you *send* him there in the first place? Seriously, do you have any idea what your lie did to him? You destroyed another human being to keep yourself out of trouble. How do you sleep at night?"

Letting out a scream of outrage, Melody launched herself at us, but Tess and I kind of worked as one super-human to shove her back before she could strike. She lost her balance, tripping backwards before she landed on her ass.

That was all it took to piss off big brother.

"Don't you ever fucking touch my sister." He grabbed my wrist, hard, and yanked me toward him.

"No!" Tess shrieked, still hooking her arm through mine so that she was dragged with me.

The cowboy reared back his fist to strike when a shout from behind us stalled him short.

He glanced over our shoulders, then abruptly released me, snatched his sister from the ground and took off jogging away with her.

"What the hell is going on?" a panting Jonah demanded, reaching us a second later so he could yank Tess into his arms and hug her. "Who the fuck was that?"

"Oh my God. Oh my God, *Jonah*." Tess burrowed into him, tucking her face under his chin and clutching him tight.

"Wha…?" He glanced meaningfully at me as he patted her back and smoothed her hair, his gaze demanding an explanation.

I cleared my throat and shifted uncomfortably. "Apparently, I'm such a badass now I have some violent enemies."

"Violent is right." Tess pulled away from her boyfriend to hurry to me and look me over as if I might actually have a wound.

I didn't but I might later. That son of a bitch had squeezed hard enough to possibly leave a bruise.

"He was going to hit you. Oh my God, Bailey. We need to call campus police. We need to—" Her voice quivered and her hands shook. Her eyes looked wild with fear as tears pooled in her lashes.

I grabbed her shoulders to steady her and said evenly, "We need to calm you down first."

I glanced pointedly at Jonah, who immediately stepped in and wrapped his arm around her from behind, kissing her hair before murmuring, "It's okay, babe. I've got you. It's okay now."

When her breathing settled, and she calmed enough to close her eyes and sink back against him, I finally said, "I don't want to call anyone about this."

Tess's eyes popped open. "But…*no*. That girl. She broke your phone. He grabbed your arm. He was going to hit you, Bailey. *Hit* you."

"But I'd just have to explain *why* Melody broke my phone in the first place. And I'd really rather not." I stared at her meaningfully, the fact sinking in that she now knew what I'd done, what'd I'd videotaped.

Oh hell. What had I been thinking? I knew I was impetuous, but pulling that phone out to shove it in Melody's face, proving I had evidence of what a big fat liar she was, had probably been one of the rashest, worst things I'd ever done. Seemed like I was setting records on dumb, rash things lately. Now Tess knew I'd made a sex tape.

Tess, my best friend on earth…

The realization hit her, and she seemed to take a step backward away from me, her eyes revealing her shock and horror.

"Why did she break your phone?" Jonah asked innocently.

Both his girlfriend and I turned to him as if he'd asked the one question he should never ask.

"I'm going home," I blurted, unconsciously rubbing my wrist and backing away from Tess and Jonah.

"But—" This time, Tess stopped herself from trying to talk me out of not contacting the campus police. Her eyes filled with sympathy. It made my heart kick.

"I'll see you later," I mumbled, whirling away and hurrying off.

For some stupid reason, I expected Beck to be there when I reached the apartment. But it wasn't even noon and he didn't think he was allowed to return until after three.

I retreated to my room, assuming a little time alone to myself would be best, but when I got there, I felt lonelier than ever. The strongest sensation lingering within the four walls was his absence.

How the hell had he managed to do that within three days? And what was I going to do when he found a life again away from here and left?

I sat on my bed, and blew out a breath, staring at the window that looked out onto the park. But the more I sat there, the more the events of the day caught up to me. I pressed the palms of my hands against my lap and began to smooth the fabric of my jean from my thighs to my knees and back again until my fingers became to tremble.

And then holy shit, suddenly, I was trembling all over, imagining what would have happened if Jonah hadn't shown up when he had. Would the cowboy really have hit me? Would he have stopped at one punch? Could I be sporting a black eye like Beck right now? Or worse?

"Holy shit," I whispered, pushing suddenly to my feet and pacing my room before going to my book bag and retrieving my shattered, mangled phone from the front pocket. I worked off the back and thankfully found the sims card inside unharmed. Thank God I had insurance and could get it replaced.

I spent the rest of the afternoon, calling the cell phone company from the apartment's landline and getting a replacement ordered. Then I tried to work on some homework, but my mind was a scattered mess. This was going to be a bad semester for me, I could already tell. I never skipped class, and here I'd done it twice this week. And now I couldn't concentrate on anything.

Anything but the fact that Tess knew I'd taken a video, and Jonah probably did too. Paige and Logan would no doubt be enlightened soon. I was so not looking forward to that. Plus, I'd almost gotten beaten up by a guy I'd had a ridiculous raging crush on for a year. And on top of that, I was becoming fixated on another dude who may or may not be suicidal and had a shit-ton of baggage to work through before he should even think about dating.

I was one pickle away from being a full barrel of whack.

* * *

By four, when Beck hadn't returned yet, I found myself pacing the front room, worrying.

"I told you guys," I muttered, chewing urgently on my fingernails. "He shouldn't have been kicked out during the day. What if someone else beat him up? What if he just up and left town and never came back?"

"Well…" Logan shrugged. "He *is* an adult. He doesn't *have* to come back."

I scowled at him, making him shift cautiously backward. "What if he *hurt* himself?" I countered.

Jonah shrugged. "He seemed pretty insistent he wasn't like that." But my glare his way made him reconsider his words. After sending me a short frown, he let out a sigh and scrubbed a hand over his head before saying, "Fine. I'll go look for him."

He grabbed his coat and stomped down the stairs. Tess moved up beside me and rubbed my arm. "I'm sure he's okay and will be home soon."

I glanced at her and realized what an annoying, pain-in-the-butt worrywart I was probably being. Opening my mouth to apologize, I stopped short as Jonah hollered up the stairwell, "Found him."

I hurried to the steps only to realize Jonah had already admitted Beckett inside the apartment and they were both starting up the steps together.

Beck lifted his face, and relief flooded me before I realized he was holding one arm where blood soaked through the long sleeve of his white thermal undershirt.

"Oh my God, what happened?" I flew down the steps to meet him halfway, clutching his arm to assess the damage. But his shirt was in the way.

"I'm fine," he assured me, his voice quiet. It wasn't filled with pain but maybe there was some hopelessness littering his tone.

"What happened?" I asked again, more rationally this time.

He shrugged and glanced away, letting me know he didn't want to tell me. "It was stupid," he said. "My own damn fault."

I just arched my eyebrows, letting him know he needed to start talking.

His shoulders slumped as I led him through the living room and toward the kitchen where I pulled his shirtsleeve up to reveal a somewhat shallow four-inch cut running lengthwise up the back of his arm.

After leading him to the sink, I began to run water over his arm, making him hiss from the chill. Once that was done, I opened a nearby drawer that housed our first aid kit.

"So are you going to talk or make me guess what happened?" I asked as I lined the wound with a triple-action antibiotic and then began to wrap it with gauze.

"It was stupid," he repeated, sighing again as if upset with himself. "I went looking for work and actually had someone offer me a job."

I looked up, gasping in glee. "That's great. Where?"

But he only frowned back. "A feed-packing plant. But don't get too excited. As soon as I started to fill out my W-2 and handed over my driver's license for proof of ID, they saw my name and tried to run me off the place, and I mean, literally, the guy charged me. So I went tripping backward away from him and stumbled into this coat rack thing he had by the door, knocking it over and slicing my arm open." He sniffed his disgust and rolled his eyes. "It was my own fault for not looking where I was going."

I didn't agree. Seriously, who would've expected someone to charge them after being offered a job? My heart cracked with pity and anger on his behalf.

"Oh, Beck," I said. "What're we going to with you?"

"I'm thinking full-body bubble wrap," he said.

I blurted out a laugh, but then couldn't control myself. I threw my arms around him and hugged him, scolding, "It's not funny. You can't keep getting the crap beat out of you every time you leave the house."

"Bailey, really." He tensed against me. "A scrape on the arm isn't exactly an ass kicking." But then he hugged me back, and for some reason I rested my head—er, rather my temple because I was too short to get my whole head up there—against his shoulder.

Behind us, Tess hissed, "She's hugging him again. Oh my God, she's hugging him *again*."

Realizing, oh my God, I *was* hugging him once again, I dropped my arms and stepped back. But he took my wrist to stop me from going away too far away.

I hissed when his fingers hit a tender spot.

Beckett looked down at my gasp and moved his fingers until he revealed a bruise. "What the hell?" His gaze sprang to mine. "Did someone hurt you?"

I was totally going to play it off, but Tess—curse her—blurted, "Yes. The cowboy guy and his sister."

"*What*?" Beck zipped a startled glance to her, making her flush and hide her face in Jonah's bicep. Then he whirled an accusing stare to me. "What happened?"

"We ran into them on campus," Tess started. When I glared at her, she slapped her hands over her mouth and widened her eyes. Then, just as quickly, she dropped her fingers and rushed, "They cornered us, bullied Bailey, broke her phone when they saw the video on it, and then the cowboy grabbed her and reared back his arm to hit her, except Jonah finally showed up and scared him off." She grinned lovingly up at her boyfriend at that part.

Beck stood there blinking for a good five seconds, before he shook his head. That's when his eyes flared with rage, and he started from the kitchen.

"I'm going to kill him."

"What the hell ever!" I leapt after him and snagged his arm, needing to put all my strength in it before he finally paused and scowled back at me. "You'll only cause more trouble," I insisted. "It's over. Let it be." He began to shake his head until I added, "Please."

His jaw bunched and eye twitched as he stared straight into me. Then he growled, "You at least called campus police, right?" When I didn't answer, he looked pointedly at Tess. "*Right*?"

She gulped and shook her head. "Bailey didn't want to tell anyone else about the vid—"

At the shriek of distress that came from my throat, Tess broke off and glanced at me. When she realized she'd been about to reveal my big secret, she clamped her mouth shut.

Beck scowled between us. "About the *what*?" he demanded, but he was already running other things Tess had said through his head. "What video was on your phone?" he asked me.

No way on God's green earth could I tell him that. But he read the guilt and humiliation clearly on my face.

His mouth fell open. "Holy shit. You took a *video*? Of me and Melody?"

Every time I'd felt embarrassed lately, it had seemed like the worst, most mortifying moment ever, but all those times were nothing compared to this one. I could barely breathe as I took in the shock on Beck's face.

I wanted to explode into a million pieces and cease to exist. Except I didn't go anywhere.

I slowly peered around us. Paige and Logan were exchanging glances, and I could read their unsaid conversation clearly. *"Who else has she filmed doing it?"*

Oh, God. I couldn't do this. Whirling away from all of them, I raced from the kitchen.

Chapter 24
BECKETT

I was too shocked to do much else than gape after her as Bailey charged from the kitchen. I just wasn't expecting to learn she'd filmed me.

Finally, I shook my head, trying to come to grips with this new development, but, yeah, this one caught me off guard.

"I'll go talk to her," Tess murmured, starting from the kitchen, but I said, "No."

When they all turned to gape at me, I said, "I've got this one."

I didn't feel as if I could trust any of them to make this better. Bailey had looked devastated when she'd fled the room. I didn't want anyone to accidentally make it worse. I wasn't sure what I was going to say to fix it, but I still felt the need to be the one to help her.

It hadn't sounded as if she'd left the apartment, so I went to her room because I was sure I'd heard an interior door slam seconds after she'd left the kitchen.

Worried she might have locked me out, I held my breath as I tried to handle, but it was open. She wasn't in the room when I stepped inside, so I went to her private bath.

"Bailey?" I blinked as I poked my head through the opened doorway into the bathroom, because she wasn't in there, either. Strange. I swore she'd gone to her room.

Starting to retreat, I paused suddenly and squinted suspiciously at the shower curtain. Instead of leaving, I stepped forward and pulled it open.

Bailey sniffed and wiped the back of her hand across the underside of nose. Hugging herself where she sat on the lip of the bathtub, she looked up at me, revealing two wet trails running under each eye.

"Hey, act impressed," I said, stepping into the tub with her and sitting next to her. "I was sober enough to check behind the shower curtain this time."

Bailey didn't answer, just kept sniffing and wiping her face.

I had to say, I'd never sat fully dressed in a bathtub that wasn't running water before. After glancing down at our shoe-clad feet side by side in the bottom of the tub, I gave a long, tired sigh.

"You know, if I'd been trapped with no alternate way out while a couple in the next room was having sex and the door was open between us, I would've looked too." I gave a negligent shrug. "It's just human nature."

Bailey brushed more tears off her cheeks. "And you would've taken a picture that accidentally turned out to be a video of it too, huh?"

I winced. Yeah, I probably wouldn't have done that. But I shrugged anyway, mumbling, "I don't know. Maybe."

When she sent me a hard glance, I cringed and admitted, "Okay, maybe not. Why…why exactly *did* you do that? Was it like an academic curiosity? Trying to take notes for future ideas?"

"Oh my God," she moaned covering her face with both hands. "I was not taking notes." Then she whimpered to herself, "This is so freaking embarrassing."

I nodded, respecting that. It was pretty freaking embarrassing for me too. I mean, I was the unsuspecting star of her porn film. This wasn't something I dealt with every day. But strangely, I wasn't mad at her. I just wanted to stop her tears and make her happy again.

Trying to go light, I snapped my fingers, coming up with a new idea. "You were gathering new material for your spank bank." Then I frowned at that term. Girls couldn't rightly call it a spank bank, could they? "Or whatever you females call your version of it."

Another hard glance shifted my way. "I do *not* masturbate. That's disgusting."

My eyebrows popped up in surprise. "You don't? Really? Like not ever?" How strange. I assumed all girls flicked the bean just as much as guys jerked off.

But Bailey's eyes widened in horror as she yelped, "No! Oh my God. That's gross. Why would I even try that if the one guy I'd ever been with couldn't even get me off?"

That was a bit too much for me to process all at once, so I lifted a finger and drew in a breath before saying, "Wait a second." Then I exhaled before shaking my head. "I thought it was harder for a dude to get a girl off than it was for a girl to get herself off."

Bailey opened her mouth as if she had every intention of arguing my point, but then she paused and frowned, tipping me a sideways glance. "Well, how the hell am I supposed to know that if I've never masturbated before?"

"Good point," I said, only to shrug and suggest, "Maybe you *should* try it then before making such rash statements." When she merely blinked at me, I grinned. "Hey, that *was* why you took the video, wasn't it? It really was spank bank material."

"It was not!" she cried indignantly. "There's *no way* the ugly heifer sounds Melody were making would *ever* turn me on enough to do *that* to myself." She flushed, looking uncomfortable and perplexed and irritated all at once.

"So you were filming her as some kind of blackmail to embarrass her?" I guessed.

"Blackmail?" Bailey wrinkled her nose. "Why the hell would I have wanted to blackmail or embarrass her? I didn't *know* her then; I didn't care what happened to her after she left that room. It was *you* I was focusing on. And I was trying to take a *picture*, not a video, anyway," She reiterated with a sniff, sending me a scowl for even suggesting the ideas I had suggested.

But I was too caught up on the other thing she'd said. "Me?" I repeated dumbly. "Why were you focusing on me?" My cheeks went hot. "Oh, hell? Did *I* look that bad, coming?" Had she wanted to embarrass *me*?

"No!" she practically yelled. "You looked amazing. That was the point. You looked so beautiful, it was like..." And then she fell quiet and her mouth popped open as if she'd just realized what she'd confessed before she whispered, "Art."

I swallowed. It was the only thing I could think to do to control the immediately reaction that sizzled through me. But my dick thickened so quickly in my pants it was freaky and embarrassing. I fisted my hands to keep from reaching for her and to control the intense images sweeping through me. Images of Bailey slipping her fingers down between my legs and stroking me through my jeans or maybe unsnapping the top button and easing her palm inside. I kind of wanted to thunk my head back against the tile wall of the bathtub and groan as if I could already feel her warm fingers wrapping around me and stroking.

But she was the one who moaned. In supreme humiliation. "Oh my God," she muffled out from between her fingers where she was covering her entire face with both hands. "I can't believe I just told you that."

"Bailey, no," I tried to reassure her. Without thinking, I touched her thigh with the sole intent to being kind and comforting. "Don't…" I wanted to tell her not to worry about something like that. I was actually flattered she'd thought I had looked like art. So fucking flattered. And turned on. But when my palm met the warmth soaking through the material of her jeans, the urge to caress her struck me hard. I mean, I think my fingers even started to move, curving around to the inside of her thigh. They wanted to move up toward her heat and cup her right between the legs.

It was so wrong and inappropriate, and I felt so guilty for almost doing just that, that I jerked my hand off her and sucked in a breath, my lungs seizing and oxygen stalling.

I couldn't fucking breathe at all. My body panicked. My mouth gaped like a fish out of water, and my hand slapped against my constricting chest.

Oh, God. I couldn't breathe.

Couldn't breathe.

Bailey noticed, glancing at my face before her eyes widened. "Dammit," she muttered, turning toward me and gripping my shoulders. "You're having another panic attack. Just breathe. *Beck*. Breathe through it."

I shook my head, squeezing her hands that were still holding onto my arms. "Can't."

"Yes, you can," she argued. "Now breathe *out*."

Looking her straight in the eye, I exhaled. When she demanded I inhale, I did that next. She coached me through the next few breaths until we both realized I was better.

Except as soon as I was better, she let go of me and stood abruptly, hugging herself. "I'm sorry. I didn't mean to creep you out to the point you had a panic attack."

She tried to step past me to leave the bathtub. But I couldn't let her go, couldn't let her think my breakdown had come from disgust.

I grabbed her arm, staying her. "No." Then I stood, shaking my head. "That's not why I freaked out."

But she wouldn't look me in the eye. She tried to pull free of my arm, not listening, too embarrassed to hear me out.

"I *liked* it," I blurted, making her pause and squint at me in confusion. I swallowed and then whispered, "I liked hearing why you took the video. I liked it a lot, like, I was about to make a pass at you before I realized how inappropriate and wrong that was. I'm sorry, Bailey." Glancing down at my hands, I tried to hide my shame. "I would never do that do you. I won't ever take advantage of your good graces. It just scared me how close I came to making a move, I…yeah, I freaked. I'm sorry."

When she didn't answer, I finally risked a glance up. She was studying me so strangely, I straightened and said, "What?"

Bailey shook her head, but then she said, "It's probably just because you feel obligated to me."

I glanced at her, wincing. "Huh?" That explanation didn't sound right at all.

"You…" She cleared her throat and glanced away. "You're confused right now. And I'm the only person who's really stepped forward to help you, so you feel…"

When she didn't come up with another word for how she thought I felt, I began to shake my head, not liking where this was headed because that wasn't how I felt at all.

But she only nodded. "Yes. You feel as if you owe me something."

Well, okay, yeah, I did feel as if I owed her *everything*, but I didn't want to sex her up because I thought it was the best way to pay her back for saving me.

Did I?

No. I started to shake my head again. But she set a hand on my arm.

"Don't worry, Beck. You don't owe me anything. So I won't let us go there."

When she calmly let go of me, I merely watched without a fight as she climbed out of the tub and left the bathroom.

My chest felt hallow and carved out, and I still wanted to argue with her. Except I felt too confused. I hadn't really wanted to make a pass at her because I just felt like I should, did I? That theory felt all wrong, and yet everything else felt muddled and confused. I had no idea what was really going on. I just understood that nothing between us would ever happen because Bailey had explicitly just said it wouldn't.

Not that I blamed her. She'd seen me with Melody. Of course, she wanted nothing to do with that. But still…it all left me strangely empty inside.

Chapter 25
BAILEY

Monday night was weird.

Beckett and I had worked out and resolved everything to do with the video, something I was sure we'd never get past. I didn't think he'd ever forgive me. And I was certain I'd never be able to look him in the eye again. But after our talk in the bathtub, we'd worked through it. And yet, it seemed like we'd opened up another problem.

The thing was, I had no idea what the problem *was*. I just felt the tension that that sprouted between us.

He waited until I was ready to turn in for the night before he took his shower, as if he wanted me to be asleep by the time he came out so he wouldn't have to deal with the moment we both crawled into bed together. So I feigned being asleep when he exited the bathroom and sadly, I heard his sigh of relief when he fell for my act.

Seconds later, the sheets on the other half of the bed lifted and the mattress dipped as he lay down beside me. But he tossed and turned for a while before he finally set a hand on my arm. At first, I thought he was trying to wake me up to talk to me, but then I realized his grip was too light, like he was worried *about* waking me. Seconds later, his breathing evened and he was out.

My lips parted with sudden realization. He hadn't been able to fall asleep until he'd made physical contact with me.

I closed my eyes, wondering what the heck was going on here. I was only supposed to be helping him out of a bad situation, and yet these feelings were surging and these wants were sprouting. Why did it affect me so freaking, stupidly strongly to realize he needed to touch me before he could settle down enough to go to sleep? I had a bad feeling I was beginning to like this guy more than I should, and I was beginning to want things from him I knew I shouldn't.

If I kept this shit up, I'd end up getting myself hurt.

I twisted around until I was facing him so I could watch him sleep. My chest constricted with this big, deep ache and I watched to touch his cheek. I wanted to lean forward and set my mouth against his. I wanted to wrap my arms around him and curl in close to his heat.

When I finally fell asleep, I dreamed about him, strange, confusing dreams of us being together and then not together, of him calling me a fat bitch the same way Chance Fairfield had and then spitting on me. And then him rearing back his arm to hit me, laughing the entire time, and telling me no one could ever love someone like me.

I woke on a gasp to my alarm sounding. Beck stirred next to me but didn't fully wake. I shut up the irritating blare and groaned in misery as I crawled out of bed, sore and extra tired from the bizarreness of my dreams.

Beckett still hadn't woken by the time I showered and changed and readied myself for the day, so I left him to sleep while I went to the kitchen for breakfast.

All four of my roommates were already up and preparing their own morning meals when I entered. I slowed to a stop, suddenly aware of the last time I'd seen them and what they all knew about me now.

Holding my breath when they turned as one unit, as if waiting for me, I wondered if they were going to kick me out because they could no longer trust me around them. I mean, how could they? I was a known sex videographer.

My heart pounded and palms turned sweaty. Beck and I were going to be kicked out on our asses. I was going to lose the only two friends I'd ever had in Paige and Tess. I was about to be just as lost and alone as Beck was. How the hell would I be able to take care of him now?

Jonah cleared his throat and sent Logan a glance, who seemed to be the one elected to do the talking. Aw, shit. They even had a get-lost speech prepared.

Logan drew in a breath before saying to me, "We decided you were right." *Wait. What?* "It's probably safer if Beck lays low for a while and doesn't leave the apartment. So he doesn't have to leave during the days while we're gone if he doesn't want to."

I blinked at him, totally not expecting him to say that. When I repeated his words through my head, it still sounded foreign. Finally, I blurted, "What?"

"Once the hoopla surrounding his case dies down, everyone will lose interest and begin to forget. He should probably wait until then to try looking for a job and new place to live."

My lips parted. At first, I was speechless. And then I was choked up with emotion. "Really?" I croaked, pressing my hand to my chest. They were worried about Beck and wanted to keep him as safe as I did?

I suddenly wanted to hug all four of my roommates at once. They still supported me and my wish to look after him. After everything they'd learned last night, I wasn't a repulsive freak to them.

Learning this was more than I could take. My chin wobbled and eyes filled with tears. "Thank you," I choked out.

"Oh, honey," Tess cooed, hurrying forward to hug me. Paige was right behind her, wrapping her arms around me as well. Their grips were suffocating and tight, yet warm and comforting. I burst out crying even harder, feeling like a total idiot.

But Tess only fussed, "That's it. Just cry it out. You're okay. It's all okay now."

"How is it okay?" I blubbered. "I'm freaking crying and *hugging* people."

"I know!" Tess, the sadist, laughed. "Isn't it amazing?"

I found it disturbing, actually, like I should go shower away such an emotional show, or kick kittens, or something.

"Here, we made you breakfast," Paige offered, leading me toward the table, where there was a plate full of waffles topped with my favorite: powdered sugar, fresh strawberries, and maple syrup.

I blinked and glanced warily at everyone while Tess pulled out my chair for me.

"What the fuck is going on?" I asked as I slowly sank in my chair, before gasping. "Oh God, one of you needs a kidney from me, don't you?"

Tess laughed as she plopped down next to me. "Oh, whatever. We can be nice to you if we want to."

"Yeah, especially the morning after you all find out I'm a—" I winced and let out a sigh. "You know I'd never do that to any of you, right? I've never overheard anything or taken pictures or—"

"Bailey," Paige cut in softly, and yet forcefully. No idea how did she that, but the woman had some strange talent with soft force. "We know that. We know *you*. And this is us trying to convince you none of that matters. We love you all the same."

I'd just taken my first bite of waffle, and it promptly got caught in my throat. Tears threatened to fall again because I knew I didn't deserve their support. These guys really were the best friends I'd ever had. Even their boyfriends were amazing, Jonah, the butthead, included.

"Here." As if reading my mind, Tess picked up my glass of apple juice and offered it to me. I nodded gratefully and scooped it up, gulping so I didn't have to talk. Then I sat it down and glanced around. Jonah wasn't paying me any mind, too busy reading the back of the cereal box beside him, but the other three offered me a warm smile.

"I kind of actually want to sing *Kumbaya* with you guys, or some shit, right now," I announced.

"Oh, God," Jonah groaned. "I'll pass."

"Yeah." Logan lifted his hands and scooted back from the table. "I'm sitting that one out too."

The girls laughed, and everything felt right with the world again.

I plowed through my waffles with gusto and was half-finished with them by the time Beck, looking pretty hot with a wrinkled shirt, messy hair, and a red sleep crease bisecting his cheek, bumbled into the kitchen, yawning and scratching his chest through his shirt.

"Good news," I hollered with my mouth full of waffle as I lifted my fork full of more waffles in congratulations. "You can stay!"

He slowed to a stop, staring strangely at me, his face frozen with an expression that clearly said he wasn't aware his stay here had been in question.

So Paige quickly clarified, "During the days. Alone. If you want."

"Oh," he said, finally catching on. This his eyebrows perked as he glanced at everyone else. "Really? Are you sure?"

"They're positive," I answered merrily for the collective whole. "Now grab some waffles and dig in. They're awesome."

I watched him as he hesitantly followed my orders, grabbing a clean plate and then filling it with waffles that were piled on a platter on the counter. He was fairly boring on the waffle front, straight up butter and syrup for him. Yawn. But I wouldn't hold that against him.

He was still nice to sleep next to, and look at, and dream about…until those dreams turned disturbing. I returned my attention to my breakfast, trying to forget the part where my dream had turned stupid.

"Are you guys heading out to your dad's tonight or in the morning?" Paige asked Tess as Beck joined the group and seated himself at the other end of the table as me.

"Probably this evening," Tess said. "You?"

"Us too." Paige glanced at Logan. "My dad says he has Trace's old room cleaned up for Logan to sleep in. It's going to be weird, but Dad seems determined to include him as part of the family, so hopefully it won't be *too* weird."

Beckett glanced curiously between the two couples before asking, "Why are all of you leaving?"

They turned to him, blinked, and then Paige kindly said, "We're going home for Thanksgiving."

He stared back a moment before releasing a breath. "Oh, shit. That's right. I forgot it was…this Thursday. Holy shit," he murmured again before turning his gaze to me. "Wha-what're *you* doing for Thanksgiving?"

I could see the worry in his eyes. He didn't know what was going to happen to him when we all took off for the holidays.

"Well," I started slowly. "I'm scheduled to work at the shop tomorrow morning until noon, and then I have to be back again at the ass-crack of dawn on Black Friday, so I was thinking we could head out early in the afternoon tomorrow and then return later on Thursday after dinner."

He blinked before lifting a finger. "Wait. When you say we…?"

"We." I motioned between the two of us. "As in you and me."

Beckett blinked again before shouting, "*What*? I can't go to your family holiday with you. Are you crazy?"

I merely sighed. "Well, what else are you supposed to do? Stay here alone through the holiday? I don't think so."

"But…" He shook his head, gaping at me as if I'd lost my mind.

I rolled my eyes. "Oh, just stop. You're coming with me. End of story."

He opened his mouth, only to close it. Then he sighed and frowned, huffing, "You didn't even ask."

Oh my God! I almost laughed and then I almost groaned. In the end, I drew in a breath before very calmly and politely saying, "Beckett, it would make me feel a million times better if you would accompany me to my dad's tomorrow and spend Thanksgiving with us and my four annoying brothers, plus one pregnant sister-in-law. So…would you, pretty please with sugar on top, just come with me?"

Again, he faltered. I knew he wanted to decline on principle alone. We all knew how it would look to my family. Single college-age guy coming home with Bailey for Thanksgiving. None of my brothers and probably not even my dad would think he wasn't my boyfriend. I didn't blame him for wanting to avoid that kind of mess. But seriously, what the hell else was he supposed to do?

When an alternative hit me, I shrugged. "I guess we could just not to go to my family's at all and stay here."

"No," he cried. "You can't *not* visit your family for the holidays because of me."

"So then you'll come with me?" I pressed.

He ground his teeth and looked up at the ceiling for a moment before meeting my gaze and reassuring me, "I'll be fine. I'll take the truck out into the country for a few days and camp out. It'll be fun."

"Right," I said slowly. "With zero cash in your wallet and zero dollars in your checking account? You'd seriously rather waste what gas you have in your truck and ration out food in the hopes you take along enough that you don't starve than just come with me and be well fed and warm inside a house with a warm, comfortable bed at night?"

"Dammit, Bailey," he muttered. "I can't go with you. I don't belong there. It would be inappropriate. And, Jesus, you can't take care of me every second of every day. I refuse to be dependent on you for the rest of my life."

"First of all, why *wouldn't* you belong? I've brought friends to Thanksgiving plenty of times before." I motioned toward my best friend. "Just ask Tess. And inappropriate? *What…*?" I shook my head before saying, "That makes no sense, so I'm just going to ignore that one and move on to all the stupid *dependent* bullshit you're spewing. Your life flipped completely on its axis barely a week ago. And as much as I know you want to, you're not going to get over what happened to you in a day. It's going to take time. A long, fucking time. So excuse me for trying to help you out until you orient yourself again."

When I stood up to leave, he sprang up from his own seat and dodged into my path. "No. Don't. Just...*stop*." He held up a hand and waited until I really stopped and lifted my brows expectantly. Then he blew out a breath. "I appreciate all your help," he started. "You have no idea how much I appreciate it. But..."

Floundering because he was out of words, I grinned and said, "It's hard for you to accept help, isn't it?"

He deflated. "God, yes. You have no idea."

I chuckled and patted his cheek. "Well, suck it up, buttercup. Because I'm here until you're one hundred percent again. You better get used to it."

Chapter 26
BECKETT

I offered to drive my truck, but Bailey insisted we take her car. I'd never thought of myself as one of those macho manly men before who always had to be in control and do the driving, but riding shotgun with *her* behind the wheel made me distinctly uncomfortable.

Or maybe that was just because she was a freaking *insane* driver.

"Holy shit," I gasped, holding onto to dashboard with one hand and my chest with the other as we narrowly missed getting t-boned by a dump truck at a four-way.

"What?" She sent me a harassed glance. "It was totally my turn."

"No." I shook my head, still seeing my life flash before my eyes. "No. I really think it was his turn."

"Was it?" Her brow wrinkled with confusion before she shrugged. "Oh well. Whatever. We lived. Relax already." She patted my thigh, and my muscles tensed for an entirely different reason. I don't think she noticed how high up on the leg she was touching me. Just a couple more inches to the right and—

No. I needed to stop being such a dog and thinking that way before we reached her dad's place. *If* we arrived. I wasn't yet convinced we'd actually make it in one piece. According to Bailey, we were only halfway there, with another hour of driving to go.

When she jerked the steering wheel in order to swerve into the lane of oncoming traffic and pass the car in front of us, I gulped and took my eyes off the road, not brave enough to watch. When we made it back into our lane alive, my fingers relaxed marginally around the oh-shit handle.

Needing a distraction, I turned to her and said, "Tell me about your family. What're we going to be walking in on? Will all four brothers be there?"

"Yep. I mean, I think so. I know my married brother Braiden and his wife, Donna, will be there, since they're bringing the turkey and stuffing. My oldest brother Brock makes pumpkin pies like nobody's business, so if he isn't around, I'll just find wherever he is and drag him home by the ear."

I chuckled at that, while Bailey finished with, "We can only hope Booth and Blaine won't be there, but they still live at home, so I doubt we'll be so lucky."

"You have two older brothers who still live at home?" I started to wonder if I'd be the type who could return to the nest after college, when it struck me afresh: I was no longer welcome home, and I no longer attended college, so all my pondering was moot.

Something akin to grief overwhelmed me. It swirled through my chest with a tight, achy hopelessness until Bailey's voice pulled me from the soul-sucking vortex.

"It's not quite as lame as that, even though they're both totally lame. They actually work for my dad on the farm, so they're more like live-in hired hands than lazy, freeloading grown children, even though grown children is exactly how I'd describe them."

I glanced at her, clinging to the light she provided at the end of my tunnel of pain. I don't know how she always did that. Just when I started to feel lost and disheartened, she said or did something practical yet quirky, and I was once again okay. She was my path back to reality, and she didn't even know it.

"You sound like me describing my sister. It was totally fine for me to call her an annoying pest, but I always wanted everyone else to think respectfully of her."

When Bailey sent me a confused glanced, I grinned. "I didn't mean to insinuate that your brothers were lazy freeloaders, and I'm sorry it came out that way, but it was a super kickass sister gesture of you to set the record straight, anyway."

She blinked, and a second later, dismay lit her face. "Oh my God, I did just totally defend those two assholes, didn't I?"

With a laugh, I nudged her arm. "It was sweet."

"*Sweet*?" She looked even more horrified than ever. "That's even worse." Pointing a threatening finger my way, she growled, "If you ever tell them I said something *nice* about them, I will cut you."

I lifted my hands, unable to stop chuckling. "Don't worry. Your secret's safe with me."

She sniffed right before her shoulders slumped. "I mean, of course I love my brothers. I just don't…"

"Want them to know that," I finished for her. "I totally get it."

Bailey glanced at me, and I could see in her gaze, she knew that I did. But that seemed to confuse her. Her eyes narrowed slightly as if she couldn't trust whatever connection we had between us where we actually understood each other.

Another stray thought flickered through me. I was glad to be here with her. I felt happy, and despite everything, there was a strange peace inside me. I was actually grateful the last week had gone the way it had, because it meant I ended up here in this car with her. There was honestly nowhere else in the world I'd rather be.

I relaxed back in my seat and grinned a smile of pure satisfaction.

That was, until Bailey simultaneously slammed her brake and horn, and then began cursing the truck who'd just pulled out in front of us before it decided to drive too slowly for her taste.

Heart pounding and muscles coiling with tension, I jerked upright, big-eyed as I glanced around to make sure we were still alive.

We were, thank God.

Okay, so maybe I was glad I was here with her, but it still would've been nice if I'd been in the driver's seat.

* * *

You'll never believe it, but we made it to Bailey's family farm without wrecking Bailey's car or running over anything or anyone in the process. Miracles did happen.

Waiting until she'd killed the engine, I unwrapped my fingers from the passenger side's door handle that may or may not have permanent imprints of my fingerprints now, and I took in her childhood home.

"Well, this is it," Bailey announced, heaving out a breath as she looked out the front window as well.

"Holy shit," I murmured, my shock instant

Dusk had fallen but I could still see enough to know she hadn't been lying when she'd said our two homesteads resembled each other. Both were two-story farm-style houses, but my parents' was white, whereas her dad's house was light blue. They both sat atop an incline and seemed to be surrounded by barren fields, laying fallow and waiting for a spring harvest. But Bailey's family had built a heck of a lot more outbuildings than mine, plus they appeared to have more heavy equipment machinery and what looked like a horse barn to the right.

Next to me, Bailey read my mind. "Freaky, isn't it?"

I nodded mutely.

When a yellow lab lazily trotted out to greet us, I blinked against the déjà vu. "Freaky's certainly one way to put it."

I pushed open the door so I could go meet her dog. He looked old and incapable of jumping any longer, so I knelt down before him and let him sniff my face as I rubbed his ears. "Hey there, big guy. Aren't you a sweetheart? It's Humphrey, right?" I asked, glancing toward Bailey when she stepped from the car and moved around to kneel next to us.

But I didn't need to wait for her nod of confirmation. The lab's tail began to thump heartily and his entire backend shook back and forth at the mention of his name. I laughed and moved my face away when he tried to lick his way into my mouth and nostrils.

Yeah, he was definitely Humphrey.

"Okay, quit hogging my damn dog," Bailey finally said, moving right up against my shoulder as if she was going to ram me aside so she could shower her pet with attention. But then she only grinned and sent me a wink.

Finally noticing her, the lab swung his big head her way, slinging drool over the both of us so he could let her scratch him too.

Crying out our dismay, we both wiped the gross off our faces before we shared a grimace of disgust, only to burst out laughing as we compared who had the most drool dripping from our fingers.

"Is that you, brat?" a voice called from the front porch of the house before footsteps sounded on the steps.

Bailey groaned and pushed to her feet, scrubbing her palms clean on the hips of her jeans as she did. I was slower to rise, following the same procedure with my own hands.

The guy strolling toward us was lean and tall and seemed to be in his early to mid-twenties. His hair was dark, but his grin was pure Bailey.

"We didn't know if you were going to make it in tonight or tomorrow morn…"

He slowed to a stop when he caught sight of me. For a second, he stared blankly before pointing. "Where the hell did you come from?" He glanced at Bailey. "Who is this guy? Did he come with you?"

I turned to her, my stomach sinking fast. I started to shake my head, denying it, but no, she wouldn't bring me home to her family without warning them who I was, without even telling them she was brining anyone with her. Would she?

She glanced at me, shrugging. "Hell, no. He didn't come with me. I thought he was one of your friends."

My mouth fell open as the man I guessed was her brother spun to me more alertly.

For a good two seconds, I froze, not sure if I should run before this fellow tried to kick my ass for trespassing or if I should try to explain I really had gotten here via Bailey. It was kind of hard to decide which of the two would land me less dead.

But then Bailey nudged my elbow with her own and snickered. "I'm just kidding. Yes, he came with me. This is Beckett." Then she pointed to the other guy, telling me, "And this loser is unfortunately my brother, Booth."

Booth eyed me up and down before he glanced at Bailey and scoffed, "Thought you said you were never going to date a guy whose name started with B."

"Yeah, except I'm *not* dating him," Bailey argued. Not that her brother was paying her attention anymore; he'd paused to pet the dog and coo lovingly at Humphrey. "And—" Suddenly, she whirled to me. "Holy shit. Your name does start with a B."

"Right," I said slowly. "We've already had this conversation."

Booth began to chant in a sing-song voice to the dog about two bees sitting in a tree.

"Yeah, but…" Bailey started only to transfer a scowl at her brother and kick him in the knee. "I said we're *not* dating, you ass clown. He's just—" She didn't have an immediate answer, so both Booth and I eyed her curiously, waiting for her to label me.

I certainly wasn't going to help her explain my presence. I was still too put out she hadn't given anyone prior warning about my party-crashing.

"He's currently family-less," she started slowly, "and didn't have anywhere else to go for Thanksgiving. *That's* why he's here with me."

Booth lifted his eyebrows as if he didn't buy that, but then he shrugged and pushed to his feet so he could fling out his arm and give me friendly backhand me in the stomach. "Well, since you're here, not dating her and all, *you* can help carry all her shit inside so I don't have to." Then he turned away to amble back toward the house, humming the K-I-S-S-I-N-G song under his breath.

"I only have one overnight bag, jackass," Bailey called moodily after him.

"Well, you usually have an entire *trunkful*," Booth shot back over his shoulder without even slowing.

"That's because I usually stay for a heck of a lot longer than one night." Then she made a face and sniffed when her brother's response was the shutting of the front door as he entered the house, completely ignoring her. "He's such an idiot." Muttering, she turned to me. "I really don't pack too much on my trips home."

I grinned, flattered she even cared what I thought. Then I lifted my hands. "No worries. That was honestly the last thing I would've believed about you, anyway."

Seemingly mollified, Bailey grinned back to me before moving toward the trunk where our two bags had been stored.

I followed her, remembering a much more important matter. "So, you didn't tell your dad I was coming with you?" I asked, dogging her heels.

She frowned over her shoulder at me. "Of course I did."

"Your brother certainly seemed surprised by me."

With a snort, she popped the lid on the trunk. "Yeah, but he's my brother, not my dad. Trust me, I told my dad."

"But did you tell him *who* I am?" I pressed, not realizing she'd grabbed our two bags together until she'd simultaneously swung the straps for them over her shoulder. At her apartment, she'd carried them both down to the car before I'd been aware what she was doing too. But I wasn't about to let her carry them now.

"Give me those," I demanded, reaching out.

The damn girl dodged around me and hurried toward the house, one shoulder loaded down with a good twenty pounds. "You're one big bruise, Bucket. You're not carrying shit."

Grinding my teeth, I started after her, determined to at least retrieve my *own* bag. "Dammit, Bailey."

The front door came open again, and a new silhouette filled the entrance. I skidded to a halt, nearly swallowing my tongue. I could tell this man was older and fuller and yet shorter than Booth. Ergo, it was probably her dad.

Great. The first impression Bailey's father received of me was of Bailey carrying my things and me cursing at her.

I was fucked.

"Bailey?" his voice called. "Booth said you were home and…" His voice trailed off when he saw me over her shoulder. "Is that your friend?" He sounded incredulous as he swerved back to her. "I thought…well, I assumed you'd be bringing a female when you said friend."

My heart sank, and anxiety rose. Bailey hadn't told him *anything* about me.

Holy shit, what were they going to do when they found out I was the great rapist of Granton University? For the briefest moment, I wanted to wring Bailey's pretty, little neck.

And what was worse, she didn't seem concerned at all as she stepped into the house and plopped both bags heavily onto the floor by her feet. "Well, that's what you get for assuming."

Her dad glanced at both bags, frowned, and then turned to me, seeing my arms were free and that I'd just made his daughter carry my things.

Face flaming hot with embarrassment, I opened my mouth to say something, but hell, my mind was totally blank of excuses.

Turned out, I didn't need to worry about explaining myself. Bailey's dad took one look at my face and said, "Jesus. What the hell happened to you, kid?"

And now I knew where Bailey had gotten her tact.

"About a couple dozen different fists," Bailey answered for me. "Over the course of a week. We'll tell you all about it over supper."

Oh, so she *was* planning on tell him the truth, then? That was relieving to learn, and yet still concerning. What if he didn't believe her defense of me? What if he didn't find me innocent? What if—

"What's for supper, anyway? I'm starving."

"Chili," her dad answered her as he continued to suspiciously eye me up and down. "We can settle him into Blaine's room, I suppose. I *did* have a mattress laid on the floor of yours, but that was before I knew *she* was a *he*."

Bailey merely shrugged. "Whatever. As long as he has a place to sleep, he'll be fine." Then she crinkled her nose. "But where's Blaine? Is he not going to be home for Thanksgiving?"

"Nope." Her dad turned away and picked up both her bag and mine before trudging up the stairs and leaving us to follow. I almost wanted to fling my hands in the air over the hopelessness of it and then shout that I was fully capable of carrying my own damn bag. "He's gone to spend the holiday with his girlfriend at her family's place up in Plainville."

"Wait." Bailey jerked to a stop so fast in front of me I nearly ran into her. "Blaine has a girlfriend?"

"Yep." Her dad sounded placid about it. "It's pretty serious too. He's planning on moving in with her this weekend."

"Holy fucking shit," Bailey breathed.

Her father kept his same monotone voice and steady pace as he repeated, "Yep. And watch your language, little lady."

Bailey glanced back at me, her eyes widening over this new development with her brother, but then she turned back and hurried after her dad. "Is she nice? She's not a bitch, is she? You know, there's room for only one bitchy chick in this family, and that's me."

"She seems sweet enough," he answered on a shrug. "And don't call yourself bitchy. You're high-spirited, impulsive and bluntly honest, but not bitchy."

Bailey gave her own shrug as if it were all the same difference to her.

Her dad dropped her bag off first, and I barely got a peek into her childhood bedroom before they were moving on to the next door down the hall. I followed everyone into what I guessed was Blaine's room—the walls covered with cowboy motif and swimsuit-model posters—just in time to catch sight of her dad setting my luggage onto an unmade bed.

"Sheets were washed last week so they're somewhat clean," he informed me.

I nodded, and murmured, "Thank you, sir. I appreciate it."

I wanted to apologize for surprising him with my maleness, but then…there were more surprises in store for him about me, and those would probably require much more groveling than a mere gender misunderstanding. I might need to store up all my sorrys for then.

My voice seemed to startle him. It made me realize this was the first time I'd actually spoken since meeting him.

He nodded before his gaze wandered curiously over the bruises on my face. "I didn't catch your name, son."

"Oh! Sorry. I'm Beck." I held out my hand to him without thinking, but a split second before he took my fingers, I remembered I still had traces of Humphrey's doggy drool all over my palm. I was about to retreat when Bailey's dad shook with me.

"Ben Prescott," he greeted. "Welcome to our home."

I wasn't too sure if he'd share that sentiment when he learned who I really was. More guilt piled onto my shoulders. Here I was, invading his home under a layer of deceit and I'd just shook his hand with dirty fingers. Feeling like a complete shit stain, I glanced uneasily toward Bailey.

She seemed blissfully unaware of my dilemma. "So, the chili's ready to eat now, right?" she pressed, rubbing her stomach. "Because I'm starving."

Her dad laughed and ruffled her hair. "Yeah, soup's on as soon as you're ready. I'll let you two wash off your travel dust, and we'll meet you in the kitchen. I like the new hair, by the way. It's a hell of a lot better than that peacock look you had before."

As he started away, she scowled after him. "It was a rainbow, not a peacock, and I liked the rainbow."

"Then why didn't you keep it?" he shot back.

She didn't answer, only frowned as we listened to footsteps on the stairs.

Once I was sure he was out of earshot, I pinned her with a stare and hissed, "You didn't tell him who I was."

She only grinned back at me, a grin that shot through my bloodstream and make me ache with the need to kiss her. "Relax, Hilliard." She bucked my arm. "And just trust me, will you? I've got this."

Then she reached up and patted my cheek. The sensation of her soft fingers against my skin must've dulled my head, because I settled immediately and forgot to keep arguing.

Her words hadn't quelled the worry in me, but her smile did remind me of one thing. I did trust her, more than anyone else in the world. Maybe she really did have this.

Chapter 27
BAILEY

"Oh, God, this is so good." My eyes nearly rolled up into my head as I moaned.

But seriously, no one made chili like my dad. Perfect amount of spice, and meat, and beans. He was a master. Setting my hand over my stomach, I sat back in my chair and grinned at Beck who was sitting across from me, taking his first spoonful. When his eyebrows lifted as if surprised—pleasantly surprised—by the flavor, I grinned. He began to smile back when Booth, sitting next to him, glanced between us.

"Thought you said he wasn't your boyfriend."

"Booth," Dad said in a warning voice.

"What?" My brother shrugged, looking confused. "It was an honest question. I mean, they were sitting there, making babies with their eyes like they—ouch!" He glared at me as the toe of my shoe made direct contact with his shin under the table.

"We're *not* dating," I bit out.

"Okay, geez," he mumbled before sniffing a scowl toward Beck as if his sore leg was all Beck's fault. "It was just a question."

"A stupid question," I mumbled, only for Dad to censor me with a measured look.

I was tempted to kick Booth again. It just wasn't fair that out of all four of my brothers, *he* was the only one around tonight. I knew Brock and Braiden didn't live here anymore and Blaine was apparently moving out, but why did it have to be the most annoying brother to stay behind?

"Who the heck is this girl Blaine's dating, anyway?" I demanded, probably startling the three males at the table with what seemed to them like an out-of-the-blue thought.

"Some girl from Plainville," Dad explained. "Name's Melody. Like I said, she's a pleasant girl. Pretty, too."

"Way too hot for an asshat like Blaine," Booth agreed.

I began to nod and ask how they'd met when I noticed Beck's sudden paleness. I blinked, wondering what was wrong, until it struck me.

Melody.

Oh, shit. No. Please, no.

My eyes grew wide as I turned abruptly to my dad. "Did you say Melody? Melody *what*?"

"Uh…" He glanced toward the ceiling. "McDaniel maybe? Or possibly McDonald. Something like that."

"McDougal," Booth supplied dryly.

I glanced between the two. "Are you sure?" I demanded. Were they positive it wasn't actually *Fairfield?* "Her last name's McDougal? It's *definitely* McDougal?"

"Yeah." Booth glanced at me as if I'd lost my mind. "It's McDougal. Why?"

He turned questionably to Beck at the same moment I did. Beck's shoulders released tension and slowly fell as relief stole through him. I could practically feel the air return to his lungs. His gaze met mine, and I knew we shared the same thought.

Thank God, it was a different Melody.

"No reason," I answered, taking a huge, deliberate taste of chili. "So, how'd they meet?"

"She was visiting one of her cousins around here and met up with Blaine at the bar, I believe," Dad answered. "It's too bad she doesn't live any closer. If they'd at least stayed around the area and not gone all the way off to Plainville, Blaine could've at least continued to work for me. Now I'm going to have to find a new hand to hire."

My back straightened. "Hire a new hand?"

He gave a worn-out sigh as he nodded. "I'm going to have a hell of a time, too. Not a lot of people have farming experience these days."

"Hire Beck!" I blurted without thinking my words through. I just knew he needed work and my dad needed a new employee. It made perfect sense in my head.

But the other three people at the table gaped at me as if I'd lost my mind.

I flushed, hoping Beck wouldn't care that I'd spoken for him. But he *needed* this. And I knew my dad would be a good, decent boss, who'd probably give him room and board too.

"He was a frat boy, sure," I started on his behalf, growing more excited about the idea the longer I thought it through. "But he grew up on a farm. I'm sure he'd catch on quick."

I met Beck's gaze across the table and nodded encouragingly. He merely blinked back. I swallowed, saying nothing as he darted a glance between me and my dad.

"But I thought…" My dad shifted his gaze from Beck to me. "Well, I guess I made another assumption that you and Beck went to school together. Doesn't he have to return to Granton for classes?" His eyebrows drew together suspiciously. "How exactly *do* you two know each other if you didn't meet at college?"

"Oh, we met at Granton," I assured, nodding quickly, while inside I cringed. I hadn't planned on telling Dad Beck's story until later this evening, after supper was full and warm in his belly and he's stretched out comfortably in his lazy boy. "Beck was a…junior?"

When I turned beseechingly to Beckett, he quickly supplied, "Senior. I was in the middle of my second to last semester there."

"But you're not attending anymore?" Dad asked slowly.

"Um, no," Beck flushed, meeting my gaze before turning back to my dad. "Due to, uh, unforeseen circumstances beyond my control, I won't be returning to Granton University again."

That answer only made my dad blink as he obviously grew more confused. "What was your major?"

"I was working toward an environmental science degree, specializing in land management," Beck rattled off.

It took me a moment for that to sink in. When it did, I swerved a gasp his way. "Wait. That's an agricultural degree."

Beck nodded slowly. "It is."

"But…" I shook my head, lost. "But you were in a *fraternity*." This made no sense.

Beckett broke out into a grin, looking amused. "Yeah, the Alpha Gamma Rho fraternity."

"Holy hell, were you really?" My dad seemed suddenly impressed. "I was in AGR when I went to college."

My mouth not-so-literally dropped to the floor. "*You* were in a fraternity?"

My own father? I couldn't believe it.

"You went to college?" Booth exclaimed, just as surprised.

Everyone ignored Booth, and Dad nodded to me. "I was. AGR is an agricultural-based fraternity, you know."

No, I hadn't known that at all.

Shock.

"But…But…" I whirled back accusingly to Beckett. "You never told me you were a real, true-blooded *country* boy."

He shrugged as if confused by my shock. "You never asked."

"But…but…"

Amusement began to glimmer in his eyes. "And my student employment was at the university barn where I fed, waterered, and groomed livestock and horses."

"But…"

That would make him almost a…*cowboy*.

"But…"

"Dear God, how many times is she going to say *but*?" Booth wondered, rolling his eyes and groaning dramatically. He sounded five instead of twenty-five.

I kicked him under the table before I pointed accusingly at Beckett. "You were wearing a freaking polo shirt, slacks and pansy-ass *loafers* the night I met you."

"Well, yeah," Beckett shrugged. "I'd just returned from a live-stock judging contest. We were supposed to dress semi-formal."

I just stared at him, wondering who the hell this guy *was*.

He gave a not-so-humble shrug and grinned. "I won runner-up in the contest, if you were curious."

"I'm confused," Dad broke in. "You only had a semester and a half of school left, you were in a decent fraternity, apparently active since you were attending judging contests and working at the university barn, yet you dropped out?"

Beck cleared his throat and shifted in his chair, but he had the courage to meet my dad's gaze—his face blushing and tense—when he answered, "I wouldn't say I dropped out as much as I was, well, *thrown* out."

The last two words tumbled from his lips timidly, and they left a silence in the kitchen that even I couldn't come up with some random phrase to blurt out in order to cloak all the awkward.

Beck's worried gaze sought me, and I knew I couldn't remain quiet any longer.

I turned to my dad, but he was already saying, "I don't understand. You were *expelled*?"

With a cringe, I answered, "Well, I was going to talk to you about that. *Later*."

Brow puckering with confusion, Dad glanced between the two of us before settling his gaze on me. "Talk to me about it *now*."

"Well." I cleared my throat and looked at Beck as I said, "Beckett's had a hard week, so I've been helping him out a little, I guess."

"What kind of week?" my dad demanded, no longer so receptive to Beck's presence, as Booth blurted, "Beckett? I thought we've been calling him Beck."

I ground my teeth. "I told you his name *outside*, moron, and besides, Beck is *short* for Beckett."

"But isn't Beckett the name of that rapist you had at your college?"

Dad froze with his gaze on Booth before flipping me an incredulous glance. I could only scowl at my brother, unable to meet my father's stare. "How the hell do you remember that?" I demanded. "You never remember *anything*!"

Booth could only shrug. "Because I remember thinking Beckett sounded a lot like *bucket*."

Beck made a sound that sounded like a mix between a choke, a groan, and a laugh. I couldn't tell if he was amused, horrified, or nervous, but I had a feeling it was a strange mixture of all three.

"Bailey Rae Prescott," my dad thundered, pointing Beck's way as he glared at me. "Please, God, tell me this is *not* the same boy who's been plastered all over the news. You did not let a rapist into my home."

"Of course I didn't," I answered immediately, while Beck silently set his spoon down and then took his hands off the table, placing them into his lap as if he were already preparing to leave as soon as he was ordered to go.

Right. As if I'd let my dad kick him out.

"He's innocent," I said simply. "He didn't rape anyone."

"And how the hell would you know that?" My dad looked disappointed and enraged all at the same time as he rose to his feet and rested his fisted hand on top of the table to glare at me. "How could you *possibly* know what he did to that girl? The news said he was released and the charges were dropped, but no one ever mentioned he was *proven* innocent. They probably just had a lack of evidence to try him. He probably had some lawyer find some technicality—"

"No," I muttered from between clenched teeth. "They *didn't* have a lack of evidence. They finally *got* some evidence. From *me*." I poked a finger into my own chest. "That's why they let him go free, because *I* was the witness who came forward and finally got him free, because he's completely *innocent*."

"Witness," Booth repeated before he let out a snort. "What, did you *watch* him screw the chick, or something?"

I flushed and couldn't help but glance at Beck. He was blushing just as red as it felt like I must be.

"Jesus Christ," my dad muttered before running a hand through his hair and pinning a glare on Beck. He sank back unsteadily into his chair. "Son, don't tell me you had sex with some girl in front of my daughter."

Beck shrank under the penetrating stare before he admitted, "I didn't know she was there."

"I got stuck in a bathroom," I was quick to explain. "And when I tried to leave, he was in the room, and they were…you know."

Booth barked out a laugh and clutched his stomach. "Oh my God, this is classic. My sister's a peeping tom. I bet he's happy you were a freaking voyeur now, though, huh?"

I glared at him. "It's not funny. Do you know how embarrassing it was to be stuck in there, listening and seeing all that, and how much worse it was when I had to go to the freaking police to have to explain it *them*?"

"Why didn't you tell me you were mixed up in tall this?" my dad demanded, looking hurt, disappointed, upset, and mad all rolled up into one.

My shoulders fell.

"You should've told me," he lectured. "And you definitely should've told me before you brought this kid home with you, before I invited him into my house to sleep in my son's bed, before he sat down at my dinner table."

"I can go," Beckett said quietly, already rising to his feet.

But I jumped to my feet as well, lifting my arm to stop him. "No." When he stopped and pierced with a hard look, I turned to my dad. "He had nowhere else to go. His family turned him out. His friends, even the university. They all turned their backs on him. He has nothing, literally nothing but a truck and a handful of clothes. I didn't tell you before we got here because if you hadn't let him come with me then I wouldn't have come either. And I just..." When my voice broke, I shook my head, cleared my throat and started over. "I wanted to see you for Thanksgiving." I cleared my throat again and straightened my shoulders. "But if you want him gone, then I'm going too. We can go right now."

I glanced at Beck, pretty much silently telling him we were leaving, but my dad boomed, "No one is leaving. Certainly not my only daughter. Now sit down." He cast Beck a nasty glare. "Both of you, *sit*."

Beck and I dropped immediately into our seats because my dad could be pretty freaking intimidating when he wanted to be.

"Now, dammit, I'm not sure why you were so worried I wouldn't believe you. You're my daughter, for Christ's sake; I was the first person to change your shitty diaper. I think I would know if you're a liar or not, and you're not. If you say he's innocent because you saw what happened, then I believe you."

My shoulders released all the tension they'd been holding. I'm not sure why I'd been so worried about my dad's faith in me. I should've known he'd come through. Maybe after seeing the way Beckett's mom had treated him had left me unsure. No idea, but I'm glad I was wrong. I'm glad my daddy believed me.

I kind of wanted to hug him now, even though we weren't the huggy type.

"But I still have questions," Dad said, scowling at both Beck and me.

"Of course." Beck answered immediately with a nod.

"This *friendship* between you two..." My father waggled his finger between the two of us. "Were the police aware you two knew each other and were friends? Why didn't that hamper the credibility of your story?"

"Oh." I wasn't expecting that kind of question. Glancing at Beck, I answered, "Well, we *weren't* friends at the time. I mean, I didn't even know him when it happened. He would've been a complete stranger to me except I bumped into him in the hall literally two minutes between everything happened."

"Then how did you become *friends*?" Booth was the one to ask.

Beckett and I shared another look. Silently, we decided to let him take this one. "When they released me, I sought Bailey out to thank her for helping me. She was the only person who believed me, the only person to save me. I didn't..." He shook his head, and this haunted expression entered his eyes. "She gave me a place to stay, and—"

"She *what*?" Dad lifted his hand to stop us before he swung his incredulous gaze my way. "Do the police know you've been letting him stay on your *couch*?"

I cringed, hoping he never learned it wasn't exactly my couch Beck had been sleeping on. "No," I answered in a small voice. "But what does it matter? They dropped all the charges, and he was completely free before I ever talked to him again."

"Hell, Bailey." My dad shook his head, clearly frustrated. "Honesty in the eyes of the law is a pretty damn important thing. If they have any reason at all to think you might've committed perjury and lied for him, your reputation could be *destroyed*."

"Dad." I clenched my teeth. "You're being ridiculous. There is nothing—"

"Bailey," Beckett said quietly, making me stop talking immediately. He lifted a calming hand and gave me a respectful nod before saying, "He's not being ridiculous. And he's right when he says a destroyed reputation would be one of the worst things that could happen to you." With a small laugh, he nodded, "I can definitely attest to that. But, Mr. Prescott..." He turned back to my dad. "You can trust me when I say no one in going to go after her for perjury. Her word wasn't the only thing that got me free. There was other evidence..." He glanced at me, and I knew we were both thinking about the video. "...that helped free me. So she's okay there. But you're also right that it isn't safe for her to continue harboring me. If any student or someone from my fraternity learned she took me in, they could begin a rumor that we knew each other beforehand, and everyone else might believe she lied. Her reputation *could* be destroyed in that way, so I *know* I can't keep staying there."

"Except he has nowhere else to go, Dad," I implored. "He's out of money, and every place he goes looking for work refuses to hire him. If I stopped harboring him, he'd literally have to live out of his truck, and he'd probably starve by the end of the week."

My dad scowled at both of us before he scrubbed both hands over his face, hissed a curse, and then dropped his arms to slap them heavily against the tabletop. "Well, I guess that settles it then. There's only one thing we can do about this situation." I glanced Beck's way, wondering what my dad thought he hand planned. When Beck glanced back, he shared our worry with a single stare, as my father announced, "When you go back to school tomorrow, Bailey, Beckett will just have to stay here and work for me."

Chapter 28
BECKETT

I could strangle her. I could literally wrap my hands around her throat and then…hell, but then I'd probably kiss the devil out of her if I ever put my hands on her again, which seemed like something that might never happen, because she'd fucking set it up so I wouldn't see her anymore after tomorrow.

I might not touch her, smell her, sleep besides her—fuck—*speak* to her again. Unable to bare that idea, I inched opened the door to her brother's room that I was supposed to be sleeping in, and I peered out into the dark hallway.

Her dad had put a lot of faith in me to let me stay here and sleep under his roof after the rape-story we'd told him. Dishonoring his trust by sneaking into his daughter's room sounded like the worst thing I could do in return. But I had to talk to her.

With the next day being Thanksgiving and more family coming in, then her leaving in the afternoon, I wasn't sure when a chance to get her alone would ever come around.

I held my breath, praying to God there were no creaking floorboards in front of the doorway as I took my first cautious step into the hall. When nothing groaned underfoot, I released a silent puff of air and took the next achingly slow step. The door to her room was ten feet away and closed. It might be locked. I wouldn't know until I made it there, but one thing I did know with all certainly, I was going to see her before the night was over. I didn't care how I made it, as long as I did.

Ten feet later, I reached for her door handle. She hadn't locked me out, thank God. My heart pumped loudly through my ears as I eased inside. When I heard the bedsprings shift as I closed the door behind me, telling me she was probably still awake, I swallowed and hurried forward, no longer so worried about how much sound my feet made as they shuffled across the floor.

Her bed was closer than I thought it would be, though, and my shin met up with the frame, jostling her entire bed an inch or so across the floor and making it screech loudly.

A strangled laugh came from the mattress. "I sure hope you're not trying to be stealthy and quiet, Bucket, because you suck at it."

Smart-ass. I grinned and I yanked up the sheet before crawling in beside her and hissing, "Shh."

She snickered.

Joy bloomed inside me, like it always did when I was with her. Instantly comforted because my curly-headed smartass was within touching distance again, I sighed out my relief, my restless nerves already settling just knowing she was near before I realized I was on my side, and she'd already been lying on hers. She hadn't been hogging the middle of the bed. For some reason, that caused my chest to constrict and remind me all over again why I really wanted to strangle her.

We'd never sleep next to each other again.

"So, you're leaving tomorrow," I whispered, laying back on my spine to stare up at her dark ceiling, feeling the doom of that fact press heavily down on my heart.

A breath passed, then she quietly answered, "Yep."

"And I'm staying here," I added. I bit my lip, trying to wrap my mind around that fact.

She had separated us. In another twenty-four hours, we'd live nearly two hours apart from each other. How could she do that? How could she tear the one person I needed most right now away from me?

Even if she did think it was for my own good, and in return, I *knew* it would be best for her too if I was out of her apartment.

How could she fucking kill me like this? My nerves began to twitch and my breathing picked up just thinking about it.

I blew out a long, steadying breath, tempted to reach out, and just touch her hair. Anything. My hands began to shake. "So how're we going to do this?"

"What do you mean?" she asked.

I clenched my teeth, my desperation and frustration mounting. "You know what I mean, Bailey. I can't fucking fall asleep if you're not right there in bed with me. How the hell am I going to sleep here without you? And what if I have another panic attack/nervous breakdown thing? Who's going to help me get past that? And… shit…" I sucked in a strange sound.

The one thing I absolutely had not wanted to happen, had fucking happened. I'd become dependent upon her.

"I can't breathe," I wheezed.

How was I going to breathe without Bailey?

She rolled toward me until I realized she was sitting up and hovering over me. My chest constricted and the panic mounted right before she cupped my face in her hands, paralyzing my oxygen even more because this was probably the last time she'd ever touch me.

"Yes, you can too breathe," she demanded determinedly. "Now *inhale*."

I tried, but it didn't feel as if anything entered my lungs. I couldn't lose her; didn't she realize that? What the hell had my life become that I needed her so much?

What's worse, I wasn't sure which notion freaked me out more: realizing how much she meant to me, or realizing I was losing her.

She waited a beat, and then ordered, "Okay, then. Try *exhaling*."

But I couldn't. There was nothing to breathe out. Just like, after tomorrow, there would be no Bailey in my life. I swung my head back and forth, gasping for air, my chest collapsing.

"Beckett," she whispered sternly. She sounded panicked and concerned. I wanted to tell her I was okay. Except I wasn't.

I clamped my fingers around her wrists where she was still cupping my face, wanting to hold onto her if this was it…if I was dying.

She shook my cheeks. "Dammit, Beck. I said *breathe*."

I floundered. I couldn't do it. I had no idea what was wrong, but it felt as if there was no air anywhere. She was leaving, and my life was over.

Hissing a curse, Bailey leaned down and pressed her mouth to mine. It was hard to tell if she was attempting to preform CPR, or what, but she didn't blow into my mouth; she just…she kissed me.

Holy shit. Her soft, pillowy, sweet lips flattened against mine, and my nostrils flared before my lungs opened, and I inhaled. Deeply.

I drew her essence into me, parting my lips and moving my fingers from her wrists so I could bury them in the satiny softness of her hair. Urging her chin up, I aligned our faces in order to taste her fully.

My mouth slanted, our tongues touched, and my body pinged with need, shooting little electrical currents out every nerve ending.

Her mint toothpaste and flowery lotion flooded my senses. I wanted more. So I rolled her onto her back and climbed on top of her, fitting myself between her thighs before I kissed her again, spiking my tongue deep and fisting her hair in my hands as I thrust my hips hard against that sweet nook between her legs.

"Oh, my God," she gasped, arching her head back so she could suck in air as she wound her legs around my waist and ground her core tighter against the straining erection in my pants.

She was so warm there; I wanted in. The need in me was strong, and I took greedily, racing my hands over her, urgent to feel every soft curve as I bit and licked my way down her throat.

She was receptive to me. So receptive. The heels of her feet dug into the top of my ass as her fingernails gouged through my shirt and bit straight into the backs of my shoulders. I latched my teeth around her collarbone and clutched her bottom, tilting her up as I rubbed myself back and forth against her, mimicking the act of entering her.

She whimpered hungry sounds that came straight from her throat, urging me on. I found the hem of her nightshirt and smoothed my hand up her thigh until I reached the back part of her panties. Her breasts pushed against my chest and her shallow pants drifted across in my ear right before she bit the lobe, making me groan. My fingers slipped inside her underwear.

She was wet. Holy shit, she was so warm and wet, and my fingers already knew how easily they could thrust inside her.

Except she jerked under me, going rigid and pressing her hands against my chest. "No. Wait."

Her rejection was so profound I almost wept. Frozen on top of her, I didn't immediately move. It took me a second to comply, my digits right there at her entrance, so close to sliding into Heaven.

"Beckett," she whispered, still applying pressure to my chest. "Stop."

I hung my head, blowing out a steadying breath, then I rolled off her to lie flat on my back, needing to cool off before I could even process thought again.

Her breathing was still labored, she was definitely still as turned on as I was. I wanted to roll back to her and try to coax more from her. I knew I could do it. I knew I could tempt her into continuing. I could make her scream and beg for more, for all of it. But I gulped and fisted my hands at my sides. My body howled in denial, unable to accept the fact it wasn't going to get what it wanted.

I realized I'd never stopped when I'd been this turned on before.

Hell, I'd never been this turned on before.

"This was wrong," Bailey finally said, turning her face my way. "It was all wrong."

I had no idea what to say to that. I wanted to argue; it had felt pretty damn right to me. It'd felt more right than anything with any girl I'd ever kissed before. How could she fucking say it was wrong? How could she not feel what I'd been feeling?

That was the biggest blow to take, realizing she hadn't felt it too.

But if she hadn't, then she hadn't, and it killed me to respect her wishes.

I blew out a breath, ignoring the buzzing of need still roaring through me. I said nothing, just rolled out of bed, and started for the door. I couldn't even apologize for kissing her, because I wasn't fucking sorry. That'd been the best kiss of my life.

She said my name, but I kept going until I reached the door. Once there, I paused and pressed my forehead and one hand against the wood, not wanting to leave with her thinking I was mad or disappointed, not wanting our last night together to end with this kind of discord.

My chest constricted, because I wasn't sure what to do, what to say.

"I'm sorry," she was the one to whisper.

I'm honestly not sure what hurt more: that I couldn't say those words myself, or that she did.

"It's fine," I answered, petting the door gently as if it were her, and I was comforting her, letting her know I couldn't hate her, no matter how much she didn't want me. Then I turned the handle and slipped out into the hall.

I'm not exactly sure what I'd hoped to accomplish when I'd snuck into her room—I'd just known I needed to tie loose ends and make sure things were still okay between us—but now I was certain that things were worse between us than they'd ever been.

I'd just fucked up royally. I'd just ostracized the only person who believed in me.

Chapter 29
BECKETT

The first Thanksgiving for me to spend away from my family was different, and yet achingly familiar.

After I returned to my borrowed room, I didn't sleep well—if at all. I tossed and turned, reliving the kiss with Bailey in my head, knowing she was still just down the hall, even though she now felt hundreds of miles of away, and she'd only move farther away by the end of the day. If worrying about how I'd just ruined our friendship hadn't kept me up all night, then her absence would have, because it really was true: I couldn't sleep without her next to me. Everything just felt wrong.

My body was stiff and sore as I changed into the clothes I was going to wear for the day. And lately, I *knew* sore. With the amount of bruised flesh, torn muscle, and battered bones I was carrying around, I knew sore on an intimate level. But the kind of sore I shouldered this morning was different, it went deeper and punched harder as if it had pierced my very soul.

Bailey was the reason. Not that I blamed her for my misery; it was more like an awareness that she'd kept this kind of ache at bay before, but now that she wouldn't be around any longer, it crept in boldly, attacking me at my most vulnerable points. It was as if the essence of me was tender and aching.

Which sounded like crazy bullshit. So I was never going to repeat that thought again.

Honestly, I didn't know how I'd make it through without her anywhere on the farm. And worse, I wasn't sure what to expect when I saw her today. Did she blame me for the kiss? Had it ruined our relationship? Would she even be able to look me in the eye now? Where did things stand between us?

Hell, maybe I *should've* apologized last night. Anything would be better than losing her completely.

My heart raced with anxiety as I opened my door and peered into the hall. The corridor was empty. A shaft of early morning sunlight flared through a window at the end of the hall and spread across the floor, pointing a diagonal path to the start of the staircase. I blew out a breath and left the room, glancing pitifully at Bailey's closed door as I passed, following the light to the stairs.

On the first floor, the smell of bacon drew me to the kitchen where Ben and Booth were up and active, Bailey's dad at the stove and her brother pulling a jug of milk from the refrigerator. I paused in the entrance, not sure what to do.

When Ben glanced over and noticed me hovering, he greeted me with a smile I'm pretty sure I didn't deserve, especially if he knew where my hands had been on his daughter a mere six hours before. "Hey, look who's up. Are you hungry, Beckett?"

"I could eat," he said, stepping forward, pressing my hands together and ready to get them busy. "What do you need me to do?"

With a grin, Bailey's dad turned to face me fully, pointing his specula at me, bacon grease dripping from it and everything. "Now, that's what I like to hear, someone willing to wade in and help out." Two pieces of toast popped up from the toaster, so he pointed his drippy spatula that way. "Get to buttering."

"Yes, sir."

I did eagerly, and Ben asked me about my potato-peeling abilities as I opened the butter tub.

"Any experience?" he wondered.

With a nod, I said, "Actually, yes. My mom put me to work peeling potatoes almost every holiday."

The first wave of nostalgia and homesickness hit then. I couldn't help but wonder who Mom had assigned to potato-peeling duty for today. From the sound of it, Britt wasn't likely in any condition to chip in. Maybe Dad had helped her. Or maybe they hadn't even felt the need to prepare a big, full Thanksgiving meal at all. Maybe with money so bad, their spirits down, and a fourth of the family—me—gone, they hadn't bothered. They could be sitting around the living room with TV dinners on trays as they watched the Macy's Parade for all I knew.

I hoped that wasn't the case. I hope they'd carried on tradition without me, that money was better, that Britt was better. I hoped they were okay.

The urge to call them rose. I wanted to check in, make sure things hadn't gotten worse. But I shook my head and finished buttering toast for Bailey's family. If my relatives wanted me bothering them, they'd call me. I'd stay out of their business.

"That'll be your first duty as my new employee then," Ben said, jerking my attention back to the present. "You can start peeling potatoes for dinner after we're done with breakfast."

I nodded, ready to earn my keep. "No problem. I'd be happy to."

Bailey showed up just before we ate, stumbling into the room still in her nightshirt and yawning, and completely getting out of cooking duty, a fact her brother decided meant she should take over clean-up then.

She smacked him on the back of the head as she passed behind his chair. He called her a brat, but she was too busy punching me lightly in the side of the arm and moving to the counters to fetch her own breakfast to immediately react.

Finally, she flipped him off with a grumbled protest before pausing at the sidebar where extra breakfast was warming.

"How're you doing, Beck?" she finally addressed me once her back was to me and she was busy piling scrambled eggs onto a plate. "Your bruises don't look so bright this morning."

I studied her, silently willing her to look at me so I could gauge her mood, but she refused to glance over.

I murmured, "I'm fine," as I turned morosely back to the table, only to find her dad watching me curiously.

I internally cringed, wondering if I looked like a lost puppy being abandoned by its beloved owner, because that's pretty much how I felt. Quickly, I lowered my attention to my plate. It took Bailey sitting in the chair across the table from me to get me to look up again.

She didn't seem changed or affected at all. But what did that mean? Was she so disgusted or humiliated she wanted to pretend it had never happened? Had seeing me have sex with Melody and then me turning to her barely two weeks later turned her off? Except, no, that wasn't her style. She was too open not to blurt-out what she thought about things. So that had to mean it just hadn't affected her at all. She'd helped stupid Beck get over a panic attack and then she'd nudged him back into his place when he'd taken it too far. The issue was probably completely over for her and out of her mind.

But that made my chest ache, because it wasn't over for me. It wasn't out of my mind. I'd kissed her, and I'd liked it. I wanted to kiss her again. A lot. Except she'd already forgotten about it and moved on.

That made me disjointed and quiet throughout breakfast, trying to orient myself to this new reality, this new environment. Bailey, Ben, and Booth were all so relaxed and at home—probably because they *were* home—it made me feel like the outsider I was. I kind of wanted to leave, except there was nowhere else to go, and Bailey was here.

This was the "different" portion of my day.

With a sigh, I powered through all the differences. Breakfast passed, and we were all assigned tasks to do, keeping us busy. Ben had Bailey whip together a cranberry salad that had nuts and whipped topping in it, while Booth helped me with the potatoes. Time passed quickly with everyone working and Booth occasionally tossing a potato peeling at Bailey, or Bailey beaning him back with pecan shrapnel. More of her brothers arrived, the oldest—Brock—baring pies that everyone gathered around, offering to taste-test, and the other brother Braiden with a pregnant wife.

Things grew louder, I was introduced as the new "Blaine" since I'd be taking over his duties on the farm, not as Bailey's friend, and every time I'd tried to back away to the fringes of the conversation and just observe, someone else would pull me back in with a question or comment I'd be forced to answer.

The Prescott family was loud and boisterous and reminded me a lot of Bailey in that they usually just blurted out whatever was on their mind, be it PC or not. That part made me smile and stay drawn in, because they were all just so…Bailey.

When we ate, the food was so familiar to everything my family had on Thanksgiving that I once again wondered how they were doing.

Bailey nudged my elbow when I'd spaced out too long. "Everything taste okay?"

"Hmm?" I glanced up and forced a smile. "Yes. It's delicious. Just like at home."

The ache must've shown in my eyes because her expression turned sympathetic. Leaning in closer, she murmured, "I'm sure they're missing you too."

The fact that she understood what was wrong with me made me feel better, but I wasn't sure how to deal with thinking of my family missing me. I kind of wanted to be mad at them for turning their backs on me when I'd needed them most, and yet, I kept hoping my phone would ring.

It never did.

Instead, the Prescotts welcomed me as one of their own, and I began to grow more accustomed to them and *grateful* to them as the day wore on.

The brother with the pregnant wife left first, with her yawning and in need of a nap. Then the oldest brother wished us a happy Thanksgiving and took his pies away. Booth received a text and cleared out just when kitchen clean-up started.

So Bailey, and her dad, and I were the only three left to straighten the kitchen. After we did, we migrated to the living room and settled on the couch as the second half of a football game started on the television. Ben kicked up his Lazy Boy and promptly took a nap.

Bailey barely sat on the other end of the couch as me for five minutes before I caught her glancing at me from the corner of my eye. So I turned to meet her gaze. An entire lifetime of feelings passed between us in that one stare. Craving, sadness, affection, appreciation, confusion, comfort. Neither of us had to say anything. We knew this was goodbye.

Suddenly, she began to blink before she turned her face away and popped abruptly to her feet, announcing, "Well…" which woke her dad mid-snore. She heaved out a long breath and rubbed her stomach like any satisfied person might after eating a Thanksgiving feast. "I probably better get on the road, so I can make it back to Granton before dark."

Ben yawned and checked the time. "Leaving already?" Then he shook his head as a glimmer of melancholy crept over his face. "Seems like your trips home keep getting shorter every time."

She paused by his Lazy Boy to kiss the top of his balding head. "If I didn't have to work tomorrow, I would've stayed longer."

"Yeah, yeah." He swatted playfully at her leg after she straightened and moved away. "I know the real truth. Your old man's just cramping your style. Time to get back to that posh, big city college life."

Bailey laughed and shook her head. "You are such a dork. I'm gonna go grab my bag from my room. Be right back."

As she trotted off, starting up the stairs, I gazed after her, feeling frozen and forlorn. This was it. She was leaving. I wanted to rebel, and yet I knew that was ridiculous. She had to return to school. But it felt all wrong for her to leave like this. Things might be fine for her—she certainly hadn't acted as if anything were wrong between us—but they damn sure weren't fine for me.

"Huh," Ben spoke up thoughtfully from his chair. "Bailey's never kissed me goodbye before. Strange."

I glanced his way to find him tenderly prodding his forehead as if the impression of her lips there had left a tangible mark on his skin. I have no idea why that spurred me into action, but I sprang from the couch where I'd been forcing myself to stay put, and I hurried up the stairs after her.

She'd already retrieved her overnight bag and had the strap hooked over her shoulder. Now she was standing silently with her back to the door as she faced her room as if trying to remember something she was sure she was forgetting to take with her.

I wanted to say, *me*, you're forgetting me. I wanted to go back with her more than anything. But I knew that was selfish, and it'd be best for both of us if I stayed.

Hearing me, she turned, and her chest expanded as she drew in a deep breath. Finally, she appeared regretful about leaving me behind. It was like a balm to my heart. No idea why. I just felt better knowing this was as hard of a moment for her as it was for me.

Suddenly, I knew I could handle this, because I knew we were in it together.

I stepped forward. "Here." Reaching out, I took her bag before she could protest. "I'm carrying this down for you."

"Oh, you shouldn't." She reached after me as I turned away. "Your ribs."

"I'm carrying it down for you," I said with more force.

When she spoke again, saying my name, "Beck..." it was soft and uncertain, and it stopped me in my tracks.

I paused in the doorway and looked back at her. Indecision crossed her face. She wanted to say something. When her mouth opened, my pulse stalled, waiting anxiously for her words, hoping she'd say something about the kiss. About…any of it. About *us*.

But then her shoulders fell, like maybe she'd chickened out, and she ended up asking, "Are you sure you're okay with this? You staying here while I…?" She didn't finish the sentence, but she didn't have to.

I shook my head, ignoring the disappointment in me. "There's not really any other option, is there?"

"No, but I…I didn't really give you an opportunity to say yes or no. I just kind of made the decision for you."

"Because it was the right decision." I stepped closer to her and lowered my voice. "In a perfect world, yes, being separated from you is the last choice I'd make." My admission made her lips part with a silent gasp, so I kept talking before she could respond. "But our world is fucked up, and this is what's best for you. You'd be crucified if everyone found out you'd been harboring me. And besides, I need to learn how to be independent again." I had to stop relying on her. "This is what we both need."

Except I needed her more, I think.

I was just too afraid to admit it. It was easier to let her go than admit anything.

"So, let's get you on the road before it turns dark," I added, tipping my head toward the hallway as I stepped out of the room, encouraging her to follow me and pretty much forcing the conversation to end there, because I was also too afraid to hear what she might say in return.

I heard her sigh after me before her footsteps entered the hall and began to follow me.

Her dad met us at the front door and walked us out to her car, where I realized the rest of our farewell wouldn't be private. I had wasted the last moment I'd had with her alone, avoiding what I really wanted to say because I'd been too afraid to speak up.

And now…now her dad was asking her if she needed any money for gas or food as I opened her back door and set the single bag into her back seat.

"I'm good," Bailey answered, glancing at me as I rejoined them. But as soon as we made eye contact, she whirled back to her dad.

"Don't work him too hard until he's completely healed, okay? He won't admit it, but I'm fairly certain he has some cracked ribs." She glanced worriedly at me as if she might be reconsidering leaving me. But then she whirled back to her dad. "Sometimes he gets these mini panic attacks. They're not bad; someone just needs to remind him to breathe and coach him through them—"

"Don't worry, Bailey," Ben said, holding up a hand to stop her from worrying further. "I'll take good care of the kid and remember to feed and water him every day." With an indignant sniff, he muttered, "I raised you and four boys on my own, now didn't I? I got this."

Bailey began to nod, her shoulder relaxing. "I know. You're right, but…" Her gaze returned to me. "Oh! His truck. It's still sitting outside my apartment. And all his things…"

But her father was already nodding as if he'd thought of that. "Booth can drive him up sometime to fetch his belongings. Now, seriously, stop." He laid a hand on her shoulder, comfortingly. "I promise, we'll take care of your boy."

I don't know why it encouraged me that she didn't argue that I wasn't hers, but it did. Happy she was at least worried about me and even amused by how cute her concern was, I teased, "I'm standing right here, you know. You can talk to me about all this."

So she turned to me as if she might do just that, but instead of rolling her eyes at my joke or punching my arm, she gulped uneasily. This was the dreaded moment, the final goodbye. Pain pierced her gaze. "Promise me you'll get better. And I'm not just talking about the bruises and ribs. I want you better, Beck."

Her gray gaze bore into me, her hope and worry striking me straight in the heart.

"I promise," I whispered, feeling my own determination in those words so strongly I could taste them. I'd never meant anything I'd said more in my life.

I wasn't sure how I'd accomplish it, what hell I'd have to go through, what obstacles I'd have to overcome, but I was bound and determined to get better.

For her.

Unable to stop myself, I reached out and pulled her against my chest, hugging her. When her soft warmth smashed against me and she wrapped her arms around my waist in return, I buried my nose in her hair, inhaled her familiar fragrance, and squeezed my eyes closed, committing every feel, smell, and sound of her to memory before she slowly peeled herself away and smiled up at me.

"Drive safely," I said quietly, only to shake my head and grin as I wondered if that edict were even possible.

As if remembering the way I'd freaked out on the way here, she smiled back, sharing the inside joke. Then she tapped my arm, saying, "I will," and turned away to climb into her car. Her gaze met mine through the closed driver's side window as her engine started.

I waved before stuffing my hands into my pockets, and she waved back. Then she put the care into drive and rolled away from me. Leaving me. My heart gave a hard, yet slow painful clang in my chest as I watched the back of her car slowly disappear down the road.

Ben shifted next to me, watching her leave as well, before he turned to me, saying, "So, you're in love with my daughter, huh?"

I glanced at him, not answering. Answering didn't seem necessary, and admitting anything aloud would probably freak me out. So I just went back to watching Bailey's car become smaller and smaller as she left me, feeling more lost than ever, because holy shit, I did love her.

Chapter 30
BAILEY

Two weeks passed.

Classes resumed. Term projects came due. Work grew busy at the store as the shopping season bloomed. And time moved on.

Life should've returned to regular programing for me, too. I should've reverted to my usual self, annoyed and secretly jealous of my constantly necking roommates or complaining about my hardest professors to whoever would listen. But I wasn't. I wasn't annoyed, jealous, or disgruntled. I wasn't much of anything really.

I sorta just grew numb.

Despondent.

Frozen in time as life went on around me.

When Paige came to me, telling me how more rumors were spreading about me—how I was a liar who helped rapists—I just shrugged it off, too discouraged by the hopelessness of my reputation to even care anymore. When Melody Fairfield showed up in the boutique where I worked and called me an ugly name before stomping out as soon she realized I was the sales clerk, I simply watched her go without a single cutting farewell remark. So untypical of me. But seriously, I couldn't make myself care. None of it really mattered, because Beck wasn't here and—

"You miss him, don't you?"

I jerked my face up from my phone where I was rereading old texts from him.

He had started texting the day after I returned to Granton, saying his phone bill was coming due, but my dad had advanced him some money to pay it this month so he could keep talking to me.

We corresponded every day, but they were always mundane conversation, about how he'd met the three horses my family owned and how I had finals to study for. We didn't discuss whether he'd had any more panic attacks without me around or how bad my name was getting smeared across campus. And we certainly didn't mention the kiss.

I still couldn't believe I'd kissed him on Thanksgiving Eve. In my defense, the guy hadn't been able to *breathe.* And I'd panicked. When I'd suddenly remembered this show I'd watched where the girl had kissed the boy to distract him out of a panic attack, I'd tried it on a whim, and it had worked. I know, mind blown.

Except he'd kept kissing me back, and then touching me, before *touching* me. What was worse, I had kissed and touched him in return. And it'd been wonderful. So wonderful. I hadn't known kisses could be that consuming or make a person that ravenous. I had wanted more, I'd wanted it all. My body had sobbed when I'd pushed him away, but I'd needed to stop it.

We couldn't just keep kissing. I mean, he must've been confused, in the wrong frame of mind, *something.* I'm sure he hadn't meant it to go that far, because why would he? No one had ever wanted me that much. Not in that way. And I knew he wouldn't feel as if he could rightly stop.

All he'd ever talked about was how much he owed me, how he wanted to pay me back, how desperate he was to thank me properly for the way I'd helped him.

If he'd suspected I really wanted what he'd been giving me more than anything in the world, he would've felt obligated to continue, whether he'd been into it or not. I couldn't trust his intentions, so I'd shut it down.

I had expected him to apologize afterward, but he hadn't. It felt strange without someone saying sorry, so I had, except I'm not sure why, maybe for making him think he had to kiss me back. I don't know. I wasn't really that sorry, though. He'd made me feel wanted, and cherished, and desired in that kiss. He'd given me a gift I'd craved more than anything else in the world. I'd been honored and thankful. Not regretful.

I only wished he'd felt the same heat and desperation and closeness to me that I'd felt to him when our lips had been locked and fingers had gripped and bodies had strained. But there was no way I'd know now, because I'd pushed him away, and we hadn't discussed it again after that.

It'd been the hardest thing I'd ever done to enter the kitchen Thanksgiving morning and act as if nothing had changed between us when I saw him sitting at the table, heartbreakingly handsome and worriedly uncertain as he looked up at me. I knew what he'd been afraid of, that I'd kick him out or get him fired before he'd even started working for my dad. But I would never do that to him. So I had pretended things were exactly the same between us so he'd know we were still friends.

We *were* still friends. That was the rub. Somehow, in less than two weeks of knowing the guy, I had fallen for him. But I couldn't let him in on that fact because he was my friend. I needed to stop being selfish and thinking only of my loneliness and secret desires, and I needed to focus on what *he* needed, which certainly wasn't a girlfriend. Not during this phase of his life. He needed to rediscover himself and heal from the wreck Melody Fairfield had turned his world into.

But then he'd confessed that he didn't want to be separated from me right before I'd left, and it made my heart clang madly in my chest, wondering if maybe he had felt something more in our kiss, just as I had. Maybe it hadn't been an obligation for him, after all.

Except he'd followed the admission with practical logic of why we wouldn't work.

So, yeah, that was why I'd waited until I was in my car and five miles from my family's farm before I burst into tears and cried the rest of the way home. And I hadn't been the same since.

"You miss Beck," Tess repeated more quietly this time as she grounded me back to the present where we sat in class, paying no attention of the professor's droning voice and trying our best to ignore the two girls behind us who were currently whispering about my lying-for-rapists ways.

We were halfway through the fall semester's dead week. I only had three finals the next week to take before winter break would begin. Last year, I'd gone home for the entire break, but this year,

Vivian had given me more hours at the shop, so I wasn't yet sure when I'd make it back home to see him again, which made the ache spread.

I really did miss him.

But I quietly muttered, "You're crazy," to my best friend anyway.

Because it was crazy to miss him. I'd known the guy less than a month. And yes, maybe I'd invited him to sleep in my bed with me way too soon after meeting him, especially after seeing him get kinky with some other girl. And maybe I'd experienced moments of connection with him that made me feel closer to him than I ever had to anyone. And sure, maybe, I'd hugged him, and smiled at him, and been softer with him than I was with anyone else, but…

Shit, I forgot where I was going with all this.

Maybe I was the only crazy facet in this whole situation.

Tess leaned closer to me, lowering her voice. "It's okay to miss him, you know. You guys were…" She shrugged helplessly. "Close."

"Shh," I hissed, frowning. "I'm trying to pay attention to the lecture."

"There is no lecture. He's just reviewing everything we've already learned this semester."

Well if that was the case… "Then what the hell are we still doing here?" I slammed my book closed and pushed to my feet, gaining the attention of the rest of the class.

Tess gaped at me. The bitches behind us stopped gossiping. The teacher paused mid-speech to focus on me.

"Yes?" he asked.

"I just remembered," I told him, stuffing my textbook and notepad into my backpack before slinging it over my shoulder. "I don't want to be here." Then I glanced at Tess. "You coming?"

She silently mouthed my name, her face turning as red as her hair. I only shrugged, so she hurried to collect her things and follow me.

Of course, she didn't want to leave with me, but it would've been more embarrassing for her to stay behind, so she rushed after me as I strolled out of the room, waving farewell to the professor and thanking him for a stimulating semester.

Once we cleared the building, Tess slapped her hand to her chest, hurrying to keep pace with me. "I can't believe you just…why the heck did you *do* that?"

I answered honestly. "I'm not sure. I just couldn't be there any longer."

Tess's eyes filled with sympathy. "It'll get better. Soon, some other hot piece of gossip will distract everyone and they'll forget they ever called you all those evil names."

I only shrugged. "Whatever. It doesn't matter." Because it didn't.

"Well, something is definitely bothering you. You haven't been right since you came back from Thanksgiving…without Beckett."

I glanced at her warningly. Maybe it hadn't been such a good idea to drag her along with me when I'd left class.

"Did you two have a fight?" she pressed.

With a snort, I shook my head. My car was across campus, but I took a slight detour toward the food court because I knew this was Jonah's lunch hour. Tess didn't even notice. "Of course not."

"So this funk you're going through is about the fact you fell in love with him and can't admit it to yourself, then?"

"What?" I slammed to a halt and whirled to face her, unable to believe she'd actually said that to me.

"I don't…That is not…" But I couldn't outright deny her words. Settling for, "You're crazy," I whirled back to the food court and hurried my pace, needing to get rid of her before she really hit a nerve.

"You're in love with him," she insisted. "And you were probably so busy denying it to yourself you didn't give him a proper farewell, so everything feels even worse and miserable now. That pang of longing inside you only grows deeper and wider every day because there was no closure in your last goodbye. You feel as if you've deserted the one person who's come to mean the most to you in his biggest time of need, so you—"

Ugh. Nerve hit, dead center, bullseye.

"Oh, look!" I nearly cried, never so happy to see Tess's annoying boyfriend in all my life as he sat on a bench by himself, eating a sandwich and reading something on his phone. "There's Jonah."

Her attention successfully diverted, Tess snapped her face up. When she spotted him, her entire expression transformed, pleasure and excitement practically sparking from her pores.

"Abbott!" I called loudly and waved big to make sure I had his attention.

He lifted his face, and as soon as he spotted Tess, he pushed to his feet, starting our way.

"Well, it looks like you should keep him company on his lunch break," I announced, pausing so I could change directions. I began to back away from my best friend. "My boss has really been needing me to work overtime a lot lately, so I'm going to head in early." I waved my fingers in farewell. "Don't you two have too much fun between classes."

Indecision warred across her face as she realized I was retreating and her boyfriend was closing in. "Bailey," she growled from between clenched teeth. "We're not done with this conversation until you have a freaking epiphany."

"Oh, I did," I assured her, backing away even faster now. "I realized my bestie was certifiably insane."

She frowned. Before she could respond though, Jonah was there, sweeping her into his arms.

I turned away, relieved, and started off. But I didn't get far before Tess hollered after me. "You'll have to accept the truth one of these days, Bailey Rae."

"But not today," I muttered under my breath as I waved over my shoulder, letting her know I'd heard her.

My hands were shaking and breathing was erratic by the time I reached my car. I unlocked it and climbed inside. Then I just sat there, not starting the engine and trying to pull myself back together. I'm not even sure why I was freaking out.

I'd walked out in the middle of class—a first ever for me.

I'd probably pissed off my best friend and would never hear the end of it when she caught up with me again.

But neither of those felt like the source of my panic.

I slid my phone from my backpack and opened up my texts to Beck. We'd last talked this morning about my dad's mare they were talking about breeding.

Yeah, we'd talked about horse sex, and it'd felt like the most real conversation I'd had all day. I ran my thumb over the screen, touching his words.

Needing to talk to him now, I typed.

"My roommate is crazy," I wrote before pushing *Send*.

He read my message almost immediately, making my chest expand with this indescribable joy, because he always made time to reply to me as soon as I wrote to him. No matter the hour.

"Tess?" He knew exactly which friend I was referring to. I loved that. **"What'd she do?"**

Right, like I could tell him anything about her insane claims. **"She's just talking crazy talk."**

He sent a laughing emoji before replying, **"About me?"**

"Now why would you think that?" I wondered, blushing because he'd guessed it right.

"No idea, but my guess certainly has nothing to do with your evasion of my answer," he teased. The brat.

A second later, he wrote more. **"Must've been something bad about me. I don't think she likes me."**

My mouth dropped open, not sure how he'd ever come to that conclusion. I'd never seen Tess really dislike much of anyone one, unless they were super awful and deserved it. Curious but also incredulous by his assumption, I typed, **"Whatever. Tess likes everyone."**

"I'm not so sure about that. She's always jerked her attention away whenever we've made eye contact, and the few times she's ever talked to me she's burrowed into Jonah as if seeking safety away from me. Are you sure she really thinks I'm innocent of that thing with Melody?"

Realizing he'd totally misread the situation, I threw my head back and laughed. Hard. **"Oh. That. Don't worry. She freaks out and turns extra shy around guys she thinks are cute. Jonah and Logan seem to be the only two exceptions since she's gotten comfortable with them."**

It took him a minute to reply. And when he did, I rolled my eyes. **"So, wait? She thinks I'm hot?"**

Oh, geez, what had I just done? **"Don't let it go to your head, Romeo."**

Except he did. He totally did. **"This is awesome,"** he cheered. **"You know, she DOES blush a lot around me, so it makes sense now. Oh man, I am so flirting with her hard the next time I see her!"**

Jealously flared to life hard inside me. I did not like the idea of him flirting with anyone. I felt a little vindictive when I wrote, **"I'll make sure to put flowers on your grave then, because Jonah will kill you for flirting with the love of his life."**

He was quick to add, **"Innocent, harmless, fun flirting. Nothing serious. I just want to see how much I can make her blush."**

"That's evil," I charged.

"As if you wouldn't let it go to your head too. You'd totally give some guy an extra smile and a couple compliments if you knew your looks flustered him."

"Okay, maybe," I allowed. Not that anyone would ever find me so attractive they became flustered and timid in my presence. But that only meant I'd definitely egg it on more if it ever happened. **"Just don't make her cry, or anything,"** I decided. **"Tess is super sensitive."**

"Ouch, Prescott. That hurts. My compliments have never made any girl cry."

"Dear Lord. I never should've told you she thinks you're pretty. You're totally letting it go to your head."

"**Hey, I'm the soul the humility over here.**"

I laughed and accidently caught sight of the time, only to sit upright, cursing. I had gotten carried away and lost track of everything but Beckett. **"Shit. I just realized what time it is. Gotta go. Almost late to work."**

"**Okay**," he wrote back. "**Text me again when you get home. AND DRIVE SAFE.**"

I rolled my eyes, but couldn't help the smile that spread. The only good part of my day came when we talked. It washed around the monotony and depression and made the world vivid and alive again. I was growing to depend on our chats more than I should.

But it wasn't because I was in love with him. That was just crazy.

I pressed the phone to my chest, before I got my butt into gear and drove to work.

I was still floating on my Beck high when I arrived at the parking lot outside.

He'd sounded better today. I absolutely didn't worry about him self-harming himself anymore. And he didn't even seem so melancholy and hopeless. He'd become—I don't know—upbeat, maybe. I would've said flirtier, except he never flirted with me. But there was definitely a certain growth of confidence in the things he said, as if he really were getting over the blow to his character that Melody had inflicted on him.

And speaking of Melody Fairfield. The chick must be Beetlejuice or Bloody Mary, or someone, and I'd thought her name one too many times today, because she was the first person I saw when I stepped inside the boutique to clock in.

Oh, for the love of—wait. Was she crying? Was she crying and talking to *Vivian*?

Why was she crying and carrying on to *my* boss?

Both women turned my way as the bell tolled over my head, announcing my arrival.

Vivian's mouth turned down and her eyes filled with disappointment and rage when she saw me. Melody had the gall to smirk.

My stomach dropped as I slowed to a stop. The shop was fairly quiet. Only two other women were shopping, one by the shoes, the other checking out slacks.

Melody pointed at me, drawing my attention back to her and my boss. "There," she sniffed. "That's her."

Vivian grew even more dour as she called, "Bailey, could you come here?"

No. No, I really didn't think I should go over there. But I did anyway, reluctantly shuffling forward, no idea what I was walking into or what Melody had set up.

Crossing her arms sternly over her chest, Vivian pinched her lips together and shifted her jaw for a second before saying, "This young lady claims you harassed her when she came in to shop last week."

I blinked, not expecting that. "Huh?"

A lie. She was trying to get me into trouble by going to my boss with a *lie*? What a stupid, lame, overused technique. I was actually disappointed in her. Did the witch have no other tricks up her sleeve?

Vivian would never believe her over me. She loved me. I was her favorite employee; she'd told me so yesterday.

"Did you call her a dirty skank and refuse to sell her a dress she tried to buy?"

"No," I said, frowning. At least, I'd never called her a skank aloud...not while I'd been working. And besides, "She didn't try to buy anything."

"I did too." Melody wiped her eyes before pointing at a dress hanging nearby from the wall. "I wanted to buy that one, but she told me no way in hell would she let me taint such a pretty dress with all my dirty skankiness."

Well, she totally would. It was an awesome dress.

My thoughts must've reflected across my face because Vivian began to shake her head. "I-I'm at a loss of what to say here, Bailey. That behavior is totally unacceptable."

"Except that's not what *happened*," I argued.

She lifted her hands as if they were tied, still shaking her head. "I'm sorry, but I just can't put up with a salesgirl who'd do something like that. I'm so disappointed in you, Bailey, and I'm afraid I'm going to have to let you go."

Behind her, Melody broke out into a huge grin and even fist-pumped the air before waving her fingers in farewell at me and then mouthing the words, "*Bye-bye now.*"

That.

Bitch.

Not only was it *her* fault Beck was a hundred miles away from me right now unable to enter the entire city or he'd be beaten to a pulp or called awful, terrible, untrue names, but now she was attacking my only means of income?

Oh, I don't *think* so.

I'm not sure how to properly explain what happened next, but I snapped. I just…snapped.

I spun to Vivian, utterly outraged. "Are you freaking kidding me?" I shouted.

She blinked, not expecting my outburst. Then she glanced toward the other two customers in the store who were peering curiously our way. "Bailey," she said in a lower, cautioning voice.

But I'd had it. "No." I pointed a finger at my ex-boss's face. "You can't fire me because I fucking quit! I can't believe you took the word of this lying bitch over me, this bitch who's had a vendetta against me ever since I actually told the *truth* about her. This bitch who destroyed an innocent man's life just so her boyfriend wouldn't find out she was cheating on him. This bitch who lies to get whatever she wants. *That's* what's disappointing. If you can't summon any more faith in me than that, then I'm sorry, but I just can't work for *you* any longer. I hope you realize you just lost the most faithful employee you ever had."

And because I was on a roll, I whirled to Melody, satisfied when she lurched backward away from me as if intimidated. "And you," I charged, aiming my finger her way. "That is the last lie you'll ever tell about me."

I had no idea how I was going to keep that promise, but damn, it felt good to make.

Both Vivian and Melody gaped as me as if I was the deranged one in this situation, as if they truly feared I was going to pull some tommy gun from my pocket and start blasting holes in the place.

And yes, maybe I'd lost my cool, but fuck them. I wasn't the one spreading lies or *believing* such stupid lies.

They were idiots. Both of them.

With a sniff, I rolled my eyes and turned away, done with them. Done with this store. Done with this entire fucking town.

A rush of adrenaline filled me as I marched from the shop. It crowded into my blood, flooding my system until I actually felt euphonic. I'd just screamed at my boss and lost my job, but damn, getting all that out of my system had felt good. It felt awesome, actually.

It was probably a bad thing to feel this way at this moment, I was juiced and ready to take on the world. Or at least ready to tell the world it could go screw itself.

Working off pure emotional steam, I made the most impetuous decision of my life.

I started packing as soon as I reached the apartment, throwing clothes willy-nilly into my bags. Thank God none of my roommates were home; they would've wanted an explanation and I wasn't in the right frame of mind to explain anything. Besides, they would've no doubt talked me out of my crazy, reckless decision of leave Granton, and college, and everything here forever. And no way did I want to hear anything rational or sane right now.

I just wanted to go. Far away. Where no one spread lies about me, where no one refused to believe me, where no one looked at me as if I was insane or a creeper pervert. Where someone just appreciated me.

I wanted Beck. So that's where I went.

To him.

I think Tess had been right. Well, about some parts. Not the love part, because, just…no. I couldn't—I *shouldn't*—love him. But I definitely did feel guilty about leaving him at Thanksgiving. I must've been so bummed out lately because I felt crappy about deserting Beckett when he'd needed me the most that I'd lost control over my own life.

So, if he needed me, then that's where I was going to be.

Maybe it would benefit us both.

Chapter 31

BAILEY

My adrenaline high had worn off by the time I reached my dad's farm, and the impact of my earlier actions was beginning to take root in my nerves, causing my hands to rattle around the steering wheel and the sweat to gather under my shirt.

Because what the hell had I just done?

Let's see…

I'd quit school, one week before finals.

I'd disrespected a teacher and stood up in the middle of class before walking out.

I'd bitched out my boss and lost my job.

I'd pretty much threatened Melody Fairfield for getting me fired, hurting Beck, and turning the entire campus against me.

I'd left my friends a horrible note that was probably going to freak them out, reason number one why I'd turned off my phone.

And then I'd run here, straight to the one person who absolutely did not need any more problems or drama heaped on his shoulders.

I began to wonder if I could somehow backtrack and repair some of the damage, and then I experienced panic when the expression on Vivian's face flashed across my memory. Yeah, there was no way I was getting my job back. But school and the professor I'd insulted…

Then again, did I even *want* to go back to that?

No, but what was I supposed to do with the rest of my life if I didn't?

My anxiety returned until I spotted Beck's truck sitting in the driveway by the barn, the severely scratched side making an ache of longing arc through me. He and my brother had come to Granton over a week ago to pick it up. I'd been in class at the time and had completely missed them. I'd moped through the entire evening, wishing I'd skipped classes that day.

Suddenly, nothing that had happened two hours away mattered anymore. Beck was here, and he needed me.

Parking by the house, I killed the engine and just sat there, staring at his truck. I wondered where he was even as a lone rider on one of my dad's mares, Lula Bell, trotted into view from the south pasture.

My breathing stalled in my chest, and my lips parted in awe. I'd never seen Beck on a horse, but I knew it was him. I could feel it deep inside me. Besides, he wasn't riding like my dad or any of my brothers did. This guy knew how to sit on a horse as if he were part of the animal under him. They moved in tandem, the mare turning toward the barn with barely a nudge from his reins.

When they disappeared inside, I drifted that way, drawn to see more but also not rushing, because I suddenly felt shy—a completely foreign concept to me. I was almost reluctant to approach him when he was like this. This was…well, it was too big for me to handle.

But Beck. My *Bucket*. He was…

I reached the opening of the barn and saw him poised at the other end as he brushed down Lula Bell from her exercise. She nickered gently and moved her face into his space, making him chuckle and nudge her away before he pulled a treat from his pocket. She snagged it from his fingers, and he gave her neck a loving stroke. Then he tied her to the door of the stall so he could heft a pitchfork and clean out the old hay inside it.

He didn't wear cowboy boots but a pair of tan Wolverine work boots. His blue jeans weren't even particularly tight, though they were nicely worn and faded in a couple of interesting places. No shiny belt buckle or pearl-snap buttons adorned him anywhere. His fleece-lined plaid jacket and ball cap which were fraying in certain spots, looked completely practical and comfortable instead of ostentatious. But holy hell, the cowboy groupie in me took immediate interest.

He was perfect. Beyond perfect. He wasn't some decorated showpiece. He was the real deal. Sweat glistened on his face as he worked, the muscles in his back and thighs flexing and stretching with every jab he heaved the pitchfork into the hay and shoveled it up before pivoting to sling it into the wheelbarrow beside him. God, just watching him made me drool.

All the raw, masculine ruggedness contained inside one person seemed too much, too overwhelming. Everything female into me gravitated toward it, wanting to grip it tight and sink my fingers into it, then quiver into ecstasy as it consumed me.

He was everything I'd ever wanted.

But the most crushing part of it all was the realization that this was Beck. *Beck*! The stumbling drunk I'd first assumed was nothing but a preppy frat boy, who had then turned into a broken man, which further transformed into…into the one person I somehow needed the most right now. How had he converted from all that into the very image of my ideal dream?

It frankly scared me. Dreams weren't real. They were something to joke about, like calling Chance—the bastard—my soulmate for that whole year before I'd actually met him. I'd known he would never became a reality because it'd only been a dream.

But the reality of Beck seemed to be turning into an unobtainable dream right before my eyes. I wanted to run to him and claw away his sexy country clothes and shout *no*, tell him to stop. He needed to stay the guy I could talk to, the boy whose panic attacks only I could stop, the friend who could sit on my bed with me and talk about anything with or text to for hours into the night.

It was as if I could already feel that person slipping away.

Finished cleaning out Lula Bell's stall, Beck led her inside before removing her bridle and shutting her door. He remained unaware of my presence as he lifted the handles of the wheelbarrow and began to roll it out the opposite opening of the barn from where I stood.

I began to back away. For some reason, this all suddenly felt like a horrible awful mistake. What the hell was I doing?

Forget thinking he needed me, I'd come because I'd needed *him*, because I missed him. And that was all wrong. Nothing could ever happen between us. I was crazy for ever thinking it might.

Because, pfft. *Me*? Really? It was laughable to even let myself imagine it. No one had ever wanted me like that. No one ever would.

Even if I did receive anything form Beckett, it wouldn't be real. He'd only feel obligated to reciprocate because I'd helped him out of a bad spot. He'd never really feel for me what I felt for him.

I began to hurry toward my car, hoping he didn't notice me leaving. I'd just cleared the barn and was still a good thirty yards from my vehicle, when I glanced over and saw him across the way.

He'd just spotted my car and was jerking to a stop, the wheelbarrow still held in his grip. His gaze swept from one way to the other until he finally spotted me. Then the handles dropped from his gloved hands and bits of hay and manure jostled from the cart as it knocked roughly back to earth. His boots ate up ground as he hurried my way.

I didn't move to greet him, paralyzed in my shoes. I just stood there, gaping, not sure what to do, my heart racing and breaths heaving.

The same moment he came close enough for me to make out the huge grin on his face, he cried, "*Bailey?* Holy shit, it's really you." He yanked off his gloves and tossed them down as he jogged the last few steps to me.

He reached me sooner than I was ready for, and shocked the crap out of me when he laughed and swept me up in a huge hug that lifted me off the ground and spun me around.

"Oh my God," he breathed into my hair, smashing my breasts against his hard chest as the smell of leather and horses and Beck swelled around me. "I can't believe this. What're you doing here? You still have finals next week."

"I…I was able to get everything finished this week," I lied breathlessly as he set me back on my feet and took a step in reverse so he could sweep his gaze over me.

"But what about work?" he pressed, his amazing electric blue eyes returning to my face as his grin stretched wider. "I thought you said your boss was going to work you most of your winter break."

I shrugged and glanced over his shoulder toward the barn. "I wanted…I just wanted to stop in for the weekend and see how things were going."

When I turned back to him, he gave a delighted laugh. "Well, things are great, even better now that you're here." He reached out to grab my hand, physically keeping me from fleeing, not that he had any clue I was scared to death and wanted to run away. Shaking his head, he murmured, "I still can't believe you're here. I love this.

Best surprise ever." His grin lit with eagerness. "I have so much to show you. Come see."

As he proceeded to lead me across the driveway toward the field, I gazed at him in amazed confusion. He still looked like Beck, though all the bruises and cuts had healed. He still sounded like Beck. But he didn't smile or talk or even walk like Beck.

This guy was so enthusiastic and vibrant and—

I shook my head in wonder. A person never would've guessed he'd been tempted by pain pills less than a month ago.

"I started a project in college that I never got to finish," he told me as we walked, completely oblivious to my shock, "but your dad said I could have a little plot here and start experimenting come springtime."

His excitement was so contagious my own heart began to race, even though I was clueless as to what he was talking about. "Experiment with what?" I asked slowly.

"Seeds." Then he laughed at himself as if he knew that answer made no sense. "I want to cross some organic-based mixtures and try to come up with a new hybrid breed. Just imagine it: heartier-growing plants that'll withstand both drought and flood but also contain more mineral-based nutrients, so they'll provide a healthier stock for consumers."

"Sounds like the best of both worlds."

Such a seed sounded like, well, him. Too good to be true.

His proud, eager grin stretched. "I know, right? It would be an awesome breakthrough."

I shook my head, my confused-yet-amazed smile returning. "Are you sure something like this is even possible?"

"Well, there's only one way to find out," he answered on a good-natured shrug, not deflated by my skepticism in the least. "But I've even got your dad interested in it after I showed him all my graphs and calculations. We both think something good will come of it. Something at least half-way decent *has* to come from it."

My mouth dropped open. "Wait. You got my *father*, Doubting Benjamin Prescott himself, to buy into this?"

When he nodded, my eyebrows rose. "Wow."

"I know." He leaned in to bump his shoulder companionably against mind. "I'm just that good, huh?"

He was a miracle, that's what he was.

Then he gave a bemused grin. "Actually, he and I play checkers a lot in the evenings. I think we've bonded."

He and my dad had bonded? Oh God, that was so awesome. It was…it was…everything. Beckett Hilliard was everything.

This animated, smiling, talkative guy wasn't the same person I'd left two week ago. This guy was perfect and amazing and beautiful inside and out. He didn't need me at all. And yet I needed him more than anything.

How sad was that?

"I've been pretty picky about what I want to fertilize my plot with," he continued, kneeling by the brown field to palm a chunk of plowed earth. He gazed at it a moment, seeing the future, and I gazed at him, seeing only my failures.

He hadn't become this happy and full of hope until he'd left me.

When he lifted his face and caught sight of my expression, his smiled dropped.

He tossed the dirt clod back into the field and dusted his hands off onto his jeans. "But you don't want to hear about manure and compost. How's everything been in Granton?" Reaching out to curl a piece of my hair around his finger, he gave an affectionate tug. "You're still blond, so I'm guessing it wasn't too bad." His grin spread and eyes lit with amusement, making my stomach clinch with longing.

God, how I had missed him.

And God, how wrong he was. I'd actually been too far gone with misery to even think about changing my hair.

Finally realizing I wasn't my usual self, he paused with his finger still in my hair. "Bailey?"

I began to blink rapidly.

Holy criminy, but what was wrong with me? My breathing was picking up, my body was going into distress, my throat was closing, and I swear I could feel moisture gathering in my eyes. If I didn't know better, I would've said I was on the verge of crying right in front of him.

What was worse, he saw it.

Worry radiated from him as he shifted closer. "Hey. What's wrong?"

I shook my head and lowered my face. I didn't even know where to start explaining what was wrong with me. I'd gone off the deep end with my problems, and I knew it. But my problems weren't even what was bothering me at the moment. It was his problems… or lack of them.

After two weeks apart, he was okay. Perfect.

Why had being away from me healed him?

Had that week he'd stayed with me, sleeping in my bed beside me, actually been preventing him from making it to this place he was at now, preventing him from getting better? I'd been growing closer to him, dependent on his friendship, bonding on a level I'd never bonded with anyone else, and he…he'd just needed to get away from me.

I felt sick. I didn't like thinking of myself as holding him back.

"Dammit, Bailey," he growled softly, cupping my cheek to urge my face up so he could see my expression. "You're freaking me out here. What's wrong? Did something happen? Are you okay?"

I just stared at him, knowing I couldn't involve him in my problems, not when he'd just recovered from his own.

His eyes pleaded right before he whispered, "Talk to me."

I backed away from him, dislodging his gentle grip on me.

"I…I shouldn't have come here."

"Wha—?" He started in absolute confusion, stepping toward me, but I only jerked back farther.

He fell to a stop, gaping at me. "Bailey?" The concern and uncertainty in his face killed me.

I couldn't do this. I might be the bold, snarky Bailey Prescott, who wasn't afraid to faceoff with anyone and spit my brutal truth right in their face, but try to make me confront my own fears and insecurities, and nothing made me run faster.

So here I stood in front of the boy I'd fallen in love with, a boy I knew I could never really have, and instead of risking rejection and a broken heart, I shook my head and gasped, "I have to go." I spun away and raced off.

"Bailey!" Alarm filled his voice. I could hear footsteps as he followed me, trying to catch up, but I only ran faster, dodging past my car and circling around my house. I'd grown up on this farm, explored it for twenty years; I knew I could escape him.

After rounding the house, I dodged into the machine shed and hurried through it so I could burst out the exit on the other side. When I crept back outside, Beckett was nowhere in sight, so I took off running again, backtracking to the front of the house where I'd left my car. But I didn't hop in it and drive off. I needed more solitude and peace. I needed my place. So I hurried back to the horse barn, rushing past Lula Bell's stall to grab hold of the ladder and climbing up into the hayloft.

Once I was there, I shuffled through the dark until I could find where the string for the single-hanging light was by feel. But as soon as I found it and gave it a pull, the overhead bulb isn't the only thing that sprang to life. Along with it, thousands of other lights bloomed, lining the rafters like a host of fireflies.

"What the...?" I spun in a circle, gaping at all the Christmas lights strung around me, making my special spot glow with the most beautiful, peaceful decoration ever.

"Do you like it?"

Sucking in a surprised breath, I spun toward the opening of the loft where Beck were lifting himself from the opening in the floor. He eyed me warily as he eased the rest of the way up and then sat directly by the loft door as if ready to leave again if I ordered him gone. Or maybe he wanted to prevent me from escaping if I wanted to try.

When I could do nothing but gape at him, he gave a self-derisive laugh and motioned around him. "Took me about three days to sneak up here and hang everything. I had a bad feeling Booth would sabotage my surprise for you if he knew what I was doing so I had to keep it on the down-low." He gave another smile-type laugh at himself as he met my gaze.

If I'd been in any other frame of mind, I would've nodded or totally agreed. Sabotage totally sounded like Booth's MO.

"Since you're an electrical engineer major, I thought the light-part would win me extra brownie points."

He seemed sad as he said this, as if he was certain he'd made no points at all. I just blinked at him. I have no idea why he even wanted extra brownie points with me, but he'd definitely gotten them. And more.

"How did you know?" I rasped.

His gaze shifted from a strand of lights to me. "What? That this was your spot?" With a shrug, he glanced around himself. "Your dad sent me up here the second day I was here to get a fresh bale of hay, and...I don't know." He shrugged again, his lips tilting with an affectionate smile. "It just felt like you, like somewhere a girl with four older brothers would go to get alone and find some peace. To dream. So I found myself coming up here in the evenings so I could find...you."

The last word was spoken so quietly I could barely hear it. But oh, I definitely felt it.

Beck had done all this for me, because he knew me, because he wanted to make me happy, because he wanted to feel closer to me.

Because he cared.

I wasn't sure how to deal with that. It was too much, too big, too amazing. I couldn't trust it. No one cared this much about me. He had to be just trying to pay me back. That's all. It wasn't…he didn't love me. Not like I loved him.

But, oh my God, his sweet, amazing gesture affected me. It rattled and devastated me.

Knees giving out, I sank to the floor of the loft and sat heavily on the wooden planks, hugging my knees up to my chest and burying my face into them so I could weep.

Chapter 32
BECKETT

Of all the things I'd hoped to accomplish when I'd jazzed up Bailey's loft, a complete meltdown was totally not on the list.

In my wildest fantasies, I'd hoped to impress her enough to make her throw her arms around me and kiss the breath from my lungs before she tackled me onto a bed of hay and...well, that was the wildest dream I'd had. But I would've settled just as happily if her response had been to grin and smack me in the arm before proclaiming, "Not half bad, Bucket."

Except she hadn't done that either.

Sobs tore from her chest as if her happiness was being peeled away from her very soul with a paint scraper.

It gutted me to bring her to this point. I didn't even know how I'd done it.

I'd busted my ass these past two weeks to become something good enough for her to be proud of, and yet it all seemed to have backfired. Unless something else was bothering her. Not that I would know; she was being so quiet and un-Bailey-like.

Worried and scared what had happened to bring her this low, I silently rose to my feet and tread carefully closer until I reached her. She didn't acknowledge my approach, I don't think she even remembered I was there; she'd fallen too far into her grief.

Needing to fix whatever was wrong more than I needed my next breath, I knelt down behind her and slowly wrapped my arms around her.

She trembled in my embrace, but she didn't push me away. Encouraged by that, at least, I tugged her fractionally closer, then closer again until I could shift her sideways so her cheek pressed against my chest.

I lowered my face to bury my nose into her hair and kissed her head as she burrowed closer, clutching my arm. Shuddering out my relief, because she wasn't resisting my comfort, I began to rock her back and forth.

I had no idea how long she cried, but each heart-wrenching sob she tried to muffle made each second feel like a year. Waiting it out until she flushed her system of some of her grief was hard. It tried my patience like nothing else. I felt helpless, unable to help the person who meant the most to me. It made my blood seethe with a pent-up frustration. But I knew I couldn't let my emotions blow; the only person I'd attack would be her, shaking her and demanding she talk to me already. That was the last thing she needed, so my nerves coiled tighter and tighter with each achingly long second.

By the time her tears had settled to an occasional sniffle, I felt exhausted by how hard I'd been holding myself in check. But I merely stroked her hair as gently as possible, determined to give her what she needed most: a shoulder to cry on.

She sat up slowly, wiping her eyes. Tears still clung to her lashes, and the red skin around them had grown swollen and tender. She dropped her fingers lamely, probably realizing she couldn't hide anything.

When she glanced at me, she looked leery. "I'm sorry," she croaked, her voice hoarse and low, full of pain.

I shook my head and reached out to calm some of the wayward curls on the right side of her head. "Don't," I begged softly. "Don't apologize to me. Just…please tell me what's going on?"

"I…" She shook her head and swiped a hand over her eyes again, growing distance. "It's nothing. I'm fine."

I snorted. "Bullshit."

"It's stupid," she mumbled, growing irritable.

All I could say was, "No, it's not stupid. It's obviously important to you. So it's important to me. Now, dammit, *tell me what's wrong*!"

Hissing out a breath, she merely sent me a stubbornly mutinous glare.

So I sighed as well. "Fine," I growled, pushing to my feet to pace the floor and spike my hand through my hair. "Then I'll just start guessing. Is it about the kiss?"

She pulled back, shocked, as if the kiss we'd shared was that last thing on her mind. "Huh?" That didn't bode well for my ego, since her reaction told me whatever was wrong had nothing to do with our kiss. She'd totally and completely moved on from it.

But it still haunted me, so I pressed the issue. "Are you pissed at me for kissing you? Did I ruin whatever friendship we had? Do you want me out of your life? Can you not see me that way because you saw me with Melody? *What*? I've always, *always* known what you were thinking before because you always just told me, but now you're not talking, and I can't read a damn thing you're thinking, and it's scaring the shit out of me. So please, Bailey, just—"

"You didn't do anything wrong," she whispered, shaking her head and staring at me as if I was insane for suggesting any of the shit that had just poured from my mouth. She pushed to her feet as well, rising to my level. "None of that…everything you said about the kiss, it's not…I'm not mad at you for *that*. Besides, I'm the one who kissed you, anyway."

"But I'm the one who took it to the next level," I insisted, watching her face closely and deciding this really didn't have anything to do with that.

"Yeah, but…" She frowned and shook her head as if confused. "You were just…" She paused again as if she wasn't sure what she was going to say was right or not.

Gently I urged, "I was just what?"

Again, her head swayed back and forth. "This isn't about the kiss," she stated more firmly.

"Then what the fuck is it about?" My patience was slipping. I was going to lose it in five seconds if she didn't—

"It's because you don't need me anymore," she blurted.

I opened my mouth, but no words came. So I pressed my lips together and blinked at her, trying to make sense of her words. Finally, I said, "What?"

"You don't *need* me," she repeated with more force, her eyes filling with tears. "You were still having panic attacks when I left. You looked like a beaten dog as I climbed into my car that afternoon.

And now, two weeks later—only fourteen days after I left—you're fine, as if nothing had ever bothered you. But how? How could you be completely healed, just like that, and...and. none of that had anything to do with me. In fact, it seemed as if I'd been holding you back from really getting better, that you couldn't heal until you cut me free. So I repeat, you don't need me."

I gaped at her, growing disoriented by her words. They felt like accusations, like my getting better was a bad thing.

Barking out a harsh laugh, I took a step away to spread my arms wide so she'd look at me, really look at me.

"You see all this," I said. "This *improvement*. I did it for you. The last thing you asked of me before you left was to get better. And I *promised* you I would. Jesus fucking Christ, Bailey. You have no idea how hard it was just to get out of bed those first few mornings, to integrate myself into your dad's world and be social again. I still wanted to burrow away somewhere and grieve because I missed you so bad. But I fought the urge, every goddamn day, because I'd made you a promise. I've even *talked* to someone about all my issues in order to get better. I was that determined to impress *you*. And yeah, maybe leaving Granton did help a lot, but it wasn't because I was away from you. Being away from you just made it that much harder to do. So don't you fucking get mad at me for busting my ass every hour of every day these past few weeks to keep my word to you. Be mad at me for…for…"

"For what?" she asked, her chest heaving with breathless anticipation and her bright eyes and glowing with hope.

I took five steps back to her. And then I took the leap. "For letting things go unsaid after our kiss. For not just doing *this* again."

Gripping her by the back of the head, I tugged her against me and smashed our lips together.

It was like lighting a fuse. We exploded. She was just as eager to grip the front of my shirt and presser closer as I was to coax her mouth open and swirl my tongue against hers. She moaned and clung to me, grabbing fistfuls of my hair and climbing my body. I backed her into a wooden beam and then lifted her by the ass, clutching two handfuls until she wrapped her legs around me.

I broke my mouth away, panting for air, only to kiss my way up her throat. She was so sweet, and hot, and hungry for me, panting and receptive, resting her head back against the support beam and staring dazedly up at the twinkling strands of lights.

I studied the soft porcelain glow of her cheeks a moment before saying, "You may be right, I don't *need* you anymore. But I sure as hell still want you, and nothing—*nothing*—has been better off without out you here."

"You can't…" She was breathing too heavily to talk in a complete sentence, but her expression told me she was still clouded with doubt when her gaze met mine. She shook her head before she winced and looked away. "You don't want me. Not really."

My eyebrow rose in challenge. "You want to say that to me again, looking me straight in the eye."

Her gaze flared back to mine, meeting my dare. "You don't want—"

I kissed her, grinding my erection against her, so she could feel just how much I really did want her.

"What don't I want?" I taunted against her lips.

With a huff of irritation, she shoved against my chest, making me stumble back. Rage filled her face, and I worried I'd gone too far for a moment until she growled, "You don't know what you're saying, Beckett. You don't really *want* me. You just feel *obligated* because I helped you through a bad situation. You're not really attracted to me. How *could* you be? I'm a fat, ugly opinionated cow who blurts out what she's thinking rashly without regard to how it'll affect other people, some people that I would never want to hurt. So…yeah. What kind of idiot would even remotely be *into* that?"

I stepped to her, hovering. "I guess this kind of idiot, because you're it for me, and I'm completely satisfied with everything you are."

Shock filled her face. "But—"

"No buts. Just…feel this." I grabbed her hand and crudely pressed it against my crotch, in case she'd missed my erection the first time I'd ground it against her palm. Under her touch, my already hard dick jerked excitedly. She gasped, her fingers twitching against me before her shocked gaze lifted to my face.

I pressed into her space until we were nose to nose. "You want the truth of what I think of you, Bailey Rae? *This* right here is the truth. My dick doesn't react whatsoever to obligation or any other measly bullshit you try to accuse me of. This guy operates on nothing but pure, unadulterated attraction, and he's been hungry for you for a while now. He thinks you're beautiful and challenging and worth his attention. *I* think you're beautiful and challenging and worth my attention. So don't try to pass that fat, ugly cow bullshit off on me. It's not going to work. I. Want. You. Not because I feel like I owe you anything, but because you're you."

No longer outright denying my claims, confusion clouded her features. "But I'm not—"

"What?" I snapped, still irritated she was questioning my desire. My *love*. "You're not anorexic skinny? Well, thank God. You're soft just where I like it soft and curvy where I like curves. You're fucking perfect *for me*."

I reached around to cup her ass and pull her flush against me until her soft breasts were mashed into my chest and she could feel my erection again. Then I lowered my face to run the tip of my nose up the side of her throat.

Her head fell back and she let out a pleased sigh. I knew she liked what I did to her. I knew she wanted me back. I just had to convince her it was real.

"Do I feel obligated to you?" I asked against her throat before kissing her cheek. "You betcha. Do I want to pay you back in the best way possible? Of course. You were the one to keep me propped up until I realized I could stand on my own. But there is so much more to you than just that. I see you, Bailey. I've seen all of you, and I've seen what you have in here," I tapped the side of her head. "And in here." Two of my fingers pressed gently against the center of her breastbone. "I've seen the real you. And I fucking adore it. I *love* it. I love *you*."

Her mouth fell open. "Wha…what?"

"Fuck obligation," I said pressing my forehead to hers. "I love you because you're you. No one else could be you if they tried. And *that's* why I want you."

Her eyes filled with tears. "Oh, Beck." She reached for my face, but I caught her hands and kissed her palms.

"But the thing is, it wouldn't matter if I didn't find you attractive. I'd still be crazy in love with you." This time when I took her fingers, I pressed it against my chest, right over my heart. "Every time we talk, this little thrill races through me, excited and eager to hear what crazy thing is going to blurt from you next. I love your loyalty in your friends, and your faith in me when I didn't even think I'd recover from this. I love your drive and determination to keep going no matter what tries to push you down. I love how you have no filter and I never have to guess what you're thinking. Until today, anyway."

She gave a noisy swallow and then shuddered out a breath. Her lips began to tremble.

I kept talking. "But I do also think you're beautiful. I used to lie awake at night just to watch you sleep because I thought you were so pretty. Your cheeks looked like a glass porcelain doll. I would reach out as softly and quietly as I could just to touch you without waking you up so I could make sure you were real. And when I'd just barely feel how soft and warm your skin was, I'd ache the rest of the night, feeling like a dumbass for wanting you so much when I knew I shouldn't, when there was nothing I could offer you."

Immediately, she began to shake her head. "Oh, but, Beck. You have so much to offer."

I sniffed out a self-derisive laugh. "Really? That why you've pushed me away every time I've kissed you then?"

"No!" She screeched, gaping at me as if I were crazy. Cupping my face in her hands, she looked me straight in the eye and said, "That wasn't why. Not at all. I just realized I loved you too, and it was freaking me out."

My eyebrows shot up before a slow smile spread across my face. "You love me too?"

Gasping, she jerked her hands off my face and smacked my arm. "Oh! You…you…You made me say it."

With a laugh, I lifted my hands, claiming all innocence. "What did I do? I didn't make you say anything."

She made a sour face. "Don't act so smug, you big..." Her nose wrinkled as if she wanted to call me a bad name but her feelings for me physically prevented her from doing so. So she just gritted her teeth and huffed. "You want to know my real problem? I came home to find this gorgeous country boy I'd always dreamed of being with, and you finally had all your shit together, and...and it *intimidated* me, okay?"

I had to cock my head to the side over that claim. "How did I intimidate you? I'm still the same old me."

"What the hell ever." She kept scowling. "This...you...you're nothing like you were when I first met you."

"Okay, fine," I allowed on a cringe. "You met me while I was going through the lowest point I'd ever gone through, but you're also directly responsible for me getting back to my old self again, so what I am right now is basically…your fault."

She rolled her eyes and crossed her arms over her chest, but didn't argue my point.

I glanced around the hayloft, at a loss of what to say or do now. I'd just poured my heart out this woman, and she'd pretty much done the same to me. And now…now we were both just standing here.

It was weird. I didn't know what to do.

I'd always kind of thought that when I told a girl I loved her she'd scowl at me a lot less than this.

"I still want to be with you," I tried, feeling less and less confident as the seconds ticked by.

"Well," she huffed, seemingly more putout than ever, before moodily mumbling. "I want to be with you too."

Okay. I cleared my throat and scratched my head.

"So, uh…" I winced and sent her what I hoped was a beseeching glance. "Where does this leave us?"

She gave another long, resounding sigh as if fed up with me for not getting with the program. "Gee, Bucket. I don't know. The room's flooded with all these romantic little lights you've hung for me, and there's a nice, convenient bed of hay right there. We both just said we loved each other. We're both consenting adults who claim to want to jump each other bones, and neither of us are obligated to anyone else. What do *you* think we should do?"

Oh, hell, yes! I liked where this was going. My body kicked into high awareness, heating and hardening instantly.

No longer uncertain or self-conscious, I started to grin slowly. "Well, I certainly don't want to play checkers."

Bailey gave the most magical reply of all. She smiled back. It lit me up from the inside and settled in all the right places, making me buzz with need. Bailey loved me back. This was really going to happen.

Biting her lip with an almost teasing shyness, she backed slowly toward a particularly nice-looking pile of hay and began to unbutton her blouse. "Neither do I."

Chapter 33
BECKETT

A knot formed in my throat when the creamy swell of both breasts and the silken edge of a lime green bra came into view. Holy shit, we were really going to…

I shook my head, not quite able to believe it. This morning, I'd woken up missing her so bad and yet certain she didn't even think of me that way, I'd taken care of myself. I hadn't thought I'd even see her until damn near Christmas. And now, here she was, claiming she loved me and undressing in front of me. It felt too much like a dream. My brain couldn't catch up with reality.

"Are you sure?" I asked, swallowing down the hope that kept rising and trying not to let it get the better of me, but also taking a step toward her when she undid enough buttons to reveal her pale stomach.

Bailey undid the last clasp and slid one side of her blouse over one shoulder. My mouth dried up and eyes widened.

Her grin was pure seductress. "What do you think?" Cloth slid from her other shoulder and her top dropped to the floor at her feet.

I might've whimpered.

"I…I…well, I think someone's going to wake me any second because I just got to the really good part of my dream. And…oh… Mother of God."

She gave a husky chuckle at my reaction to her slipping her fingers into the waistband of her yoga pants and then pushing them down over her hips as she simultaneously toed off her shoes. Bending enough to help them billow down around her ankles, she shuddered and rubbed her arms from the chill as she stood in front of me in nothing but her green bra and black panties with hot pink stripes.

When I saw goosebumps rise on her arms, I held up a finger, unable to tolerate letting her get cold. "Wait. Hold that thought. Don't move. I'll be right back."

"What?" she shrieked, hugging herself as I rushed backward toward the opening of the loft because I didn't want to turn my back on her and miss a second more of this view than I had to. "Beck! What the hell? I'm doing the best striptease of my life, and you're *leaving*?"

"No! No, I'm not leaving. I'll be right back, I swear. I'm just going to run and grab something real quick." I help up a finger, silently asking her to stay put, and pleading with my expression, hoping she didn't kill me, as I felt behind me and began to climb through the hole in the floor. Before I completely lowered myself from view, I pointed at her again, this time more commanding-like. "Don't remove another stitch until I return."

"Beckett," she cried, letting me know she wasn't willing to forgive me for this. But she would. As soon as she saw what I was fetching, all would be okay again.

I flat-out ran toward the tack room, flinging the door open and hurdling myself inside. A brown, fleece blanket lay folded and draped over the back of a chair. I snagged it as I darted past, only to skid to a stop at a shelf against the wall that housed a couple of small, battery-powered portable space heaters that were used in the bitter cold of winter to keep the horses warm. Tucking one under my arm, I next hurried toward the bathroom where I'd seen a half empty box of condoms in the medicine cabinet the other day when I'd been looking for a bandage.

They probably belonged to Bailey's brothers. I didn't care. They were mine now.

Arms full, I plowed my way from the tack room, the door banging shut behind me, only to skid to a halt when I nearly ran into Bailey's father who was standing there in the center aisle, his back to me.

The box of condoms, which had been sitting loosely on top of the blanket and heater piled in my arms careened forward and spilled to the ground, littering the hay around my feet with little foiled packages.

Oh, shit. *Oh shit, oh shit, oh shit.*

Ben began to turn. I slid my foot over the box, covering some of the condoms but not all. My heart racing and smile too bright, I gasped out a too-innocent, "H-hey."

He seemed surprised to see me. Scratching at the whiskers growing on his cheeks, he motioned toward the opening of the barn. "Hey. Booth and I were about to go into town and catch a meal at the diner. The special's meatloaf today. But we saw Bailey's car when we stepped outside." Glancing around as if confused, he asked, "Have you seen her?"

"I, uh…" *Don't look down, don't look down.* When he turned back to me and focused on the things still piled in my arms, frowning at them, I blurted. "Yeah. She's in the…in the grove."

"In the grove," he repeated slowly. "Why? And what the hell is she doing home?"

"I, uh…" Finally I just shrugged. Would he kill me first, and then fire me, if he saw the condoms? Or fire me and then kill me? I didn't want to find out. "I'm not sure. She seemed upset but wouldn't say what was wrong, so I dragged her out there to talk. Except it seemed cold, so I came back to gather this, hoping it'd warm her up and relax her enough to open up to me."

Ben blinked at me as if I'd lost my mind. I flushed, knowing I'd just spewed the worst lie in the history of lies. But then he hummed, "Huh. Bailey's upset but *won't* talk about it? That's new."

I tripped out a nervous laugh. "Yeah. Isn't it, though? Totally not like her."

"Huh," her dad repeated before he shrugged as well. "Must be about girl problems, then." Reaching out to heartily slap my arm, he added, "I'll leave that to you to fix. Good luck. We're still going to get some meatloaf. Want us to bring you guys any of it home?"

"Uh…no thanks."

"All right then. Your loss."

When he turned away, all the air I'd been holding in my lungs escaped in relief. I was about to reach down and fetch the condoms when Ben paused and suddenly turned back. I froze, half bent over and back to holding my breath.

He narrowed his eyes a moment before declaring more than asking, "You'll tell me if there's actually something seriously wrong with her."

I nodded immediately. "Of course."

He nodded too and finally left.

Oh dear Lord. My heart wouldn't stop pounding.

This time, I waited until I heard the engine of Booth's truck start before I gathered the condoms. Blowing away a chest full of dread, I returned to the loft at a more sedate pace.

Bailey had pulled her shirt back on, but hadn't redone the buttons, and was currently shimmying the pants back up her legs.

Damn.

"That was your dad," I said, setting everything on the floor by the opening so I could close the hatch.

"I heard." Her fingers shook as she rushed to pull buttons through their holes.

I scowled, not really a fan of all the disappearing flesh she was hiding away. As far as I was concerned, we were still going to do everything my body was screaming to do.

"You should probably take that back off," I told her easily, turning the heater on and aiming the warm blast radiating from it toward the flattest pile of hay. "Unless you wanted me to take it off you, which might be fun too."

"*Excuse me*?" Bailey spun to me, her mouth falling open as she watched me flick the blanket open and settle it over the hay before smoothing down the edges. Her gaze shifted from the heater to the condom box sitting beside it. "What the hell are you doing? We just about got caught"

"But we didn't." I rose to my feet. "I'll tell him when he gets back from supper we're together now if that makes you feel better. But right now, I want to finish what we started."

She didn't answer. Her lips parted in awe. Then her gaze moved to the box.

"You got condoms."

I nodded, so she shifted her gaze.

"And a heater and blanket."

"You looked cold."

Her throat worked as she swallowed. Stepping toward me, she slowly reached out to touch my shoulder. "You thought of everything."

I lowered my gaze to the front of her shirt. "I only thought of you." She'd only gotten two buttons together. Slowly, I freed them again. "But then, you *are* everything, so that makes sense."

Chest heaving as she drew in a deep breath, Bailey shook her head. "How the hell did I get so lucky as to land you?"

Before I could even contemplate an answer, her fingers gripped the front of my shirt. Then she jerked me close and stamped her mouth to mine. I kissed her back hungrily, ripping her blouse open and back over her shoulders before flinging it off somewhere into the hay. She plowed her fingers through my hair and tried to tear the roots from my scalp as she sucked on my tongue. I came back just as rough, peeling off her pants and underwear together before smoothing my palms over her bare ass and then squeezing two palm-fuls.

"God, you're so soft and warm," I breathed, lowering her to the cushioned blanked. My hands skimmed her body until I flipped down the cups of her bra and popped a hard, pink nipple into my mouth.

"Beck!" Shock littered her voice as she jolted under me, her fingers clamoring to grip something and hold on for dear life while I licked and sucked. After palming a full lush hip, I smoothed around to curl over the rounded globes of her ass.

My arousal grew and breaths turned shallow. I came in from the back to find her wet and ready. We sucked in a surprised breath together.

"Oh, God," she moaned.

I moved my attention to her second breast but couldn't give it the same amount of attention as the first. Not when my fingers were soaked from her. Needing to taste this, I eased down, kissing and breathing in every inch of her along the way.

When she realized where I was headed, her muscles tensed and the fingers in my hair clamped down harder. "Oh, no. You're not… holy shit, are you really?"

Oh, yes. I was. Really.

I paused my decent to the apex of her thighs so I could grin up at her. She gulped, so I returned my attention to the pale blond curls in front of me.

Reverently, I brushed the backs of my fingers over them, making her shudder. "You really are a true blonde."

When I glanced back at her face again, she blushed and set a finger against her lips, silently asking me to keep her secret.

With a wink, I leaned in and licked her secret, dipping my tongue across the lips of her sex and opening her to my explorations.

"Holy…fucking…shit." She bowed up under me, gripping my hair and spreading her legs wider.

Mmm, I think she liked this. I certainly did. Bailey tasted good.

Finding the little nub I sought, I licked to one side of it and then the other, under then over.

Bailey went crazy, gasping out unintelligible words, arching and twisting in an attempt to get my mouth where she wanted it, panting and glistening with sweat. I almost lost my shit I wanted her so bad.

I could already picture her clawing my back and biting my ear when I finally got inside her. It prompted me to rush things along. I had wanted to draw this out and make her really sweat, but reaching my own limit, I thrust two fingers in her and plunged my tongue right where she wanted it.

She gasped. She arched. And then she fell apart, coming hard and fast.

It was nirvana. I couldn't wait to feel all this wrapped around my cock.

As soon as the last big spasm claimed her and her legs fell limp around either side of my face, I sat up to gaze down at her, eager to catch her expression.

She looked dazed, her plump lips were wet and dewy and her eyes were glossy and unfocused. But when she peered up at me, she still managed a smile. My dick twitched in my pants, growing even more painfully confined. But I didn't care because I was gazing at the most amazing view on the planet. Bailey Prescott, post-orgasm was a sight to behold.

"My God," I murmured, overwhelmed. "You are so fucking beautiful."

Her cheeks glowed pink. Then ducking her face to the side in the first act of bashfulness I'd ever seen her display, she said, "You're not so bad yourself, Bucket. But you're making me all freaky self-conscious down here, being totally naked while you're still completely dressed."

I chuckled. "I think it's hot."

"Well, I think it's not," she argued, growing bolder as she turned back fully to me in order to scowl. "Now, take 'em off and show me the goods already, Hilliard. What exactly have I purchased here?"

"Purchased?" I arched an eyebrow meaningfully, even as I removed my boots.

"Well…" She shrugged, not quite able to make direct eye contact since she was too busy watching me undress. "I do own you now, don't I?"

Her gaze finally lifted to mine as she sent me a challenging stare.

I grinned. "About as much as I own you, I guess." And to prove how much control I had over her body, I flicked my finger up her abdomen, toward her breast, making her shudder from the delight.

"Damn, you're good at that," she had to admit, her nipples turning hard and eager for more. "I mean, seriously, Beck. I was certain I wasn't even capable of having a…well, you know. But you… and it happened so fast, like…wow. How the hell did you do that?"

She seemed to be reliving what I'd done to her; she didn't even notice I'd stripped down to my boxer shorts.

Glad I'd made such a good impression on her, I decided to let her in on my secrets.

"Here," I murmured, taking her hand and coaxing it to follow my lead where I lowered it to between her legs. She let me until I moved her pointer fingers over a spot that made her jump.

"You feel that right there?" I murmured. "That slick little nub?"

When I moved her finger across it again, her body gave another jolt.

Oh, yeah. She definitely felt it.

"Yeah," she answered in a high voice, her face filled with a glazed tension as she bit her lip.

I grinned, loving her willingness to let me play. "That's your clit." I urged her fingers to circle it. "You don't touch it directly. Not at first, anyway. You go around it as close to contact as possible, tease it, drive it mad with desire, until it's cursing you and crazy for direct contact. That's the key to arousal. You don't give your body what it wants at the beginning. First, you make it want it, make it need it, make it so desperate for the pleasure you can give it that by the time you finally do touch it where it really makes a difference, it just…"

"Explodes," Bailey answered for me, her voice breathless and full of that rising need and desperation.

"Exactly." I kissed her hair and backed my hand away so she was the only one touching herself. Watching her with her hand buried between her legs was the hottest thing I'd ever seen. "God, that is so perfect." I bit my knuckles to keep from reaching out and interfering with her administrations.

My gaze followed the movement of her fingers for a few seconds longer before it rose to her face to find that she was watching my expression.

Her bottom lip was wet and dewy as if she'd been biting it, and her eyes were glossy with a primal awareness. She knew exactly what she was doing to me.

She gave a low, husky laugh. "You're teaching me how to masturbate, aren't you?"

My eyebrow quirked. "Maybe." Laying down on my stomach so my face was between her open thighs, I said, "Don't stop."

"What're you—?" She cut herself off with a chocked cry as I entered her with my tongue. "Ohmigod, ohmigod, ohmigod!"

Her fingers worked faster so I thrust deeper. Within seconds, she was gasping and going off again, filling my mouth with a decadent flavor I'd never forget.

"Oh, damn," she breathed, staring straight up at the ceiling. "Oh, holy God. That was unreal."

"It's not over yet, darling." Crawling off her like a crippled old man—er, more aptly like a horny, twenty-two-year-old guy with a painful erection that needed some serious attention—I peeled off my boxer shorts and grabbed a condom.

I was so beyond ready for this part, I swear the throbbing was pounding through my head now. My mouth was freaking watering as I returned my attention to Bailey, ready to climb on top of her. But when I caught her hesitant expression, I paused.

She nodded immediately, but I could tell she was having some doubts.

Remembering the way she'd described her first encounter, I threaded my fingers through hers and whispered, "Hey," until she stopped gaping in fear at my cock.

Her eyes lifted and I pressed my forehead to hers. "It's not your first time anymore, so it's not going to hurt, okay? Not at all."

She nodded as if she understood and believed me, but then she gulped. "You're so much bigger than he was though."

I couldn't help it; I grinned. Smugly. "Well, thank you."

Growling, she smacked my arm. "That wasn't a compliment."

With a chuckle, I nodded. "Oh, yes it was." Kissing her temple, I said, "Want to know what my favorite part of sex is?"

She shifted her face so she could brush her cheek along mine. "What?"

"That first moment I push inside." I positioned myself above her, aligning myself right at her opening. "When it's the tightest and most unprepared. The initial shock of sensation, your body receiving mine, the two of us joining. There's nothing else like it."

She shuddered out a breath and tightened her grip on my hand. "Show me."

I plunged forward, stretching muscles and igniting nerve endings, sending sparks of pleasure along my dick and down into my balls. The friction of male into female was overpowering. Gasping together, Bailey and I clutched and kissed, our tongues copying the wet thrust of our bodies. She curled up her legs along my sides, allowing me to go deeper. Faster. Harder. Then she sank her fingernails into my back with one hand and clutched my ass with the other, holding me inside her.

I choked out a breath when the first wave hit, spiraling up my cock and bursting out of control. Afraid to come without her, I reached between us, but I barely touched her clit before she erupted as well.

We held each other through the rapids until the orgasmic sea calmed and only the occasional lap of a lowering tide swept over us.

My forehead collapsed onto her shoulder and my body went from all to nothing, zapped completely.

Under me, Bailey gulped loudly. "My pussy," she uttered in a dazed voice. "My poor, poor pussy. I think you killed it."

Rolling off her, I landed on my back with a refreshed sigh and sent the Christmas lights above me a satisfied grin. "Then my work here is done."

Chapter 34

BECKETT

"Okay, that was unreal. I mean, that was really just completely and totally unreal. It didn't happen. It *couldn't* have. Because holy shit. I just came, like, three times. Three. In a row. I've never come before in my life, and you just stroll in and…*three* times? No. Just…no. I have to be dreaming." Bailey rolled her face my way. "Tell me I'm dreaming."

I grinned. "You're not dreaming."

Once we'd recovered from everything, she'd started talking and she couldn't seem to stop. Apparently, I'd blown her mind, which was pretty much, yeah, awesome. Until her eyes narrowed suspiciously.

"You've done this before," she accused. "I mean, *a lot*. You *had* to have done this a lot to be this good. I know the first time I met you, you hooked up with Melody, sure, but with everything that happened after that, I'd kind of assumed you weren't a big, man-whore player, except holy shit, how can you be this good without practicing it hundreds and hundreds of times."

She looked so worried and insecure, I immediately sat up and lifted my hands to calm her. "Whoa, hey, calm down. I haven't…" Well, I wasn't sure how many times I'd done it. I did know with how many women I'd been with, though. "Five," I said, spitting out the number and admitting all, even though I'd always heard you were never supposed to share you past with your current woman. "There have been five total, four before you. My high school girlfriend, a summer fling before college, then Jana, Melody," I made a face at her name, still tasting all kind of vile whenever I thought of her. "And then you. That's it."

Thank God, my word-vomit of a confession seemed to calm her. Her face relaxed and body released all its worried tension. But then she started blinking as if confused. "But you're so good. And you made me…" She shook her head, not understanding.

"Well," I said slowly, thinking it through logically. "You're definitely the best I ever had, and *you* don't have tons of experience."

That eased her mind for a second until she started again, unable to stop worrying completely. "But I was just following your lead." Her big gray eyes gazed at me, revealing all her insecurities. "You're the one who did all the mumbo-jumbo awesome shit with your tongue and that big boy handing down there."

I sighed and gave up another secret. "Okay, fine. Jana used to send me all kinds of self-help sex videos to watch." When Bailey blinked at me as if she totally didn't believe me, I turned a little defensive. "I mean, not because I was awful at it. That was just her thing. She liked investigating new tips and ideas." The last of my explanation came slower and slower the more I worried about upsetting her by talking about my relationship with another woman.

But all she said after ten second of gaping at me was, "You're really serious, aren't you?"

Relieved she wasn't jealous, I grinned. "What? You thought you were the only person who's ever seen other people have sex?"

Her mouth fell open, and she snorted out an amused sound.

I shrugged, growing more entertained by the second, even though it'd always kind of irked me when Jana had sent me a new video, like she really *had* been trying to tell me I sucked. "Honestly, the most helpful one I watched was actually some guy just fingering some fruit as he explained the best places to touch."

Bailey threw back her head and laughed. "Oh my God, I have to see that one." Grasping my arm, she ran her hand up it as she smiled at me. "Remind me to thank Jana for sending you all those."

My heart thumped hard and heavy in my chest and emotion overwhelmed me. I wanted to thank Jana for more than just that. She'd always made me feel as if I wasn't worthy enough, as if no matter what I did for her I needed to try harder. She had never appreciated me for just being me. She'd never made me feel like a Casanova. She'd never made me want to just grab her face and kiss the fuck out of her. Not the way Bailey did.

The lack of what Jana had done for me made everything that Bailey *did* do feel all that much bigger and more powerful. It was like starving a man before serving him his favorite meal, so he could truly appreciate the different between heaven and hell.

Bailey was my heaven: spunky and bold and even argumentative enough to keep me challenged and on my toes, but sweet and soft and perfect when I needed an emotional pillow to lay my head on.

I honestly wasn't sure if I had ever loved anything as much as I loved her in that moment.

Her lips parted as she read my feelings. "Why are you looking at me like that?"

I shook my head. "Like what?"

"Like…I don't know." She bit her lip. "Like you love me. Like I amaze you."

"Because I do love you," I said. "And you do amaze me."

I cupped her face in my hands as tears glittered in her eyes. "Oh, wow," she rasped. "This is…it's just so surreal. Are you sure it's really happening?"

"If it's a dream, then it's my dream too."

She pressed her lips together before whispering, "Thank you."

My eyebrows crinkled with confusion. "For what?"

Sniffing, she shook her head as if she didn't want to talk about it. But then she said, "For showing me what love could be like." Her fingers rested against my chest, right over my heart. "What sex could be like." She gave a wonderful, watery laugh. "I mean, I've listened to Paige and Tess talk about it with their guys, and I just, I don't know, I assumed they were exaggerating because they were just in love and wanted to play their boyfriends off as superhuman lovers. When Tess said Jonah had given her two orgasms in one round of sex, and Paige claimed Xander had given her three, I thought they were full of it, but—hey! What're you doing?"

After her pushing her back down on the blanket and crawling over her, she gaped up at me as if I'd lost my mind.

"What?" I asked, blinking down at her as if confused by her confusion. "You just said the record was three orgasms in one round. I've given you three, and our round's technically not over yet, so, challenge accepted. We're breaking the damn record."

"Oh my God," she groaned in annoyed disbelief, even as her eyes glittered with glee. "You don't seriously think you can—oh! Oh my God!" This time, the phrase was gasped in pleasure. "Okay, maybe you can," she finished in a high, strained voice while I licked my way up the inside of her thigh. "Jesus, Beck." Her fingers burrow in my hair, encouraging me on. "You win. You already win."

Yeah, well, now I wanted to win bigger. I teased her pussy, making her groan and arch toward my face. We were both still fully naked and stretched out on the blanket in the hay, her on her back and me on my stomach as I lay between her legs. Just when I decided to give her clit some direct attention, something scurried across my bare ass.

At first, I thought it was her fingernails, teasing and tickling. But then it struck me, where I was laying, there was no way her arms were long enough to reach down that far.

Jerking my face up, I mumbled, "What the hell?" and glanced over my shoulder in time to see a grey ball of fur with a long pink tail dash cross the loft floor toward another pile of hay.

"Holy shit!" Beyond freaked, I sprang upright, forgetting about my O-challenge and making Bailey spring upright, demanding, "What? What?"

When she caught sight of the fur ball, she yelped and covered her breasts. "Ohmigod, was that a rat? That looked like a rat."

A shudder of revulsion consumed me. Immediately denying it, I shook my head. "No. No, maybe it was a kitten. There are a couple gray kittens around."

Yeah, I could handle a kitten running across my naked butt.

Bailey looked at me as if I'd lost my mind. "That was a freaking rat."

I freaked and gave another tremor of eww, before grabbing my boxer shorts. "Okay, that's just wrong. It ran across my fucking bare ass."

Bailey watched me yank on my clothes a second longer before she burst out laughing, not in a hurry at all to dress herself.

I scowled. "Creepy little pervert."

She only howled harder, grabbing her stomach and rolling across the blanket until Creepy Pervert's little friend sprang up from a piece of hay beside her and scampered across the blanket right next to her, chasing after Creepy Pervert Number One.

Suddenly, she was screaming and as freaked out as I was, grabbing her panties and yanking them on.

"Yeah, that's what I thought," I taunted, pulling on my jeans and zipping them up.

"I feel so violated." She hiked up her pants and gave a full body shiver. "I bet the little voyeurs watched us the whole time too, the sickos."

With a grin, I winked. "At least they didn't take a video."

"Ohhhh…." Shock filled her face when she realized I'd just made a dig at her. "You bastard." Grabbing the condom box, she flung it at me. "That was low."

I laughed, rebuffing the blow with my arm. "Oh, come on. It was a little funny."

"You just compared me to a pair of peeping-tom *rats*!"

Okay, maybe it wasn't so funny. I winced and paused before putting my overcoat on to kneel beseechingly in front of her. Taking her hands, I said, "I'm sorry. Honestly, I will be forever grateful you watched me that night."

Her scowl dropped, but she didn't appear completely swayed, so I kissed her hands and continued, "After that night with Melody, I thought being with her had been the biggest mistake of my life. But if I had it all to do over again, I would in a heartbeat. Up until this very moment, that's the way I saw it."

Her eyebrows puckered, showing her confusion. "So you don't regret sleeping with her anymore?"

"Oh no. I still totally regret it," I corrected. "Just thinking about it makes me want to scrub my dick clean with some turpentine and a wire brush. But no matter how awful and traumatizing it was, I'd go through it all over again. Because it ended me right here with you. We never would've spoken again after that night, or seen each other, or hell, probably thought of each other if it wasn't for what she did. And that's why I'd bear it over and over again no matter how many times I was given a repeat. Because I'm here with you. So, honestly, I love and appreciate your voyeuristic ways."

She smiled and touched my cheek. "Okay, I forgive you." But then she gripped my arm and hauled me too my feet with her. "But still…rats just watched me have sex. That's creepy. I want to take a shower now."

I laughed. "Yeah. Rodent paws just groped my ass. I'm right there with you."

So, as I bent to retrieve the space heater, she scooped up the blanket and condoms. Then we hurried from the barn and made our way to the house, where no one was home but us.

* * *

Shower sex wasn't quite what it was cracked up to be. The water proved to be less of a lubricant and more of a resistant. It was hard to prop a sexy wet, slippery woman against a cold wet, slippery wall, and equally impossible to get a good hold on anything to provide a nice hearty thrust.

Oh, but we still got the job done, of course. No worries there. We just laughed more and moaned less, I probably bruised my elbow by smacking it against the shower wall, and Bailey stubbed her toe, but I did make her come again. She said it didn't count as number four because we'd put our clothes back on and changed locations, but I totally counted it.

I was the O-champion. The winner! Not that any of the other guys even realized they'd been in the competition, but still…

I ruled.

I definitely felt like I was on top of the world when I glanced over at Bailey and watched her sleep heavily, passed out on her stomach in her bed with her cheek nestled deep in her pillow. Yeah, I was definitely the champion.

She was so precious and full of life. I'd had no idea someone could come to mean so much to me.

I touched her naked back before drawing the blanket up further to warm her.

Just as I removed my hand, my cell phone rang from my pocket. People called me so rarely it was a little startling to hear. Only Bailey or her dad rang me these days.

Wondering if it was Ben, I fished it from my pocket to stop the sound from waking Bailey.

I didn't recognize the number, but went ahead and answered to quiet it.

"Hello?" I asked with plenty of caution.

"Is Bailey there with you? Please, God, tell me Bailey's with you."

Thrown off by the lack of greeting and harried question, I didn't immediately recognize the voice. "Uh…who is this?"

"It's *Tess*," she screeched, growing more insistent by the second.

Tess?

That would make sense why I hadn't recognized her voice—the girl rarely talked around me—but I still had no idea why Bailey's best friend would contact *me*.

Maybe it was another Tess...not that I knew any other Tess. My brain was still kind of mushy from post-coital satisfaction. I'm not sure anything could really alarm me or make me think completely straight right now.

"The same Tess who's too shy to talk to me because she thinks I'm hot, Tess?" I asked.

"YES!" She growled. "Now focus. Is Bailey with you or not?"

"Yeah." I glanced down at the sleeping naked goddess next to me. Oh, yeah...she was definitely with me. "Of course. She's right here. Sleeping. What's going on?"

"I have no clue. That's why I'm talking to you, you idjit. She's not answering her phone, and no one here knows where she is or what's going on. All we have is this stupid, vague note she left, saying she was dropping out of college and she'd be back sometime to pack her things and move out."

It took me a second for all that to really sink in. But that second later, I jerked upright, completely alert now. And utterly alarmed. "Say what?" She hadn't said anything to me about quitting school.

Though that would explain what had been going on with her when she'd first showed up.

Still, I felt the need to say, "She didn't drop out of school. Why would she drop out of school? That would be crazy," even as my gaze moved to her sleeping form, and dread built in my stomach.

What would prompt her to drop out of school?

I had a bad feeling it had something to do with me.

"Well, Crazy's her middle name," Tess exploded. "She stood up and walked out of the middle of class today, too. And then...then her boss called, wanting to discuss the incident at work."

I shook my head, clueless. "What incident at work?"

"I have no clue, *Beckett*," she growled. "That's why I'm talking to you."

"She wasn't herself when she got here," I admitted. "But she hasn't mentioned school, or work, or classes, or any of that."

"Oh my God! If she hasn't told you anything, then what the fuck have you two been doing since she arrived? It's been *hours*."

Hearing Tess say the word fuck was a bit staggering. I knew I didn't know her well, but I had the feeling she didn't say it a lot. So I just said, "Uh…" not sure how to properly answer her question.

"Find out what's going on, for God's sake," she demanded. "And then make her call me. Oh, and please inform her she's also dead for telling you about my stupid shy gene around hot guys. The traitor."

I started to laugh, but Tess had already hung up on me. I could get used to Bailey's friend. She was funny. Her angry mode was cute, like a soft furry bunny flashing its fangs at you. You still wanted to pet all its adorableness and only chuckle in amusement when it bit you.

But the reason she was freaking out wasn't funny at all. Absorbing all the claims she'd made, I turned my attention to my sleeping girlfriend and let out a long sigh.

I didn't want to wake her. I mean, after the way I'd worn her out, she needed her rest. But there was obviously something going on, and I was going to find out what it was.

Then I was going to fix it.

Chapter 35
BAILEY

I came awake slowly to the soft brush of fingers through my hair, and my lover gently cooing my name. Relaxed and refreshed and warm in my own bed, under my own blankets, I rolled onto my back and opened my eyes to smile up into Beck's face.

He smiled back, looking awed by me, which awed *me*.

"God, you look perfect, waking up naked in bed with me," he whispered, tracing the backs of his fingers over my cheek.

I sighed sleepily. "You look pretty good yourself, Mr. Hilliard. Feel free to wake up in bed with me any..." When I glanced around, realizing it had turned dark out and wasn't a new day yet, I finished with, "time," instead of morning.

"Deal." The affection in his gaze lasted another second before he scowled. "Now, would you like to tell me what the fuck's been going on in Granton?"

I blinked, not expecting that question. "Wha—what?"

He folded his arms over his chest. "Tess just called my phone."

"Oh." Dread pooled in my stomach. Not able to face this conversation lying down and naked, I sat upright and pulled the sheets to my chin.

"Oh?" He repeated, starting to lose his cool. "I just found out from someone else—because you sure as hell didn't seem like you were going to tell me—that you quit school and maybe even your job, and all you have to say is *oh*?"

"I didn't quit my job," I mumbled to my knees. "I was fired."

"Fired?" he cried. "Why in the hell would your boss fire you? I thought she loved you and always praised you for doing a good job."

"She did." I sighed and turned away, not wanting to talk about this and break the perfect time we'd been having. But Beck caught my arm and urged me back to him, his electric blue eyes piercing as he watched me and waited for an answer.

I closed my eyes, knowing he wasn't going to like this. "Melody came in and told Vivian I refused her service. And Vivian believed her, not me."

"Melody," he said slowly. "Melody Fairfield?"

"Well, it certainly wasn't the Melody dating my brother," I answered bitterly, only to wince and shake my head. "Sorry. I didn't mean to snap at you, I just—"

"That *bitch*!" he exploded, springing off the bed to pace the room and spike his hands through his hair. "I can't believe she... I'm going to kill her. She went after you because of me. She can't go after you because of me. I won't...I'm just not going to allow this."

Okay, yikes. I knew he wouldn't be pleased, but I hadn't expected quite this level of rage. Crawling off the mattress after him, I grabbed his arm, forcing him to look into my face. I kind of thought being naked would help distract him, but he was too busy fuming to even notice my lack of clothes.

"No one's going to hurt you because of me."

Though I loved his passion and the fervor and feeling behind his words, I needed to calm him down. "It's not because of you," I insisted. "She's just mad at me for outing her. And attacking me every chance she can get."

But that only set him off again. "What do you mean every chance she can get? What *else* has she done to you?"

I cringed. Dammit, why couldn't I watch my mouth sometimes? "I just,well, you know how some of the rumors have been going around that I lied to get you free?"

His eyes grew wide. "They're *still* saying that?"

"I'm pretty sure Melody's been fanning the flames. The gossips gotten worse instead of better."

He blew. "Motherfucker!" Spiking his hands through his hair, he spun away as if to go do something about the injustice of it that very second, but then realized he couldn't do anything.

He whirled back to me. "I can't believe she's still after you. We need to stop her and get this straightened out so you can—"

I shook my head and grasped his wrists to gain his attention. "No. Don't worry about it. It doesn't even bother me."

With a snort, he muttered, "Yeah, that's why you dropped out of school *days* before semester finals, because it doesn't bother you."

There was no way to argue that. I stared at him mutinously before mumbling, "You dropped out of school too."

"No," he growled. "I was kicked out. Big difference."

"Well, you left Granton," I argued. "And look at you now. Everything is better for you away from there." My eyes pleaded as I dropped my hands limply to my sides. "Maybe everything will be better for me too if I leave."

Affection and symphony filled his gaze as he cupped my face in his hands. But then he softly said, "No. You're not quitting school. My problems were the consequences of my own stupid actions. *You* didn't do anything wrong. You don't deserve any of this. They're picking on you because of me, because of what *I* did. And I'm not going to let them scare you away from your own future."

I only shook my head. "You didn't deserve what happened to you, either, Beck."

He pressed his forehead to mine. "Whether I did or didn't, I've adjusted to and dealt with what happened to me. This one's about you, baby. And we're not going to lay down and take it when they turn on you. We're going back to Granton and getting your life back. Tonight."

When I looked at him, I wanted to argue—maybe just for the sake of disagreeing—but I couldn't deny there was a part of me aching to return to my normal life, my future.

I didn't have to say anything, but I knew the moment he realized I'd given in.

He took my hand and nodded. "Let's go."

* * *

It was nearly eleven when we reached Granton. I was ready to crawl back into my bed and hide away from the world, but Beck was ready to barrel ahead, full bore. He had no qualms about knocking on my roommates' doors and rousing them all from bed for a meeting in the living room.

Tess and Paige hugged me when they saw me, and Tess even took my hand and held onto it as she sat us side-by-side on the couch. A month ago, I never would've allowed such touchy-emotional treatment. Now it just made me feel warm and loved.

Beck paced the living room as he filled everyone in on what had happened—the me dropping out of school, being harassed and losing my job part, not the three orgasms part.

Paige just shook her head, looking tormented. "My God, Bailey. I knew things weren't good but I didn't realize how bad they'd gotten."

"Well, they have," Beck boomed. "Everyone went after her because of me. They might go after all you next because of her. We need to stop it here and now before anyone catches any more heat."

Paige arched her eyebrows. "You don't have to sell us, you know, we already want to help Bailey."

"Oh." He seemed surprised by that. "Well, then good." He rubbed his hands together. "Does anyone have any ideas of what to do?"

Jonah shrugged. "I say we take out this Melody chick."

Tess gasped and slapped his leg. "Murder, Jonah? Really?"

"I didn't say we should kill her, just take away her ability to torment anyone anymore."

Beck pointed at him. "I like where you're going with that. Keep thinking." Before Jonah could respond, someone knocked on the front door, the sound echoing up the stairwell and making us exchange confused glances, because who would be visiting us at eleven o'clock on a Thursday night. Beck motioned to Logan. "Get that, will you?"

I sat up straight, really confused, because he was the only one not acting surprised by the knock. "Are you expecting someone?"

Beck didn't answer me, his attention back on Jonah, "We need to find out everything we can about her, where she works, lives, hangs out, talks to, everything."

Wondering who the heck was at the door, I eased up from the sofa just as Logan climbed up the steps with—

"Sam!" Paige cried in surprise. "What're *you* doing here?"

The single mother who headed the grief group at Granton had helped both Paige and Logan as well as Jonah through some traumatic shit. She'd visited the apartment a handful of times since we'd all moved in together this summer. But she'd never showed up after dark and unannounced like this before.

With a bemused shrug, she gave us all a peppy wave. "I was summoned," she announced.

"But…" Logan glanced around, frowning. "Who…?"

Beck stepped forward. "I called her." He held out a hand. "It's nice to meet you in person."

My jaw dropped as I watched Sam and Beck shake hands and look each other over before she told him it was nice to meet him right back.

"Wait." I waved my hands. "You know Samantha? How do you know Samantha? You don't know Samantha!"

His lips quirked with amusement. "I told you I've been talking to someone to get better." He tipped his head toward Sam. "She's who I've been talking to."

"And he's been the nicest, young man." Sam glowed at him before glancing toward me and winking. "You picked yourself a good one, Prescott."

I could only blink, because…what? What was happening here? Beck knew Sam. He'd been talking to Sam? And she already knew we were a couple?

This was so bizarre.

"So, what's the situation?" Sam asked, taking off her coat and rubbing her hands together as if ready to get down to business. Then she plopped down onto the loveseat next to Paige and squeezed her knee affectionately, joining the group discussion with ease.

"They're going after Bailey," Beck said. "The rumors about her are getting worse. And it's not like she can really stand up for herself with proof that she's not lying."

"Right," Samantha murmured. "Because of the video. If they don't label her a liar, then she'll be that dirty little peeping tom." After crossing her arms, she tapped her chin thoughtfully. "I see the dilemma."

Oh my God. I whirled to Beck, feeling my face drain of color. "She knows about the *video*?"

He finally sat next to me, grasping my shoulder and pulling me back against his side to kiss my temple. "Don't worry," he said into my ear before lifting his face to Sam. "And Melody's been harassing her. She went to Bailey's boss with some lie that got her fired. Now Bailey's trying to drop out of school and leave Granton for good."

Hey, I wasn't trying to drop out.

I *had* dropped out.

"It's one thing for them to ruin my reputation and send me packing," Beck added. "But I'm not going to just stand around and do nothing while they turn on Bailey too. *No one fucks Bailey.*"

My heart thudded hard inside my chest as I tipped my chin up and gazed at the man so adamantly defending me. No one had ever done anything like that for me before. I wasn't sure how to deal with it. My eyes and throat began to burn as emotion, overwhelmed me.

Next to me, Tess fanned her face and leaned more fully against Jonah before saying, "That was so romantic."

Beck tightened his arms around me as if he knew I was about to burst. But how could I not? He loved me. He really, freaking loved me.

I turned into him abruptly and buried my face in his chest to hide the flow of tears. He kissed my forehead and smoothed my hair, and I knew that no matter what happened, everything was going to be okay.

Beck loved me. There could be no doubt about it now.

"That really burns my ass," Sam growled, startling me from my mini meltdown. "I can't handle people who lie to save their own butt, especially when that lie hurts others. I wish there was some way to..." Her words faded off as this strange expression filled her face.

"What...?" Frowning, I glanced to everyone else, since they seemed to know her better than I did. "What's she doing? What does that look mean?"

Jonah grinned. "It means she has a plan."

"An evil genius, probably not fully on the up-and-up plan," Logan added.

"Oh, no." Sam held up a single finger. "It's not my plan. It would be totally wrong and unethical for me to come up with such a plan as this."

"It'll be my plan, then," Beck immediately claimed responsibility as he shifted her way, eager to hear more. "What's the plan?"

"Well..." Sam paused a dramatic moment to gather her thoughts. "I can't have any part of it."

"Don't worry about it," Paige assured. "We'll take care of the dirty work."

Sam winced. "But none of you should have a part in it, either. If any of you are caught tampering with school equipment—"

"This is for Bailey," Tess cut in. "It's worth it."

Sam cringed, still hesitant. But then she sighed and said, "Melody works for the university's Admissions office as a campus tour guide, right?"

"Uh..." Beck shook his head, his expression completely blank. "I have no idea."

"The answer is yes, yes, she does." Sam gave a satisfied grin. "After you told me about her, I looked her up. And it just so happens one of her stops on the tour is the human health department, where..." She cleared her throat and pressed her hand to her chest, "I just happen to volunteer as a counselor over their grief group. So I know for a fact that Deb, who gives the health department's presentation to new student recruit tours, only talks for a couple minutes before she pops in a video and leaves the room. Meaning, if someone—a person's who's totally not me, because this isn't my idea at all and probably shouldn't be any of you either since it could get all of you into trouble—were to *replace* that video with something else..." She glanced meaningfully in my direction, it's possible the truth about Melody could get out without anyone accusing our Bailey here of, you know, peeping tom things."

My eyes widened. "Oh my God," I whispered, gaping at Sam in awe. "You are so diabolically brilliant; I think I just fell in love with you."

Sam laughed, then blushed and self-consciously tucked a piece of hair behind her ear. "Well, thank you," she demurred, only for her gaze to seek Beck. "But it'd be even better if the idea could bring *everyone* to justice, not just the people in this room who were wronged."

I glanced at Beck, wondering what she was talking about. At first, he squinted, clearly not understanding either. But after a moment, his gaze cleared and eyes widened. "You mean...?"

Growing somber and sympathetic, Sam met Beck's gaze and nodded. "I do. I think this just might help her a lot."

Chapter 36
BAILEY

I tugged the hood of my sweatshirt more snugly around my face and kept to the rear of the group as Melody began the tour, introducing herself. Then I shimmied my phone from my front pocket and opened it to look up the picture Beck had given me of Daylon Raider. After I scanned the high school seniors gathered with their parents in front of me, my pulse began to kick into high gear.

He's here, I typed before hitting *Send* to the group. **We're a Go!**

My phone vibrated about five times simultaneously as I stuffed it back into the front pocket of my hoodie, probably everyone telling me good, and now to get out of there because my job in *Operation Truth* was complete. All I was supposed to do was ensure Daylon Raider was part of the tour. Then I was supposed to evacuate.

Except running wasn't in my blood today. I *had* to stay and see, to watch everyone get what was coming to them.

We'd worked all weekend, scheming and planning, working through alternative after alternative to get everything just right. Four days later, Monday morning, and our plan was coming to fruition.

"Alright then." Melody clapped her hands to gain everyone's attention. "If you'll move this way, we'll visit the McCuffrey Hall, the science center first." She traipsed over the campus lawn, leading us like a mother duck with her younglings and talking about the type of tree we passed. Not once did she mention this was the very ground where a crazed gunman had killed nearly a dozen students a year before, or that it was between this building and the next—Jamison Hall, the Art Department—where he'd finally killed himself.

She was kind of a sucky tour guide if you asked me.

I yawned inside my hoody and kept out of sight in the back as we moved through the science building, then the art building, then the food court.

After two more stops, and my feet aching from so much stupid walking, we finally, *finally* made it to the Human Health Department.

And just as Sam had described it, Deb the Human Health spokesperson led us into a room with a huge projection screen hanging down in front of one wall. After we all sat, I grew a little more ill at ease because Melody remained standing next to Deb as she addressed us. If she looked at me, *really* looked at me, she would recognize me.

I slumped lower in my hair, cringing when my phone buzzed loudly in my pocket. At least it felt super-loud.

Finally, thank God, Deb announced she had a video for us to watch, and after she started it, she moved to the door where she turned down the lights and then slipped silently from the room just as the usual beginning started that she was used to seeing.

I breathed out a breath, glad she hadn't stuck around, while the rest of me tightened with anticipation. This was it. It was going to happen right now.

I glanced Melody's way where the glow from the screen splashed perfectly across her face so I could gage her expressions. She looked completely bored, her arms crossed over her shoulder and her back propped against the wall. She had no idea what was about to happen.

Two rows in front of me, Daylon Ralder looked equally bored, slouched low in his own chair where he was flanked by both his parents.

I have no idea how Paige's fake email invite to him had coaxed him into coming to campus today and taking this very tour, but I loved her persuasive skills.

"We at the Granton Human Health department are committed to providing services for all students in all manner of health needs," The voice over began as the screen panned from the entire campus and on to this building, "ranging from your physical to mental to emotional well-being. Our clinic provides medical, dental and women's services for either walk-in or appointment visits, along with a twenty-four hotline for therapy and counseling, plus in-house along with volunteer psychologists willing to work with students one-on-one or in group sessions."

This is where the video changed from the original beginning to our happily tampered-with portion. The voice-over changed from a male to female (Tess's voice). And the scene moved from the building to one of the rooms inside the health center.

Melody didn't seem to notice as she yawned and checked the time on her phone.

"One of Granton's Crisis Counselling sessions for raped and sexually abused victims would be particularly beneficial to your very own tour guide, Melody. Melody *Fairfield*, that is."

At the mention of her name, Melody perked to attention, shoving away from the wall and shrieking, "What the hell?"

A shocked murmur spread through the group.

Excitement raced through me. I sat forward, as the screen stopped zooming in on a group in the middle of having a meeting to a picture of Melody's face we'd taken from her Facebook profile.

"Melody was raped right here on campus at a fraternity party on the night of November Eleventh."

Slapping her hands to her face, Melody slowly began to back away from the screen as if it were suddenly toxic.

"Or at least, that's what Melody *claims*," Tess's disbelieving voice continued. "But if you'd like to see what really happed to sweet, innocent Melody on the night of her quote-quote *rape*, just stick around. We actually have a video of the event, and we'd be happy to show you the truth."

"Oh my God, oh my God! *No*! Someone turn this shit off." She rushed toward the podium computer stand and grabbed the mouse to end the presentation. But someone—ahem, Paige and Logan—had already been in here to change the setting so that she needed a password to get in to the video controls.

She did not know the password, even though I did. It was *IAmALiar*.

Clueless, she screamed and pounded on the mouse, getting no results, while the video on the wall turned to my homemade peepshow.

"Oh my God, Beck! Right there. Right there," her voice squealed through the speakers, making the real her slam her hand to her chest and gape in horror.

All the parents in the group gasped and tried to urge their high school children to stop watching, even though most of the high school students whooped and cheered. A couple of them pulled up their phones and began to take a video of my video. I'm pretty sure one guy was even live-streaming it to his social media account.

"It looks like maybe Melody Fairfield needs a bit of a lesson on what rape *really* is." Tess's voice reprimanded as she continued. "That's why we here at the Student Health Services center are more than willing to educate her. You see, Melody dear, rape is *not* when your boyfriend catches you screwing another guy, and you lie and tell him you were forced so you don't get into trouble. Rape is where you tell the boy no, and you're *not* a willing participant. Rape is when you really are forced. Like sixteen-year-old Brittany Hilliard. Now Brittany really *was* raped this summer by Daylon Raider. And it just so happens Daylon is in the crowd with us today. Why don't you stand up, Daylon, and show yourself, so Melody can see what a true rapist looks like."

Daylon's father surged to his feet, fuming. "What the hell is this? What's going on here? I will sue this entire school if you don't shut that video off right now."

"After Brittany told him no and tried to struggle to get free from him, he pinned her down and held his hand over her mouth as he forced his body into hers."

The screen flashed to a picture of Brittany, pale and cowering in a sweatshirt with her wet hair plastered to her head. But the centerpiece of the photo were the bright purple bruises on her neck, arms, and face.

"Brittany was raped. Melody was not. Brittany still wakes up screaming from the nightmares she has of him covering her mouth and cutting off her air flow. She's been admitted to a mental health facility twice since the attack and cloisters herself in her room when she's home. She's also dropped out of school and stopped talking to her family completely."

Pictures of Brittany before and after her attack flowed across the screen. It was obvious, she'd been completely scarred by what had happened.

"Melody, on the other hand, still attends class and leads tour guides, smiling and happy, as if nothing bad happened to her. Because nothing bad *did* happen to her."

Before Tess's voice could continue, Daylon Raider kicked the computer's mainframe, sending wires and sparks flying. The video on the projection screen went dead and the room fell dark.

A few people screamed. Chaos reigned as a mad scramble toward the exit ensued. Amidst the fear, some laughed and some demanded an explanation.

Suddenly, the lights popped on as Deb flew into the room, crying, "What in the world is going on in here?"

I decided that was my que to leave.

But just as I ducked out the back door with a family of three—the mom and dad trying to shield their daughter form the nearby rapist—I glanced back just in time to make eye-contact with Melody.

Shock marred her face just as she pointed my way. I gulped and rushed through the door.

Oh, crappity, crap, crap!

This could be bad. If Melody knew I was behind this—

Well, duh, she had to know I'd been involved in some way; it had been my freaking video of her with Beck on that screen. I could totally get into trouble for interfering with the campus tour, scaring off prospective students that might've actually been interested in attending Granton, and tampering with Human Health Services' property.

Oh, hell. Why hadn't I thought of just how *much* trouble I could get into?

And it really seemed like it'd be worse if I was caught actually *at* the tour. Crap. Why hadn't I listened when everyone had told me to skedaddle? I suddenly knew why they'd wanted that.

Hurrying from the building, I waited until I'd reached the History department before I glanced behind me. I wasn't expecting Melody to actually follow me, so I nearly pissed myself when I caught sight of her exiting the building behind me and frantically glancing around as she talked on her phone until she spotted me.

When she started after me, definitely zeroed in on me, I whirled away and took off running.

Shit on a monkey stick, I think she'd just called in reinforcements. I ran faster.

Reaching the edge of a building, I veered around a corner, still running full out. I started to race toward the other end so I could turn again, but my pace was already lagging.

Unfortunately, I think Melody was more inclined for this running shit than I was, so when I passed a side entrance of the building, I darted inside. Glancing over my shoulder as the glass door slowly swayed shut behind me, I saw she'd turned the corner and had spotted me entering. So either I needed to get lost in here, or I needed to find another exit and make a mad dash for my car.

I have no idea what she thought she'd do when she caught me, but I really didn't want to find out either. She'd ruined Beck's life and gotten me fired from my job; her evil powers sure *seemed* limitless.

Since speed of escape wasn't my strong suit, I hurried up the first set of stairs I saw. They were padded with carpet and made my flight quieter, which I totally appreciated.

Once I was on the second floor, I searched for the first bathroom I found, and pushed my way inside.

My breathing was harried and heart was racing as I locked myself in a stall and sat on the toilet, fully clothed, before pulling up my phone and sending out an SOS to the group.

Good News: The plan worked beautifully. Bad News: Melody saw me and chased me to the Science building. Oh, and she called in some kind of reinforcements, I'm pretty sure. So I'm hiding out in a bathroom on the second floor for a bit.

My phone immediately buzzed with replies.

We told you to leave BEFORE the tour! That one was form Jonah. He was *so* concerned about my welfare, the big jerk.

Which bathroom? I'll be there in a second.

At least Tess had my back.

Logan and I will look around for Melody.

And so did Paige. Damn, I had the most awesome best friends ever.

Beck, however, didn't answer, which made me frown. What the heck was he doing? My life was in danger here and he was, what, out getting a slushie or something? Humph. Some boyfriend he was.

Not that I was really in danger. At least, not at the moment. I'd probably be screwed once school administration got hold of me. But whatever. It was worth it to get both Beck and his sister a little bit of justice and truth.

"Are you sure she came up here?" a familiar voice asked as the outer door to the bathroom came open, making me lift my feet up and tuck my knees to my chin so this stall would look empty.

"Where the hell else would she go?" Melody huffed. "She's too fat to keep running for long."

Hey. Rude much? I scowled at the stall door, so badly wanting to snarl, *I totally could've kept running if I'd wanted to, bitch.*

I just hadn't wanted to.

The room grew quiet. Scarily quiet. I think they'd discovered me. I could picture them dorkily outside my stall, making hand gestures to each other, indicating I was in here.

My phone shook in my hands. I was about to tell my cavalry it was too late; I'd been discovered. But at the last moment, I didn't. I swiped into my camera mode and set it to *Video*. On purpose, this time.

Suddenly, the door to my stall burst open and would've smacked me in the legs if I hadn't already tucked my knees up to my chin.

I screamed and dropped my phone.

In front of me, Chase the fake cowboy, lowered his boot. My mouth gaped open. Had he really just *kicked* my freaking bathroom stall door open?

"I could've actually been going pee, you know," I charged, scowling at him.

He reached in, grabbed my arm and yanked me from the toilet. I yelped from the pain, surprised. The bastard nearly tore my arm out of its socket and I didn't have time to catch my footing so I pretty much skidded out on my knees.

"Hey…" I tried to smack at him with my free arm to no avail.

Anger and indignation was replaced with fear when he grabbed my hair and yanked my head back, forcing me to stare into his livid eyes. "I told you to stop messing with my sister."

Oh, God. This wasn't playtime anymore. Shit had gotten real.

I gulped, straining against him but unable to break free.

"Tell her to stop messing with me first," I had the gull to reply.

His face went angry-red. When he lifted his gaze to his sister as if seeking instruction, she ordered, "Slap her."

His hand swung out, cracking against my cheekbone. I cried out from the shock and pain, totally not expecting that.

But what the hell? These psycho siblings were totally fucking crazy.

"Are you out of your ever-loving minds?" I started, only for Melody to motion a finger my way and simply say, "Muzzle that ugly mutt."

"No! I—"

The bastard cowboy jammed his hand over my mouth, er, actually kind of into my mouth. The side knuckle of his index finger pressed in against my teeth, practically gagging me, so his thumb could wrap around my face and dig into a sensitive part between my jaw and ear. It hurt like fucking hell. Tears sprang to my eyes and what was worse, he could control the tilt of my head and keep me from biting him very hard.

I couldn't move, struggle, talk, scream, bite, or anything, but stare up at him from wet, dazed eyes.

He smirked down at me.

Melody's face appeared over his shoulder where she smirked at me too. "That's better," she crooned. "Now where we were?"

I lifted my hand to flip her off.

"Behave," Chance growled, smacking the side of my head into the wall and making me see stars.

Unable to admit I was beaten, I fought harder, attempting to sink my teeth deeper into his hand, then rearing my head back before slamming it forward, right into his.

The impact was brutal. Oh God, so brutal. More stars. Lots of stars.

But it also caused him to curse and lose his grip on me. For the briefest second, he stumbled back, holding his head. I took a moment to lean into the wall and orient myself, before pushing away and lunging for the door. Hoarse air gasped from my lungs. I was three feet from making contact with the handle when a hand landed in my hair and yanked me backward, causing me to cry out.

"Oh, no. You're not going anywhere yet," Melody said, tossing me back to her brother, who flung me into the wall.

I hit so hard, everything went momentarily black. But I didn't fully lose consciousness. I ducked my head down, protecting my face and squeezing my eyes against the agony. Chance's head moved in closer, and this helpless surge of fear and surrender swept over me. I'd never be able to overpower him enough to escape. I might actually die in this bathroom.

A wave of images flashed through my head. Beck. Tess. Paige. My dad. Even my brothers. Everything good in my life swelled up and surrounded me, like a big hug, trying to protect me from harm. And I embraced it back, not ready to deal with what whatever the Fairfield siblings planned to do to me.

Except, whatever they'd planned never happened.

The door sprang open, and Beck's voice cried, "*Bailey*?"

Chapter 37
BAILEY

With a roar of rage, Beck shoved Melody aside and launched himself forward, tackling Chance against the wall, much the same way Chance had just pinned me there. Since the wannabe cowboy still had a hold on me, I sustained enough of a jarring impact that I cried out, even though it also helped me break free.

Beckett's gaze sought mine. Our eyes met, and I could only guess what he saw when he looked at me. My eyes were wet and something dripped from my nose, maybe blood. But the fear—absolute terror—in my expression is probably what prompted him to turned back to Chance and swing his fist into the guy's face.

I wrapped my arms around my stomach and backed away from them, as I watched my tormentor become the tormented. Beck showed no mercy, pounding away at Chance's face until the guy passed out.

When two hands wrapped around my shoulders, I jumped and spun, only to find Tess there, and Paige too, swarming me and hugging me, Tess crying and telling me how sorry she was. My gaze shifted around the bathroom until I found Logan corralling Melody toward door, keeping her back, while Jonah rushed past them to catch Beckett around the neck and drag him off the limp, bloody Chance.

"He's out, man. No more."

Beck puffed out an angry snort and kept glaring at Chance's crumpled form, but he didn't struggle against Jonah's chokehold.

"Let me by," Melody sobbed, shoving at Logan. "That's my *brother*."

When he stepped aside to let her through, she rushed to Chance and knelt before him, shaking his shoulder and repeating his name until he gave a weak groan and began to stir.

Beckett turned to me. Devastation flooded his face as he took me in. "Bailey," he croaked, stepping forward. Tess and Paige parted so he could pull me into his arms and kiss my hair before setting his cheek against me and tenderly keeping me close.

I buried my face in his shirt, inhaled his familiar scent and tried not to completely lose it. Around me, everyone started talking about what they needed to do, but I didn't care about any of that. I just wanted Beck to take me home and hold me until I fell asleep and this whole nightmare was in the past.

Until Tess announced she was calling campus police.

I lifted my face. "No," I said, shaking my head. "Beck's not allowed to be on campus. If they found him here, beating up another student—the brother of the girl who claimed he raped—what do you think's going to happen to him?"

"Fuck that," Beck said. "They *attacked* you, Bailey. We're calling it in."

But I kept shaking my head. "They'll tell them what we did, how we tampered with the video. We'll all get into trouble."

"Bailey, it's okay," Paige reassured me, petting my arm. "We'll face what we did if we have to, but honestly, what do you think will hold more water? Them physically assaulting you? Or us switching a silly video?"

"You sabotaging my tour," Melody announced, getting to her feet to glare at all of us. "My brother didn't touch anyone. He came in here and saw that *rapist*..." She pointed at Beck, "attacking Bailey, so Chance tried to stop him."

Tess scoffed. "Oh, really? You're going to try to *lie* your way out of this one too? Who do you think everyone's going to believe this time? You or Bailey?"

"Me," I said, stepping out of Beckett's arm. Remembering my phone I'd dropped, I checked the bathroom stall I'd hidden in to find it still laying on the ground. When I picked it up, I was happy to see it hadn't been smashed and was still recording. It probably hadn't shown much of anything but the ceiling, but I'm sure I had picked up everything Chance and Melody had said.

I pushed *Stop* and began to play it again. When it reached the part where Melody cried, "*Slap her*," Melody closed her eyes and cursed under her breath.

"That's right," I murmured. "This time they'll believe *me*. Now take your brother and get out of here, or I will show this to everyone. If either of you bother any of us in this room again, I will show this to everyone. And if you try to tell the school administration who switched that video on the tour…"

"You'll show everyone," she finished lamely, glaring at me, but resigned to her fate.

I smiled. "That's right." Nodding, I glanced at my tribe. "I think we're done here."

* * *

I really loved my bed. It was so soft and comfortable and warm. Despite how much my entire head throbbed and my side ached, my beautiful, wonderful bed just kept hugging me, telling me it'd take good care of me.

I kept my face nestled deep in my pillow as I came awake. It was late Monday afternoon, and I was grateful I didn't have a final until tomorrow—yeah, somewhere in there, I'd decided to return to school, after all—because I was in no condition to take a test right now. I swear, every inch of my body hurt.

Beckett and the two couples had taken me home straight form the incident in the bathroom, harassing me the whole way and trying to convince me we should've turned Chance and Melody in to the police, but I'd stuck to my decision. This way would keep us all safer. So they'd pampered me and helped me into bed. Someone made me soup and hot tea, and gave me aspirin, and then I'd fallen asleep in the arms of the man I loved.

The only problem with my wonderful, beautiful, comfortable bed now was that Beck was no longer in it with me. But I could hear the low rumble of his voice. So I opened my eyes and rolled my head that way to find him standing at the window with his back to me as he spoke on his phone.

"Yes, sir," he was saying as he nodded. "Yeah, I'll make sure. I got it. Okay. Thank you. Bye." After hanging up, he gave a long-exhausted sigh and rubbed his hand over his head as he stared out at the park across the street.

"Who was that?" I asked, surprised when my voice came out rusty.

Beckett spun to me. "You're awake? Are you okay?" He hurried to the bed so he could sit next to me and press his hand to my forehead then the side of my face, worry lining his seeking gaze.

"I'm fine." I brushed his hand away. "I mean, other than feeling like shit because some shithead siblings attacked me, but yeah, I'm great. Who was on the phone? You looked upset."

He gave a low laugh. "I'm not really sure what I am, but I know I'm not upset." Then he ran his hand over his face, appearing strangely contemplative.

"Who called?" I repeated.

"Everyone." He laughed and dropped his hands to send me a helpless look. "I swear, since you went to sleep a few hours ago, everyone I've ever known has called me."

"Wha…why?" I grew instantly worried and gripped his thigh. "Is everything okay?"

"Yeah," he murmured, seemingly lost and confused by that. "Everything's great, actually. Our, um, our video switch made it viral. It already has thousands of views. The university was the first to call me. They apologized for expelling me after I was found innocent. I've been okayed to return to campus next semester and finish my degree. They even okayed it with my professors to take all my finals late to catch up from this semester."

My mouth fell open. "Really. That's great."

He nodded, looking distracted. "Yeah. And then my fraternity called. I can return there if I want to. Chance dropped out. Then my boss at the barn called. I can have my job back. Max called." He glanced at me before rolling his eyes. "I hung up on him."

I nodded. "Good."

He nodded too. "Yeah. And then…then my dad called."

My eyes sprang open wide. "Your dad?"

"Yes. He, um, I guess Daylon's father, Mr. Raider, wasn't the controlling interest in the company. His older brother was. And when *he* saw the video splashed all over social media and learned what his nephew had done, he forced Mr. Raider to step down. Dad got his old job back, and Daylon's uncle is encouraging them to proceed with pressing charges against Daylon. Britt actually came out of her room when she heard that. She ate lunch with my parents and spoke to them. She wanted them to tell me…" He blew out a breath before saying, "She wanted them to tell me thank you."

I sucked in a happy breath and grabbed his hand. "So you're back in the family?"

He glanced at me and squeezed my fingers. "I think so. At least, if I want to be. I might." He shrugged. "I'm not sure yet."

I drew his hand to my mouth and kissed his knuckles. "You don't have to decide now. You'll figure it all out when you're ready."

He nodded and smiled sadly at me. "And that last call is one *I* made. To your dad." He shook his head. "Ben was the only guy to give me chance on faith alone, and he was the one who got screwed in this whole deal. Now he's going to have to find a new hired hand."

A slow grin spread across my face. "So you're coming back to school, then?" I asked, growing encouraged.

He gave another shrug. "That depends. I know I don't want to return to the fraternity, so…think you can you handle another roommate?"

"Yeah," I murmured. "I think I can handle that, no problem."

"Good." He learned toward me to kiss me, only to pause and frown. "You have a bruise."

His fingers barely traced over my cheek before I growled my frustration, grabbed the front of his shirt and yanked him toward me, smacking our mouths together.

The kiss was just getting good, our breaths mingling and fingers gripping when a knock came on my door.

"Hello?" The door slowly swung open. "I heard voices. Are you awake?" Tess popped her head into the room. When she saw Beck and me on the bed, she grinned. "Oh, good. How do you feel?"

The door flew all the way open and she bounded into the room, skipping forward to join us on the bed. Sitting on the opposite side of me as where Beck sat, she took my hand and looked me over. "Your head still hurts, doesn't it?" She snapped her fingers at Beck. "Go get her more pain relievers."

He laughed, but stood to follow her orders. As soon as he disappeared into the bathroom, Tess turned back to me. "So, the truth is out, and everyone welcomed Beck back to his regular life. That's good, huh?"

I nodded and struggled to sit up. "That's amazing. What else did I miss while I was sleeping?"

"Not much. I'm not shy around your boyfriend anymore, though, that's for sure."

I smiled. That meant he was a keeper. Something I already knew. But I'm glad she knew it too.

"But I still can't believe that jerk ruined the computer and cut off the video right before I got to the moral and lesson in all this," Tess was ranting, already moved on to a new topic. "Because that's what Melody needed to hear most of all, you know. Rape is serious and awful and can really mess up people's lives. To lie about something like that is an insult and slap in the face to all the true victims out there, devaluing the trauma they go through and—"

"Uh, Tess." I patted her hand to shush her. "We heard all this the first time you recorded it. You don't have to repeat it."

Tess scowled at me. "But it really bothers me that she did that. I mean, at first, I was just mad at her for the way she treated you and Beck, but then...then it really started to sink in how wrong she was to so many *more* people out there. People like her…they just—"

"I know, sweetie." And I really did. "I know."

Tess stared at me for a minute, mutiny in her eyes, letting me know she wanted to keep raging over the topic. But a moment later, she blew out a breath and murmured, "Yeah, you do. It just...it really sucks."

"It does," I agreed. "It kind of makes you want to go Sweet/Vicious on all those bastards out there who hurt women and take justice into our own hands."

Tess's eyes lit with excitement. "Exactly. I'll be Ophelia. You can be Jules."

I sniffed. "What the hell ever! In no universe ever would I be the sweet, sorority girl, Jules. I'm totally Ophelia. *You'd* be Jules."

"But Jules is blond," Tess reasoned. "And you're blond now."

"And Ophelia dyes her hair funky colors, so that's definitely me. Ooh, I'm so going to go green on my next dye job. In honor of Ophelia!"

"Who's Ophelia?" Beck asked as he returned to the room with a bottle of Tylenol. After handing it dutifully to Tess, he plopped down on the bed next to me and curled his body around me so that we were touching everywhere, just like Tess and Jonah and Logan and Paige always did.

"Oh, just some character on this TV show we love..." I glanced at him and grinned, touching his face, because I could. "You know what? I'll just make you watch it with me."

Epilogue
BAILEY

Years and Years and Years Later

"Bethany! Baxter! Brynlee!" I yelled up the stairs. "Hurry your asses up. We're leaving in five minutes."

As I moved to the hall closet and pulled out four coats, the first pair of footsteps sounded on the stairs. They were loud and pounding, letting me know my youngest daughter was tromping down first.

"Mama," she started in before she even rounded the corner, hands on her hips and ponytail swinging indignantly behind her. "Baxter says I have to wear a dress, but Daddy said I didn't have to. So I'm *not* changing."

She glanced down at her outfit, which consisted of nice slacks, cowboy boots, and a gray vest over a grey and orange plaid long sleeve. For my tomboy, that was as dressy as she got.

I sighed wearily, tired of getting stuck in middle of these endless battles my second and third daughters were always forging. "We already told you, you don't have to wear a dress or skirt or any other girly contraption."

"But Baxter—"

I help up a hand to shush her. "Just stop listening to Baxter." Then, to appease her, I hollered up the steps again, "Baxter, she doesn't have to wear a dress."

"Well, she'd look better in one," Baxter lamented as she finally appeared at the top of the steps, decked out in a long-sleeved black and gold number, pantyhose and high-heeled pumps. Her mahogany hair fell down around her shoulders with a gold clip holding up one side. "We're supposed to be honoring Daddy tonight. She doesn't look very respectful in that ugly, gaudy—"

"She looks just fine," I ground out, lifting my eyebrows meaningfully as my girly daughter swept down the stairs.

With a dramatic sigh, Baxter rolled her eyes. "Fine, have it your way. She looks like a heathen, but whatever."

"She looks like Brynlee, which is exactly how your father wants her to look." I passed Baxter her coat before tossing Brynlee's her way. "Just as you look like Baxter, which is perfect for you."

I started to slip my arms into my jacket as the last set of footsteps clattered toward us. "Sorry I'm late. I just had two more pages until I finished the chapter."

Bethany, my bookworm, was too busy stuffing her kindle into her purse to watch where she was going that she tripped on the last step before catching herself. She wore a long, flowing skirt, nice top and flat pumps, but wasn't nearly as decorated as Baxter. I couldn't help but grin as I asked, "Did you brush your hair?"

Her hand went to the side of her head. "Oh, shoot." She began to whirl around and race back up the stairs, but Baxter rolled her eyes and groaned.

"Don't bother. I have a brush right here." She opened her own purse to pull one free.

"Oh! Thank you." Bethany turned her back to Baxter and let her younger sister comb the tangles from her hair. As the two worked and Brynlee discovered a piece of gum in the pocket of her coat before plugging it into her mouth, Bethany glanced my way. "Is Daddy nervous?"

"He says he's not." I handed her her coat. "But you know he is."

"He keeps messing with his hat?" All three girls guessed.

I nodded and grinned. "Oh, yeah. Big time."

"I'd be peeing my pants right now if I were him," Baxter announced as she finished with Bethany's hair only to aim her brush Brynlee's way and immediately be batted away.

Brynlee snorted. "I seriously doubt Daddy's pissing his pants."

Baxter sniffed. "And I seriously doubt a twelve-year-old girl should be saying piss."

"Bite me."

"Oh, I'll—" Baxter lifted her brush threatening, only to be stopped by Bethany, who snagged it neatly from her hand, and me who hollered, "Girls! Cut it out. This is Beck's big night. Don't—"

Before I could threaten them within an inch of their lives to behave for their father, the front door opened and he stepped inside, rubbing his gloved hands together. "The car's warmed," he started to say, only to pause and beam at us. "Well, look at all my honey Bs. You ladies look lovely."

"Daddy," the girls cheered in unison and rushed toward him, all three of them hugging him at once. My twelve, fifteen, and seventeen-year-olds could barely see eye to eye or agree on anything, except their complete and utter adoration for their father.

He opened his arms wide to encompass his honey b's, a term he'd started using after we'd decided to go the B route and coin all our children with names that stated with the letter B. And just like Beck and I had despised it when we'd been young, Bethany, Baxter, and Brynlee hated it too. But one day…one day, they'd get it.

Beck met my gaze over their heads, and his eyes sparked with love. "Hey," he said softly.

I gave an internal sigh. Damn, he could still melt me with a single look. "Hey, yourself. Nervous yet?"

He touched his hair, letting me know he didn't even have a hat to mess with, ergo no nervous habit to be had.

Bethany pulled back to grin up at him. "We're so proud of you, Daddy. You worked hard for this. You deserve it."

"You do," Baxter seconded as she lifted up onto her toes to kiss his cheek.

"Yeah, we should go out to celebrate at Colton's afterward," Brynlee chirped.

"There's going to be food at the award ceremony," I reminded her.

Her nose wrinkled. "Yeah, but nothing good. I want steak."

"I heard a rumor there would actually *be* a steak dinner served," Beck said as he tugged at Brynlee's ponytail.

Our youngest gasped, her eyes lighting with pleasure. "Oh, wow, Daddy. You really are getting full-service treatment tonight."

He chuckled. "I most certainly am. I'm going to be surrounded by the four most beautiful women in the county." His gaze rose to mine again.

Love bloomed, warm and liquid in my chest, before it flowed through my veins like a stimulant, exciting everything inside me. "We better get going," I murmured, and our daughters peeled themselves away from Beck before they tromped out the door in a line. He started to follow them until I caught his arm and swung him back to me.

"Wha…?" he began to ask in confusion.

I merely gripped his shirtfront and pulled his face down to mine, kissing him warm and long, before I pulled back and murmured, "I'm proud of you too."

Beck tenderly touched my cheek and pressed his forehead to mine before growling suggestively. "Now *I'm* ready for the after-party. You wanted steak too, right?"

I laughed and slugged him in the chest for his crude, but not unwanted, suggestion. Then I grew serious as I gazed into his eyes. "Did you ever think we'd get here to this point in our lives?"

Tonight he was being honored for running the state's business of the year. The momentous thing about that was this was his first year running the spraying and fertilizing company he'd built from the ground up. It really was a momentous honor. The governor was supposed to be there to congratulate him personally.

"Of course," he said with a shrug. "I have you. I can accomplish anything with my Bailey Rae by my side."

I kissed him again, and Brynlee popped her head back through the doorway. "My God, would you two quit sucking face already. They're going to give the award to the runner up if we're late."

From outside on the porch, Baxter's annoyed voice groused, "They are not going to give Daddy's award to the runner up, you dummy."

"Well, they might." Brynlee sent Beck and I arched eyebrows. "Let's go already so we don't have to find out."

Beck chuckled and took my hand, leading out into the cold winter chill before we all marched through a snow-packed walkway and climbed into the SUV Beck had warmed for us. The girls kept trying to bicker and pick fights all the way there, but I'd just warningly cleared my throat, and they immediately told Beck how excited they were for him.

After doing this twice, he sent me an arch glance and dryly asked, "What'd you threaten them with?"

I winked. "A mother never reveals her secrets."

Sometimes, it still wowed me that I was a mother now. I'd had seventeen years to adjust to the idea but, yeah, it still managed to blow my mind, as did the fact I was married. Married to Beckett Hilliard, of all people, the annoying drunk bucket-head who'd changed my entire life in a single night.

I'd had no idea I could be loved or feel loved until he'd come into my life.

I'd never been so wrong about something.

And I couldn't be happier.

We made it to the event building just before the time we were supposed to arrive. The coordinator led us inside to our table where most of them around us were already filled. Tess and Jonah, and their redheaded boys sat at one. The Xanders and their daughter, Kayla, took up residence at another, then my family, Dad and my brothers with their assortment of children and significant others, took up about three other tables, before Beck's parents and still-single sister sat at the last.

It was strange how some things worked out in the end, but they always seemed to sort themselves through, one way or another, for better or worse. Something good, a hope to hold onto, always bloomed from the tragedy and suffering, making every dark patch worth fighting through.

And while Bailey-met-Beckett-on-the-night-of-the-worst-drunken-hookup-of-his-life wasn't exactly a story we'd be telling our grandkids, it was something I'd always be grateful for, anyway.

THE END

Acknowledgements

Thanks to my family who puts up with me through everything! Kurt, the best husband I could ever have, I love you more each day. To Lydia and Sadie, thank you for keeping me going during those times I want to be lazy and stay in bed! And to Holly, your purr had the most calming effect! Then to everyone else in the extended family. It's nice to know I can fall back and rely on you anytime I need. Love you guys.

Thanks a ton to the beta readers for your insight and opinions: Zasharie Rodriguez, Amanda Klinger, Alaina Martinie, Shi Ann Crumpacker, Ada Frost, Lindsay Brooks, and Amisha D'Lima! You have no idea how helpful you guys are with just your bits of feedback!

And thank you to the awesome team at Omnific who helped bring Believing Bailey to life, like my editor Kateasa Langston, Melissa Simmons, then Elizabeth Riley and Lisa O'Hara. I appreciate everything you guys have done.

Thank you to my PA, Ashley Gibbons. You're always out there, giving me a shout out! Big hugs.

And thank you to God for, you know, being you!

About The Author

Linda grew up on a dairy farm in the Midwest as the youngest of eight children. Now she lives in Kansas with her husband, two daughters, a cat named Holly, and their nine cuckoo clocks. She works a day job in the acquisitions department of a university library and feels her life has been blessed with lots of people to learn from and love. Writing's always been a major part her world, and she's thrilled to finally share some of her stories with other romance lovers. Some of her works include Fighting Fate and Loving Lies. Feel free to visit her at her website www.Lindakage.com

www.ingramcontent.com/pod-product-compliance
Lightning Source LLC
Chambersburg PA
CBHW020335120726
47904CB00002B/422

* 9 7 8 1 6 2 3 4 2 2 5 1 6 *